PUPPY LOVE 2: BUILDING A FAMILY

JEFF ERNO

Seattle, WA

Published by Fanny Press
PO Box 95462
Seattle, WA 98145

Cover design by Sabrina Sun
Cover illustration by Paul Richmond
(PaulRichmondStudio.Com)

Contact: info@fannypress.com

ISBN-13: 978-1-60381-436-2 (Paper)
ISBN-13: 978-1-60381-468-3 (Cloth)
ISBN-13: 978-1-60381-437-9 (ePub)

To my dear friend, a fellow author, Michele L. Montgomery, whose loving words of encouragement have inspired and motivated me. You're my most loyal fan and one of my closest friends. I love you.

And in loving memory of my best friend and soul mate, Jason Scruggs; you have always been to me as Drew is to Petey. You are my sweet Drew, and you'll remain in my heart forever. I love you.

Contents

1

The four of us were riding together back from Fort Lauderdale. Matt and I were in the front seat of his parents' SUV, and Alex was with Drew in the back. They'd been on their spring break vacation while Matt and I had gone on our cruise. It was the most awesome vacation of my life! I curled up next to Matt as he drove, resting my head against his shoulder. None of us were talking much, all feeling rather exhausted from the ten days of sunshine and partying. That morning when Alex and Drew picked us up at the docks, I had gushed to Drew, telling him every detail of our trip. The four of us had lunch together in Fort Lauderdale before we began our four-and-a-half hour drive north to Tampa.

I was not really all that excited about going home, for I knew that things were not that great with Kathie. She and I had quarreled a few times about my relationship with Matt, and it seemed that it was more and more difficult to find common ground upon which we could communicate regarding this issue. When I had rejected her friend Cameron, choosing a relationship with Matt over Cameron's so-called equality, it had not set well with Kathie. I suppose she had convinced herself that she knew what was best for me, and that a minor thing like my own free will was merely an obstacle that stood in the way of my own true happiness. It seemed ironic to me that she disliked Matt so intensely. She felt he was too controlling, yet she herself was the one who was trying to manipulate me.

The real turning point in my life had been the day I returned to Matt, leaving Cameron behind in the restaurant and bolting down the street towards my true hero. It was then that I had decided with whom I would spend my life, and how I would find the contentment I'd so long desired. After that pivotal decision had been made, the rest seemed to just sort of fall into place. Drew and I had begun discussing plans for me to move in with him and Alex, and I was making plans to attend university at the start of the fall semester as opposed to community college.

This would mean that I'd be going to a different school than both Matt and Drew. Whereas Drew would remain in his teaching position at Hillborough Community College, Matt was planning to attend Stetson University to pursue a degree in business administration. My first impulse was to follow Matt and attend this college as well, but he dissuaded me from doing so, urging me to consider which school would be best for achieving my own personal goals. Ultimately I decided on the University of Tampa.

Alex was gearing up for his graduation and had already begun an internship with a software distributor in Tampa. It was pretty much a foregone conclusion that he would be taken aboard as a full-time associate within the company upon the completion of his degree. Drew had confided in me that once Alex had settled into his new position and was happy, he was going to approach Alex about the possibility of returning to school to complete his graduate studies. Secretly I'd hoped that Drew would elect to attend the University of Tampa with me, although I knew realistically that even if he did so, it would not necessarily mean we would see much of one another on campus. It just was sort of comforting to know that there would be someone there that I already knew.

The night of my birthday party and the days immediately following had been a time of significant turmoil for me. I was so emotional about the decision I'd made to be committed to Matt that I wanted to jump into everything with both feet. I wanted to move out of the apartment immediately and start doing all of the things I'd been reluctant to do previously. Drew started taking me to the Gay Student Union meetings with him, and I started wearing an earring that displayed rainbow colors. I even bought a rainbow flag bumper sticker, which I attached to the frame of my bike. If Matt had allowed it, I'd even have worn my collar 24/7, but actually he was the rational one during this transitional period for me. He persuaded me to remain calm and to wait things out at the apartment until the end of the school year. "Pup, wait til after the end of this semester, or at the very least until we get back from vacation. There is no reason for you to be making a major change just yet. Plus, I don't want you doing anything out of anger. When you make life decisions, you have to think with your head, not your heart."

"But when I decided on you, I thought with my heart, Sir," I protested. "Didn't I?" He had looked down at me smiling and ruffled my hair affectionately.

"Yeah, it was your heart and your feelings that led you to make the decision, but still you had to think things through, right? Don't you remember? I told you I wanted you to think about it really hard."

I nodded in agreement. He was right, as usual, and so I elected to just chill out a bit and try to maintain a low profile around the apartment. I made a very valiant effort, I felt, to remain respectful of Kathie at all times. Things just felt odd, as if there was a constant underlying tension that existed between us. We were cordial, but not close to one another like before. She seemed to also have a way of getting her digs into me about Matt, saying things to get a point across without actually coming right out and being blunt. The day before we left on the cruise she had said to me, "Not all of us have a rich boyfriend." She was responding to a question I'd asked about if she and Carter were planning any vacations together in the near future.

Whenever she said these things to me, it would cut me to the quick, and invariably I'd run to Matt, either emailing him or talking to him on the phone or in person, telling him verbatim what was said. He just seemed to brush it off, downplaying my emotion, and led me into a rational way of thinking. "Pup, you gotta understand, it is normal for her to be a bit jealous. All these years she's taken care of you and watched out for you. Now she prolly feels that you're being taken away from her, and in some ways you are."

"But why can't she just be happy for me? I mean, I'm happy for her having Carter!"

"Once she sees how happy you really are and really gets on with her own life, I bet you two are gonna be really close again. The bond you have is strong enough to hold you together, no matter what else happens."

"Yeah, at least I used to believe that. I don't know though now. She just is so different."

"You're both different, pup. People change. They grow ... it's all part of life, but she's gonna be your sister forever, no matter what."

Sometimes it scared me the way I depended upon Matt so very much. He was my voice of reason, my conscience, my emotional stabilizer. I worried that he would eventually tire of me, get disgusted by my weaknesses and dependencies. I feared that he would ultimately seek a partner who was stronger and more mature. What was it that he even saw in me? Why did he put up with my insecurity and my quirkiness? Drew had explained it to me one day when I confessed my fears to him. "Petey, Matt likes you because of all those things, not in spite of them."

"But how is that possible?" I'd responded. "How can he like that I'm a crybaby?"

"You're not a crybaby. You are just sensitive and emotional, and you have this air of innocence about you. It is like you are so very transparent, you have nothing to hide. Matt sees in you an honest person who is very trusting. Sure, you're weaker than him, but he's the kinda guy who likes to look out for the underdog. He's like a superhero or something."

"Yeah ... you're right about that. He is totally a superhero. Does that mean I'm like Lois Lane?"

"You're a lot cuter than Lois Lane ... plus she's got a pussy."

I turned my back towards him, thrusting my butt in his direction, "So do I!"

As we drove back from Fort Lauderdale, I slid my hand onto Matt's thigh, easing it down to the inner part of his leg near the groin. I rested it there affectionately as I lay against him. I was not wearing the shoulder-strap seat belt but merely had on the middle lap belt, leaving the far right seat vacant. Alex and Drew sat behind us, both apparently dozing serenely. "I love you so much, Sir," I whispered to Matt. "Thank you for the cruise. Thank you for everything." Matt shifted slightly in his seat, bringing his arm around my shoulder, pulling me into him tightly. He steered using only his left hand.

"You're my pup. I'm glad you had fun." As I leaned into him peacefully and closed my eyes, suddenly I felt his body tense and instantly my eyes shot open. He was gripping me firmly, holding me close to him as we came over the crest of a hill. Immediately in front of us was a huge pileup of cars, and Matt reacted promptly by slamming on the breaks and holding me tightly at the same time. He gripped the wheel tightly with his left hand as the truck went into a skid. We had been traveling at a speed of about 75 mph and were suddenly coming to a screeching halt. Alex's cell phone, which had been sitting on the back seat, flew through the air and crashed into the windshield. I felt the impact of both Alex and Drew as their bodies were slammed into the back of the front seat, jolting us as I pressed my firmly-planted feet against the floorboards. The only thing that kept me from slamming my own head against the dash was Matt's intense grip around my shoulder.

"Fuck!" he screamed, as he steered the vehicle frantically, trying to regain control. The back of the truck spun around, causing us to fishtail as I heard the deafening squeal of the brakes, the tires leaving behind black streaks of rubber on the pavement. The truck spun around so that we were sliding sideways across both lanes and then finally skidded to a jolting halt. We had not hit anything, but were facing the wrong direction. The truck had stalled.

"Oh my god!" Matt yelled. "What the fuck! Are you guys all right?" He craned his head backwards to see Drew and Alex pushing themselves back into a seated position.

"Yeah ... fuck! What happened?" Alex yelled.

"There's an accident. I gotta get this fucker outta the road before someone slams into us!" Matt pulled his arm from around me, pushing me away from him. I knew it was not a gesture of unkindness, but an act of survival. I leaned away from him, allowing him space to restart the ignition. He fired up the engine again, threw the automatic transmission into drive, and gunned it, driving immediately over to the shoulder of the road. We were facing the wrong direction, but Matt kept driving. He continued until he was back to the top of the hill we had just come over, and then he pulled right out into the middle of both lanes, immediately flipping on his hazard lights. "Everyone out of the truck! Petey, grab your phone."

Drew and Alex piled out of the backseat hurriedly as I reached under the dash to press the latch release for the rear door. I then unbuckled myself and shoved the door open, climbing down to the ground. I ran to the back of the vehicle and pulled open the rear door which was slightly ajar. I grabbed my duffle bag and unzipped it as quickly as I could, digging inside to find my phone. "Call 9-1-11!" Matt ordered. "Come on Alex, there are people still in those cars down there. Drew, you and Petey stop any traffic from coming through, but stay the fuck off the road!" He and Alex raced back down the hill on foot as I dialed the emergency number.

"Fuck, there must have been ten or fifteen cars piled up down there!" Drew said to me. "All these cars came booking over this hill and just crashed into each other!"

"There's a big accident! Please help!" I screamed into the phone. "Drew, where are we?"

"On Interstate 75, northbound, mile marker one-forty-three," he responded.

"I-75 at about mile marker 143; there's a huge pile up ... ten or twenty cars! ... Yes, we are safe, but there are people hurt ... Yes! Please hurry!" I clicked off the phone and ran to the front of the SUV, looking down the hill to see Matt. He and Alex were already almost out of sight, checking each vehicle to see if anyone needed immediate help.

"Oh my god!" Drew screamed. "That truck ... it's upside down! ... It's leaking water or something."

"Fuck! That's not water, Drew...it's gasoline!" Matt and Alex were beside the truck, and Matt dropped down to a crouching position peering inside the driver-side window. He grabbed for the door latch, jerking against it with all his might, but it did not budge. He turned to Alex, yelling something to him, and Alex headed back up the hill towards us.

Drew had turned back around and was waving at the oncoming traffic, urging them to stop before they approached us. "Stop! Stop! It's an accident! Stop!!"

"Get a tire iron!" Alex screamed to me. "From the truck!" I ran immediately to the rear of our vehicle and started hurling our luggage behind me onto the ground. As soon as there was a bare spot on the floor of the truck, I reached for the latch to lift up the spare tire compartment, shoving all the other contents that remained on the floor out of the way. I grabbed the tire iron hurriedly as Alex approached me, handing it to him quickly. He did not say anything but spun back around and ran down the hill. I started to follow him but stopped at the top of the hill as I remembered that Matt had told me to wait.

I watched as Alex handed over the tire iron to Matt, like a runner passing a baton. Matt spun around and bolted towards the opposite side of the upturned pickup. He was swinging the tire iron against the glass of the passenger window. He did it three times, and I saw shards of glass flying around him. He used the tire iron itself to quickly clear off the broken pieces of glass that were still stuck in the window. Then he dropped down to his knees, crawling into the truck. I panicked and headed down the hill at full speed.

"Petey, what are you doing?" Drew yelled from behind me. "Wait!" I did not listen to him but ran towards the pickup truck, which was continuing to pour the contents of its gas tank on the pavement. As I approached the truck, Alex grabbed me.

"What are you doing?" he demanded. "Get back up the hill."

"No! That truck is gonna explode! It's leaking gas!"

"Get back up the hill!" Alex repeated.

"Matt!" I screamed, as Alex grabbed tightly a hold of my shoulders. Matt backed out of the vehicle.

"I can't get in there! Fuck! There's a woman in there ... unconscious! I can't fucking get in!"

"Let me do it!" I screamed.

"Petey, I told you to stay by the van!" Matt yelled at me.

"Sir ... please! That truck is gonna explode! Please ... let me do it ... I'm small enough to fit!"

He looked up at me as he knelt there beside the broken window. "Get over here! Fast!" Alex released me and I ran to Matt. "Watch the glass ... now, listen to me ... you gotta get over to the seatbelt and unlatch it. She's gonna fall forward when you do ... right on top of you. You gotta use all your strength to push her towards me ... and hurry!"

I crawled inside, my heart pounding in my head. The adrenaline within me was racing so fast I did not have time to be afraid. I heard Matt behind me, instructing Alex to get the rest of the people out of their vehicles as quickly as he could, and I scurried into the upside-down pickup, crawling on my knees. As I inched my way across the ceiling of the truck, which was now of course the floor, I winced, feeling a shard of glass stab into my leg. The woman that I moved towards was still conscious, I immediately discovered, but moaning. "Can you undo your seatbelt?" I asked her. She did not respond, as if she couldn't hear me at all. I pushed myself closer to her. The weight of her body had pressed her head down flush against the ceiling of the pickup, but the seatbelt was still holding her in place. When I got close enough, I tried to pull against the seatbelt, but there was no slack. I reached above my head into the section of the seat where the belt was clasped. "I'm gonna undo your seatbelt ..." I said to her, "and you're gonna fall onto me. It's okay though, I will get you out." Again she did not respond to me at all; I wondered if she was in shock.

"Hurry Petey!" Matt yelled behind me, and I reached up to the seatbelt clasp and pressed into it. I had to extend both hands, pressing into the release using both of my thumbs. Finally I felt it give way and the seatbelt popped out of the clasp. As Matt had said, the woman immediately fell forward. I reached for her, thrusting my body under hers, and her weight shoved me backwards, right onto the steering wheel. I cried out in pain but quickly stifled it as I concentrated on using all my energy to hold onto her. She was not a big person, but her body was limp, like a rag doll. She was not cooperating at all. I pressed my hands against her shoulders and shoved her backwards, away from me, as I felt the steering wheel pressing into my back.

"Unghh!" I cried, as I shoved with all my might. I moved my hands downward on her body, gripping the waistband of her jeans. I tugged hard, suddenly realizing that her leg was pinned underneath me. I wriggled around frantically, shoving her whole body as I did so. When I'd freed myself from the position of being pinned, I finally was able to get a good grip around her waist. I tugged hard, now being back in a kneeling position on the ceiling of the pickup. Gradually I inched her closer to the window. Matt's upper body was leaning inside; he was reaching for her.

"Just a little more, pup!" he yelled. "Come on!" I gasped, as I felt my own tears stinging my face. I didn't think I could do it. "Petey, push hard ... NOW!" Then with all my strength I shoved her body towards Matt. He finally was able to grab her, sliding his hands under her arms and pulling with all his might. She slid out of the window smoothly as I scurried behind her. When I made it out, Matt was already a good fifteen yards away from the pickup, dragging the woman to safety. I pressed my palms against the pavement and pushed myself up into a kneeling position, gasping for breath. "Come on, Petey!" Matt screamed as he turned to look for me. "Get away from the truck!" My leg was throbbing, but I scurried to my feet and ran after them.

In the distance I could hear the emergency sirens. "Is everyone out of their cars?" I yelled. Alex was now beside us.

"Everyone is out ... except two people."

"Where are they?" Matt turned to him. "We gotta get them out!"

"No ... no, they ... um ... there's no saving them."

Matt turned his attention to the girl in his arms. He laid her flat on her back on the grass. We were in a field at least fifty yards from the pileup on the highway. "She has a pulse ... she's breathing ... but she isn't conscious. Alex, go get a blanket! Petey, are you all right?"

"Yes Sir," I said. "I just cut my leg."

"Oh my god ... it's gushing. Sit down and put pressure on it. Sit right here ... next to her. I'm gonna go get the paramedics." Just as he said that, a huge explosion erupted behind us. The truck from which we had just escaped had gone up in flames. "Fuck!" Matt screamed. He jumped up and ran down the field, down well past the wreckage and back onto the highway. I heard the sirens loudly now as I sat there, staring down at the woman. I hoped she was going to survive. This didn't even seem real to me.

Alex returned with a blanket and covered the woman, again checking her pulse and breathing. "I think her leg is broken, and she has a head wound." he said. "Petey, you're bleeding everywhere!" He moved over towards me. "Lie down!" I obeyed him, lying down on my back. He reached down to my calf, where the glass had cut into my leg, and tore the fabric of my khakis clean away from the wound. "There's still a piece in there. I gotta pull it out, Petey." I winced as he jerked the shard of glass from my leg. Then immediately he leaned into me, pressing down with his palm firmly over the wound. I could hear people running as I lay back, closing my eyes. It was Matt with the paramedics.

The rescue workers gave their immediate attention to the woman who apparently had suffered a very severe blow to her head when her truck had upturned. More paramedics arrived, and a young guy in his mid twenties knelt down beside me. He was blonde with a very boyish face. "Eww ... nasty cut," he said, as he smiled down at me. "Are you hurt anywhere else ... besides your leg, I mean?" I shook my head.

"No ... uh ... no Sir," I said. Matt was kneeling on the other side of me.

He reached into his bag and pulled out a bottle of something, uncapping it and pouring it over the wound. I grabbed Matt's hand firmly as I winced from the sudden sting. "Sorry," said the paramedic. "I know it stings. My name is Eric, by the way. You're gonna need some stitches for this, but I'm just gonna wrap it real quick." He proceeded to bandage me up, tying a white piece of cloth around my leg securely. "You gonna be all right? I gotta move on to help these other people." I nodded. "I don't think you need to go in the ambulance ... we've stopped the bleeding. One of the officers can drive you in to emergency."

"Thanks," said Matt. "We have our own vehicle. We weren't in the accident."

"Oh, okay," said Eric. "Take care of him!" he said, as he turned from us and headed down towards the wreckage.

"Do you think she's gonna be okay?" I asked Matt, referring to the woman we'd saved. "Is she still unconscious?"

"I don't know, Petey, but she is still alive. And if you hadn't crawled in that truck to get her, she wouldn't be. You're a hero, you know."

"No ... no, you're the hero, sir." He reached down and brushed my hair off my forehead.

"I can't even believe this," he said. "Look at that truck ... those cars. They're gone." We watched as fire trucks approached, and the workers began to focus on extinguishing the inferno. There were people around us everywhere, and suddenly we were invisible. Matt reached under my shoulders and slid his hands into my armpits, pulling me up against him. He stretched his legs out on either side of me as he repositioned himself into a sitting position. "I'm just glad you are all right. You could have been hurt so bad."

"So could you, Sir ... I knew that truck was gonna explode. I knew it."

"Yeah, but I told you to wait up on top of the hill."

"You wouldn't have saved her though ... you couldn't have fit into that window ... the truck was too smashed."

"I know, pup ... but still—" he did not finish his sentence but just hugged me very tightly. He rocked me back and forth in his arms. "I love you pup," he said, as we sat there and waited for it to be over.

* * *

"Now you have battle scars," said Drew, as we walked out of the hospital together. "If you can handle the pain from getting those stitches, you should be ready to get your tattoo, no problem."

I laughed. "Yeah, but they don't give you a local anesthetic for a tattoo, silly."

"We still are getting you that tattoo though, pup," said Matt. "Just not til you've moved out of the apartment."

"I can't wait, sir," I exclaimed. "I can't wait to be marked by you."

"Are you guys as hungry as me?" asked Alex. "I'm totally fuckin starving."

"I'm so hungry I could eat a ... uh ... dick," said Drew.

"You'd be hungry for that even after a full seven-course meal," I said.

"True," he laughed.

"Where do you wanna eat, pup?" Matt asked. "You decide since you're the hero today."

I blushed. "I'm not a hero, Sir. I don't like to decide stuff like that. Will you decide ... please? I like whatever you like."

Matt sighed. "All right, let's just go to that restaurant over there across the street. We can walk. In the future though, if I tell you to decide something, ya better do it ... or else." I looked down at the pavement in front of me, thinking I was being genuinely scolded. "Or else you will get tickle tortured!" Matt yelled, reaching out and grabbing me around my sides, digging his fingers playfully into me. I burst into giggles.

"Okay! Okay! I decide we go over there!" Matt pulled me into him and put his arm around me as we walked together across the street. I was feeling no pain in my leg at this point because the anesthesia hadn't yet worn off, and I'd changed into a pair of shorts instead of my khakis.

A sign above the doorway of the restaurant boasted, "Homestyle Family Cooking", but as we entered, it became obvious that the establishment was simply a little diner. It sort of reminded me of that little greasy spoon that I'd seen on the re-runs of the show "Alice"—Mel's Diner. It very much had a small-town feel to it and appeared to be patronized mainly by local, working people. A sign just inside the door told us to "Please seat yourself", and we did so, Matt selecting a booth in the non-smoking section.

As we were sitting down I looked across the room to spot a group of people in uniform, obviously medical workers. Suddenly I realized who they were—paramedics. My rescuer Eric was amongst the group. "Look Sir," I said quietly to Matt as I nodded in their direction, "it's Eric, the one who bandaged my leg."

"Oh, yeah," he acknowledged, and as he did so Eric looked over to make eye contact with Matt. He raised his hand to us in an informal, waving gesture. The four of us took our seats in the booth, Matt and I on one side and the other couple opposite us. Drew and I were of course seated on the inside, next to the wall.

"I'm getting a burger," Drew announced. "Extra greasy."

I made a face. "How can you eat that stuff?" I asked. "Don't you realize how many fat grams there are in that? Plus it is red meat."

"Whatever," he said.

"This place is totally a blast from the past," said Alex. "It's like retro or something."

Just as he said this, a waitress appeared carrying a tray with four glasses of water. "Ev'nin, gentlemen. Can I start you with somethin t' drink?" We gave her our drink orders and she disappeared.

"I wonder if her name is Flo," Drew said. "You know, like from Mel's Diner." We laughed. I had just picked up my menu and was reading it over looking for anything that might not be too unhealthy, when Eric approached our table.

"Hey guys," he said. He looked directly at me. "How's your leg, little guy?"

"Fine, sir ... thank you." I quickly looked back down at my menu, feeling suddenly shy. I did not like being the center of attention.

"I heard about how you guys helped all those people today. It was amazing ... wanted to say thanks. I'm Eric," he reminded us, "In case you didn't remember."

Matt extended his hand to greet Eric, and they shook. "Matt," he said, offering his own name. "This is Petey, of course, and these are our two friends Alex and Drew." Eric then shook Alex's hand.

"Nice to meet you," he offered. "So, are you guys from around here, or just passing through?" He casually pulled up a chair from the table behind him, placing it in front of him as he sat in it backwards, his legs straddling the seat. He crossed his arms in front of himself, resting them on the back of the chair.

"We're on our way back to Tampa," Matt answered. "We were on a cruise, Petey and I. Alex and Drew were vacationing in Ft. Lauderdale."

"Really?" said Eric, "I'm gonna be moving to Tampa myself in a couple o' weeks. "Just got a full-time job offer. Gonna be a full-fledged paramedic."

"Cool. Congrats," said Matt.

"Where in Tampa?" asked Alex. "I mean, where's your place gonna be?"

"I'm renting an apartment over on the east side, on Gennessee Avenue."

"Cool, that's not far from our place," said Alex. "Drew and I have an apartment on Wilder."

"So what are the hot spots in Tampa?" asked Eric. "Any good clubs?"

"Wherever we're at," said Matt jokingly, "that's the hot spot."

"No doubt," said Eric, looking over to smile at me. "You dudes seem pretty cool."

"What kinda clubs you like?" asked Alex. "We've got all kinds."

"Um ... alternative, I guess. Maybe dance clubs." Alex's face sort of lit up when he said this. Alex was sort of the activist in our group, being the president of the Gay Student Union at our community college. I think his "gaydar" kicked in when he heard the words "alternative" and "dance" used in the same sentence.

"Yeah, we can show you a few clubs like that," Alex said.

"You guys should come to a party tonight. My friend Adam is throwin this big bash. Lotsa cool peeps gonna be there."

"We still have a two hour drive home," said Matt. "But thanks anyways."

"Could always spend the night, drive home in the morning," Eric suggested. "You could crash at my place if you wanted."

"Sounds cool, but we better not. Been partying our asses off anyways all week. Be cool to go out some time, though, when you get moved to Tampa. Let me give you my number."

As they were writing down each other's number, I spoke up. "Eric ... um ... how's that lady doin? ... the one from the accident."

"Oh, well I'm not sure, but I think she's gonna be just fine. She was talkin and everything by the time we got her to the hospital. Her name is Brenda."

"You shoulda seen that truck," said Alex. "The one side was so caved in that Matt couldn't even fit through the window."

"Yeah, Petey went in," interjected Matt. "He's our hero today."

"Well she owes ya big time. If you hadn't gotten her out, she'd 'ave burned up."

"We only did what anyone else would do," I said, feeling my face redden. "I wouldn't have even known what to do at all if not for Matt."

"Still, you're the one who saved her, Petey," said Matt. "No one can take that away from you."

"You guys sure you don't wanna hit that party? You can stay at my house. It's better than driving all that way."

"None of us have to work or go to class tomorrow," said Drew.

"Yeah, and drivin two more hours right now would totally suck," said Alex.

"What about you, Petey? You wanna go to the party?" asked Matt.

I looked up at him wide-eyed and said very quietly, "I want to if you do ... but what about Kathie? She'll be worried."

"Well that's no biggie. You can call her if we decide to go." Just as he said that, our waitress returned with the drinks.

"Well, talk it over, guys," said Eric, "I'll be here a few more minutes." He nodded to us as he got up from the chair and returned to his table.

* * *

"No, really I'm okay ... everyone's okay. I just got a little scratch on my leg." I was talking to Kathie on my cell phone.

"You wouldn't have needed stitches if it were only a scratch. Stay where you are, I'm coming down to get you right now." She was starting to freak.

"No ... please ... it's okay. You don't have to come down to get me. We will be back in the morning. It's just Matt and Alex don't feel like making the long drive tonight. Please ..."

"Put Matt on the phone! I wanna talk to him," she demanded.

"He's not here, he's … uh … he's in the bathroom right now." Matt reached over and held out his hand, being that he was sitting right next to me.

"Give me the phone, Petey," he said calmly.

Worriedly, I obeyed him. "She's pissed," I whispered to him as I covered the receiver with my palm.

"Hello?" said Matt into the phone. "Yeah, everything is fine." He paused for a minute while listening to her response. "About eight stitches. He got a piece of glass stuck in his calf. He actually was very heroic today. Crawled into an overturned truck to pull out a woman who was trapped. You'd have been proud."

Matt remained calm while Kathie yelled into his ear. I could hear her going off, even though Matt had the phone pressed tightly against his head. He got up from the table to step away. Drew raised his eyebrows as he looked over at me. "You'd think she'd be happy that you're all right," he said.

"All she can think is that I could have been killed, and I bet you anything she's gonna blame it on Matt. She blames everything on him; I'm so sick of it!"

"She just is being protective of ya, that's all," said Alex. "Don't worry about Matt. He can handle it just fine. He doesn't need anyone else's approval."

"I'll just be glad when I get moved in with you guys. Then she won't know what I'm doin every single second."

Matt had returned to the table, and I looked up at him inquisitively, awaiting his report on the phone conversation. "Everything's cool," he said. "I told her I'd have you back safe and sound tomorrow by noon." I reached under the table and placed my hand on Matt's thigh.

"I'm sorry, Sir, that she yelled at you."

He shook his head. "Didn't really yell. Just got a little excited, but only cuz she was worried bout ya. Everything's cool."

We followed Eric over to his apartment. It was a large two bedroom, and he informed us that two of us could share the one spare bedroom and the other two could crash on the hide-a-bed. Alex immediately volunteered to take the hide-a-bed for himself and Drew, and of course Matt and I got the bedroom. We hauled our suitcases in and deposited them in the bedroom and then joined the others in the living room. "You guys want a beer?" offered Eric.

"Sure," said Matt. "Could use one about now." Alex also accepted the offer, but Drew and I declined. I'd wait until the party if I had any alcohol at all. The five of us sat in the living room making small talk. Matt was sitting on this big comfortable sofa, and I sat Indian-style at his feet. Drew was sitting next to Alex on a love seat across from us. To be honest, I wasn't sure I was even up for a party, but I was thankful we did not have to go home just yet. I loved spending all of this time with Matt, and as I realized that our vacation was coming to a close, I did not want to be separated from him again.

After conversing with Eric a few minutes, it became apparent that he was not really familiar with the Dom/sub lifestyle that the four of us had embraced. His references made it clear to me that he considered us to be "boyfriends" rather than owner and pup. This did not seem to bother Matt at all, and he actually seemed to adapt to the perception of our host. Instinctively, I knew to refrain from addressing Matt as "Sir", and he called me by my own first name, rather than "pup".

But then after we had sat there a few minutes, and Eric had turned on the stereo, Matt suddenly surprised me by something that he did. He reached down and handed me his beer bottle. It was empty. "I need another one," he said, and without even thinking, I jumped to my feet to get it for him. Eric looked over to us without saying anything, and I suddenly wondered what he thought of me waiting on Matt like that. I obeyed Matt's orders so frequently and so automatically that it just seemed natural to me, but to an outsider, it may have been a bit startling.

When I returned to the living room, I resumed my position at Matt's feet. He took the beer from me without acknowledgement and spread his legs apart slightly so that I could slip back into my comfortable position between them. Eric was telling Matt about his recent trip to Mexico, and occasionally Alex or Matt would interject a comment or question. Drew and I both sat quietly.

When the conversation got around to career stuff, Alex told Eric about his internship and his job with the software firm. Matt explained the situation that he was in with the impending inheritance of his father's business, but Drew never spoke up to explain that he was a college professor. I found it to be a little bit ironic that the one person amongst us who was the most successful career-wise, did not even bother to talk about it. When Eric finally did ask Drew about his profession, Drew simply stated that he was a teacher and did not elaborate.

As I looked over to Drew, seeing him sit there at Alex's side, I suddenly realized just what an amazing person he was. He was without question one of the least self-centered people I'd ever known. He was the perfect sub. Never once had I heard him ever question his owner, Alex. He never expressed feelings of jealousy or anger—never whined about anything. He obeyed every instruction given him, and always strove to stay out of the center of attention, deferring always to his owner.

I wondered if I ever would become half the person that Drew was. I was so very thankful for him and for all of the help and reassurance he had given me over the past months. He seemed to understand every feeling or insecurity that I had, and he always helped me to do my very best to serve my owner. Never once had he said a single word of criticism to me about Matt. Even at the times when I was being disciplined or the times when Matt chose to be away from me, Drew continued to show Matt the utmost respect.

After Matt finished his second beer, he suggested that we get ready for the party. It was already about nine o'clock, and Eric quickly concurred with Matt's suggestion. He informed Matt and me that we could use his bathroom in the bedroom, and Alex and Drew were shown to the bathroom off the hall. Eric said he had some stuff to do while we got ready, so we then separated.

I followed Matt into the bathroom and shut the door behind me. Matt turned to face me and then stepped forward, causing me to back up against the doorway. He reached up above my head with both hands and placed his palms flat against the door. Then he moved them down so that they were on either side of my head. He was leaning over me and had me trapped between the door and himself. I smiled up at him, trusting him completely, and becoming immediately thankful that we were finally alone together.

I sensed from Matt's demeanor that he was in the mood for a little more than just a shower. During our cruise, he had taken advantage of many opportunities to use me for his sexual satisfaction, but it had been nearly a day and a half since we had had any real privacy. I was about to slide down the door and drop to my knees when he spoke to me. "Pup was a very good boy today," he said softly. His voice was dripping with sexuality, and just the authoritative sound of it made me instantly hard.

"You remember what I told you before about actions and consequences, pup?" he asked.

I nodded silently as I looked up at him. I was staring wide-eyed into his face, and then I finally spoke. "Yes Sir, I remember. Every action has consequences."

"That's right," he said. "When you do things that are bad, the consequences are bad. When you are good, you get rewarded."

"But Sir," I said, starting to protest. "I did not do anything to be rewarded for. I disobeyed you, actually." I looked down, away from his face, as I said this. "You told me to stay by the van, but I didn't. I ran down the hill instead."

"I know, pup," he said, moving his hand from the wall to gently push up my chin. He forced me to look up at him. "Why did you do that?" he asked.

"I was afraid, Sir. I thought you were in danger," I confessed.

"Pup, do you think I'm so strict a Master that I would punish you for trying to save me?"

"You are always fair, Sir," I said to him sincerely. Tears welled in my eyes. "I didn't mean anything bad about you."

"I know you didn't pup, but listen to me. Do you realize what exactly you did today? You saved another person's life. That is incredible! Can you think of anything more heroic than saving a life?"

"You saved me though, Sir. Remember? That is how we met. You saved me from Devin and Kyle when they were beating me up."

"Yeah," he nodded, "and I knew that what I did was good. You need to know that what you did was good too. There is nothing wrong with feeling good about yourself. You should feel good, cuz you deserve it."

"Okay," I said finally, "but I don't see how what I did was any better than what you or Alex did. It's not like I could have saved that lady all by myself."

"True," he admitted, "but we aren't talkin bout me or Alex right now. We're talkin bout Petey. In a minute you're gonna strip off your clothes for me and take me inside of you." My heart raced as he verbalized his intentions. "And I'm gonna fill you with my load ... you know why?"

"Cuz it's my job," I said to him sweetly.

"Yeah, and cuz what else?"

"Um ... cuz good pups deserve owner cum?"

He nodded. "That's right. Good pups get owner cum, bad pups don't. But that's not all. I'm gonna give you something else ... something 'sides my cumload."

"What?" I asked eagerly.

"That will be later. It's a surprise." And with these words, he leaned in and kissed me. As he pressed his lips against my own, I reached out to him, grabbing him around his waist. I slid my hands upwards, feeling the hardness of his body as I tilted my head slightly, having learned how to effectively respond to his kisses.

His tongue entered me, as he moved his hands down the door until he reached my own waist. He leaned forward as he grabbed my shirttail and pulled it up my body. Briefly we pulled away from one another as he peeled the shirt over my head. Then instantly he reconnected himself to me. I could taste the beer on his breath and smell the masculine scent of him with which I was now so accustomed. I pulled myself towards him, pressing my body against his, as he ran his hands across my smooth back.

"Take off your shorts ... strip for me pup," he ordered. I did so, all the while staring up at him. I stood there then, wearing only my white briefs and socks, my leg bandaged just below the knee. I reached down again, this time grabbing the elastic waistband of my underwear. He smiled as I slid them down over my butt, all the while staring directly into his eyes. I stepped out of them, and then immediately fell to my knees. He did nothing to discourage me.

As I knelt there, I positioned my weight so that I wasn't putting pressure on my sore leg, but honestly gave it little thought. I'd have walked over a mile of broken glass to serve him at that moment. My own cock was rock hard, and my heart pounded in my chest. Even after having served him all of this time, I still got just as excited when I knew it was about to happen. Initially I'd been so modest around Matt, not wanting him to see my puny body, but at this moment it excited me to be so exposed. I loved the fact that I was smoothly shaved, marked as his property, and that he could see how rigid my cock was—proof of my eagerness to please him.

I took my eyes off from his face and focused my attention towards the bulge in his pants. I reached up reverently, touching it gently with my fingers, excited like a small child in a candy store. Just as my fingertips brushed against the fabric of his pants, he stepped backwards, distancing himself from me. I was surprised and disappointed, immediately looking back up at him. He looked down into my eyes, gauging the eagerness that I was obviously conveying to him. He took another step backwards, positioning himself in front of the bathtub. He was about three feet from me now. I continued to kneel in the exact position that he left me, knowing I was not to move until given permission.

He then took off his baseball cap, his movements being very slow. It was almost seductive the way that he paced himself. He turned the cap around, adjusting the back to make it slightly smaller and tossed it to me offhandedly. "Put it on," he said simply. I obeyed, turning the cap backwards before placing it over my head.

Then he pulled his polo shirt up, peeling it off his torso and over his head. He carelessly tossed it on the floor in front of the vanity. He stood there then, shirtless, towering over me. He was wearing khaki pants, and the waistband of his boxers was visible above the waistline. His abs were tight and smooth, caved in somewhat in the region of his innie belly button. My cock was literally throbbing as I stared up at him in awe. His chest was so smooth and hard, his pecs being well defined. He was not bulky though, just muscular and toned. When he reached above his head to grab the shower curtain bar, I saw his biceps flex and took in the sight of his neatly trimmed armpits. He was the embodiment of absolute perfection!

Involuntarily, I whimpered as I looked up at him. I craved him so badly. I wanted him inside of me, wanted to taste him, to feel him, to be of service to him. He responded to this audible expression of my desire, by merely smirking. He looked so cocky, so very self confident as he stood there. Then oh-so seductively he reached down with his right hand and positioned it in his groin area. He moved his legs apart slightly and assumed a position of absolute authority. He then brought down his left arm, quickly pointing to his crotch as he grabbed himself arrogantly with his right hand, squeezing his own hard cock and his balls. "This what you want, pup?" he asked sarcastically.

I could barely find my voice as I knelt there before him. I nodded my head automatically. "Yes Sir," I finally said, not recognizing my own voice as I did so. It was so quiet and timid, even more so than it normally was.

"What?" he demanded. "What did you say?!"

"Yes Sir!" I repeated, this time a little louder, but my voice was still shaky.

He unclasped the button on his khakis, allowing them to loosely slide down his hips. The outline of his cock was clearly visible within the confines of his white cotton boxers. I could see it pointing upwards, angled slightly to the left of his groin. He rubbed himself, allowing me to see the throbbing responsiveness of his rock-hard shaft. He neither moved towards me nor indicated that I had permission to crawl to him. He merely continued to rub himself, finally reaching up with the thumbs of both hands and grasping the waistband of his boxers. He pulled them down slowly. First his khakis slipped the rest of the way down, and then he proceeded to pull down his underwear.

He stepped out of them slowly, shoving the clothing into a pile with his foot. Now we were both naked. Unlike me, Matt sported a thick growth of hair around his pubic region. It was medium brown in color, just like the hair on his head. He had an almost-invisible trail of hair that ascended from his groin and went part way up his abdomen. Other than this, he was smooth from the waist up. His arms were mildly hairy, covered with a very faint-colored layer of brown hair. It was just his forearms really, as he was smooth for the most part.

Everything about him was the opposite of me. He was tall with very broad, masculine shoulders. He had a very clearly defined chest, and tight, rock-hard abs. His groin was covered with pubic hair, and his legs and forearms were slightly hairy. I, on the other hand, was very skinny, puny compared to him. My chest was not cut like his, but merely smooth and flat. My shoulders were narrow, and my body was entirely smooth. I had very soft features and big, brown eyes. It was with these eyes that I then looked up at him imploringly, pleading with him as I conveyed nonverbally to him my hunger to serve. I knew that this hunger was in turn feeding his desire to be served. We fit together so well, each providing for the other the very thing that we craved so intensely.

He did not command me to crawl to him. I think the only reason was simply because he was aware of my bandaged leg. Instead, he stepped back to the position where he'd just been moments before. He positioned himself above me in a manner that commanded authority, planting his feet firmly on either side of my slender body. My face was merely centimeters from his rock-hard cock, and I made virtually no effort to back away or to even look up at him. I simply stared at the part of him to which I was most enslaved. My mouth fell open as he grabbed my head with his left hand. He used his other hand to hold firmly to the base of his cock, guiding it into the warm, comfortable hole that was made for it. He released his cock and grabbed a hold of the other side of my head, thrusting smoothly as he slid into me.

I heard him moan as I felt his rigid cock make contact with my tongue. I carefully clamped my lips around the shaft, concentrating on providing him a smooth entry. I'd become expert at this by now, and cranked my jaw at the exact moment his cockhead reached my throat. He continued to slide in with one smooth movement, burying himself balls-deep. He did not start to thrust into me, or pump me on his shaft, but instead savored the warmth and tightness of my mouth. I felt the intensity of his grip and realized he was flexing the muscles of his ass, relishing the heaven-like feeling of my deep, hungry throat.

He finally pulled me back up his shaft, bringing me to the very tip of his cock. As he held me there I rolled my eyes to look up at him. I knew this was what he wanted. He wanted to see the hunger, my desire to please. He held my capped head there in his hands, staring down at me authoritatively. "Suck my cock!" he ordered simply, and then he began pumping. He had developed an ability to coordinate the downward pump with his own hip thrusting. My mouth and tongue had long since memorized the shape of his cock. I knew every vein, every single inch of him. It was similar to the way our tongues familiarize themselves with the inside of our own mouth. That was how well I knew my owner.

He continued with the synchronized thrusting and pumping, fucking my throat as fiercely as if it were an ass or a pussy. He'd trained me well, teaching me how to take him deep without gagging. I knew where to go mentally to block out all of my feelings of pain or discomfort. I knew how to give up virtually every shred of control that I had over my own body. I had learned how to be his hole.

I wish I knew the very thoughts that flashed through his mind as he rocked himself in and out of me. On more than one occasion I'd asked him about this, trying to get him to offer me some insight. He always gave vague answers, telling me he thought about how good he felt and knowing how right it was, how it simply was "the way it should be."

His thrusting became more rapid, and his grip tightened on my head. I knew I would soon have my reward. I focused on continuing to provide him with the suction that his cock deserved. I wanted to please him more than anything in the world. He slammed himself in and out of me, verbalizing his pleasure by saying "Oh yeah! ... Fuck yeah!" Then finally he gripped my head tighter than ever and slid all the way into me, forcing my nose flat against his groin. Then I felt the cumload firing into his throbbing cock. I felt it with my own tongue. It was coming!!

He erupted, pumping his load deep into me, and I felt his cock spasm in my mouth. After three or four heavy spurts I began to taste the load that was backing up in my throat. I gulped quickly, being unable to breathe, but not even thinking of it. "Ahhhhhhh ... uh ... ahhhhh!" he moaned as he emptied himself. I swallowed eagerly. He pushed me away from him quickly when he was finished, both of us gasping for breath. He leaned against the countertop of the vanity, staring at himself in the mirror. "Oh fuck! That was hot! Pup, get in the shower."

I quickly rose to my feet and stepped in the shower, adjusting the water to the temperature that I knew he'd like.

2

Alex and Drew rode with Eric over to the party, and Matt and I followed in Matt's SUV. I sat quietly alongside of Matt during the ride as I most often did. Generally when he and I were alone together, this was typical behavior on my part. Sure, there were times that I would get excited about different things and would ramble. This seemed to amuse him, and he'd allow me to go on and on, looking at me occasionally and smiling. Other times it seemed that Matt would deliberately provoke me to debate him, bringing up topics of which I was strongly opinionated and then playing the devil's advocate. I would most often avoid arguing at all costs, but when I did finally express myself, he'd tell me it was okay for me to have my own opinion, even if it was wrong. At that moment, though, I could think of not one single thing in the world over which to argue with Matt. He had made me so genuinely happy. All that I really wanted to do was to find ways to show my devotion and appreciation to him. As I spent more and more time with him, I did not resent the fact that he had control over my actions and behaviors. Instead, I became more and more comfortable with the feeling of security that he provided me. He, in turn, seemed to become awakened to the reality that he was naturally designed to be the person in charge.

I noticed this tendency in other aspects of his life besides our relationship. With his social connections and platonic relationships even, Matt was always the decision maker. He was the one whom other people looked towards for guidance and approval. He was the one who spoke up when certain things needed to be said. He did all of this in such an unassuming and confident manner that it was for the most part unremarkable. The people who knew him understood that Matt was Matt.

To me, though, Matt was so very much more than just a figurehead of dominance. He was the one who had saved me, single-handedly taking on my bullies and sweeping me to safety. Then he had selected me, lured me into his life, and ultimately claimed me as his own. He taught me so much, constantly challenging me to believe in myself and to be the best person I could be. He was always there behind me to catch me if I stumbled, yet he allowed me to walk on my own, helping me to grow stronger. In some ways it seemed ironic to me, for on the one hand he was training me to serve and obey without question, yet on the other he was instilling within me a sense of self pride and independence. I think he enjoyed watching me grow, become emotionally stronger, face my fears; but he also was always aware of his own status and of how it was so natural for me to submit to him.

As I sat there next to him, I started to grow a little bit excited as I remembered his words to me earlier in the bathroom. He'd promised me a very special reward later this evening. I had no idea what it could be, but I trusted him so completely that I knew it must be something extraordinary. Never had I been disappointed by him before when he made a promise to me. He always kept his word, reinforcing the trust and faith that I had in him.

We saw Eric pull his jeep into a long driveway and up onto an area of lawn that was obviously designated for parking. There were about fifteen to twenty other vehicles already at the party when we got there. As Matt pulled his big van-like vehicle up next to the jeep, we both unfastened our seatbelts and climbed out. Immediately I heard the rap music blaring from the house we were about to enter. I quickly hopped out of the vehicle and stepped in line behind Matt as we headed towards the center of the party. Eric, Alex, and Drew walked with us as we approached the building. When we got to the door, I carefully reached up to place my hand against Matt's lower back. He made no indication to me that this was unacceptable, so I lowered my hand and looped my fingers just inside the waistband of his pants. It felt safer to me, in these new surroundings, to simply be touching him, to be attached to him and behind him. He acted as if he did not even notice.

Eric was very polite, immediately introducing us to the party's host, his friend Adam. Adam was a somewhat cute, though rather effeminate, dark-haired, preppy-type guy, probably in his mid-to-late twenties. His hair was sort of spiky, and he displayed a wide toothy grin as he greeted us. Everything about both him and his home seemed impeccable, even his fingernails being expertly manicured. As Eric and Adam chatted with one another, bringing Alex and Matt into the conversation naturally, Drew and I both sort of moved towards one another. I carefully let go of my grip of Matt and turned to Drew, who then asked me if I wanted to go with him to get a drink. I agreed without hesitation, but moved myself over to the side of Matt first, allowing him to see me standing there.

When there was a break in the conversation and Matt looked down at me, I said to him, "Drew and I are going to get a drink, would you like something?" Matt requested a beer, as did Alex, but Eric declined, stating he'd get his own in a minute. We headed towards the area of the house which was obviously the kitchen and found two large tubs of iced beverages displayed prominently on a large round table.

"This place is huge," said Drew. "Did you notice the artwork?"

I shrugged. "I didn't really notice it." I looked up to scan the room, noticing the details of the home. The kitchen alone was as spacious as our entire apartment. "Wonder what this guy does. Maybe he's a doctor or something."

"Maybe. He is friends with Eric," Drew stated, referring to the possible connection of their medical professions.

"I want to go outside for a smoke in a minute," said Drew.

"I thought you quit," I reminded him.

"Yeah, but this is a party! Can't drink and not smoke at the same time," he rationalized.

"Whatever," I said.

After getting the beers for Matt and Alex, I found in the selection of beverages a berry-flavored wine cooler for myself. Drew fixed himself a vodka and tonic, and then we headed back towards the living room. The music was much louder than when we had first arrived, and several more guests were pouring into the house. The room was becoming crowded, and I actually had to look around to locate where Matt had gone. I saw him over in the corner, but Alex was not with him.

"Just a second," I yelled to Drew above the music. "I'll take this to Matt and then meet you outside."

"Okay!" Drew yelled.

I pushed my way through the crowd then, inching my way closer to Matt. As I approached him, I noticed that he had his hand against the wall, leaning against it, as he looked down. He was talking to someone who was standing there in front of him. I recognized the person but could not remember from where. When I got closer, it suddenly dawned on me. It was the guy Matt and I had met at the bar the single time we had gone there. His name was Ryan.

Instantly I recalled the feelings I'd had that night when we had first encountered Ryan. I had swelled inside with jealousy, for Ryan was sub like myself, and was obviously interested in Matt. I'd been rather rude to him, and Matt was displeased. He ordered me to apologize to him.

That particular evening had ended sweetly for me, though, as Matt made it abundantly clear to Ryan that he was with me. Ryan had actually witnessed me serving Matt in the backroom of the bar and then had exited swiftly. But now here he was again, and this time Matt was leaning in to talk to him. All those feelings of jealousy and insecurity suddenly overwhelmed me once again.

"Hello Ryan," I said, as I approached them. "I never expected to see you here."

He smiled broadly at me. "Yeah, what a coincidence, huh?"

"You want a beer, Ryan?" asked Matt.

"Oh, no Sir ... but maybe a wine cooler or something."

Matt looked at me intently, and I immediately handed over my wine cooler to Ryan. "Here, I can go get another one." I handed Matt his drink as well, and then turned to head back towards the kitchen. This was like a replay of the night at the bar. Matt had made me go get us drinks while he stayed and talked to Ryan. All the while, I was consumed with feelings of jealousy and fears of what they might possibly be talking about.

When I finally made it back to the beverages, I had to wait, for there was a crowd of people milling around the table. Most of the party guests were guys, but a few women were in attendance. Seemed to me that a lot of gay men had very close female friends. A few of them always showed up for the gay parties. After getting another drink finally, I decided to head outside and find Drew. I was very concerned about Matt being alone with Ryan, but I knew that by horning in, I'd probably only make matters worse for myself. I did not want to again be punished or scolded for being rude.

When I did find Drew, he was over on the side of a big patio deck, smoking a cigarette and talking to some girl. As I approached them, Drew introduced me. "Petey, this is Cammie. We just met," he laughed.

"Hi Petey," she said sweetly. Cammie was a petite blonde, with a short, boyish haircut. She was wearing a very feminine-looking, summer dress and sandals. "Nice to meet you," she said. "Are you two boyfriends?"

Drew laughed. "Hardly! Petey's not my type. He's not bossy enough."

"Ohh ..." she said. "So how do you know Adam?"

"We don't actually," said Drew. "We met his friend Eric just today. He was one of the paramedics who was at the scene of that big accident out on the Interstate."

"Oh my god. Were you in the accident?"

"No, but we helped some of the people who were hurt before the paramedics got there. Well, at least Petey did."

"You did? Wow." I looked down at the ground when she looked over to me.

"Well we all did really," I said.

We chatted for a few more minutes while Drew finished his cigarette, and then Cammie left us. "Guess who else is here!" I finally said to Drew.

"Who?" he asked.

"Remember that guy Ryan? The one I told you about that was hitting on Matt at the bar that one night."

"Oh yeah? Well, don't worry. You know Matt isn't interested in anyone but you."

"I don't know. He's in there talking to him now."

"You think he wants to do something with him?" Drew asked.

"I don't know! What if he does, Drew? I mean they were being pretty friendly with each other. I hate that guy so much! Why doesn't he just go and find himself someone else, and leave Matt alone!"

"Just chill out, Petey. Even if Matt does decide to do something with him, doesn't mean he cares any less for you. Ya already know that Alex does that sometimes. He even wanted me to pimp you for him before we met Matt. Remember?"

"Yeah, well I don't know if I can handle it if he does that. I'll be too jealous." I was starting to become emotional, finding myself wanting to cry. It was a struggle for me, for I had been trying to act more maturely and not be such a whiner. But then how was it that Matt could do this tonight? Why did he tell me earlier today how much he loved me, then make love to me in the bathroom and promise me a special reward tonight, and then turn right around and hook up with some other boy? I then wished we had headed straight home from the restaurant and not accepted Eric's invitation to come to the party.

As I was standing there, allowing these thoughts to race through my brain, the patio door opened behind me. It was Matt, and he had Ryan with him. "Hey pup, wondered where you disappeared." I smiled up at him sheepishly.

"Sorry Sir. It's just that it's so crowded in there, and I knew Drew was out here having a smoke. So Ryan, how have you been?"

"Oh dude, I'm doin great. I totally can't believe I came all the way down here to this party and ran into you guys. Matt told me about what happened to you today. That's pretty wild, especially the way you crawled into that truck and saved that woman. That's pretty awesome."

"Thanks," I said quietly. "So how is it that you ended up coming to this party anyways? You must know someone here, huh?"

"Well, I met Adam online. We have chatted on and off for a couple months, and so I decided to drive down to his party. He has been tryin to hook me up with his friend Eric, the paramedic dude that you guys met."

"Small world, huh?" said Drew.

"Eric doesn't really seem like your type though," I added. "He isn't, um ... you know, very ..."

"Dominant?" Ryan finished the sentence for me.

"Right," I nodded.

"That whole thing is kinda new to him, I guess. I met Adam in the leather chat room of gay dot com. Adam is sub himself, but has been friends with Eric for years. He is confident from the conversations and stuff he's had with Eric that there is a Dom in there waitin to bust out." He laughed as he said this, and Drew and I both smiled back at him.

"It's true though," said Matt seriously. "If he is truly dominant, then all it'll take is a good sub to awaken that within him."

Ryan raised his hand as if waiting to be called on in class. "That would be me," he said cheerfully.

Drew and I glanced at one another, and I thought *Oh Brother!* "So did I awaken that within you, Sir?" I asked.

Matt put his hand on my shoulder as he looked down at me. "Nah, pup, sorry. You don't get the credit. Already knew I was Dom. Had known that awhile. Do have to say, though, that you are the first pup I've ever owned, and only one I ever want."

I beamed up at him, but then suddenly thought of how he'd phrased that. The smile slipped off my face as I looked up into his eyes. "You mean, Sir, because I'm such a pain that you'd never wanna put up with anyone else like me?"

The three of them laughed in unison at my expense as Matt looked into my eyes. "No pup, cuz you are all I need."

"Aw, that's so sweet," chimed in Ryan. For some reason he just totally annoyed me. I wanted to encourage him to just go away, to go find Eric or some other unattached guy instead of hanging around my owner and me. Instead I just ignored him and continued to look up at Matt. "Hey, I'm ready for another drink. You need one too Petey?" Ryan asked. "Anyone else?"

It surprised me that Ryan was being so polite to me, but I then turned to him and graciously declined. "No, but thanks Ryan. I just got a drink a minute ago."

"Well, when you're ready, I'll get it for you, okay? Right now I'm gonna go get one for me and then try to find Eric and Adam."

"Sir, do you know where Alex is at?" asked Drew.

"Sorry, lost track of him when I started hangin with Ryan. Probably he's with Adam and Eric somewhere."

"Okay, I'll go with ya, then Ryan," said Drew.

We spent the next hour or so mingling with some of the guests at the party. I pretty much stayed by Matt's side, and we danced a few times together. Intermittently during the evening, Ryan would return to us, constantly offering to replace our drinks for us. He was being surprisingly polite and friendly towards me, so I was starting to feel a little bit guilty for having had such strong feelings of dislike and jealousy towards him just a short time ago.

I was so happy with how Matt was treating me too. He was showering me with so much affection and attention, pulling me close to his side, touching me and holding onto me publicly. It made me so happy to be viewed by all of these people as Matt's boyfriend, his property. Even the times that Ryan would interrupt us, offering his comments or asking if we wanted another drink, Matt did not seem to be very concerned with him at all. I was sure then that my fear upon first seeing Matt with Ryan earlier in the evening, was total unfounded. Matt quite obviously had eyes only for me this evening, and as always, I myself thought only of him.

Finally at about half past eleven, Matt informed me that we were gonna split from the party, but Alex and Drew were going to stick around a while longer. Alex assured Matt that they'd just ride with Eric back to his house, so we said our goodbyes to the host and headed across the lawn. Suddenly I noticed Matt motioning to Ryan with a head movement. Ryan immediately came over to us. "We're ready to go," Matt said to him.

"Okay cool, or I mean yes Sir," he said, smiling up to Matt. "I'm ready."

Ready for what?! I wondered, as I immediately was puzzled. Was Matt taking Ryan with us? "Sir," I said to Matt, tugging against his belt loop, "are we giving Ryan a ride somewhere?"

"Yeah," said Matt flippantly, "We're taking him back to his motel room." His tone was very matter-of-fact, and so I did not ask any more questions but just stood there behind my owner. When we got to the SUV, I was right behind Matt. Usually when we used this vehicle, we both would enter from the driver's side door. He'd unlock and open it, and then I'd climb in, sliding partway over in the seat. Then he would get in behind the wheel. This time, however, I waited to see what I was supposed to do. I wasn't sure if I'd be riding up front with Matt or alone in the back. Matt stopped and opened the back door for Ryan and then looked at me, waiting for me to crawl in front. I smiled up at him, relieved, and quickly crawled in the vehicle.

As we headed over to Ryan's motel room, I wondered why Ryan didn't just get a ride with someone else or didn't just drive his own car. He certainly must have driven himself to the party. We drove for about ten minutes, Ryan instructing Matt where to turn, and then finally pulled into a small strip motel. "I'm in room 124, Sir," Ryan told him. "Over there, that red Ford Ranger is mine." He pointed to the small pickup truck. It was the same type of vehicle that Drew owned. Ryan must have gotten a ride from someone else over to the party.

Matt parked the SUV in the parking place next to Ryan's truck and turned off the ignition. He then turned and spoke to me for the first time since we had left the party. "Come on Petey," he said casually, and opened his door. My hands were shaking as I slid out behind him. So Matt was gonna do something with Ryan, and he was gonna make me watch. This can't be happening! I had no choice, though, but to follow them inside.

When I stepped inside, Matt told me to close the door. He had already moved over to the other side of the small room and was seating himself in a chaise-type chair in the corner. Hesitantly, I obeyed him, and then stepped closer to him. Ryan was on the other side of us, standing in front of a dresser. "Strip fag!" ordered Matt, and I thought he was talking to me. Ryan, though, began removing his clothing immediately.

"Sir," I said quietly, "would it be okay for me to just wait out in the truck?"

He looked at me intently, as if he were perplexed by my question. "No, don't be silly pup. You can't wait outside. Now get over here and stand in front of me." Tears were starting to well in my eyes as I stepped over to him. I slipped myself into position, standing between his outstretched legs. "What's the matter? Why are you cryin?" He had moved his hands up onto my upper arms, pulling me closer to him.

"Nothing Sir," I said to him, my voice almost a whisper. "I'm sorry."

"Pup, answer me! Why are you cryin?"

"... Um ... oh Sir," tears were now streaming down my cheeks. "Sir I'm sorry. You know I accept it, no matter what you do."

"Accept it? Accept what?" he said to me sternly.

"For you to be with whoever you choose ... if you choose to be with ... him," I pointed to Ryan, "I accept it. It's just I feel bad. It hurts me inside." He then pulled me into him, twisting me so that I was sitting on his leg, and he grabbed my chin with his fingers, positioning my face to look up directly at him.

"Pup, did you forget again what I promised you?" he asked softly. "Huh?"

I looked at him, remembering how he'd promised me in the very beginning that he'd never ever hurt me. "You promised to never hurt me," I meekly said to him.

"Yeah, and I promised you something else, just a few hours ago. Remember?"

"That you were gonna give me a surprise—a reward," I said.

"Bingo!" he said. "I didn't say I was gonna hurt your feelings and make you cry. I said I was gonna reward you.

You think I'd get it on with this fag in front of you or something, and tell you that's your reward?"

I shook my head, suddenly feeling ashamed of myself. "I thought you forgot, Sir. I thought you wanted him instead of me."

"Look at that," Matt said, pointing his finger towards the mirror that was on the wall opposite us. "What do you see?"

I looked over and caught our reflection, Matt looking as powerful and strong as ever, hot as hell. He was sitting there confidently and I, the miniature version of him, was sitting on his leg. My legs dangled down, toes barely scraping the floor. We looked so perfect together, so very well-suited with our matching haircuts and similar clothing. "I see my owner, Sir. I see him and his pup."

"You got that right. It's just you and me. You belong to me—my only pup, and there is no other. You understand?"

"Yes Sir," I said, finally smiling at him.

"Fag! Get over here," Matt suddenly barked. It startled me to hear him speak this way. He obviously was directing his order to Ryan, but it surprised me for he'd always been so insistent on me showing Ryan the utmost respect. Ryan literally jumped to attention, moving directly in front of us. He was now completely naked. "Kneel!" Matt commanded, and Ryan dropped to his knees immediately.

I stared down at Ryan, wide-eyed, uncertain as to why he was kneeling in front of us. I felt a sudden urge to get off from Matt's lap and step aside, to allow Ryan to bow before his superior. Matt, however, held me firmly in place. Then Matt's voice softened as he re-directed his attention to me. "Pup, why does this fag kneel to us?"

I looked into Matt's eyes, thinking carefully before answering. "Because he is less than you?" I stated with uncertainty. "He is inferior to you. He's sub, and you are dominant."

"True," Matt said, "but he kneels before us both, not just me."

I then thought that Matt was trying to teach me that I should immediately have moved, as my first instinct had told me. "I'm sorry Sir. I will move for him to worship you." I squirmed in his lap then, trying to rise, but he held me in place once more.

"Stay!" Matt commanded. "Do not move unless ordered to do so."

"Yes Sir," I said.

"Fag, why do you kneel?" Matt said loudly to Ryan. Matt and I both looked down at him as he himself looked down at the ground in front of him.

"Sir, I kneel to serve you. I kneel because I was ordered to do so by you, my superior."

"And why do you kneel before the pup?" Matt asked.

"Because he is yours, Sir. He is your property, greater than this humble faggot slave. So this slave kneels here to serve both you, Sir, and your pup."

"Very good," said Matt, "well-stated.

"Pup, I promised you a special reward. This fag is what I'm using to give it to you. Do you understand?"

I shook my head slowly, not comprehending what this whole scene was even about. "Sir, it is not my place to be served. I don't understand. I am a sub myself, born with a need and desire to serve without expecting any form of reciprocation. You have taught this to me, Sir. I know it is true."

"And you were chosen by me, your superior, to be my pup, so you are very valuable property to me. It is this distinction that makes you superior to this fag and deserving of his worship. I've employed the use of this fag to reward my pup. Don't resist, or you'll be resisting me. You understand?"

I then looked Matt in the eyes and slowly nodded, suddenly realizing what this visit to the motel room was all about. At the party, Matt must have been speaking to Ryan about using him. He must have persuaded the sub somehow to agree to service me. Or perhaps he had merely told him that he needed his services and had not explained the details to Ryan. In any event, Ryan was here now kneeling before me, ready to do as my owner commanded.

"Pup, I don't want you to make this about him. He is nothing more than a hole for us to use for pleasure. He knows this, and he knows this night is about you and about me rewarding you. Let's keep this special, between just you and me. Think of the fag as being an extension of myself, a tool I'm using to give you pleasure. Do you see what I'm sayin?"

"Yes, Sir," I responded. "I think so. You want me to be served the way that I serve you, and you are gonna use him to do it."

"Exactly," he smiled at me. He then pulled my head into him, pressing his lips against mine and kissed me so passionately. It instantly was as he had said. We were alone in the room together. Ryan did not even exist to me as I swooned in Matt's embrace.

"Fag, take off his shoes and worship his feet," Matt commanded. I looked into Matt's eyes with astonishment.

"Sir, I do not deserve to have my feet worshipped," but as I was saying this, Ryan was already unlacing my shoes. "Thank you, Sir," I said to Matt. "Thank you so much." I stared into Matt's eyes then as I felt the fag kneeling at my feet slowly remove each of my shoes and peel off my socks. When the warmth of his tongue touched the skin of my feet, I squirmed a little for it sort of tickled. "Sir, it's tickling me!" I giggled.

Matt playfully dug his fingers into my side. "You mean like this?" I busted up laughing then. He then reached down to the tail of my shirt and grasped it, pulling it smoothly over my head. I continued to sit there on his lap while Ryan licked my feet, slowly and reverently kissing them in between the lapping of his tongue. As he did this I reached up and touched my collar with my fingertips, running them back and forth against the leather.

"I'm gonna take you to the bed," Matt informed me, and he then stood up, scooping me up in his arms. "Stay on the floor fag," he said to Ryan without looking at him. He then carried me to the bed and placed me down, flat on my back. He unbuttoned my jeans then and removed them from me. Then he pulled off my briefs. I was suddenly naked there before him, while he remained fully clothed. He sat on the edge of the bed and looked down at me, staring into my eyes. "Pup, you've never felt a mouth on your cock, have you?"

I shook my head, "No Sir."

"Well, for the first few minutes, I want you to just lie back and enjoy the sensation. Don't cum though. Don't you dare cum until I tell you, okay?"

"No Sir, I never would!" I assured him.

"Good boy. Now look at me, right into my eyes. I want you looking at me when you slide your cock into the hole." Just as he said that, I felt Ryan between my legs. I spread them apart slightly as his fingertips brushed gently against my balls. I was excited, my heart racing, and I felt my cock throbbing in anticipation. I dared not look down at him though, but instead fixed my gaze upon my owner.

"Sir, it feels so good to be touched like that. It sorta tickles though. You know how ticklish I am ... down there," I giggled as I confessed this to him.

"Just relax," Matt told me. He then leaned in to kiss me again, and as he did so, I knew that I was by now rock hard, my cock throbbing against my belly. I felt Matt's tongue enter my mouth as I felt the other tongue lapping against my nut sac and then moving slowly up the shaft of my cock. I wrapped my arms tightly around Matt, pressing myself into him as I felt the passion of his kiss overwhelm me. He then slowly pulled away from me, continuing to stare into my eyes. Then I felt it, a sensation unlike anything I'd ever felt before. I felt the warmth of Ryan's mouth as he slid it around my throbbing cock.

I stared right at Matt, my eyes getting wider as I resisted the urge to close them and moan in response to the indescribable pleasure I was experiencing. "Sir, ohh, oh god Sir ... it feels so good." The feeling of the warm mouth was so extremely different than what I'd ever experienced previously. Before this, the only stimulation I'd ever had to my penis was by either my own hand or by Matt's. The feeling of a mouth, though, was so extremely warm and soft. It was like my cock was sliding into a warm, cozy hole. I did not want the feeling to end—ever!

"Oh Sir!" I whimpered to him, "This is how I make you feel when I serve you?"

He smiled at me, nodding. "Even better," he said, "cuz you're so damned good at it." I smiled as I looked at him, reaching up to run my small hand across his rock-hard chest.

"I love you Sir. I love you so much." I then lay back, closing my eyes and relaxing, just as Matt had instructed me, and I felt the warm hole sliding up and down on my cock. It went all the way down to the base of my shaft, completely engulfing my hard prick. I felt the tongue press against me, sliding against the underside of my shaft as the hole bobbed up and down slowly.

"Gonna start to pump him on ya, pup," Matt said. I opened my eyes and looked down, seeing Matt's hand firmly gripping Ryan's head as he pumped him up n down on my cock.

"Oh Sir, it feels good! Oh thank you Sir!" I cried out. "I love when you make it go all the way in, when you make it go deep!"

"Like this?" he asked, as he shoved Ryan's head down forcefully, completely impaling him with the full length of my seven-inch hard-on.

"Ahhh, oh yes ... yes Sir! Oh Sir, it feels so good!"

"You pump it, pup," Matt instructed me. "Grab his head!" As I reached down to grab a hold of Ryan's head, Matt let go of it and grabbed two pillows that were on the bed beside me. He slid his arm behind me and pushed me up, shoving the pillows under my head so that I was propped up. "Take control, pup. Pump his head on your cock just like you're alone in your room jackin off. Go for it!"

I was now sitting up on the bed, comfortably propped up with the pillows, my legs stretched out in front of me. Ryan was lying flat on his belly in between my legs, gently resting his palms against my thighs as he took my cock into his mouth. I reached down, as Matt had instructed me, and wrapped my hands around the sides of Ryan's head. He rolled his eyes to look up, and I saw for the very first time ever the same look of servitude and worship which Matt must have seen every time I knelt before him. Now, however, the tables were turned, and it was I who was in the throne being worshipped; I was for once in a position of power and control.

As this reality suddenly struck me, my first impulse was to release him, to simply let go of his head and pull away. It did not feel right to me, for all I could think of at that moment was that he must feel so humiliated. I did not want to hurt him in any way, and I was afraid I might do so. I loosened my grip on his head and pulled back, my cock suddenly starting to go soft.

"Pup, what are you doin?" Matt asked me. He leaned into me, cupping my chin in his palm and turning my face to look at him. "What's the matter?"

"Sir," I said, "I don't think I can do it. It ... um ... it doesn't feel right."

"How does it feel to you when you serve me?" he asked.

"It feels wonderful Sir. It feels perfect."

"Why?"

"Because Sir, it just does. It feels like it is where I'm supposed to be. It's my job to serve you."

"Exactly," Matt agreed with me, "just like it's Ryan's job to serve you. His status is less than you, pup. It's his duty to serve you. That's what he's for."

"Sir, will I serve him afterwards, I mean when he is done serving me?"

Matt looked me right in the eye then, with a look of stern, unwavering certainty. "Absolutely not! You are mine, boy, and you belong to me. You never, EVER serve anyone but me. You understand?"

"Yes Sir," I said. "I'm sorry, Sir. It's just it doesn't seem fair to use him like this."

"It's not fair," Matt stated matter-of-factly. "Not supposed to be fair. It's right though; it's the way it should be. How would you feel if when you went to serve me, I told you no, never mind, cuz it wouldn't be fair?"

"But Sir, it's not the same! It is who I AM! I am born to serve; I'm your pup!"

"And he is born to serve, too," Matt said, pointing to Ryan. "Now it's your job to just enjoy it. Take it for granted that you deserve it because you're above him, and when you do, think about how you make me feel when you serve me. This could be the only time in your life you'll ever be served. Do it pup! Fuck the fags face! Do it for me, your owner!"

His words to me had sent a wave of excitement through my body, and I was instantly rock hard again. I smiled up at Matt and then quickly looked down at the fag boy between my outstretched legs. I grabbed his head then again and pushed it down as hard as I could onto my cock. "Yeah!!" I screamed as I felt my cock slide into his tight throat.

"Sir, I love how the tongue feels against my cock!" I pumped the cocksucker on my shaft quickly as I said this. "Oh Sir, thank you so much. It feels so good!" Ryan was offering no resistance but had yielded himself completely to my control. "It feels best when it's all the way in like this—" I thrust his head down forcefully, ramming myself balls-deep into his throat. Instantly his gag reflex kicked in, and he started to choke.

By reflex, I quickly let go of his head. "Don't stop!" Matt said to me. "Not your job to worry bout whether or not he gags. Just do what feels best to you." For some reason this comment struck me as being so funny, and instantly I smiled, starting to giggle. Matt laughed back at me, and then said, "Now pump it, pup. Jack your cock til you're ready to shoot!"

I then grabbed a hold of the fag's head again and pushed it down into the position that felt best to me. My cock was all the way in his throat, but this time he did not gag. Then I started to pump. I did not pull him all the way up on my shaft, but only part way, so that I could feel the warmth of his mouth around my shaft the entire time and so that the most sensitive area of my prick was quickly sliding in and out of his tight throat. It was exactly like Matt had said to me. It was just like jacking myself off, although the sensation of the mouth on my cock was a thousand times better than my own hand.

I was getting more and more excited as I continued to pump the cocksucker on my throbbing cock. For the first time ever, I got that incredible rush of confidence that Doms must experience on a daily basis—that comes from being in control and from having power. I smiled to myself as I thought about the fact that I was gonna use this fag until I was ready to drain myself, and that when it was over, I'd owe him nothing. There'd be no reciprocation, for it was my right to be served, and it was his job to serve me. *Fuck yeah!*

"I'm so close, Sir!" I screamed. "I can feel it!"

"Push him all the way down, pup! Go balls deep!"

I tightened my fingers around Ryan's head then, digging into his scalp, as I rammed him all the way down on my cock. It felt like nothing I'd ever experienced before.

"Drain it!" Matt ordered. "Shoot your load!"

It was like those last four or five seconds before I shot were in slow motion. It was the most unbelievable feeling of ecstatic build-up and release that I'd ever known. I felt like I was a volcano about to erupt. It was right there, the cum already having fired into my shaft, and I prolonged the release just a few seconds by tightening the muscles in my pelvic region. Then I pumped it, letting go completely! As I did so I moaned loudly and gripped Ryan's head tighter than ever before. "Oh god!! Fuck yeah!!" His warm hungry mouth remained tightly clamped around my shaft as I emptied my cum into him. Jet after jet fired from my cock, as Matt leaned into me, pressing his lips against my neck. My body was shaking, and I was sweating profusely as the waves of pleasure washed over me. Then as I began to return to calmness, Matt started kissing me. He kissed my neck and made his way slowly up my chin as I lay there, eyes closed, gasping for breath.

Then I released Ryan, shoving him away from my cock quickly and carelessly as I grabbed a hold of my owner. "Oh my god, I love you, Sir!" I said, repeating it over and over as I pressed my small body into his rock-hard torso. "I love you so much! Thank you, Sir! Oh god, thank you!"

Matt wrapped his strong arms around me then and kissed me with unbridled passion, driving his tongue deep into my mouth. I squirmed in his embrace, trying to push my body as close to him as possible, but he grabbed my sides and moved me away from him, releasing me. I looked up at him, eager to touch him, my cock still throbbing even after just draining my load. He reached down and quickly stripped his shirt off, pulling it over his head. Then he kicked off his sneakers and undid his jeans, stepping out of them and tossing them aside.

Ryan had moved over to the side of the bed and was kneeling beside Matt. He reached up and grabbed the waistband of Matt's underwear, pulling it down. Matt allowed him to do this, lifting up each leg one at a time to step out of the boxers. Then Ryan looked up at him after having taken in the sight of my owner's cock for the first time. The look in Ryan's eyes was one of unbelievable astonishment. I could relate well to that shock, remembering how I'd responded the first time I'd seen Matt naked and in a state of arousal. The eye contact that Matt had with Ryan lasted only briefly, though, for he then reached down to Ryan's shoulders and pushed him backwards. Matt was not excessively forceful, but delivered to him a clear message. He was not interested in being served by him. The fag had already done his job and it was over. Matt then turned back to me as my heart swelled with tremendous pride.

"Roll over!" Matt commanded me, and immediately I assumed the position. I quickly got on all fours and started to back myself up to him so that I was at the edge of the bed, but before I'd even done so, he had grabbed a hold of my hips and literally pulled me into place. "Lube it!" Matt stated to Ryan, and within five seconds I felt the warmth of Ryan's tongue again on my body. This time he was licking my ass, driving his tongue into me, saturating my hole with his spit. I guess Matt had not been completely done with the fag after all, but then when Matt was finally satisfied, he once again pushed Ryan aside and stepped back into position.

With one very smooth movement, Matt drove his cock into my ass. This position, doggy-style, was by far my least favorite, for it generally was not as comfortable for me. Plus, I could not look into my owner's face while he fucked me. None of that mattered now, though, for all I cared about was pleasing him. I wanted him inside of me so badly that I pressed my buttocks backwards, forcing them against his body, even though he was already completely buried within me. He moaned with pleasure as he felt my tightness, and I myself was so hot for him that I scarcely noticed the initial pain. "Oh Sir!" I cried. "I love when you're inside me!"

His rock-hard, nine-inch prick jabbed deep into me, slamming against my prostate. My already hard cock stiffened all the more as I whimpered in response to the powerful pleasure-pain mixture that swept throughout my body. He was holding onto my hips, gripping them tightly, as he began to drill my ass unlike he'd ever done before. He had positioned himself against the side of the bed, his shins pressing against the mattress and his feet planted firmly on the ground. He took total control of me then, plugging me mercilessly, maximizing his own pleasure with every thrust. He would fuck me for awhile with quick staccato thrusts and then slow it down, grinding into me slowly. Obviously he was loving the sensation and made every effort to prolong his pleasure.

I myself was beginning to approach a point where I was gonna shoot another load, trying desperately to refrain from doing so, for I knew better than to do it without his specific command. "Fuck yeah!" he said as he drilled his cock into me. "You like your owner's cock up your tight ass, boy? You like that pup?"

"Yes Sir! Oh god! Sir! It's—" I was trying to speak in between my gasps for breath. "It's gonna make me shoot again Sir! Oh god!"

"Yeah? You wanna shoot another load for your owner, pup? You wanna shoot a load while I'm drillin your tight fag ass? Huh?"

"Oh yes Sir! Oh god!! Oh please!"

He then rammed himself into me deep, holding it there all the way. I knew he was gonna pump his cum into me. "Shoot it!" he screamed, and we both fired our loads at that instant. Mine went spraying up against my chest and all over the bedspread beneath me. I felt my body trembling; I was suddenly so weak as I shook from the powerful sensation of the orgasm. Matt leaned into me, pulling me backwards onto my knees as he wrapped his arms around my chest. He used his finger to scoop a big wad of my cum off my belly and held it to my mouth. I licked his finger clean, feeling as if I were literally melting into his body.

I then looked over, catching Ryan out of the corner of my eye. I turned to take in the sight of him completely and saw him kneeling on the floor in the position where Matt had left him. He had been jacking himself, and his own cock was covered with his sticky cum. He looked up at me then, not saying anything. Quickly I twisted my body around to stare into the eyes of my owner.

"Let's get cleaned up," Matt said. "Go jump in the shower, and then we're gonna split."

"Yes Sir," I said, and grabbed my clothing from the floor and proceeded to obey him.

As I reached the bathroom door I heard Ryan say to Matt, "Sir, please—um—may I keep your boxers?" Quickly I turned and saw Matt toss Ryan his underwear.

"You did a good job," he said, and Ryan smiled up at him.

After we had showered, Ryan was sitting by the window smoking a cigarette. Matt reached in his pocket just before we exited the room. "Oh Ryan," he said, pulling out his wallet. "Here is some money for the motel room." He placed a fifty on the bedside stand next to the door. "See ya." Then we left.

3

As promised, Matt had me home by noon the following day. After going back to Eric's house when we left the motel room, Matt and I were both ready to crash. I slept so peacefully, snuggled up safely in the arms of my owner, grateful for his showering of affection towards me. Then when we got up in the morning, we said our goodbyes to our host, and Matt politely thanked Eric for his hospitality.

I was startled to come face-to-face with Ryan in the hallway. "Hey, when did you get here?" I asked.

"Oh, I headed back to the party last night after you guys left. Eric brought me home with him," Ryan winked at me. He then lowered his voice. "I think that Adam was right about Eric; he just needed to be awakened to his Dom side. Believe me, it was wide, fuckin awake last night!"

"That's so cool, Ryan," I said. I was feeling something for the sub now that I'd never felt before. Previously my view of him had been so tainted due to my own jealousy. Now I sort of felt pity for him, in a way. He'd wanted Matt so desperately that he had even begged him for his boxer shorts. He craved his approval so intensely that he had lowered himself to serve another sub, yet when rejected had then turned to another Dom, one he obviously was 'settling' for. "I'm glad for ya, Ryan," I said. "I think Eric is gonna be a great Sir for you."

Ryan grinned. "Hung like a horse too, though not quite as big as Matt."

I placed my hand on his shoulder. "You did such a good job last night. Probably better than I would've."

59

"Doubt that," responded Ryan in the sincerest of tones. "There must be a reason why Matt has chosen you. You must be really good, or else damn lucky."

I remembered Ryan's words to me all the way home, thinking he was right; I was damned lucky. Matt certainly could elect to be with just about anyone he chose, male or female, and for some reason he chose me. During all of the previous months, this awareness was so troubling to me. It made me insecure, knowing he could dump me at any time, but I actually was beginning to look at the situation a little differently. Matt's opinion of me was starting to matter so much to me that it sort of made me feel better about myself knowing that he'd chosen me.

If Matt, having the choice of so many possible partners, would choose to be with me, then there must be something about me that was of value. In some ways this reality smacked of irony, for one might think that by subjugating myself to another person, I'd be lowering my self esteem; yet Matt's feelings for me tended to actually boost my ego somewhat. When he'd repeatedly told me the night before that my status was above Ryan—because Matt declared it so—how could I help but feel special?

And special was precisely how I felt when I stepped into my apartment after having been gone for two weeks. My sister Kathie swooped down upon me, showering me with hugs and kisses. "God, I've been so worried about you! Let me see your leg," she said. Gently I pushed her away.

"It's okay, I'm fine," I was smiling and laughing, as was Matt. "You know you worry way too much."

"I just can't believe what you did! I don't know what I'd have done if something happened to you." Tears were welling up in her eyes.

"Well, nothing bad happened, so don't cry! You're gonna make me start cryin. Hey, I brought you something!" I suddenly remembered the souvenir I'd picked up for her. "It's in my suitcase." Quickly I picked up the smaller piece of my luggage that was on the floor beside me, flinging it onto the couch. "Here, I hope you like it," I said as I opened the suitcase and retrieved a small package for her.

"Oh Petey, you didn't have to get me anything," she said, wiping the tears from her cheeks. "What is it?" she asked.

"Unwrap it and see," I encouraged her. "Did you get my postcard too?" I asked.

"Yeah, honey. I got it yesterday. How'd you mail it when you were at sea?"

"Oh, the ship docks every so often. I mailed the card and got you this gift when we were on one of the islands."

"Oh it's beautiful, Petey!" Kathie exclaimed, as she unwrapped the jewel-encased, beaded necklace that I'd gotten her.

"Those gems are very rare. They are only found on that particular island," I explained to her.

"I love it!" she said, and once again hugged me. I looked up and rolled my eyes at Matt while in my sister's embrace. He smiled down at me approvingly.

"You know, I'm gonna have to get home myself," he said to us both. "Petey's gonna need to go into emergency or else his doctor in about a week to have the stitches removed," he told Kathie. "He has some ointment in his suitcase and some pain pills if needed. Hasn't needed any so far though, so you probably can just flush em once he's healed."

"Matt, I'm so sorry I overreacted yesterday," Kathie said to him sincerely. "It was very brave what you both did. You should have been praised, not bitched at."

"I understand. You were jus' worried bout your baby bro. It's no problem."

"Thanks," she said. "And I've got a big dinner planned for you tonight, Petey. Baked lasagna, your favorite."

"Wow, that *is* my favorite. Better turn on the air conditioner though. This apartment's gonna be a hotbox."

"Okay, Petey, wanna walk me out?" asked Matt. I knew it was a polite way of ordering me in front of my sister, but I played along.

"Sure," I said. "I'll be right back," I told Kathie.

When we were alone in the hallway, Matt grabbed me and kissed me. "Thanks for a great vacation, pup," he said. "You gonna talk to Kathie about moving in with Drew?"

"Yes Sir, but if it's okay I wanna at least wait until tomorrow. I don't wanna spoil anything tonight."

"Sure, whenever you feel is best. Just play it by ear."

"Thanks for everything, Sir," I said to him honestly. "You gave me the best vacation of my whole life."

"My pup deserves the best," he said to me, flicking the visor of my cap affectionately. "I'll call you tomorrow sometime, probably in the afternoon."

"Okay. I'll miss you!"

"Miss ya too." He then turned from me and walked down the hallway, waving one last time before rounding the corner.

That evening was so relaxing, Kathie and I kicking back together and simply enjoying one another. It was almost the way that it was before Matt had come into the picture. I sincerely wished that there were some way to bring the two of them together so that both could remain an important part of my life. I feared, however, that Kathie would never be comfortable with the type of relationship that Matt and I shared. She distrusted him completely, and it seemed there was nothing I could do to convince her otherwise.

There hadn't been any mention of Tracy since the big blowup that occurred on the night of my birthday. After Tracy and Alex's girlfriend Kelly had ditched Matt and Alex on their three-day vacation to the cabin, Matt did not seem to be seeing her at all any more. He had not come right out and promised me that he'd never sleep with another woman, but his behavior indicated that he seemed to have no interest in it whatsoever.

This deterioration of the relationship between Matt and Tracy did not bode well with Kathie, I feared. Although she had had her own battles with her long-time friend, when push came to shove, she always was right there to defend Tracy. It was like Kathie harbored major resentment towards Matt, thinking him the bad guy simply for not loving her friend the way that Kathie wanted him to do. I found this logic to be extremely biased, for she seemed to completely side with Tracy against me. I realize that I should not have taken my sister's viewpoints personally, for she simply came from a mindset of ignorance. She didn't understand what it meant to be in a Dom/sub relationship, and what was more, I doubted that she fully accepted that two men could love one another as deeply as a heterosexual couple.

Clearly she knew about my sexual orientation, and she even accepted and supported me in this regard. She wanted me, though, to seek out some other gay guy who was similar to myself. She couldn't comprehend the notion that it was possible that a guy as masculine, athletic, and stereotypically straight-acting as Matt could actually be attracted to men more than women. The only rationale she could come up with for Matt making me such a huge part of his life was that he must have some sort of ulterior motive.

This reasoning made virtually no sense, though, for clearly I had nothing to offer Matt other than myself. I was not wealthy like he was. I wasn't smarter than him. I wasn't even a great physical trophy. If it were some great-looking, socially-acceptable partner that he wanted to publicly cling to his side in order to make him look good, certainly he'd have opted for Tracy over me. How could Kathie not see that the reason Matt was with me was because he loved me? Period.

The course that my relationship with Kathie seemed to presently be on was one of silent denial. She and I both knew that it was best not to discuss the topics upon which we disagreed. We just acted like there were no problems, that my relationship with Matt was not an issue. Hopefully Kathie would eventually come to understand that what Matt and I shared was very sincere and very genuine. Until this happened, however, there was little that I could do to heal my relationship with my sister.

This evening, though, Kathie and I had forgotten all of this tension and had simply enjoyed our time together. We rented a couple of comedies and sat together in front of the television laughing hysterically. Eventually our conversation became more serious and the two of us began reminiscing about the times when our mom and dad were alive. It was a series of, "Do you remember the time that—'s". As the evening drew to a close, I was certain that I wanted to do nothing to spoil the camaraderie that Kathie and I seemed to have finally rekindled, so I pointedly made no effort to broach the subject of my moving out of the apartment. To my surprise, however, Kathie herself became serious and told me there was something she needed to discuss with me. I was all ears.

"Honey, things are getting very serious with Carter and me. He's asked me to move in with him." I looked at her wide-eyed, feeling an overwhelming sense of relief sweep over me. She, however, must have misinterpreted the reaction. "Of course, Petey. I declined his offer. I told him there was no way you could afford to keep this apartment yourself. Then Carter really surprised me, yah know. Guess what he said?"

I shrugged my shoulders, "What's that?"

"He said he'd love for you to move in with us. He wouldn't dream of asking me to abandon you. Honey, I want you to just think about it, okay ... Now, I know this isn't something you can decide right away, and if you don't wanna leave the apartment, I understand. Carter and I can shelve our plans to live together for awhile–indefinitely, if we have to—"

"Kathie," I said, interrupting her. "It's okay. I want you to go ahead and move in with Carter. There is somewhere else I can go. I was gonna talk to you about it anyway."

"What do you mean, Petey? You're not thinking of—um—moving in with Matt are you?"

"No, not now anyways, but–well—you know my friend Drew? He and Alex have offered to rent me a room."

"So when exactly were you planning to tell me this?" she asked defensively. "You've made all these plans to move out and didn't even feel it necessary to inform me of them?"

"No, Kathie, wait—" I sighed. "It's not like that, honest. I hadn't made any plans. We just were talking about it, tossin it around, is all. I'm just sayin that if you do decide to move in with Carter, it's not like I'm gonna suddenly be homeless or something."

"Petey, you and I are family! You'd rather live with some strangers—some people you just met—instead of me, your own sister? We've been through so much together."

"I know. I know we have, Kathie. But ya know, I have to grow up sometime. It's not like I can plan on living with you forever. Plus, is it really fair for you or Carter to begin your lives together with a third wheel always hangin around?"

"Petey, Carter likes you so much. Neither one of us would ever feel that way about you."

"No, I don't mean it like that. It's just I would feel that way, ya know. I would feel like I was such an intruder. You two deserve your privacy, and you know what? I deserve mine too."

"So that's what this is about, huh?" she asked, suddenly awakening to a realization that she thought she had. "You don't want me telling you what to do any more."

"Kathie, no, it's not like that! I didn't mean it that way. I just mean that I know you have–um—questions about Matt and me. You don't like him very much."

"Let's not even go there. My feelings for Matt are not even relevant. Whomever you have chosen to be in your life is your business. I can't believe you'd think that I'm trying to pressure you into letting me choose your friends for you."

I simply smiled at her then. "No, of course not. I don't think that at all. It's just that this is good news, really, for both of us. You and Carter are ready to move in together, and I have some options of what to do. It's all gonna work out. When is the lease up on this apartment?"

"The end of the month. Actually, that's why we started to talk about it in the first place. The other possibility is that we could just rent this apartment on a six-month lease. It'd give us some time to decide for sure what we wanna do." Her voice was again calm, almost gentle and loving.

"Kathie, it's gonna be so hard for us not to be together. You've been the most important person in my life for so long." I reached across the sofa to place my hand on top of hers. "But I think we have to just go for it. No matter where we end up in life, we always will be brother and sister. Nothing or no one can ever change that. Not Carter. Not Matt."

As I looked at my sister, her face then softened and her eyes became misty. "Oh Petey, I knew this day would come, of course I knew it. I couldn't expect for you to be a kid forever. You're growin up, but ya know what? You're always gonna be my baby brother." She leaned into me to hug me then, and I responded by wrapping my arms around her.

"I love you Kathie," I whispered to her.

"I love ya too."

***

"Guess what?" I was on my cell phone talking to Drew.

"You won the lottery?" he quipped with me.

"No, but close. I can move in with you any time."

"Oh my god! Really? What about your sister?"

"Drew, it's so cool how this has worked out. Kathie wants to move in with Carter. She wanted to talk to me about it last night but didn't know how, so when I told her about the idea of me moving in with you, she didn't really argue much at all."

"So you didn't mention to her that Matt's the one who wants this?" he said. I could almost see him smiling into the phone.

"Duh! Like that'd go over like a lead balloon, ya know."

"It's so cool that this worked out, dude! So when ya gonna start packin?"

I sighed as I leaned back on the bed. "Well, maybe you should talk to Alex, find out when I can start actually movin my stuff in."

"Yeah, of course, but I'm sure he'll say right away. He already has okayed everything. This is so exciting Petey! We're gonna be roommates."

"I know! I hope it doesn't hurt our friendship though, ya know?"

"How? How could it hurt our friendship; that's silly."

"No, not really," I said. "People that live together can get on each other's nerves after awhile. I mean look at Kathie and me."

"Yeah, but she's your sister. I'm your best friend. Aren't I?"

"Hmm, let me think about it," I laughed. "Yeah, I guess so."

"Shut up, fag!"

After Matt had collared me, my restriction on calling him had been lessened. Initially I was only allowed to call him on his cell phone if it were an absolute emergency. Then when he collared and tagged me, he'd actually had his phone number engraved on the back of my dog tag. Still, I was very cautious about when to utilize this privilege and reserved it only for things that were extremely important. I already knew that if he were in a situation where he couldn't talk to me at the time, he'd just send me to voicemail. If there were an actual emergency, I could dial his pager and press 9-1-1 before I called his cell phone.

"Cool," he said when I told him about my conversation with Kathie. "So call Drew and Alex and tell em you wanna start movin in right away."

"I already called Drew, Sir," I said.

"You called Drew before me?" he questioned.

"Um ... Well, yeah—or, yes Sir. But only because I get so nervous about callin your number, Sir."

"That's silly. Why'd ya be nervous about that?"

"Remember last time? When you had to–um–spank me, Sir?" I felt my face turning red.

"That was different. You get too hung up on things in the past, pup. Anyways, from now on, call me first if it's something important. Least leave me a voicemail or something. Then you can call Drew or whoever."

"Yes Sir. Sorry."

"Kay. Now can you get your stuff ready by this weekend?"

"Yes, Sir. I can get it ready by this afternoon. All I have is the stuff in my room. Gonna leave my kitchen stuff for Kathie probably."

"Isn't that your stuff though? I mean, you do all the cookin, right?"

"Well, she's the one who bought all of that, Sir. It belongs to her."

"Just don't want you getting cheated outta the stuff that belongs to you."

"No Sir. Kathie wouldn't ever cheat me outta anything. Honest. We sometimes fight about stuff, but she isn't like that."

"I know. Just gotta look out for yourself sometimes. We can get you anything you need for the kitchen or whatever after you get moved in. Plus Drew pretty much has everything already."

"Yeah, he likes to cook too."

"All right, well today is Monday, so ya got four days to get your stuff ready. I'm gonna pick you up this afternoon at three. When you gotta work again?"

"Not til next Monday, Sir. Remember? This is still my vacation. Where we goin today? I mean when you pick me up."

"You'll see. Okay, gotta run. Be ready at three."

"I love you, Sir!"

"Later babe." He then disconnected.

I rested my head against the pillow then, dropping the phone beside me. This was just too awesome to believe. I was gonna be moving in with Drew and Alex. I wouldn't ever have to worry any more about there being misunderstandings about Matt owning me. I wouldn't have to explain myself or defend him or conceal things any more. I could be myself finally! There now would be no interference between Matt and me; he would have 100% access to me and 100% control. My heart raced a bit as I thought of it.

I began making a mental inventory of the things I'd need to move over to Drew's. I had to pack my computer for one thing. There still was the big box that it came in, stored in the far corner of my closet. I had my desk, bed, dresser, and nightstand to move. That was about it for furniture. Then I had all of my clothes and a few personal belongings. Probably wouldn't be more than a single pickup truckload altogether.

I'd have to stop over to the grocery store at some point to get three or four boxes for my things, and I could pack my clothing items inside my luggage set. Also I had all of my bathroom and toiletry items to pack up. Maybe I'd better make a list, just so I remained organized.

By three o'clock when Matt arrived, I already was just about completely packed. I let him in the front door of the apartment and immediately ushered him into my room, proudly showing him how prepared I was.

"Good job, pup," he said, leaning down to kiss me. "Maybe we can get you moved tomorrow then, instead of waitin til the weekend."

"I'd like that, Sir," I said.

"Okay, now let's get goin. Grab your b-cap."

"Yes, Sir," I said, and then followed him back out into the living room. "I wonder when Kathie's gonna be actually moving out," I said.

"Well, when you find out, let me know. It's only right for us to help her get moved too. After all, you two shared this apartment for a long time."

"Thank you Sir," I said. "I was hoping you'd say that."

"You must think I'm some sorta meanie or something, huh? Don't I usually treat people fairly?"

"Yes Sir, of course. It's just—um, well—Kathie is sometimes sorta mean to you. I'd understand if you didn't wanna help her."

"Well it's not really just about her. It's about my pup. You gotta own up to your own responsibilities and do the things you know are right. She's your sister and has been your roommate a long time, so you can't just bail on her. Right?"

"Right." I smiled up at him. "You're about the fairest person I know, Sir."

"I'll remind you of that statement the next time you're in chastity." I didn't take my eyes off of him.

"Okay."

"Let's go," he said, and I followed him out the front door.

I was a little bit surprised when we got downstairs and I noticed that Matt was driving his pickup. Most of the time when we went somewhere together it was in his sports car. Between his parents and him, their household had no shortage of vehicles. They had the family SUV, each of his parents had a car, and Matt owned both a truck and a BMW sports car. The contrast between his financial situation and my own was quite striking. It was all I could do to be able to afford bus fare and keep my bike in good condition, yet he had a plethora of transportation options.

I followed Matt to the driver's side door, and he unlocked and opened it. First I slid in and scooted half-way over in the seat. Then he got in behind the wheel. It seemed so wonderful to be alone with him. For the past couple of weeks we'd spent an enormous amount of time together, but for the most part we were always around other people. Secretly I hoped that whatever plans he had in store for us today would be exclusive to the two of us. I loved Drew and Alex so much, and the time we spent with them would never be something I'd regret, but at this moment I so craved the one-on-one intimacy that only my owner and I shared.

As Matt pulled out of the parking lot I leaned into him, resting my head against his shoulder and placing my hand on his thigh. "I just love being with you, Sir. I never wanna be away from you. Never."

Matt did not respond verbally to me but instead removed his right hand from the steering wheel to place it on my knee. He squeezed gently, in such an affectionate way. I squirmed a little, reacting to the tickling sensation, but did not pull away. I nuzzled my body even closer to him.

Finally after we had driven for awhile, it became apparent that Matt was taking me out of the city. We were following a familiar route, heading in the direction of his cabin. It was about a forty-five minute drive from my apartment, and I'd been there a couple of times with Matt. It was in this locale that Matt had collared me. He'd brought me there on our birthday weekend, and we'd made passionate, beautiful love together. I must mention that it was during this weekend that he also mercilessly tickle-tortured me after tying me spread-eagled to the bed, and he fed me my dinner as I knelt at his feet, begging like a canine pup. He could be so gentle and loving, the epitome of romanticism; then when the mood suited him, he could be so powerfully dominant and controlling. He had introduced me to things that were previously unimaginable to me. I'd never have dreamt that I'd kneel to drink the piss of another man or bow to worship his feet. All of these fit together so beautifully within the context of our relationship, though. He was my owner, my best friend, and my lover.

When we finally approached the road that I recognized as the turnoff to go to the cabin, it surprised me that Matt did not take the turn. Instead he kept driving, and I knew that we were heading towards Bradenton. "Sir, where are we going?" I asked, my curiosity finally peaking.

"Since when do I have to report where I'm goin to passengers, especially passengers who are pups?" he asked.

I looked up into his eyes to gauge his level of seriousness. During the earliest stages of our relationship, such remarks from him would have caused me an inexorable amount of distress, but I'd since learned that his sometimes-blunt statements such as this generally were intended to be lighthearted. His look was serious, though.

"Oh, I'm sorry Sir. Guess I'll just wait and see."

Neither of us spoke again until Matt pulled the truck off the road to stop at a convenience store/gas station. "Want something to drink?" he asked.

"Um ... sure. Thank you, Sir. Could I just have a water please?"

I waited in the truck while Matt went inside. When he came out, he was carrying a bottle of Mountain Dew, presumably for himself, and a large, thirty-two-ounce bottle of spring water for me. "Thanks, Sir," I said, "but a small woulda been fine."

"Drink up," he said. "You got ten minutes to have it completely empty." I had slid over in the seat and was leaning against the passenger door. Quickly I turned to look directly at him, again trying to figure out if he was actually being serious with me.

"Sir, I can't drink—"

"You got a problem takin orders today or somethin?" he said sternly, interrupting me.

"No Sir," I said and took a big gulp of the water immediately. Matt's demeanor was so confusing to me, and I was starting to get a little bit nervous. He hadn't seemed the least bit angry with me when he'd arrived to pick me up. Then when we got in the truck together, he'd allowed me to snuggle with him and had even touched me affectionately. Now within the last ten minutes it was suddenly as if he'd grown so cold towards me. I wanted to ask him if he was angry at me. Perhaps something that I'd done wrong had suddenly occurred to him and he was extremely pissed. That wouldn't be typically characteristic of him, though, for if anything bothered him about me or my behavior, he simply would tell me point-blank. He'd never keep his thoughts and feelings about something bottled up inside and wouldn't ever harbor resentment against me.

As I looked over to him, he did not return the gaze but simply put the truck in gear and pulled back out onto the highway. I shifted in my seat nervously and took another big swig of the water. Then I turned to look out the passenger window and suddenly remembered an event that had happened a few weeks previously. Matt and I had been over to Alex's apartment. I was visiting Drew while Matt and Alex went to the gym to work out, and when our owners returned they immediately called us into the living room. We were ordered to kneel, and I then for the very first time, I learned how to definitively demonstrate my worshipfulness and humility. Drew and I knelt and served our owners' feet while they watched television.

This session of non-stop worship had lasted for nearly an hour, and when we were done, Matt immediately had informed me that we were leaving. We got to the parking lot, and Matt directed me to a dark alley behind the apartment complex dumpsters. He then shoved me against a fence and was about to begin a hot scene of rough pseudo-violent sex with me. Immediately, though, I freaked. I began to have flashbacks of being attacked by my homophobic classmates, and I covered my head, begging Matt not to hurt me.

Afterwards I'd felt so extremely guilty, realizing that Matt hadn't had any intention of hurting me in any way. He was merely creating a hot scene. I also regretted the fact that we did not actually go through with the scene that night. For every time that Matt presented me with any variation of our sexual behavior, it was hot. I'd promised both Matt and myself then that I would from that point forward trust him completely. I would always remember that he'd promised never to hurt me.

Another thought that flashed into my mind was his repeated assurance to me that if ever he were angry with me, he would make that abundantly clear. He had drilled it into my brain that it was not acceptable for me to make assumptions about his feelings, but instead to simply obey. So this is what I then focused on doing. I would not allow myself to worry about his mood but would just obey him without question. Perhaps he was setting us up for some sort of scene, or maybe he was thinking about something else entirely. Maybe he was just in a more serious mood. Whatever the case, I would trust him. I looked over to him once more and took a third, huge gulp of my water, this time emptying the bottle by a third.

We rode in silence for the next few minutes, and I continued to take gulps from my water bottle. I kept checking the time on the dashboard clock, counting down the remaining minutes of my deadline. I realized that I had only three minutes left and my bottle was still nearly half full. I was feeling very full myself, actually, and was starting to get extremely worried. How would I be able to finish it in time? Should I say something to Matt? Should I apologize and tell him I simply couldn't finish it? I was a little fearful of saying anything at this point, for I knew that it clearly was not conversation or lip service that Matt expected of me right now. His attitude conveyed to me that the only thing he wanted from me at this moment was compliance. He wanted me to simply obey.

Previously it would have been my gut reaction to ask why. What difference would it make if I drank all this water in only ten minutes? Why did he give me this order in the first place? I was realizing though now, finally, that if Matt chose to give me an order for any reason, it was my job to obey him. He may simply be issuing a command merely for the sake of seeing me obey him. He may have other reasons that I didn't understand. Worrying about these things, though, was truly not my job.

So I then took a deep breath, looking down once again at the clock and seeing that it was beyond the two minute mark. I brought the bottle to my lips and tilted my head back slightly, beginning once again to gulp the water. I raised my arm and cocked my head back even further as I swallowed furiously, gulping down as much of the water as possible. When I pulled the bottle away I looked at it, seeing I'd emptied over half of what was remaining. I was gasping a bit, trying to catch my breath.

Matt didn't even appear to be aware of what I was doing. Never once did he even look over at me. In fact, I never even noticed him look at his watch or at the clock in the truck. On the other hand, I was watching the digital readout intently, and when I saw it change to the one-minute mark, I once more moved the bottle back to my lips. I slowly took a breath and released it, then quickly tilted the bottle upwards as I shifted my head backwards. I was determined! This time I drained the remaining contents.

When I was done, I smiled to myself, quickly looking over to my owner. He did not turn to look at me but seemed to be focusing on his driving. Then he surprised me by saying, "And with only thirty seconds to spare."

"Yes Sir," I said, cautious about saying any more than that.

We drove on for another five minutes or so and I stared out the window, watching the scenery. We rode in silence, as I was compelled to keep quiet by my owner's solitude. Finally he did speak to me, and once again it was simply to give me an order. "Get on your knees, under the dash." Almost reflexively I then slid from my seat and turned my body sideways, lowering myself onto the floor of the truck. Obeying him was becoming automatic to me. "Slide closer to me," he said, and I inched my way over, squeezing my small body between the dashboard and the seat.

I was now right beside his leg, wanting to touch it, but knowing I'd have to wait for his command. I stared up at him, resting my palms against the seat in front of me. As he glanced down at me, I noticed the very stern expression that was on his face start to soften a bit. I wondered what thought had flashed into his mind. Perhaps he thought it was cute the way I knelt there with my hands in front of my body. Maybe he thought I resembled a real pup, sitting pretty for its owner, but as quickly as the gentle expression appeared, it then vanished and was once again replaced by his air of superiority.

"Still thirsty?" he asked me, and I almost wanted to laugh. It was such a ridiculous question, for I'd just finished an entire quart of water in less than a ten minute period. I knew though, that this was not the reply he was seeking.

I continued to stare up at him and responded, "Sir, I'm always thirsty for you." I felt myself getting hard in anticipation of what I was expecting to occur next. My heart was beating rapidly, and I felt that exhilarating feeling of excitement sweep over me—the same feeling that I always had when I knew I was about to serve.

As I watched him, looking up with awe and genuine adoration, he appeared so god-like to me. He sat there looking so confident, leaning slightly backwards in his seat.

He was comfortable with his legs spread apart casually as he drove. I wanted so very much to touch them, to slide my hand up inside his thigh right then. I wanted to bury my face in his groin and lap up the drops of sweat from his balls. I wanted to taste him, to smell him. Oh god, I wanted to serve so badly!

He turned the steering wheel sharply and started to brake the truck. I had no idea where he'd turned off for I had no visual of our surroundings, but I was anxious for him to stop the vehicle. I knew that once he'd stopped, I'd be allowed to finally serve. The truck continued to slow and it became apparent to me that we were in some sort of parking lot. I saw a lamppost out his window as he parked the pickup. He then shifted the automatic transmission into park but left the engine running. It was too hot to sit inside a vehicle with no air conditioning.

He looked down at me again, this time not allowing his face to soften as before. "How thirsty?" he asked, his voice resonating with confidence and authority.

"Oh Sir, I can almost taste you. I'm so thirsty for you, it makes my mouth water."

He laughed sarcastically. "You gotta do better than that!" he said. "Convince me how bad you want it, boy. Say what you want."

"Sir, I want to drink you! I wanna take your cum! Oh god Sir, oh please, I'm begging you!" My voice was high-pitched, sounding more like a whine. It got this way when I was so overcome with excitement. I wondered if he heard the yearning in the tone of my pleas. I wondered if he sensed how very true the words that I was saying actually were. "Sir, it's all I want, all I ever want. Serving you is my greatest pleasure. I've never wanted anything so bad!" I was gasping now, my voice sounding choppy and breathy. "Please! Oh Pleeeze!" My crotch was pressing against the truck seat in front of me as I stretched my body upwards, imploring my owner even with my body language.

He reached down and grasped the elastic waistband of his basketball shorts. I stared at his crotch, my eyes widening as I anticipated what was going to happen. "Why?" he suddenly asked, stopping himself from pulling down the shorts. "Why should I let you serve?"

Oh my god! I couldn't take it! Why was he torturing me like this? "For you Sir! Please Sir! Let me serve you for your pleasure!"

He then laughed. His laughter was literally dripping with sarcasm and arrogance. "You fuckin want me to give you what's mine, and you say it is for me? I just asked you why I should give it to you! Why do you deserve it? Huh? Why?"

I felt so debased then, so lowered and humbled. He was right, I truly did not want to serve him for his pleasure. I wanted it for my own gratification. I was begging him to serve because of how it made me feel, not him. Every time I knelt to take my owner's piss or cum, I attained a sense of validation, a feeling of worthiness and purpose. Every time I served, I felt complete and satisfied. Honestly I must admit that this desire to serve was far more about me than it was about him. How could I have not understood this before?

I then hung my head, looking down at the seat in front of me. "Sir, I don't deserve it. I don't even deserve to serve you."

He removed his right hand from the waistband then and brought it over to my chin, cupping it and repositioning my head so that I was looking up into his eyes. "You are mine. You belong to *me*!" he said, "and you deserve only what I say you deserve. You understand?"

"Yes Sir," I said.

"So why do you deserve to take my load, boy?" he repeated the question to me.

"I deserve it ... um Sir ... I deserve it cuz you say I do. Only cuz you say I do, because you own me."

"That's fuckin right, boy! You are worthy cuz I've declared you worthy. I've made you mine. You're my boy, my pup."

"Yes Sir!" I whined to him excitedly.

"You want it boy? You want your owner's cum?"

"Oh god! Oh ... oh ... oh yes!"

Quickly he again grabbed the waistband and thrust his hips forward slightly to raise his butt from the seat, sliding the shorts down in one smooth motion. "Pull em off!" he commanded, and I grabbed them and pulled the shorts down his long legs. He was wearing nothing beneath them. He then grabbed my head and shoved it into his crotch, my mouth sliding around his semi-hard cock.

As I remained in my submissive position at his feet with his cock in my mouth, I felt him growing harder. I responded by wrapping my lips entirely around his shaft and sliding my tongue against the underside. His hard-on grew even more rapidly in my mouth. I heard him moan in pleasure. I could smell the dampness of his crotch, my nose pressing into his pubic hair as I sucked on his semi-hard prick.

I was so hungry for him, wanting desperately to now proceed with draining him of his cumload. Matt, however, had very different intentions, for very abruptly he grabbed my head with both hands and jerked me away from his cock. I was leaning into him, not resisting his guidance or defying him in any way, but clearly expressing my strong desire to keep him in my mouth. My head was bent downward and my mouth open wide; I craved having him inside me so very passionately. "Please Sir!" I begged, "please feed me your cum." My plea was merely a whisper, for I was almost too excited to articulate anything at all.

"No!" Matt commanded. He pushed me away, and I returned to my kneeling position beside him. I stared up at him imploringly, yearning for more of his cock, but instead he ordered me to pull his shorts back up. "You'll get my cum when you earn it, boy."

My hands were literally trembling as I gripped the waistband of his basketball shorts and pulled them up over his long legs and knees. The taste of his cock in my mouth and the smell of his sweat were so powerfully erotic to me, and I felt my own hard-on throbbing in my briefs. I dare not touch myself though, for surely this would displease him immensely. My job was to serve him without regard for my own pleasure, and I was determined to do exactly that. As I pulled up his shorts, I pressed my lips against his beautifully masculine legs, kissing his calves, his knees, and then his thighs. I gently and reverently pressed my lips against his flesh, trying desperately to demonstrate my servitude to my superior.

He thrust himself forward when I finally reached the point where the shorts had to be pulled up over his buttocks. I pulled them up and leaned into him, pressing my lips again into his crotch, kissing it worshipfully. He momentarily maintained the position, allowing me to kiss his bulge several times, and then dropped backwards to rest himself again comfortably in the seat. "Get back in the seat," he said to me calmly, and I slid away from him and pulled myself up, finally twisting my body and sitting back down next to the passenger door.

As I looked out the windows, I realized we were in a parking lot. It looked like some sort of shopping mall. I also realized another thing almost instantly. As my hard-on started to subside, I had to take a piss in the worst way. It suddenly felt as if my bladder was going to burst. I turned back to Matt then, afraid to speak at this point but realizing that I actually had no choice. "Sir?" I said meekly, "I really have to go to the bathroom. I'm sorry—"

"Hold it," he said without emotion, and simply remained in his seated position, saying and doing nothing at this point. After about two minutes, he finally reached over to turn on the stereo, and as he did so, I squirmed a bit in my seat. I'd just swallowed thirty-two ounces of water, and I had to piss so badly that it was all I could think of.

The fullness of my own bladder was making me so uncomfortable, and I didn't think I could hold it for very much longer at all. I began to shift nervously in my seat and to tap my foot against the floorboard of the truck, trying to act as if it were in rhythm to the music which had begun to play.

Matt looked over at me smugly and said to me casually, "Sit still and quit that. It's annoying." Oh my god! I was gonna piss myself!

I looked back at him, starting to feel very panicked. "Sorry, Sir ... um ... I don't think I can hold it." I was tightening the muscles in my pelvic region, feeling the pressure of my bladder as it demanded release. It was as if Matt had not even heard me, and rather than responding to me, he again reached for the stereo and turned up the volume slightly. I sat there in misery while he listened to the remainder of the song. He was acting very unconcerned, and it was almost as if he didn't even notice me.

Finally Matt turned to me, speaking up so that his voice could be heard over the music. "If you gotta piss, better go inside." He obviously meant the huge shopping mall that was in front of us. Actually we were in the very rear of the lot, so it was gonna be a very long walk for me, but I quickly grabbed the door handle and jumped out.

"Thank you, Sir!" I said. "I'll be right back." I then turned to close the door and was about to bolt when he stopped me.

"Wait," he said. I pulled the truck door back open and looked up at him while I teetered back and forth from one leg to the next. I had to piss so bad. "I think I'll go with ya," he said. "Get back in."

I obeyed him, of course, but did so with much reluctance. It wasn't that I demonstrated any hesitation in complying with his order; it just was that I was starting to be in serious pain. I knew I couldn't hold my bladder for very much longer at all. The very last thing I wanted to do was piss my pants, especially not in his truck. I felt my face getting hot, and I fidgeted in my seat, unable to remain perfectly still due to my discomfort.

Matt then turned the ignition key to start the truck and put the vehicle in gear. He then drove around the parking lot, apparently looking for a parking space that was closer to the entrance. The truck was moving so slowly, and had the driver been anyone but Matt, I'd have just jumped out and ran inside myself. I'd have gotten there much quicker for sure.

When Matt did finally park the truck, he did not act as if he were in a really big hurry, but opened the door slowly, at his leisure. I jumped out the passenger side door and ran around to stand beside him. I knew that it was not proper for me to run ahead of him. As we approached the entrance to the mall, my need to empty my bladder was stronger than ever. I was literally ready to scream, for I didn't think I could last a minute longer.

When we got inside, I quickly glanced around, looking to see where the restrooms were. I rushed over to the kiosk, which displayed a mall map, and I realized that we were not far from them. Quickly I turned to Matt. "Sir, is it okay for me to run ahead? The bathrooms are just around the corner."

"No, it's not okay," he said. "We're not gonna be usin the bathrooms."

He had to be joking! I looked up at him in disbelief, tempted for the very first time ever to simply defy him. This was ridiculous! I was about to burst, or at the very least to piss myself right here in this mall in front of all these people, and he was making me wait! I took a deep breath, though, and calmed myself. Suddenly it occurred to me that he may interpret this as being an exasperated sigh. His response, though, was merely to look over at me and smile.

"Sir," I said, looking up at him. "Honest, I can't hold it any longer. Please let me go."

"Okay, go ahead." *Oh, thank god!* I shot a smile back at him and quickly turned, ready to dash off to the bathroom. "Go ahead and piss right here," he said. I swung back around to look up at him once again, not believing what I'd thought I had just heard. "You are gonna piss yourself. Right here in public."

I felt my face getting suddenly red, not from anger or from being flushed, but purely from embarrassment. He couldn't expect this of me, could he? He wouldn't actually make me do something so utterly humiliating. I must have had a terribly shocked look on my face, and I did not know which I wanted to do more—challenge his order or cry. However, I did neither. I just stood there for a few seconds thinking.

If I started to bawl like I did when he wanted to fuck me in the alley that night, I knew I'd later regret it. If I argued with him now after he'd given me a direct order, I knew he'd be disappointed in me and possibly angry. If I obeyed him, it would be mortifying, but it wouldn't hurt me in any way. Shit, I didn't even know for sure where I was. None of these people here knew me or recognized me. Even if they did, wouldn't any amount of embarrassment be worth it in order to obey my owner?

I looked right back in Matt's eyes then, and said to him boldly, "Yes Sir!"

He then gave me specific instructions. "I'm gonna go over to the end of the main walkway, over to where those benches are." He pointed to where he was describing. "Gonna sit there and wait for you. Then you are gonna walk around me in a big circle. Soon as I nod to you, you're gonna start to piss. Gonna do it slow, and gonna keep walkin as you do it. You're gonna piss yourself til you're totally empty, and gonna keep your hands at your sides and act like it's totally normal. You're not gonna stop walkin til I nod to you a second time, and then you're gonna stop right where you are and stand there like a statue. Soon as I get up from the bench you're gonna head for the hallway that leads to the bathrooms and gonna wait for me in that hall. You got it?"

"Yes Sir," I said.

"Go down and wait in front of the Foot Locker store and watch for my signal. Now go!" he said.

I turned from him and dashed down the main walkway of the mall. My heart was pounding in my chest as I suddenly became aware of what was about to happen. I was gonna be pissing my pants right here in this huge public mall. What was worse, I would be doing it just a few feet from the bathroom and most likely there would be people walking past me. They'd wonder what in the hell I was doing, possibly think I was some sort of lunatic. People might even laugh at me or ridicule me. I couldn't even say anything to defend myself or even act like I knew Matt.

When I made it to Foot Locker, I once again had an overwhelming temptation to just disobey. I was just feet from the bathroom now, and could dash in there and relieve myself, and this would all be over. Matt surely would be upset with me for not doing what he said, but he couldn't hold it against me forever. And was he gonna dump me just for not doing something so totally absurd as degrading myself like that in public?

I couldn't disobey him though—not now—not after all he'd taught me and all he'd been through with me. I had to do as he said, to obey him at all costs. It was not my job to worry about how other people would respond when I was carrying out an order. It was not my right to question Matt's judgment about the things he wanted, even if those things might make me feel humbled or even humiliated. It was my job to simply listen carefully to what he instructed me to do, and to then do exactly that. I turned in my tracks then and clasped my hands behind my back, watching the benches where my owner had told me he'd be.

Several other mall shoppers were milling about around me, all of them going about their shopping as if I weren't even there. Some of them were shopping alone and some in pairs or groups. Some gave me quick glances, probably wondering why I was just standing there like a statue. They just looked at me quickly and then looked away, not seeming to care at all. Regardless of their reactions, I was self conscious each and every time. My heart was pounding in my chest and I felt myself right on the verge of tears. I would not cry though; I absolutely refused!

Then finally I saw him. He walked around the corner and headed towards me, coming right down the center of the walkway. I looked directly at him, trying to make eye contact. He acted as if he were just one of the other shoppers though. He was about twenty feet from me, and it oddly seemed to me that he was moving in slow motion. The whole thing just didn't even seem real. When he got up to where I was standing, he did not say anything to acknowledge my presence but simply walked right past me. I watched him intently as he headed over to the benches. Then he casually sat down, kicking back in a relaxed position. He cupped his hands behind his head and slid down in the seat slightly, and then finally looked over to me and nodded.

Slowly I took a few steps forward, beginning to walk in the direction of my owner. When I released my piss, it was like a dam that was breaking, for I'd held it inside of me for so long. It came out of me forcefully just like water firing from a faucet turned to full force. It was such an incredible feeling of release, and I instantly felt the warmth of my own piss in my crotch. I knew the wet spot was growing in my beige khaki pants as I quickened the pace of my steps, and I knew with certainty that this would be extremely visible to anyone who happened to look in my direction. As I emptied myself, it seemed that I wasn't going to ever stop; my underwear and pants were getting soaked and I even heard the piss dripping down onto the floor at my feet.

The people that were close to me then got a very clear view of me and looked at me with shocked expressions. There was a pair of middle-aged women who each quickly looked at one another, took a step further away from me, and hurried past without a word. I glanced over to Matt quickly, being careful not to stare, and noticed that he was smiling. I felt how hot my face was; this was totally humiliating! There was another person coming towards me. It was a guy, possibly a teenager. I wanted to quickly turn from him and head in the opposite direction, but I knew I had to just keep walking and obey Matt's orders. I knew my face must be as red as an apple at that point, and I was soaking wet. By the time the guy got up to me, I was finally done pissing. He glanced over at me and then said rudely, "Dude, get a fuckin diaper!" and then proceeded beyond me snickering in disgust.

The wet spot in my khakis had grown huge. My entire crotch was soaked, and the piss was dripping down my leg and onto the floor around me. Other people were looking at me, and I felt that I was about to start crying. I wouldn't let that happen though! I wasn't gonna be a cry baby this time like I'd been so many times before. I was gonna prove to Matt that I could obey, no matter how embarrassing it was. I kept walking, trying to ignore the stares and the comments of the people around me. I walked around that big circle, remaining at all times in plain sight of my owner. I kept glancing over to him, waiting for his signal, praying to myself that this soon would be over.

Finally I saw him nod for the second time. Immediately I stopped in my tracks. I was positioned dead center in the middle of the walkway and people were all around me. I stood there motionless, hands at my side, as I looked over to Matt and watched him slowly get up. A group of three teenage girls walked by and suddenly stopped, staring right at me. They were less than three feet from me, and I watched their eyes as they looked me up and down.

Suddenly they turned to each other and all three busted up laughing. Then they walked away quickly, making jokes about me to one another. I continued to watch Matt, following him with my eyes as he walked across the fairway towards the restrooms. I finally could not restrain myself any longer, and I felt my eyes welling with tears. He wouldn't see, thank god. He wouldn't see me crying.

As soon as he was out of sight and around the corner of the hall, I wiped my eyes quickly, suppressing my emotion. Then I took off behind him, hurrying to meet him where he'd instructed. As I rounded the corner, I saw him casually standing in front of me. We were alone, at least for the moment. It was a busy mall, and I knew people walked through this passageway to the restrooms constantly. He motioned for me with a movement of his head and then turned to face a door that was at the end of the hall. He pulled a key out of his pocket and opened it. I hurried to catch up with him and stepped in behind him. As soon as the door was closed he grabbed me and forcefully shoved me against the wall. "I told you as soon as I stood up, you were to meet me here by the door! What the fuck took ya so long to move?"

Finally the emotion I'd been holding back burst forth, and my vision blurred as my eyes welled up with tears. He leaned into me forcefully and pressed his body against my own, grabbing my head with both of his hands and kissing me passionately. I felt his tongue as he forced his way into my mouth, completely overpowering me with his strength. I responded by reaching to him, wrapping my hands around his body, pressing my piss-soaked clothing against him. Oh fuck, why did I let him see me cry? He then kissed and clawed at me savagely, slamming me against the wall over and over. He was so hungry for me I could almost feel the desire radiate from his body. "Fuck yeah!" he moaned to me, expressing himself in a tone that seemed more a growl to me than an exclamation. His hands were tearing at my clothes as he drove his tongue deep into my mouth, covering my lips completely with his own. Never before had I sensed such intense hunger from him. Never had I felt so much the object of his desire.

"I own your ass! I fuckin own it!" he moaned as he continued to kiss me. "I want you so bad! Wanna be inside you! Wanna fuck your tight puppy ass! You're fuckin mine! You belong to me!" He continued with this tirade of verbal pronouncements as he edged me further down the corridor, kissing and groping me all the while.

Finally he pulled himself away from me and grabbed me by the collar of my shirt. "Get down the hall!" he ordered. I looked in front of us and saw that this was some sort of passage that led to the rear entrances of the mall shops. I could hear pounding around us; some sort of construction was taking place very nearby. I hurried my pace, rushing forward down the hall, with Matt walking briskly behind me. "Right here!" he said, and once again he grabbed me and shoved me into one of the entrances. It was an empty room with large sheets of plywood blocking the front windows. Obviously the room was a vacant mall store. It appeared they were in the process of renovating it for a new owner. I could hear the construction sounds loudly now, the hammers and power tools being used in the room next to us. In front of us there were a couple of wooden sawhorses with a piece of plywood resting atop. Next to them there was a small gym bag.

I heard the door close behind me. Matt was shutting and locking it. "What is this room, Sir?" I asked.

"Shut up!" he said, walking briskly towards the gym bag that was on the floor. He leaned over and scooped it up, unzipping it hurriedly. Quickly he pulled something from it and dropped the bag back down on the ground. He stepped towards me and instinctively I took a step backwards. He grabbed a hold of the front of my shirt and pulled me towards him. He spun me around and said to me authoritatively, "Open your mouth." I did as ordered, and immediately he stuffed something in it. It was some sort of gag, and he pulled it tight around my face, attaching it together in the back of my head. I heard it snap as he connected the straps together. The part of the gag that went into my mouth tasted like leather. I bit down on it, unable to do anything else really. Then he pushed me forward, directing me towards the sawhorses. Quickly he grabbed the edge of the plywood piece that was on top of them and flung it to the ground. Then he pushed against my neck while positioning me in front of the sawhorse, bending me over. I felt my body slam into the wooden structure and moaned from the sudden jolt. I reached out to grab the sawhorse in front of me while my body was bent over the other.

Matt then grabbed a hold of the back of my waistband, firmly gripping my khakis. He pulled against them, yanking very hard. I heard the fabric tear as I gripped the sawhorse tightly to brace myself. He jerked again, tearing them further, and then finally a third time, ripping the back of my pants right off my ass. Then he grabbed the fabric of my underwear, tearing it apart though leaving the waistband intact. He was exposing my ass to himself while leaving my crotch encased in the piss soaked clothing.

I knew what was about to happen. I knew he was planning to fuck me. He'd never done anything like this before, fucked me in a public place like this. We could hear people in the room next to us. We could hear the pounding, the construction workers yelling out to one another above the sounds of their equipment. Matt also had never fucked me like this with no form of foreplay. He'd always used a lubricant of some sort. I didn't think I could even begin to take him without some kind of lube. He moved quickly back to the bag he'd just discarded on the floor and pulled something else out of it. Then I felt him place his hand against my neck, pushing my head down so that I was looking at the floor, and he squeezed some sort of gel into the crack of my ass. I heard him spit. He squeezed another big gob onto my ass cheeks and tossed the tube of lubricant carelessly on the ground.

He then released his grip on my neck and stepped back. He was pulling down his shorts, removing them as he stepped up behind me, and I felt him smear his cock around in the gob of lube that was on my ass cheeks. He then stepped even closer to me, sidling himself up behind me so his legs were pressing against the back of my own. Then with one swift movement, he impaled me!

I started to scream from the pain, biting down hard into the gag. My screams came out muffled, sounding more like moans. Out of pure reflex I pushed myself forward, trying to pull away, but he was now holding onto my hips. I tried righting myself, moving more into an upright, standing position, but he pushed me back down, using only one hand in the center of my back. He grabbed my hips again and began to thrust. He slid his cock all the way into me and then back out. I felt him ramming deep into me; the pain was severe though thankfully somewhat lessened by the lube.

"Fuck yeah!" Matt said as he enjoyed the tightness of my hole. "You fuckin faggot pissboy. How'd it feel to piss yourself in front of all those people, huh? Huh? You fuckin fag. You're my hole. You're just my fuckin pisshole and my cumhole, too. You're mine. I own your faggot ass! I fuckin *own* it!!" As he said these things, he rammed himself deeply into me. Each verbal assault was accompanied by a physical one as well, as his cock tore into my guts. It felt like he was slamming me so hard he was gonna poke himself right through me.

I bit down hard into the gag and gripped the sawhorse with both hands. I was powerless underneath him and had no choice but to take whatever he doled out to me. He was now riding me, holding onto both hips intensely as he rocked himself in and out of me. I heard and felt his legs slapping against the back of my own as he drove himself into me, and I could not help but respond verbally myself, crying out from the pain as he stabbed me fiercely. My cries were not heard by him though, for the gag completely muted me, making the cries sound like moans. He did not know if they were moans of pain or pleasure.

At a certain point, I did not know either. The pain was subsiding and the drilling of his cock into my prostate was exciting me. I felt my own hard-on pressing into my piss-soaked underwear. I was moaning more loudly now as he continued to fuck me without mercy. He quickened the pace, fucking me now harder than he ever had done before. His staccato thrusts were of course to maximize his own pleasure, yet they were bringing me so close to the verge of orgasm myself. I did not wanna shoot in my pants, not without his express order to do so. I couldn't even speak to him though. I couldn't even tell him I was about to cum.

"Shoot in your pants, fag!" he said, as if somehow reading my mind. "Shoot your fuckin load while I drill your ass. Do it!" I moaned loudly then, bracing my feet against the tile floor beneath me, and felt my body tremble as I drained my load into my already soaking-wet clothes.

"Fuck yeah!" Matt yelled, "Fuck!" He slammed himself all the way into me, burying himself balls deep as he held tightly to my hips. I felt his cock swell inside my sphincter as he drained himself, shooting his hot load deep into me. "Annnghhhh!" he moaned.

It took a full fifteen seconds for him to finish pumping into me, and then he grabbed my shoulders and pulled me into a standing position, wrapping his arms around me. He buried his face into my neck, kissing me passionately, all the while remaining buried inside my ass.

He then reached up and ripped off the gag, tearing the snaps loose hurriedly and tossing it on the floor. I gasped madly, trying desperately to catch my breath as he planted his lips over my own. He drove his tongue inside my mouth, kissing me with such passion and intensity that I thought I may just cum again right then. He then pulled out of me quickly and spun me around, pulling me into himself with an all encompassing, protective embrace. He wrapped his arms completely around me and pulled me to his chest, and I reached up with my small hands and felt his rock-hard body. I melted into him, feeling his strength and security, and most of all his love.

"Good boy! You were such a good, good boy! I'm so proud of you!" he said, as he held me there. Finally after all this time, I began to sob, burying my face into his chest. "Why you cryin pup?" he said softly. "Why you cryin now?"

My tears were not tears of sadness or even of shame or humiliation. They were simply tears of relief. I'd had all this emotion bottled inside of me and was trying so desperately to obey and make my owner proud. When it was over, I simply had no choice but to release them. "Did I do it right, Sir? Did I obey you?"

"You did! You did it exactly right ... perfect! And you didn't freak, not even once. So why you cryin now?"

"I don't know, Sir. I ... um ... I just am ... overwhelmed I guess." He then kissed me again, this time a soft and loving kiss, slowly pressing his lips against mine.

"Was it hot, pup? Did it turn you on?" he asked.

"You made me cum, Sir. You made me cum in my pants without even touching myself."

He laughed when I said it, "Cuz you had your owner inside you, usin you the way ya need to be used."

"Yes Sir," I said. "Thank you Sir."

"Go over to the bag on the floor. There's a plug inside of it. Want you to wear it the rest of the day. Keep my cum inside ya."

"Yes Sir," I said, and hurried over. "Sir, what am I gonna wear now? How can I go back to the truck like this?"

"Look in the bag. There's clothes."

"How? How'd you do all this? How'd you get the key to that hallway?" I asked.

"This is gonna be our newest gym," said Matt. "My dad closed on the deal last week when we were on the cruise."

"So you had it all planned?" I asked.

"Was testin ya, pup. Wanted to see if you could handle it rougher. See if you could take a little humiliation."

"And ...?"

"And you did it all. You passed!"

I smiled at him broadly. "Thank you, Sir. Thank you so much."

"Let's hit the showers!" he said. They're around the corner."

4

Drew arrived at my apartment at ten o'clock the next morning. He and I both had the entire week off, not having to return from spring break until the following Monday. Alex had already returned to work, and Matt was busy with his own business. With the purchase of the new gym in Sarasota and the renovation of the gym he'd taken me to the night of my birthday party, he definitely had a full plate. Drew volunteered to come over with his Ford Ranger and start moving me right away. The heaviest item we had to transport was my bed, and between the two of us, we'd be able to manage it with little problem.

"You would not believe what Matt did to me yesterday," I said to Drew excitedly. "I was so excited I about pissed myself. No, wait! I *did* piss myself." I laughed as I looked over to him. We were in my bedroom, packing up my computer.

"What do ya mean?" he asked, smiling over to me.

"Oh god, you totally won't even believe it. Matt came to pick me up yesterday afternoon, and well, he didn't say where we were goin or anything so I thought it was just like this big surprise."

"Yeah?" said Drew, urging me on.

"Well so we get into the truck and he is like acting like he's all pissed at me or something. It was weird. I thought he was really mad or something. I didn't say anything though, cuz you know how sometimes I overreact and get too sensitive and stuff."

"Oh really? Never noticed that," he said sarcastically.

I smiled at him, pausing before I continued. "Well then he stopped at a gas station and buys me this huge bottle of water. Orders me to drink the whole thing in ten minutes. I was thinking, 'There's no way I'm gonna be able to drink all this water so fast', but I didn't argue with him. I just did it. I was really proud of myself too, when I actually finished it in time."

"Why'd he want you to drink so much water?" asked Drew.

"Well, that's what I was wonderin too, but I didn't wanna ask him. He wasn't really in the mood to be explaining himself. Thought it best for me to just obey him without botherin him with annoying questions. Well then next thing I know he orders me to get down on my knees right there in the truck."

"He make ya blow him while he was drivin?" asked Drew excitedly.

I shook my head. "No, why? Have you done that before?"

"Sure," he said, as if it was a stupid question. "So why'd he have you kneel then?"

"Well, then he pulled over. I had no idea where we were cuz I couldn't see or anything, but I could tell it was some sort of parking lot. I could see a lamppost out the window. Well, he parks the truck and makes me beg for his cock."

"Oh my god! Then did he make ya blow him?"

"Shut up and let me finish the story, would ya?" I said, laughing. "No, then I had to piss like a fuckin racehorse. I'd had this huge bottle of water. I thought I was gonna burst. But he wouldn't let me get out of the truck to piss. When I got up from the floor I saw we were at a shopping mall. He wouldn't even let me go inside."

"So you pissed yourself right there in his truck? I'm surprised he wasn't worried bout his seats getting wet."

"No, he didn't make me do it there. He went into the mall with me. Made me piss my pants right there in the fuckin shopping mall, right in front of a whole bunch of people."

"Oh my god! How embarrassing! Petey, did you cry?"

I shook my head, smiling broadly at my friend. "Nope, can you believe it?"

"So did you have to wear your pissy clothes the rest of the day?"

"No, you are totally not gonna believe what happened next. After I pissed myself, and I mean I was totally fuckin soaked, he drags me into this corridor and fucks the shit outta me."

"No way! You're making this up!" demanded Drew.

"No, honest I'm not. He had a key. They're puttin a new gym in this mall. He dragged me into the corridor and then pushed me into this big empty store that they were working on. It was part of the gym. That's where he actually fucked me. He bent me over a couple 'a sawhorses."

"Oh wow, that's so unbelievable."

"It was the hottest thing that's ever happened to me. Ya know, I've never seen him like that."

"So aggressive, ya mean?" asked Drew.

"Nah, he's been aggressive before. This was somethin different. It was ... um ... like he was—I don't know."

"What?" asked Drew. "What was he like?"

"He was like hungry for me or something. He was like an animal."

Drew's mouth dropped open, "Whoo hoo! So he had passionate animal sex with you in the fuckin shoppin mall. That is way hot!"

"But Drew, he was like so different, I mean before he even fucked me. When he pushed me against the wall in that corridor, he started kissin me real hard like. He was like tearin my clothes apart and shit. He kept sayin shit about how much he wanted me and stuff. I felt so—"

"Desired!" interjected Drew.

"Yeah, it felt like he really did desire me!"

"Watchin how you pissed yourself for him really turned him on, I guess," Drew told me. "To have that much control and to see you obey him without freakin like you sometimes do, it must've made him real hot for ya."

"He said it was like a test for me, and that I passed. He said he was so proud of me, and that I did everything perfect."

"Oh god, that is like one of the hottest things I ever heard. So did he buy you some new clothes before you left? I mean after he ripped yours to shreds and stuff?"

"He had new clothes for me there already. He had the whole thing planned. Can you believe that shit?

"You know the hottest thing about it was how he made me feel when he was kissin me in the hallway. I was thinkin bout it last night, and it's sorta like he wanted me even more than I wanted him. I just never felt like that before. I always just knew that it was my job to serve him, and I did so cuz I craved him so bad. But this time it was like he was the one craving me."

"Isn't that the most incredible feeling?" asked Drew. "Alex was like that with me in the beginning. Sometimes he still is actually, but there's nothin like that feeling."

"Then after he fucked me, he kissed me so much Drew. He just held onto me and kissed me over and over. Then we took a shower together. It was so romantic. He washed every inch of my body too, almost like he was worshipping me."

"Oh my god! Now you're gonna make *me* cry!" said Drew.

"I couldn't help myself. I dropped down to my knees in the shower and sucked his cock, even after he'd just fucked me like a wild man. He didn't cum again though; he just let me suck him for awhile." I giggled as I shared these intimacies with my best friend. "I think he was letting me suck him as a reward. He could tell how much I wanted him in my mouth."

"Are you sore today, I mean after the way he brutalized you?" asked Drew.

"Yes! Oh my god, my ass has never been so sore. Plus I have a bruise on my hip where he slammed me against the wall. I gotta make sure he doesn't see it somehow though."

"Why? You should just show him, Petey. It's no big deal," Drew said sincerely. "Let me see it."

"I just don't want him to feel bad about it. It's not like he hurt me on purpose." I turned to the side and unbuttoned my pants, pulling down the waistband slightly to show Drew the bruised area.

"Wow, that's pretty nasty. Does it hurt real bad?"

I shook my head. "Surprisingly, no. It really doesn't. I think it looks a lot worse than it feels. Matt's gonna be busy for the next couple days, so hopefully it will be healed some before he even sees it."

"Petey, don't you ever learn anything? Call him today and tell him about it! Don't you remember when your chastity was cutting into you and you hid it from him? He was so pissed."

"This is different, though, Drew. I'm not being hurt right now; it's something that's already happened. Not like we can do anything bout it now." I raised my eyebrows to him as I refastened my pants.

"Just tell him though. Tell him before he sees it himself." Drew put his hand on my shoulder. "You don't want some stupid bruise to ruin the hottest sex you ever had, do ya?"

"No, you're right. I'll tell him. I promise. He's gonna call me this afternoon, and I'll tell him then. He probably already knows there's a chance I'd be bruised anyways."

"Maybe. Hey, do you have a box for this printer?"

We continued our packing and started moving the boxes downstairs to the truck. We actually got everything loaded into the small pickup bed except for the clothes. We took the first load over to Drew's apartment and then returned for all my clothing. After vacuuming out my room and checking the rest of the apartment to see if I'd left anything else behind, I wrote Kathie a note and placed it on the dining room table, telling her I'd come back over in the evening to see her and to say goodbye. I felt a wave of sadness and nostalgia sweep over me as I signed my name to the note. Saying goodbye to her was gonna be so hard, for we'd been together so long, but this chapter in our lives was through now. It was time to move forward ... for both of us.

* * *

I spent the majority of the day getting settled into my new room at Drew's house. When Alex got home from work the three of us went out for pizza. It seemed kind of odd to be hanging out with the two of them, for generally when Alex was around, so was Matt. Drew always seemed a bit more reserved when in the company of Alex; the sub in him seemed to pretty much take over. I imagined it was like that with Matt and me as well. I always was aware of my status and was guarded in the things I said and did when he was right there to observe me.

Matt never called me that afternoon as I had expected, so I didn't tell him about the bruise on my hip. We had actually remained so busy that I hadn't really even given any thought to the notion of Matt calling me. After we had devoured our pizza, Alex offered to take me back to Kathie's house. I'd told him that I needed to stop in to say goodbye to her and to make sure I'd gotten all of my stuff.

When we got there, Alex and Drew came with me up to the apartment. I used my key one last time to enter and immediately called out for Kathie. She came around the corner from the kitchen, smiling broadly as she greeted us. "Oh honey, I can't believe you're leaving! I looked into your room and it was empty, and I can't stop crying." Her voice quivered, indicating she was on the verge of tears again.

"Don't cry!" I chided her. "I'm not even goin that far away. Just a few miles. We can still see each other every day if you want."

100

"I know. I know, honey," she said. "Come here, give me a hug." I walked over to her, extending my arms, and we embraced. "I want so much for you to be happy, kiddo. I'm always gonna worry bout you, ya know."

"I know," I said. "I'm gonna miss you so much." I was on the verge of tears now myself as she held me. As we clung to one another she moved her hands down my back, squeezing me tightly. Involuntarily, I winced a bit from the pain, for she'd moved her hand onto my bruised hip.

"What's the matter?" she asked. "Are you hurt?"

"No–um–not at all," I said. "Why do you think that?"

"Cuz you just jumped when I touched your back," she said defensively. "Did you hurt your hip or something?"

Quickly I looked over to Drew. "No, I'm fine. You just were tickling me."

"Bullshit. Let me see," she insisted. "Pull up your shirt."

"No! I told you I'm not hurt. Please," I said. "We've gotta get goin anyways."

"Petey, you're not leaving this apartment until I see your back. Now lift up your shirt now," she demanded.

I sighed loudly and turned away from her. She grabbed the tail of my shirt and pulled it up, exposing the big bruise I'd been concealing. "Oh my god!" she exclaimed. "How did this happen?"

"I fell. It's no big deal. Please, just forget it."

"You're goin to the hospital, Petey. You need x-rays," she said in a very matter-of-fact tone.

"No! I don't need x-rays. I'm fine. Nothin 's broke. Please, Kathie. Just forget it; I'll be just fine."

Alex had then stepped over to look at my back. "Maybe you should at least get it looked at Petey," he said. "It looks pretty bad."

"Where did you fall?" asked Kathie. "Did someone do this to you?"

"Stop it! Both of you, please." Quickly I looked up to Alex. "I'm sorry–um–um—please, let me wait. Matt can take me to the hospital tomorrow."

"This is *not* gonna wait til tomorrow," said Kathie. "And what does Matt have to do with it? You don't need him to drive you to the hospital; I'll do it right now."

"I'm gonna call him," I said. "Just wait–let me call him first, please."

Kathie placed her hands on her hips, looking at me intently with an expression of utter exasperation. Alex looked down at me. "Go ahead. I think you should call Matt about it," he said. "He'd wanna know."

Once I'd pressed the speed dial option on my phone to ring Matt, I quickly turned away from the others and stepped towards the other side of the room. "Hello," he said, and immediately I was relieved to hear his voice.

"Matt," I said, knowing that by using his first name he'd understand I was not alone. "I have to talk to you about something."

"What's up?" he said. "Somethin wrong?"

"Um—no, not really. Well, sorta." I stepped further away from the other three and into the kitchen. "I have this bruise. It's from yesterday."

"Really? Are you all right? How bad is it?" he asked.

"It doesn't hurt. Really, it's no big deal, but I'm over at Kathie's house and she wants me to go to the hospital. Alex is with me; he said I should call you."

"All right, stay there. I'll be over there in about fifteen minutes."

"I'm sorry, Sir. I tried not to let her see it."

"Don't worry about it; just stay put til I get there. Okay?"

"Yes Sir."

"Bye."

I turned back around and walked into the living room. "He's gonna come over here. He'll be here in a few minutes," I told them.

"Oh Christ!" said Kathie. "I told you I'd take you. Why can't he just meet us there?"

"Kathie, he said for me to wait, and I'm gonna wait."

She sighed as she looked over at me. "Okay, well, you guys want something to drink?"

Drew spoke up finally, "I'll have something. Diet Coke if you have any." I think he was trying to distract Kathie before she started in again about my bruise. It didn't really work though, for she was ranting about it already while on her way to the kitchen.

"Petey, I wanna know how this happened. How'd you get all bruised up like that? Is that the only place you're injured?" she bombarded me with questions.

"I'm not all bruised up. I just fell and got a little bruise. Big deal. Ya know, I'm not as fragile as you think. So what if I get a bruise once in awhile? Doesn't mean I gotta rush to the hospital every time."

"Well Petey," said Alex. "It could be worse than you think. If it hurts to even touch it, maybe you fractured something. Best you at least get it looked at. Where'd you fall anyways?"

"It was when we were moving. Drew accidentally pushed me into the staircase when we were carrying down my computer desk," I lied. Drew looked over at me wide-eyed.

Alex then turned to Drew. "And you never bothered to even make sure he was okay?" Alex asked him accusingly.

"Um—well, I'm sorry, Sir." Drew stammered. "I didn't know. I didn't even think he was hurt."

"It wasn't his fault!" I quickly interjected. "I lost my footing and started to stumble. That's what made him run into me."

The room got quiet and we all sort of were just looking at one another. Finally I sat down on the couch, and the other three also found a seat. We waited a few minutes and finally Matt arrived. I jumped up from the couch when I heard his knock on the door.

"Let me see," he said, after he'd stepped through the door. I pulled my shirt up and he reached down to gently touch the deep purple bruise. I gritted my teeth, willing myself not to wince, but as he gently pressed against it, involuntarily I jerked a little. "It's probably just a bruise, pup, but you should get it looked at, just in case."

"No shit, Sherlock!" retorted Kathie, who had then stepped over next to us.

Matt looked up at her as he gently pulled my shirt back down into place. "Kathie, you know I'd never hurt him on purpose."

"What?" she exclaimed. "I knew you did this to him. You fucking bastard!"

"He didn't do anything to me!" I yelled back at her. "I already told you, I fell against the staircase when we were moving. Didn't I, Drew? Tell her!" I looked over to Drew, praying he'd back up my story again.

"Petey, don't lie to your sister," Matt said to me calmly. "It was an accident. I never, ever would hurt him on purpose. I didn't beat him or anything; it just was an accident. That's all."

"It looks like you beat him with a fucking baseball bat. That was no accident. I'm not fucking blind!" Kathie was not even being reasonable, her anger seeming to have reached a boiling point. For a split second it occurred to me that the emotionalism, which so often controlled me, must be a genetic trait.

"Just calm down!" said Alex sternly, now dragging himself into this shouting match. "There's nobody here who thinks that Matt would ever hurt Petey on purpose, and no one is accusing him of anything."

"Speak for yourself!" said Kathie. "Petey please! You don't have to let him do this to you. You don't have to be his punching bag."

"Oh for chrissakes! I'm not anyone's punching bag. Matt did not beat me, and nobody else did either. If you must know, we were making passionate love and I slammed into the wall, or maybe it was the wooden sawhorses I was bent over. I don't know for sure. But it sure as hell was not from being beaten!"

Kathie's mouth dropped open then, having no immediate rebuttal to offer. I looked over to Drew and he was stifling a grin. In spite of my anger, I almost laughed myself.

"Oh," said Alex, and then turned away immediately. "Drew and I are goin back to the apartment. We'll see you there later." Drew quickly stepped up behind Alex as they headed for the door.

"I was willing to take the blame for it, honest I was," said Drew on his way out the door. I just smiled up at him, not saying anything.

"This is unbelievable," said Kathie, her voice being completely calm and nearly monotone. "Matt, don't you realize how much bigger than him you are? Don't you realize you could hurt him?"

"And don't you think you may be being just a bit overprotective, Kathie?" Matt asked. "Haven't you ever gotten carried away in the heat of the moment before? Haven't you ever suffered any battle scars from–um–from wild sex?"

"Where were you doing it that there were sawhorses?" At this point she didn't seem so angry any more, but genuinely curious.

"You don't wanna know," I said.

"Oh, really I think I do," she said. "I really, really do." She then actually laughed. "One time I thought I'd sprained my wrist when I fell off the bed. Carter was gonna take me to emergency, but I wouldn't let him. He felt so bad afterwards."

"See!" I said. "And you never even told me. You knew it wasn't his fault cuz you knew he didn't hurt you on purpose. It was just an accident."

"Yeah," she admitted, "you're right. I'm sorry. I'm sorry, Matt, that I accused you."

"It's no problem, but I do think he should at least have it looked at."

"Please Matt," I said to him. "I don't wanna go to the stupid hospital again!"

"We can just go down to Urgent Care. They can do an x-ray there in like ten minutes. It's no big deal, Petey. Then we'll know for sure that it's all right."

"I can take him, Matt," offered Kathie. "I know you probably weren't planning on this tonight."

"I know," said Matt, "but since I was the one who caused the injury, I'll take the responsibility. You can go with us if you want."

"Hmm, okay. I'll go," she said. "Let me grab my purse from the bedroom."

When she left the room I looked up at Matt and whispered to him, "I'm so sorry Sir. This is so much stupid fuckin drama!"

"Don't worry bout it," he said.

The ten minutes that Matt had referred to turned into an hour-long ordeal, and when it was over, the bruise ended up being officially called a "bruise". We stuck with the moving story, and I was sternly warned not to be lifting things heavier than I could carry because I was just "a little guy".

"You've gotta know your limitations," the big, husky female nurse scolded me. "You're just like my grandson Darren. He thinks he's superman or something. I always tell him, 'Darry, you're gonna hurt yourself one of these times,' but he never listens to Grandma." I just laughed at her as she smiled affectionately.

I was given a prescription of pain medication, which I doubted I'd even fill, and when we finally left Urgent Care, Matt offered to take us out for ice cream. Surprisingly, Kathie acquiesced, and we headed over to Baskin Robbins. "This reminds me of when you sprained your ankle in the sixth grade," said Kathie as the three of us sat down at the small round table in the ice cream shop. "Remember? You had been climbing on that huge monkey bar thing and jumped clear from the top. Landed on some sorta hard plastic thing."

"It was a cow," I said as Matt laughed. "Seriously, it was a cow. It was this hard plastic cow. It didn't even break either, but my foot almost did."

Kathie had busted up laughing. "Bobby Fortune came running to our front door screaming at the top of his lungs, 'Petey landed on a cow and broke his foot!' You should have seen the look on Dad's face! All I could think of was this big barn animal walking around in the playground. I kept visualizing it and laughing." The three of us all were laughing at this point.

"Have you ever broken anything, Matt?" Kathie asked as she took a bite off her ice cream cone. "Other than someone's heart, I mean."

He half-grinned at her, not verbally responding to the last part of her question. "Yeah, I had a couple sports injuries. Broke my wrist when I was ten, and sprained my ankle when I was a freshman."

"Did you cry?" I asked. "I mean, when you were ten?"

"Hmm, don't remember. Probably I did. Was only ten."

"I can't picture you ever cryin, Matt," I said. "Not even when you were that young."

"Why? You think I don't have emotions? I'm human, ya know. I've cried before." I reached under the table and placed my hand on his leg. "Sometimes you can't help it. If you are in pain, it's natural to cry."

"Speaking of pain," said Kathie, "you still planning to get that tattoo?" I couldn't believe she was bringing up the topic. I looked to Matt before answering. When he didn't answer I turned back to Kathie.

"I want to. I'll get it if Matt wants me to," I said to her sincerely.

"But is it what *you* really want, Petey?" she asked.

"Yeah, I'm looking forward to it actually." I then looked back at Matt, smiling warmly.

"Well I decided that I can't freak out every time you make a decision about your life," Kathie said. "Carter and I were talkin bout this earlier today. I gotta just let go. I know Mom and Dad would've wanted me to butt out and let you live your own life, so I'm gonna try to be less of a bitch about things."

"Kathie, you've never been a bitch to me. You just care a lot, that's all, but I owe you so much. You've always been there for me."

"And you've been there for me too. We've been there for each other. I'm sorry I overreacted earlier at the apartment. Matt, I shouldn't have accused you of anything."

"No problem," he said. "I'd be pretty upset too if I thought someone had hurt my family–especially Petey." I looked up into Matt's eyes then, realizing what he'd just said. He had just referred to me as being a member of his family. Gently I squeezed his leg with my small hand, letting him know I was aware of the importance of the statement.

I was so thankful for him then, and so very proud to be his pup. We finished our ice cream together, and then he took Kathie home before delivering me safely to my new apartment. Things were gonna work out just fine. Even Kathie knew I belonged to him now.

"Petey, you know I did not hurt you on purpose yesterday, don't ya?" he asked before I climbed out of the truck.

"Sir, you didn't hurt me," I responded quickly. "I just bruise easy. It's cuz I'm such a wimp. Please don't say you hurt me, Sir."

"I want ya to start martial arts classes. The new wing at the gym is just about completed. Gonna be ready to open it and start classes in a week or two."

"Yes Sir, of course. I'll do whatever you say," I said to him sincerely as I shifted in my seat to face him squarely.

"I know you will, pup, but I want you to do this for yourself. I want you to get stronger. That's not cuz I think you're a weakling either, so don't go thinkin that. It's that I want my pup to be safe—to know how to defend himself." He reached over to me, motioning for me to get closer to him.

"Do you have any idea how much I love you, Sir?" I asked as I looked into his eyes.

"Really?" he asked. "Thought you just loved my big cock."

I reached into his lap then, gently resting my fingers against his crotch. Then I smiled at him. "Well, yeah, it's mostly that." We laughed together as I ran my fingers over the outline of his bulge. "Want me to suck it again, Sir?" I asked hopefully.

"No!" he said firmly, pushing my hand out of his lap. "You already had your treat for tonight," referring to the ice cream, I assumed. "I'm gonna pick you up tomorrow morning though. Eleven o'clock. We're gonna go get your tattoo."

"Oh Sir! Really?" I asked excitedly. "Can Drew come?" I asked quickly.

He looked down at me, gauging my response carefully. "Why you want Drew there?" he asked. "This is something special between you and me."

"I know Sir," I said apologetically. "I just am nervous, that's all. Cuz—um—what if it hurts real bad?"

"Well, tell ya what, I'll call you around nine or ten tomorrow morning. We'll see how ya feel about it then, and you can talk to Drew tonight and see if he even wants to go. He should ask Alex first anyways."

"Yes Sir," I said. "It doesn't matter, long as you're with me."

"Okay, get some good sleep tonight, all right?"

I nodded. "Sir, I'm sorry for ruining your plans tonight, just cuz of this stupid bruise."

"Didn't ruin anything. Nothin's more important than my pup."

I then quickly bent over and kissed his crotch. "I had to at least touch it!" I said. He laughed and pulled me up by the shoulders. Then he leaned in and kissed me on the mouth, wrapping his arms around me and holding me against himself. God I loved him so much!

5

Had Matt actually known how I'd be affected by knowing in advance about the tattoo, I'm sure he would not have even told me. That night I was so anxious that I got myself worked up beyond the point of being able to even get to sleep. Instead I stayed up and tried to get my belongings unpacked and organized as well as I could in the new room. I was extremely concerned about keeping the noise level to a minimum and was literally tiptoeing across the room so as not to disturb Alex and Drew.

Drew had been almost as excited about the tattoo as I was, and when I told him he grabbed and hugged me tightly, suddenly remembering about my bruise and releasing me abruptly. "Oh Petey, I'm sorry. Did I hurt you?"

I just laughed. He could have gut-punched me at that point, I think. I was too ecstatic over the knowledge of my tattoo to even care about the bruise. "Drew, I'm so scared about it, though. Will you go with us?"

Drew put his hands on each of my shoulders. "Of course I will, Petey," he said. "Sure."

I was about to thank him when Alex piped up. He was sitting in the living room, in the same recliner where I'd both worshipped my owner's feet and where I'd been spanked in front of Alex. "No Drew, you're not goin." Immediately I wanted to question him, to ask why, but bit my tongue. I definitely did not want to sound insolent towards Alex on my first day in their home. Alex then explained himself, "The tattoo is between Petey and his owner. If Matt wants you there, he will have to ask." Alex was watching television and hadn't even bothered to turn and look at us.

"Sir," I said meekly. "Matt told me I could talk to Drew about it, but that he needed your permission."

"Did he say it was okay for Drew to be there?" Alex asked dryly.

"Um—no Sir. Not exactly. He said he'd think about it and then call me in the morning."

"Okay. Well if Matt says okay, then fine."

"Thank you, Sir," I said, smiling broadly at Drew.

"So where you getting it?" asked Drew. "I mean, what part of your body?"

"I don't know," I said, suddenly realizing we'd never even discussed that. "I never even thought about it. Where do you think he will put it?"

"Maybe your arm or leg—where it's visible," suggested Drew.

"Probably your ass," said Alex. "Doesn't need the tattoo to be visible, not when ya got a collar already."

I raised my eyebrows to Drew. Alex was probably right. I wondered if he and Matt had already discussed this. Maybe he'd be making Drew get a tattoo next.

"Well, honestly, I don't even care where he puts it on me. I'm just happy that I will be marked by my owner."

After brushing my teeth and changing into some sleep pants and a tee shirt, I padded off into my bedroom, all comfy and wearing my glasses. I closed the door gently and picked up a box of my belongings, placing it on the bed. I then sat there, crossed-legged, sorting through the contents of the box. When I was younger, we used to refer to this sitting position as "Indian style". The box contained mainly personal things such as pictures. I pulled out the picture of my parents and me, the one that Kathie had given me for my birthday. I remembered my dad showing me his tattoo, explaining to me how he'd gotten it while in the Navy. It made me wonder what he'd think of me now, getting a tattoo of my own. Probably he wouldn't be all that proud though. He'd gotten himself inked to prove his manhood, to demonstrate his masculinity. I, on the other hand, was getting marked to signify my status as owned property.

What would Mom and Dad think of all this, if they were still alive? How would my father feel about having a son like me? Probably it was the absolute worse-case scenario for him to have ever imagined. What father actually wants to even think about the possibility of their son growing up to be a fag? It would have been particularly worse for him, I reasoned, being that I was his only son.

Mom probably wouldn't have been as bothered about having a gay child. Honestly, she may have even come to the point where she actually enjoyed it. As a small child, my mom was always the one who defended me. When I selected girl toys over the boy toys, she was the one who ran interference. She insisted to my father that it didn't matter, that I should be allowed to play with whatever toys made me happy. She embraced the softer side of me and accepted me totally for who I was.

My dad never made me feel that way, though. When I was around him, I felt almost as if I had to focus very hard on maintaining a certain image. I had to control my mannerisms and my speech and had to pretend to like things I did not. I did not feel resentment about any of this. If anything, I felt guilt. I thought there must be something wrong with me. These masculine things should have simply come naturally to me. It never should have been a matter of pretending.

I'll never forget how utterly humiliated I knew that my father was the day I was cut from the Little League team. Dad had taken me to the park every single day for over a month, tossing a ball to me, teaching me the correct way to throw and catch. Really, his attempts were so futile. Even to this day, when I try to throw a ball, I know that anyone who is watching is thinking how pathetic I look. All through school I always was teased and taunted, always accused of "throwing like a girl". The vast majority of applicants who tried out for Little League were accepted onto a team. The majority were boys, but actually there were a few girls in the mix as well. The handful of kids who did not make the cut were sent back to the "Minor League." This league was sort of in between T-ball and Little League. It was a stepping-stone, of sorts. The really lousy, non-athletic, sissy types like myself never actually made it out of the Minor League. When they finally got too old to continue, they would drop out. This system of rejection was a very simple way of remedying an embarrassing problem.

I remember that day so very clearly, as I stood there on the sidelines of the Little League field. The six coaches for the respective teams were standing before us. Each coach read aloud in a monotone voice the names on their roster, and then as the name was called, that player would step forward and move over to stand behind his coach. My heart was pounding so loudly in my chest. It was not that I particularly wanted to be on a team in the first place. I only wanted to please my dad. "Oh please!" I prayed. "Please let him call me!" With every single name that was called, I repeated that prayer to myself. I was begging and pleading with God to just allow it to happen. It never did.

Finally after the last name was called there were only seven players left standing. We were curtly instructed that we'd been assigned to a Minor League team, and that we were to report to our practices on Wednesday evenings. Then the coaches turned away from us, casting us aside, and focused their attention on their own excited team players. I felt the tears welling up in my eyes as I ran off the field and headed towards the bathroom. God, I did not want anyone to see me cry! That definitely would have added insult to injury. Already I was the laughing stock for not even making it onto a team, but to then be humiliated by bawling in front of the entire Little League, that would have been the ultimate mortification.

My dad found me crouched in the far corner of the back bathroom stall, sitting alone on the top of the toilet tank. He dried the tears from my nine-year-old face and took me out for ice cream, trying to cheer me up. It only made me feel worse, though, for I knew in my heart how terribly ashamed of me he must have been.

That was why this particular picture was so incredibly meaningful to me. When I'd received that award for my essay and had to go up before all of those people to accept it, I saw a pride in my father's eyes for the very first time in my life. He actually seemed to be almost exuberant as he congratulated me. I was so very thankful for that one memory. It truly was amazing, though, how on that very night, my feelings of exceptional happiness could so quickly change to horror and terror when my dad was suddenly rushed to the hospital with his heart attack. Maybe he died with pride in his heart for me, I reasoned. Maybe.

As I reflected upon my memories of my parents, I suddenly realized that I was again crying, and quickly set the photo aside. I wasn't gonna let this happen, not tonight. This was a happy night for me—first night in my new place with my dearest friend on earth. Tomorrow morning I'd be getting my long-awaited tattoo. Everything seemed to be going extremely well between Matt and Kathie. There really wasn't anything to be sad about. I set the entire box of pictures aside then, and turned my attention to the computer.

Alex and Drew had just converted their internet service to a cable modem system. Prior to that, they'd used a dial-up connection. Alex had offered to allow me the use of the second phone line, as long as I was willing to pay the monthly fee. This would give me access to the internet at any time I wanted on my own private line, and I would never have to worry about tying up their main household line. Matt was very agreeable with the offer and assured me that if I had difficulty paying the monthly fee, he'd help out.

I crawled down under the desk then and began connecting the various electric chords and adapters, realizing what a myriad of confusion this was going to be. Systematically, though, I proceeded to plug each item in, one-at-a-time, and finally was ready to turn on my computer. Once I realized that it was running properly, I attempted to log onto the internet. Everything seemed to be working fine, and so I immediately emailed Matt and reported my success with the computer hardware. I also told him about Alex's comments about Drew going with us in the morning, and I assured him that whatever he decided was certainly fine with me. The last thing I wanted was for Matt to ever feel that I was overstepping my boundaries and trying to second-guess his decisions.

By the time I was done with the computer connections, I realized it was after one in the morning, and I dimmed the overhead light and crawled back up on my bed. I reached over to my nightstand and picked up a book that I'd placed there. It was the birthday present I'd received from Cameron, the book about gay athletes. It was sort of coincidental that this book would surface now, right after I'd been reliving my own athletic fiasco, but I picked it up and started to thumb through it. Finally I settled in, burrowing under the covers, and began to read the book. I must have read for an hour or so, for I was halfway through the book when my eyelids became so heavy that I started to nod off.

Suddenly it was eight o'clock the next morning, and I awoke with the opened book lying neatly on my chest and my glasses still on my face. I must have slept like a rock, without even tossing and turning, I thought. Then almost instantly, the reality of my situation hit me. It was now morning and in three hours I'd be getting my tattoo! I threw back the covers then and crawled out of bed, heading straightway towards the bathroom. After relieving myself, I returned to my bedroom and logged back onto the internet. Already there was a response from Matt.

Pup

Been thinkin bout it a lot. Want this to be between just you and me. Tell Drew we appreciate him being willing to go with you, but explain I want it to be just the two of us.

See you around eleven.

M

I sighed to myself as I read the email but then quickly thought about his words. He was correct, actually. This should be an event that was shared exclusively by Owner and pup. I could tell Drew all about it afterwards, like I did with just about everything else, but the actual tattooing was something I wanted only my Matt to be a part of. He was so wise with his decisions, I realized. I was so lucky to have him in my life.

The next three hours seemed an eternity for me. I went out to the kitchen, made a pot of coffee for Drew, and then turned on the television at low volume and began watching the Today Show. I heard Alex get up about ten minutes later and stumble out to the kitchen. He pulled a carton of orange juice from the refrigerator and began to drink from it, not bothering to get down a glass. He then walked into the living room, shirtless and wearing only his boxers, and stood next to me while still holding the orange juice carton. "How'd ya sleep?" he asked, his voice sounding a little different than normal. It was weird how people had that sleepy voice when they first woke up.

"Oh, very well, Sir. Thank you. I hope I didn't wake you with the television."

"Nope, gotta get ready for work. Help yourself to breakfast if you want. I'm getting in the shower." He then went back to the kitchen to put the juice carton in the fridge before heading down the hall to his shower.

When Drew got up about five minutes later, I immediately told him about Matt's email. "It's okay, Petey. I kinda figured he'd decide that. You can come right back here and show me, though, when you're done. I can't wait to see it."

"Thanks Drew," I said. Truly he was an amazing person–the most understanding friend I'd ever had.

When Matt arrived at the apartment at a quarter to eleven, Drew and I were sitting together at the kitchen table. We were discussing boy bands and laughing, trying to create a diversion to distract me from worrying about getting tattooed. It was so funny, for I was so incredibly nervous that I felt like a person who was about to undergo major heart surgery or something. The feeling was altogether surreal, and although I was anxious to get it done, I also was very much afraid of the procedure itself. When Matt knocked on the door, I literally jumped in my seat, and Drew laughed at me lightheartedly. "Little jumpy?" he asked, as he got up to get the door.

"Hey, how's my pup?" asked Matt as he walked into the dining room. He seemed so cheerful and upbeat as he approached me, placing his hand on my shoulder. In his other hand, he was carrying a plastic bag. Already I knew enough not to question him about its contents. The mystery did not go long unsolved for me, though, for he almost immediately turned and handed the bag to Drew.

"Drew, want you to do me a favor. Take Petey in the bedroom and put this chastity on him. Bring me back the key." He stated this so matter-of-factly, that it seemed as if it were absolutely no big deal to him at all. It was as if he were asking him to perform some mundane task, like getting him a drink of water. Drew also seemed unfazed and nodded immediately.

"Yes, Sir," he said. Then turning to me he said, "Come on, Petey."

I got up and followed Drew into his bedroom. "Okay take off your pants and lie down on the bed," Drew instructed me.

"Why do you think he wants me to wear a chastity?" I asked Drew as I unfastened my khakis. "Do you think maybe I did something wrong?"

"Nah, of course not. You should have expected to be in chastity when you go to get a tattoo. You probably are gonna have to take your pants off to get it. I bet Alex was right; he's gonna mark your ass."

"So?" I said. "What's that got to do with wearin a chastity?"

"Well the tattoo dude is gonna see your privates," explained Drew. "Matt probably wants him to know they belong to him. Plus maybe he doesn't want you poppin a boner."

"Yeah, like that's gonna happen!" I said. "Like I'm gonna get a hard-on from someone ramming a needle repeatedly into my ass cheek."

Drew laughed. "Well don't question him. Just obey. Now get up on the bed and spread your legs." I did as Drew instructed, not even feeling a bit modest. I'd become so comfortable being around Drew now that it was no big deal for me to strip in front of him. Plus he and I had jacked off together that one time, with Matt's permission of course. "You did a good job shaving, Petey," Drew commented. "I doubt you could get any smoother."

I smiled down at him as he knelt on the floor beside the bed. "I shave every single day, just to make sure I'm totally smooth."

"Matt must like that, huh?"

"Yeah. I'm not allowed to have any hair below my neck."

Drew then pulled the CB2000 out of the bag. "I see he removed the points of intrigue gadget. That's good."

"Oh yeah, thank god!" I agreed. Then Drew quickly slid the chastity onto my soft penis. He had not touched me at all prior to doing so, probably to make sure as to not stimulate me in any way. It had to go on when I was completely soft. He wiggled it around a big, getting it to where it belonged and then asked me if it was comfortable. "Yeah, it's fine," I said. He then attached the lock.

"Okay, wait here and don't get dressed," said Drew. "I'm gonna take the key back to Matt and see if he wants to inspect you before you put your clothes back on."

"Okay," I said, cupping my hands together behind my head. Drew left the room and then returned less than sixty seconds later. "He says to get dressed and come back out in the living room. Wants you to wear that jockstrap instead of your underwear too."

I jumped up and pulled on the jock and my khakis. "I wonder why he didn't just have you put on my chastity out there." I stated.

"You ask too many questions sometimes, Petey." He put his hand on my shoulder then, "But I love ya anyways." He then leaned in and sweetly kissed my cheek. Afterwards I turned and grabbed him, hugging him tightly.

"I love you too, Drew. I love you so much!"

"Come on, let's go. Can't keep your owner waiting."

***

On the ride over to the tattoo shop, Matt did not say much to me but did allow me to sit right next to him in the front seat of the SUV. At first I wondered why he was driving this vehicle instead of the pickup, but as I thought of it, the thought of me having to sit on my tattooed ass on the ride home provided a very feasible explanation. If it were actually my butt that was getting inked, I'd probably need to lie down for the ride home. It was sure to hurt too badly to immediately sit on.

Matt reached onto the dashboard as he drove down the street, pulled out a piece of paper, and handed it to me casually. When I looked at it, I realized it was a copy of the graphic he'd shown me earlier. It was the dog tag in the shape of a bone, just like the one that hung from my leather collar. "Do I have to give this to the guy at the tattoo place, Sir?" I asked quietly.

"Nope. He already has one. I talked to him already and he'll have everything ready for us when we get there. There is a pair of basketball shorts in the backseat for you to wear when it's done. Just grab the whole duffle bag before you get out of the car."

"Yes Sir," I said. "I'm so nervous!"

He moved his arm around the back of my head and slid it completely around my right shoulder, pulling me tightly against his body. He just held me there securely as he continued to steer with his left hand. No matter what happened, I knew I'd always feel secure in this place. His arms were my favorite place in the whole world. I pressed my face against his torso while placing my hand on his thigh. I truly did belong to him; being his pup was the greatest desire of my heart.

When Matt pulled the vehicle into the strip mall and found a parking place, I thought my heart was literally gonna pump right out of my chest. I slid over to the passenger door, knowing I had to retrieve the duffle bag as instructed, and opened the door, lowering myself slowly down to the pavement. Suddenly a wave of nervous nausea overtook me, and I was certain I was going to vomit right there. I pressed my hands flat against the side of the door as I stood there in the parking lot, bending over slightly. I was trying to regain control of myself before I completely lost it.

Matt was right behind me. "You all right?" he asked.

"I'm sorry Sir," I said, feeling suddenly as if I was gonna cry. "I'm so sorry I'm this way."

"Don't be sorry, pup. You're just nervous, but I'm with you, so don't be scared."

"I'm not Sir. I'm so sorry. I'm not scared; it's just I get sick when I'm so nervous."

He then grabbed my shoulders and gently turned me to face him. "Think of me, pup. Think of how you're doin it for me."

I nodded to him as I looked up into his eyes. "Yes Sir!" I said, and grabbed him and hugged him so tightly. "Thank you. Thank you for letting me do it."

Matt then opened the rear door and pulled out the duffle bag. "I'll carry it," he said, and put his free arm around my shoulder. We walked to the entrance together.

The proprietor of the tattoo business immediately put my mind at ease when I first saw him. He was sort of a fatherly looking man, probably in his late thirties or early forties. He had dark hair and big dark eyes and spoke very softy. "Hey, you must be Petey," he said, walking over to me and extending his hand.

"Yes ... um ... yes Sir," I said.

"I'm Niko," he said. "So you want a tattoo huh?"

"Oh yes. Yes Sir. I want one very much," I assured him as I looked up into the eyes of my owner. "But I'm kinda scared a little."

"Oh, well don't be scared. I know that's easier said than done. Here, come over here and sit down. I'll show ya a couple of my tattoos and explain exactly what we're gonna do here today." He gently grabbed my wrist and led me over to a chair in the corner of the room. He then pulled up a folding chair in front of me and sat down in it backwards, resting his arms on back of the chair. "See this one?" he said, rolling up the cuff of his shirtsleeve. It was a tattoo of a big dragon, prominently etched into his bicep, complete with multiple colors. "Now this one took quite awhile to do, and it was sorta painful too, but yours is gonna be simple compared to this. Yours will be just one or two colors, and it will be on your backside, so it won't hurt as much."

"Really?" I asked. "Why is that?"

"Well cuz there's a lot more padding back there," he laughed. "What I'm gonna need you to do, is to try to lie as perfectly still as you can. If it starts to hurt real bad, try to distract yourself. Think of something that makes you happy or something like that. Ya know what I mean?"

I nodded to him quickly. "I already know exactly what I will think about." I smiled and looked up at Matt.

"How long you two been together?" Niko asked.

"Little over six months," answered Matt.

"Well you two look great together," Niko complimented us. "You can be with him the whole time. I think that will help distract him from the pain too. Just keep talkin to him. Keep his mind off it." I thought it was odd the way they were talking about me as if I was not even there. Matt simply nodded to Niko, though, demonstrating his complete trust in Niko's expertise.

"Can you stand up for me now, little guy, and turn around?" asked Niko. "Pull down your pants and let me see." I stood up and turned around so that I was facing away from him. I unbuttoned my khakis and pulled them down below my buttocks, exposing my bare ass to him. "Cool," he said, "Nicely smooth. Don't even have to shave ya. Well let's go into that backroom there and you can take your pants right off and climb up onto the table."

I did as Niko said and walked into the room where he'd directed me. I then toed off my shoes and undid my pants again, this time removing them. I turned to look for my Sir, and Matt was standing right behind me. "Should I take my shirt off?" I whispered to him.

Niko walked in behind me, laughing, "Yeah, Petey, why don't you take that off too, or at least pull it up." Matt stepped in front of me and grabbed the tail of my shirt. I lifted my arms straight up over my head as he pulled off my shirt. I then climbed up onto the table and lay face down. I suddenly felt modest for the first time but was so thankful that Matt was there beside me. He pulled up a chair and placed it by the table in front of me, and then he sat down. I had tucked my arms under myself, crossing them so that I could rest my chin on the back of my hands. Matt reached out and placed his hand against my arm and smiled at me. I wanted so much then for him to bend down and kiss me.

"Okay, I'm putting some solution on this gauze and am gonna wipe the area clean to sterilize it," Niko informed us. He held the square of gauze out for me to see as he soaked it with clear fluid. I could smell that there was alcohol in it. He then wiped the gauze across the right cheek of my buttocks. He was doing it so gently that it almost made me shiver. I laughed a little bit—sort of a giggle. "Ticklish, huh?" he asked. "I like that!"

Matt laughed then himself. "Yeah, he's very ticklish."

"Figures," said Niko, "that a cute ticklish pup like this would be already taken." He then sighed. I looked up at Matt to gauge his reaction and saw that he was smiling. Perhaps he agreed with Niko that I was a cute, ticklish pup, or maybe he was pleased by the fact that it was he who had "taken" me.

"Now I'm gonna explain how we do this, Petey," said Niko. "Have you ever seen those little temporary tattoos? The kind you find in a Cracker Jack box?"

I nodded. "Yes Sir, I know what you mean."

"Well, to start with, we're gonna use something like that. I'm gonna transfer this design onto your skin just like ya do with those temporary tattoos. Then I'm gonna use this gun here to color in the design with ink." He pointed to this electric tattoo gun that was sitting on the counter. "Here, I'll show ya the designs that you have to choose from."

He held up the transfers in front of me, and I smiled as I looked at them. Both were identical designs of the bone-shaped dog tag, but the first one bore the inscription "Property of Matt" while the second stated "Matt's Pup". I looked at them carefully and then up into my owner's eyes. "Sir, which one should I choose?"

"It's up to you pup—your choice," he said.

"Really? And it doesn't matter which?"

"Nope, your choice," he repeated. "Which do you like better?"

"I like that one better, Sir," I said, pointing to the "Matt's Pup" inscription. "Because it says what I am—your pup. I think it sounds more personal than 'property'." I reached out and placed my hand on top of his.

"Yeah, I think you're right," Matt agreed, moving his hand out from under mine and placing his on top. He squeezed my fingers together gently in his palm.

"Okay, 'Matt's Pup' it is," said Niko, and he placed the other transfer down on the counter and proceeded to peel off the backing of the transfer that remained in his hand. Then he smoothly pressed the adhesive side of the transfer on my exposed right butt cheek, firmly smoothing out the air bubbles until it was completely flat. Then with one smooth movement he ripped it off my behind, leaving behind the temporary ink design. "Now, talk to me about colors," Niko said, this time directing his comments right at Matt. "We can do the whole thing in black or we can just make the outline black and the inscription in the color of your choice. Or actually, we can do it however you want."

"Black border with red inscription," Matt stated confidently. Niko nodded.

"All right. Gonna do the inside first. We'll start with the inscription." He then turned towards the counter and picked up a cylindrical container of red ink. He then unscrewed its cap and attached it to the tattoo gun. He placed a clean square of gauze on the counter and began to squeeze the trigger of the gun, doing this very rapidly and repeatedly, until the red ink began to appear on the gauze. It reminded me of blood.

"Petey," Niko said, "are you ready for me to start?"

I looked up at Matt, suddenly realizing that this was it. He was still holding my hand, and I moved my fingers slightly within his grip, squeezing the inside of his palm. "Yes Sir, I'm ready."

Then Niko positioned the tattoo gun against my buttocks, lining up the needle with the outline of the inscription. He held the gun in his right hand and a solution-soaked square of gauze in his left. When he first pulled the trigger on the gun, I felt a very sharp stabbing pain as the needle entered my flesh. I looked directly into Matt's eyes and held his hand fiercely. The initial pain was the worse, perhaps because of the shock of it, but then as Niko continued, I realized that the firing of the needle into my skin felt more like an annoyance than actual stabbing pain.

As Niko continued to stab me with the needle of his gun, rapidly transferring the ink from his gun into my skin, he used the gauze square to wipe away the fluid that was seeping from my flesh. The needle pricks were making me bleed, and Niko quickly assured me this was normal. "It's gonna bleed a little bit, just like any wound," he said. "Then it will scab over, sort of the same way a scraped knee would do. You're gonna have to keep the skin very moist though, apply lotion every couple of hours."

As Niko continued to trace the design, I had to grit my teeth, for the constant stabbing was becoming tedious to me. The irritation was at times bordering upon genuine pain. I remembered what Niko had told me before we started. He'd said to think of something that makes me happy. I squeezed my eyes shut tightly and lay my head against the crook of my elbow, trying to visualize the way that Matt had made love to me the very first time. He had taken a bath with me and had bathed me so romantically. Then he carried me to the bed and showered me with passionate kisses. It was purely heaven. This is what I thought of as I lay there on the tattoo table, holding my owner's hand.

The relentless stabbing continued as Niko proceeded to etch the design of the artwork into my skin. He stopped only one time, and this was to get a fresh piece of gauze, then continued. I was thankful for the brief respite and was almost tempted to ask him to wait before he continued. I endured though, and he was done with the inscription in less than fifteen minutes. It was like after a few moments of stabbing me with the needle, the pain actually did not seem to exist. It seemed to be more of an annoyance to me, and I was anxious for it to be over with. At last, though, he set the gun down and told Matt that he was done with the inscription. Matt stood up completely and leaned over me, admiring Niko's handiwork. Niko wiped the area clean with a fresh piece of gauze as Matt sat back down in his chair. "It looks good pup," Matt said. "How ya doin?"

I smiled up at him. "Okay Sir. It really doesn't hurt that bad."

I turned my head towards the counter to watch what Niko was doing. He'd removed the red ink and had replaced the cylinder with one of clear solution. He squeezed the gun's trigger rapidly, placing the needle tip against a gauze square that was on the counter. The red ink oozed out onto the gauze as he did this, becoming paler in color as he continued. He kept squeezing until there was no red left in the gun and only the clear liquid was oozing from the tip of the needle. Then he removed the cylinder of solution and screwed on one containing black ink.

"Okay, we are about half done, Petey Pup," he said. "You hangin in there?"

"Yes Sir," I said. "I'm fine."

"I gotta say, little guy, you're doin a lot better than some of the big tough biker dudes I've tattooed. It's funny; some of those mean looking guys are real babies when it comes to pain. You haven't even complained once though."

"Thank you, Sir," I said as I looked up at Matt. I was hoping he was proud of how I was doing, especially after Niko's compliment.

Niko then repositioned the gun against my buttocks, and said, "Here goes." He then started to trace the outline of the dog bone. After restarting, the pain seemed to be worse, and I moaned a little bit, biting down on my lip, trying to think my happy thoughts. Maybe Niko's compliment had come too soon. The wave of pain that swept over me only lasted briefly though, and as he continued I was able to block it again from my mind. I lay there, trying to be as still as possible, looking up into Matt's face as the stabbing continued.

This second interval of time seemed to take much longer than the first, and I was getting very eager for it to be over. "We are almost done, Petey," Niko said to me. "Just relax." I must have been tensing up my legs or something for him to have offered me this instruction, and I tried to do as he said, focusing on relaxing my body completely.

Then suddenly the stabbing stopped, and Niko placed his gun down on the counter. He reached into the upper cupboard and retrieved a bottle of lotion, squirting a small dab of it onto my wound. Gently he rubbed it into my tender flesh. "Wanna take a look?" he said to Matt, who was already standing up and leaning over me. Matt nodded and let go of my hand. He walked around the table then and stood behind me.

"Yeah, it looks great! Perfect," he said.

"Okay! Glad you're happy with it. I thought I was gonna screw up on the one corner, but it turned out really good I think. Now Petey, you'd better be a good boy the next couple of weeks. Don't wanna get any spanks on this tattooed ass of yours. Least not til it's healed." The three of us laughed at his comment. "What you're gonna need to do is get some unscented lotion. Keep the area moist at all times. I'm gonna put a bandage on it, which will need to stay on for about an hour or so. Then after you get home, remove the bandage and apply some more lotion. Repeat this every hour or two for the first day. It's gonna scab over, but you gotta keep it from drying out. There's gonna be some blood at first, but don't worry about it. Just keep it clean and moist. Got it?"

"Yup," said Matt. "We'll take care of it."

"Sittin down might be a little painful for the first couple days. If you want, I can give you some sports cream, which will deaden the pain a bit. Petey, you wanna see your tattoo before I bandage it?"

"Yes Sir. Yes please," I said excitedly. "Okay, slide down off the table and go over to the corner there. You can see it in that set of double mirrors." Carefully I slid my legs over to the edge of the table. It hurt a little bit to move at first. As I walked over to position myself in front of the mirror, I noticed that Matt and Niko were staring at me. I positioned my butt in front of the one mirror, so that I could see its reflection in the other. There it was, my cute little dog-bone tattoo. I was now permanently marked by my owner! I was so happy!

"Bet he smiles like that when you're ticklin his feet," said Niko.

"That and other places," said Matt.

On the way home I lay in the backseat of the SUV, so excited to be going home to show Drew. I sort of wished that Drew had been able to be with me for it, but in a way I was thankful he wasn't. Now I'd always have this special memory that was just between Matt and me. I think I must have smiled all the way home, not really even thinking of the pain in my tender ass.

6

Matt kept me in chastity for the duration of the next two weeks. I was not bothered much by this, other than the fact that it meant I had to sit down to urinate. Sitting wasn't exactly easy at first with the tattoo. Within a couple of days, though, I did not even notice any discomfort. Drew was extremely helpful with the applications of lotion that I was required to make. He was really impressed with the tattoo itself, stating that it was very tastefully done. For the most part I did wear only a jock strap and loose fitting pants during that healing stage.

The following Monday I returned to my regular work and school schedule. I was starting to heal enough to wear my normal attire, and I did not have to make the frequent lotion applications any longer. I was thankful that I'd been afforded almost a full week of time wearing the chastity device before I had to return to my normal routine. This allowed me time to get used to it.

Matt did not even once express a desire to fuck me while my tattoo was still healing. On the one hand I was thankful for this, but on the other, I sort of hoped he would. I would have been willing to endure a little bit of pain in order to serve him. It did appease me though, that he allowed me the privilege of servicing him orally during this period. In fact, I think that I did so literally every day at some point or another. The afternoon that we got back home from the tattoo shop, Matt stayed at our apartment for several hours. He sat comfortably on the sofa with his legs kicked out in front of him, and I stretched out beside him, resting my head in his lap. When Drew came into the living room to inform us that he was gonna run down to the store for a few minutes, Matt realized that we were totally alone in the apartment and proceeded to order me to blow him.

I was thankful that Drew was gone for a good hour, for it allowed me the time to suck on Matt slowly, taking his entire shaft into my mouth. I sucked it like a baby nursing from a bottle. That first time sucking Matt while in chastity, I was very much aware of the fact that I was wearing it. My cock got rock hard like it always did when I served, and it pressed against the hard plastic that encased it. This was not very comfortable at all, and within seconds my erection subsided. Of course Matt was not aware of any of this, for my cock was tucked neatly away in the plastic cage, which was in turn tucked within the tight-fitting pouch of my jockstrap, which was covered by the basketball shorts that Matt had given me to wear.

This is exactly the state within which my cock remained for the next two full weeks. It was always flaccid. When Alex came home that evening, Matt volunteered to spring for a bucket of chicken. The four of us hung together and watched some movies, and finally before leaving, Matt handed Alex a key to my chastity. "Can you have Drew unlock Petey every couple days to shave him? He's not to get hard." Alex said sure and shoved the key into his pocket. After that one time when Alex had insisted that Matt punish me for being disrespectful, I got the feeling that he would love an opportunity to catch me in some misdeed which he could then report back to my owner. I was determined, though, while under his roof, to tow the line.

The next evening I went over to Matt's house. His parents were gone for the entire night and he had the place to himself, so he seized the opportunity to spend some time alone with his pup. We used the pool when I first got there, and Matt pushed me in six times. The first time was very shocking to me, and we laughed about it together as I shot up out of the water sputtering and flailing my arms in protest. The second and third times were amusing as well, though not really surprising. By the fourth time, I was starting to get a little bit annoyed. I almost snapped at Matt the fifth time he shoved me in but simply bit my tongue. Finally on the sixth occurrence I was downright pissed.

I marched up the steps at the end of the pool, holding onto the railing and not even looking up at Matt who was standing there staring down at me. Why was he doing this to me? This was getting just totally fucking stupid, I thought. I stomped over to the patio chair that was on the deck, picking up the already-drenched towel to dry myself with. I was completely ignoring Matt, not wanting to say anything to him that might get myself into trouble, but then also wanting desperately to do exactly that. I wanted to tell him he was not funny any more; he was just being a jerk.

As I buried my face in the towel, wiping away the beads of water that were dripping down from my hair, I felt Matt walk up behind me. "Frustrated?" he asked. Unwilling to look at him, I merely shook my head. "Huh?" he said. "I can't hear you?"

"No Sir!" I snapped back at him suddenly, turning around quickly to face him.

He laughed as he looked down at me. "You seem frustrated," he said casually. "Actually, you seem pretty much pissed off."

"Well I'm not!" I shot back at him. "Why would I be pissed? Just cuz you've thrown me in the water *six* times in a row? I'm just really fuckin enjoying every second of it!"

"Okay," he said calmly, and then immediately pulled me into him and scooped me up with both arms. "Guess we'll go for seven then."

"No! Please Sir! Why are you doing this?" I protested, as I kicked my feet and tried to push myself away from his body.

"Hmm. Well, probably just cuz I want to," he said. "Isn't that reason enough?" He walked over to the edge of the pool, holding me tightly in his arms.

"But it isn't very nice, Sir! It isn't very nice at all!" I yelled.

"I know," he said in an emotionless tone, "but who said I always have to be nice?" He then flung his arms forward and hurled me back into the pool. I flailed helplessly as I felt the tidal wave of water splash around me, and I sank below the surface, inhaling deeply before I actually went under. As I surfaced the water, I also felt my anger starting to surface. In fact, it was boiling within me. I shot up out of the pool and again stormed up the steps, walking over to face Matt who was standing in the exact spot where he'd just so carelessly tossed me into the water.

"Do you have any idea what that feels like, Sir?" I yelled at him. "It really is frustrating, you know!"

"Yeah. I do know. That's part of the fun of it. I can do it as many times as I want to, and there's not a damned thing you can do about it." He then leaned over and quickly grabbed my shoulders, pushing me easily right back into the pool for now the eighth time.

This time when I surfaced the water, I did not even want to get back out of the pool. What was the point? He'd just shove me back in again. But why? Why was he doing this to me? I just looked up at him and stared, watching him as he looked down at me smugly. "May I get out now Sir?" I asked, "or are you just gonna throw me back in, for the *ninth* time?"

Matt shrugged, showing no regard for my feelings whatsoever. "Don't care what you do. Suit yourself, but if I wanna throw you in again, I'll do it. If I wanna do it a hundred times I will. I'm really enjoyin it, to be honest."

In pure frustration, I then splashed my arms angrily against the water, spraying my own face far more than Matt. He laughed at me again as I moved quickly over to the ledge of the pool and began to hoist myself up. Matt stood there watching me as I climbed up out of the pool, righting myself to a standing position. "Come here, pup," he said finally. "No hard feelings, all right?" Instantly my anger subsided and I stepped over to him. He was just messin with me obviously. Why'd I even let myself get so mad.

Just as I leaned into him, about to bury my hot face against his chest, Matt grabbed a hold of me tightly again and shoved me harder than ever before. Tripping over my own feet, I sprawled backwards right into the pool, shocked worse than any time before as the water instantly engulfed me. I was spitting and sputtering as I surfaced the water, and now tears were stinging my face. I didn't know if it was the teardrops or the pool water that blurred my vision as I stared up at him. I immediately turned from him and rushed to the far end of the pool, heading for the steps. By the time I reached the top step, Matt was standing there in front of me, towering over me.

I was crying hard now, overcome with anger and frustration. He reached out to grab me again and quickly I spun away from him, moving to his side. "No!" I screamed, almost unable to believe the sound of my own voice. "Stop it! Damn it! Stop doing this to me!" I demanded. "You're being a jerk to me, and it's not fair! I don't have to take it!"

In spite of my protests, Matt again grabbed my shoulders, but this time he did not push me towards the pool. Instead he held me there in front of him as I glared up at him defiantly. "No pup, you don't have to take it! You don't ever have to let people push you around!"

"What?" I asked incredulously. Was this whole scene some twisted idea of a life lesson that Matt was trying to teach me? "I'm really mad at you right now!" I spat at him. The sound of my anger as it spewed from me was truly shocking to myself. I was so furious that my body was actually shaking, and my voice was quivering as I struggled to keep from crying.

"I know!" shouted Matt as he smiled down at me. "You're really fuckin pissed."

"Yes I am! Yes I fuckin *am*!"

"Good!" he said, "and it's about damned time. I thought you were never gonna stand up for yourself."

"Sir, I don't understand! Why are you doing this to me? Why are you being so mean all of a sudden?" Tears rolled down my cheeks as I looked up into his face. I couldn't even believe he was smiling at me.

"Petey, listen to me," he said calmly. "Don't you see what just happened? Don't you see what you just did?"

"Yeah, I see," I said. "What I just did was fall into the fucking pool nine times after the one person I trusted more than anything kept throwing me there!"

"And ...?"

"—and I'm pissed!"

"Yeah, but you've been pissed before, haven't ya? So what's different about this time?" He was prodding me like he so often did when he was trying to get me to come up with the right answer.

"It's ... um ... different cuz I blew up, Sir. I got so mad that I yelled at you." My voice was now becoming calmer, and I was no longer crying. Suddenly I realized what I was doing and the horrible things that I was saying to my owner. "Oh my god!" I said, throwing my palm over my mouth. "I'm so sorry Sir."

"No! No, no, no!" he said. "Don't be sorry! Be proud of yourself. You stuck up for yourself. You showed spunk and courage. You showed that you're not some wimp that just lets himself be pushed around."

"But Sir, you're my owner!" I cried. "You have the right to push me around."

"And I did. Doesn't mean you gotta like it though, does it?" I continued to stare up at him, not knowing what else to say. I shook my head in answer to his question.

Finally I spoke. "So does that mean you want me to argue with you about stuff, Sir? To challenge you?"

"Try it and see what happens," he said, suddenly sounding very serious.

"What then Sir? What am I doin wrong?"

"Pup, do you think I want you to be a doormat? Do you think I want you to let people treat you bad while you just sit back and take it? How many times do you think I'd let someone throw me into a pool without getting pissed?"

"Zero," I answered quickly.

He laughed. "Well depending on the circumstances, maybe one time tops. But the point is, I don't let people abuse me, and I don't expect you to either."

"But Sir, I just don't understand," I said sincerely. "All this time you have taught me to obey you and never question you. Now you are praising me for blowing up at you and calling you a jerk."

"Oh, well you're gonna pay for that 'jerk' comment," he said, smiling at me broadly.

"Sir, please! I'm being serious."

"So am I," he said, still smiling. "What I'm saying is that I wanted to discover if what I've been wanting and trying so hard to grow in you—that instinct to defend yourself—was finally starting to come out. I wanted to see if you'd eventually stick up for yourself and express your anger, or if you'd just fall apart and start cryin."

"Like I always do ..."

He nodded. "Like you always *used* to do."

"So how do I know when it's okay to talk back to you? How do I know when I have the right to say what I think?"

"Petey, you've always had the right to say what you think. You know I always have wanted your opinion. You just gotta have the balls to say it!"

"And what if it is the exact opposite of what you think, Sir?"

"Then you still have the right to your opinion, even if it is wrong."

Now I was finally smiling at him. "Yeah," I nodded, "even I have the right to be wrong."

"So what if I decide I wanna throw you in the pool fifty times?" he asked. "What if I did that, huh? And what if I did it for no reason at all, other than to amuse myself?"

I felt the smile on my face starting to fade as I looked at him seriously. "Sir, you'd be a total jerk for doin it, and I'd tell ya so, even if I couldn't stop ya."

"Good boy," he said. "Now blow me!"

Immediately I dropped to my knees, thinking of only one single thing. *I must obey him!* He towered over me then, looking down and saying nothing. He stepped back away from me, and I inched my way towards him, my body still dripping with water. I continued to crawl towards him as he kept backing up. When he finally allowed me to get near him, I looked up into his face and saw that he was smirking as he stared down at me. He seemed to tower over me like a giant, a king who was receiving worship from one of his subjects. He was wearing nothing but his swimsuit, and his rock-hard body seemed statuesque to me, the embodiment of perfection.

Without a single word, he reached for the waistband of his swim trunks and pulled them off from himself smoothly, stepping out of them and tossing them aside. His groin was only an inch from my face, and his cock was already fully erect. It commanded the full focus of my attention. "Kiss it!" he said. "Show some respect."

Feeling then more humble than I ever had my entire life, I pressed my lips against his shaft reverently. No matter what events transpired within our lives, no matter how much we both would change as our relationship developed, one thing would always remain exactly the same. This was my place. Kneeling here at his feet, humbly and worshipfully, I knew my status. I was there to serve him and always would be. I even was now branded as his property and was securely locked in his chastity. I belonged to him. I lived for one purpose–to obey him. Every single one of these thoughts and feelings were suddenly translated into action as I pressed my lips against his hard flesh, making love to it, worshipping it, and craving it with every fiber of my being.

"Please Sir! Oh god, oh please!! Please let me serve you!! I beg you. You own me, Sir. Please use me. Please allow me this privilege. Oh god, oh please ... Please!"

I kept repeating these pleas to him as I continued to press my lips against him, sliding my mouth gently up and down his rock-hard shaft. Never once did I look up, striving to convey my respect and humility to him with my every gesture. I felt the hardness of the tile beneath me as my knees rested against the slate. It felt so very right for me to bow this way. It felt so utterly perfect.

My pulse was racing, and my cock was throbbing within the confines of the chastity device. I felt the gripping pain of the cage, as its hard and unyielding plastic casing kept my cock from growing to its full size. As it throbbed mercilessly, I willed myself to focus my attention on serving and to not think about my own discomfort. I continued to kiss him, now adding my tongue, as if I were frenching his beautiful, hard cock. It surprised me to notice that even during my excitement and eagerness to please my owner, my cock started to go flaccid. The chastity was causing me to become reconditioned, to respond sexually in a different way than I'd known thus far. I directed every ounce of sexual energy into my service at this point, caring nothing for my own pleasure or lack thereof.

I felt his hands upon my head and pulled myself away from him only slightly, just enough to be able to glance up at him. He took a firm grip of my head then and stared down at me. Then he swung me around, steering me towards a large, circular flowerbed that was behind us. We were about fifteen feet from it, and he began to inch me towards it, making me crawl backwards. He started to pick up the pace of his steps, forcing me to crawl faster. I continued to stare up at him as he moved me into the position of his choosing. Finally I felt my feet rub against the brick wall of the flowerbed, and I pushed my feet out from under me, landing flat on my butt. My neck was level to the edge of the wall behind me and he pushed my head backwards so that I was staring upwards, facing the sky.

It was an awesome sight to see him then, staring down at me as he towered in his position of supreme dominance. He had placed his feet firmly on each side of me, and his knees were pressing against the same ledge upon which my head rested. He thrust his groin forward, pointing his cock at my opened lips. Then he very smoothly eased his way into me, driving his cock deep with one swift motion. He moaned with pleasure as he grabbed a hold of a large urn behind my head. He was using the pot to steady himself while he forced me to deepthroat him.

I cranked my jaw open wide and instantly felt his cock stab into my throat. I struggled to suppress the urge to gag but did not succeed completely. He ignored my discomfort and continued to grind in as deeply as possible. He kept it there for several seconds, savoring the tightness of this hole, which seemingly was made for the express purpose of sheathing his throbbing hard-on. I felt it throb within me, knowing he was doing this deliberately. He was literally flexing his cock inside of my throat. I knew this was to assert himself over me and also to maximize his own pleasure. I was trying desperately to breathe through my nose but was unable to even inhale for he was blocking my air passage. When he finally pulled back slightly I took a very deep breath, but it was immediately followed by a fierce and determined thrust of his cock, back in all the way to where it felt best to him.

He humped my throat like this for at least ten minutes, controlling every single thrust. It was as if I existed only as a hole to him. When he finally came, he did so while buried balls deep in my throat. I gulped down his load as it shot from him like a volcanic eruption. Then he pulled out of me quickly and turned away. He walked over casually and picked up his swim trunks, stepping back into them without comment. Then he went inside as I lay there against the wall of the flowerbed, gasping for breath.

* * *

Drew and I spent quite a bit of time together that weekend. It was so sweet to be able to spend all of this time with one another, to go to bed and wake up in the same home, to share so much of ourselves. I had previously thought that Drew and I were about as close as two friends could be, but I had no idea how very wrong that actually was, for we were growing closer all the time. Friday night we stayed up until almost six o'clock in the morning talking softly to one another. Our voices were barely above a whisper as we lay on my bed. Drew had positioned himself so that he was lying with his head at the foot of the bed next to my feet. He rolled over on his elbow as we shared our pillow talk, disclosing our feelings and memories and hopes that we had for the future. It surprised me somewhat that Alex allowed Drew this privilege without coming and calling him in to his own bed. There were times that I was concerned that Alex may grow jealous of my close relationship to his boy.

Thursday had been the day that I'd served Matt poolside, Friday he drained his load into me while in his truck, Saturday he came to the apartment and had me suck him in my bedroom, and Sunday we were alone together at his house. It had been five full days since I'd had an erection myself, and of course this meant I had not cum either. Twice Drew had removed my chastity to shave me as per Matt's instruction. Drew was so very gentle in the way that he handled me. When he was finished, I softly kissed his sweet lips, thanking him for what he'd done.

Finally Monday morning had arrived, and I had to once again begin my classes. It would only be a matter of five weeks until finals from this point. After that, we'd be on summer break, and I would be beginning classes at the University of Tampa in the fall. I was scheduled to work in the afternoon and truly was anxious to return. It had been a fantastic vacation, and the cruise was extraordinary. Plus I'd gotten my tattoo and had moved into a new home. I felt like a new person, in a way.

I was not expecting to see a new face when I arrived at the bookstore that afternoon. After punching in at the time clock, Mr. Bartlett called me into the office, and for a few seconds I was concerned that I may be in trouble already. Quickly he assured me this was not the case and explained to me that I'd be training a new employee. "Peter, you've been with us for quite awhile now, and you know how impressed I've been with your work. I wanna put you in charge of training the new employees from now on. We have a new guy starting today, and I think you'll be a good example for him to follow. How do you feel about it?"

I sat in the chair in front of his desk, feeling somewhat small as I looked up at him. "Sir, thank you so much for ... um ... having that much confidence in me. I would like it very much to be able to do this if you think I'm capable."

"Well I do," said Mr. Bartlett confidently, "or else I wouldn't have suggested it." He laughed as he said this, and I returned his laughter with my own obligatory chuckle. "His name is Jason, and he's about your age. This is his first real job, so go easy on him. I mean, try to make him feel comfortable, ya know."

"Yes sir," I said. "I'll be very nice to him."

"Well make sure you explain the rules and procedures to him. I don't mean you should baby him. Just wanna make sure he feels comfortable. Most people are really nervous on their first day, and I'm sure he will be no exception."

"I understand, sir," I responded. "What time does he start?"

"Same as you, so he should be here any time. How was the cruise?"

I smiled up at him. "Oh, it was wonderful. I've never had a better vacation. Thank you."

Just then there was a knock on the open door behind me. I turned in my chair to see a very slender young man with glasses standing in the archway.

"Come on in, Jason," said Mr. Bartlett. "I was just telling Peter about you. You're gonna be working together today."

I immediately stood up and turned to face Jason, extending my hand to greet him. He looked down towards the floor as he shook my hand and smiled nervously. "Nice to meet you, Jason," I said, and we both sat down.

Jason was about three or four inches taller than me and very thin. His waist was not more than twenty-eight inches, and I guessed he did not weight more than 130 pounds. He had long slender fingers, and his mannerisms were rather soft and graceful. I thought it was sort of cute the way he looked when he pushed his glasses up on his nose. He seemed to do this often, probably out of habit more than necessity. His hair was a very light brown, and he had rather pale blue eyes. I noticed how his clothes seemed to hang rather loosely on his thin frame, and I couldn't help but wonder what he'd look like naked. Immediately I liked him, for he seemed so vulnerable to me. His very presence seemed to exude sincerity and openness. I was certain I was gonna enjoy working with him.

At first Jason said very little to me and merely responded when I spoke to him. As the afternoon progressed, though, he started to relax and become a little more talkative. I was truly impressed at how quickly he picked up on the new tasks I was teaching him. I discovered he was sort of a computer geek and was attending a technical school in town. Of course the biggest question I had about him was whether or not he was gay, but I dared not ask such a thing. Eventually he would hopefully drop me some sort of hint, or perhaps I'd do the same with him. I had very little doubt that he was in fact a fag like me, but I was afraid to overtly make this assumption.

That week I was scheduled to work literally every day, for I had already had my days off over the weekend. Jason was there working with me for three of the five days, and I enjoyed it tremendously. I told Drew and Alex about him when I got home Monday night, and both of them were in agreement that he probably was gay. Matt teased me when I told him, jokingly accusing me of checkin out other guys behind his back. I assured him quickly that I was not, and that even if Jason were gay, I was sure he'd be sub. Matt just laughed at me and said he'd stop in some day to the bookstore to check him out for himself.

Friday night when I got home, Drew quickly ushered me into the kitchen. He was speaking to me in hushed tones and seemed extremely agitated. "What's wrong?" I asked Drew worriedly.

"It's Alex!" he said. "He had a fight with Matt I think."

"Oh no," I said, suddenly feeling a wave of panic wash over me. "What did they fight about?"

"I don't know, really. I think that Matt was pissed because Alex saw Tracy yesterday and told her something about Matt. Well anyways, she ended up callin Matt about it. Now Matt is all down on Alex cuz of what he said, but I don't know exactly what it was."

"Shit!" I said. "I hope they don't stay mad at each other. Do you think Alex is gonna tell you that ya can't be friends with me?"

Drew shook his head furiously. "No, he'd never do that. I'm sure he wouldn't."

"Where is he at now?" I asked.

"He's in the shower. I think he's getting ready to go out somewhere. After he leaves, you should try to call Matt."

"I don't know Drew," I said. "If Matt is really pissed he might not wanna talk about it. Plus he'll probably tell him it's none of my business."

"So, can't you make up some other excuse to call him. Petey, please! If those two don't get this worked out it could be really bad for you and me. Matt might end up making you move out."

"How can you say that, Drew? You just insisted that Alex wouldn't forbid you from being my friend, but you think Matt would?" My eyes were starting to fill with tears as I began to become extremely overwrought with emotion.

Drew put his hand on my shoulder. "No, I'm sorry Petey. I didn't mean it like that. I'm just worried that's all." His tone really had me worried as well. Up to this point, Drew had always been my calming voice of reason. Every time I had gone off all half-cocked with worry and anxiety, he'd been the one to help me think things through and to re-center myself. Now he was the one who was freaking, and I did not know exactly what to do.

"Hey, are you hungry? I'll make us some dinner," I offered, trying to change the subject.

"No. I don't wanna eat anything right now. I'm gonna go see if Alex will let me into the bathroom. Maybe he will end up saying something. I'm sorry Petey; I just never thought Matt and Alex would be getting into a fight."

"I know! Me either," I replied.

I was sitting at my computer twenty minutes later when Drew walked into my bedroom. His hair was still wet from the shower, and he was wearing only a towel. "God! He fucked my brains out, I think! Bent me over the sink and just totally pounded my ass."

"Been there, done that," I said without emotion. "So did you find anything out?"

"Yeah," he said sitting on the bed. "He's gonna be leaving in a couple minutes and then I'll tell ya. What are you doing?"

"Oh, I'm just doing some research for one of my classes. I can't really concentrate on it right now though, so I think I'll just wait."

"Well, I'm gonna get dressed, and I'll be right back. Don't worry, Petey, everything is gonna be fine. This is just gonna blow over, I think."

I looked up at Drew hopefully and saw he was smiling again. It was amazing how a hard cock up the ass could always do wonders to set the world aright again. When I finally heard Alex leave out the front door, I dashed down the hall and into Drew's room. He was standing in front of the mirror, gelling his hair. "So what happened?" I demanded.

Drew made eye contact with me in the reflection of the mirror. "Well," he said, "apparently Alex tried to set up a double date for him and Matt with Kelly and Tracy."

"You've gotta be kidding me!" I said. "They are the same ones who dissed them at the cabin. Why would Alex do that?"

"I don't know. Wanted pussy real bad, I guess."

"And Matt got all pissed at that? That's crazy. Why didn't he just say no; what's the big deal?"

"Well I guess Matt had made some comment about not fucking you for all this time since you got your tattoo, and so Alex thought he would do Matt this big favor by finding him some pussy. When Matt said no, Alex got all offended and spouted off about it. They ended up yellin at one another."

"Shit. So what's gonna happen now?"

"Alex is meeting Matt tonight. They're goin to a club, so I think they'll just end up working it out."

"Thank god! I wonder if I should try to call Matt then after all."

"Yeah, or at least leave him a voice mail or something. I wanna make sure he is not still pissed."

Suddenly I remembered what I had witnessed in this very apartment on the day of my birthday party. I had walked in and saw Alex kneeling to serve Matt. While I stood in the corner I watched Alex suck Matt off, and Alex had no idea I'd even seen it. I knew at that time that my owner was superior to Alex. I knew that Alex really idolized Matt and wanted to please him. It all sort of made sense, all of a sudden. The two of them were best buds, and Alex knew that Matt was bumming cuz he'd gone awhile without fucking, so he was tryin to impress Matt. When he screwed up and Matt rejected his offer, it must have embarrassed Alex and hurt his feelings. That's why he shot his mouth off the way he did. He'd probably actually been angrier at himself than he was at Matt, but he had misdirected his emotion. Matt was sure to understand this and definitely would allow Alex to get back within his graces. At least this was what I hoped.

"Hey pup," said Matt, knowing it was me from his caller I.D. "What's up?"

"Sir ... um ..."

"What's wrong?" he said, immediately sensing the hesitation in my voice.

"Oh nothing Sir. Um ... Is everything okay with you? I mean, with you and Alex?"

"Yeah, everything's fine. Why?"

"Um ... I don't know. Just worried, that's all." I bit my lower lip and waited for his response. Suddenly I was concerned that this phone call was not such a good idea after all.

"No, everything is fine between us. Alex got a little freaky on me today, but whatever. We're buds; shit like that is no big deal. Why you worryin about stuff like this anyways? Not a pup's job to be worried all the time."

"I'm sorry Sir. I just don't want anything to happen. I don't want you and Alex to get into a fight or something."

Matt laughed then. "Pup, you want me to come over there and spank your tattooed ass?"

I laughed in response, "Well ... um."

"Yeah, dumb question, huh? Of course you do! But anyways seriously there is nothin to worry about. So just chill. We're gonna go get some brews together in a few. Alex is supposed to be here any time, in fact."

"Yeah, he left already, Sir."

"You bonehead! Then why ya even callin me?"

"I don't know Sir, I guess I *am* a bonehead."

"I'm just messin w' ya pup."

"I know," I said, feeling a broad smile creep across my face. "Sir, I love you."

"You hangin with Drew tonight?" he asked.

"Yes, Sir," I said.

"Well make sure he knows not to worry too. Got it?"

"Yes Sir."

"Okay, I'll talk to ya later. Bye."

* * *

Drew and I spent the rest of the evening together, relaxed in front of the television. He volunteered to shave me, and I readily agreed because it felt nice to get that thing off of me, even if only for a few moments. We were curled up together on the couch at 1:00am when Matt and Alex walked in. I had dozed off and was sleeping with my head against Drew's shoulder. He'd turned the television down to low volume but was still engrossed in a movie, so he just let me sleep. The sound of the door roused me and I looked up to see Alex and Matt standing behind the sofa. I reached up to touch Matt affectionately, but he did not even seem to notice.

"Drew, get up," said Alex. He then stepped over by the recliner that was opposite the couch. Drew scurried over to him without saying a word and stood before him. "Kneel," Alex ordered him, and Drew instantly dropped to his knees. Then Matt stepped over to stand next to Alex, looking down at Drew in his servile position. Alex extended his hand to Matt and they shook, the way bros do, not businessmen.

"He's all yours, bud," he said to Matt. "Use him as you like." Then Alex stepped away from Drew and Matt immediately moved into the exact spot where Alex had been standing.

"Dude, have fun, all right?" said Matt. "Go get some pussy!" I watched Alex as he casually walked back to the apartment entrance and closed the door behind him as he left.

Drew immediately lowered himself, pressing his lips against the top of Matt's hiking boots. At this point, I was wide awake.

7

I did not have to be ordered to kneel before my owner, for
when I saw my best friend bowing humbly in submission to
Matt, I knew it was only appropriate for me to do the same.
Quickly I slipped off the couch and slid onto my knees,
crawling across the floor to lower myself before my superior.
Drew had not looked up, continuing to press his lips
reverently against the top of my owner's boot. He was
undoubtedly awaiting Matt's instruction. I eased myself up
beside my friend, respectfully lowering my face to the
opposite boot in a manner that mimicked his position. We
knelt there silently, kissing Matt's boots, while he lowered
himself into the recliner behind him.

"Take 'em off," he instructed us, and then immediately
Drew and I began to unlace Matt's boots, using only our
teeth. Matt shifted in the chair, extending his feet further in
front of him as he assumed a more relaxed position. Drew
and I scurried to follow his feet, trying to keep our mouths
pressed against his boot laces. Finally I was able to grasp the
end of the lace in my teeth, and I pulled my head back
quickly, loosening it with ease. Then painstakingly, I moved
my face back down to his boot, concentrating my attention
upon the task of loosening each of the laces that crisscrossed
the top of his hiking boot.

Matt sat there comfortably relaxing as he settled into the
chair. I realized he must have picked up the television
remote as I heard him begin to surf through the channels on
the TV. He seemed to be ignoring Drew and me and simply
taking our servitude for granted, for I then heard him click
open his cigar lighter, and I recognized the sound of him

puffing quickly as he ignited his stogie. When we had finally unlaced his boots successfully Matt offered us further instruction, curtly informing us to use our hands to remove his boots.

"Then strip," he said, in a moderate, emotionless tone. Both Drew and I were quick to obey his commands, carefully but hurriedly pulling off each of his boots. I held my palm under Matt's heel as the boot slipped off, making sure his leg did not drop suddenly to the floor. Then I reverently lowered it back to the floor, resisting the urge to begin kissing his foot in the process.

I glanced over to Drew as I stood to remove my pajama bottoms. My heart was racing with excitement as I realized what was surely about to happen. Matt was going to use both Drew and I for his pleasure. Apparently Drew had been offered to my owner by Alex. Perhaps it was Alex's means of atonement for the childish way he'd blown up when Matt refused his suggestion that they fuck pussy. Briefly it occurred to me that Drew may be unhappy about this situation, but as I looked over at his face, I was fairly certain this was not the case. Drew seemed to have an almost lustful look in his eyes as he hurriedly peeled his shirt off and began to step out of his sleep pants.

Drew and I dropped immediately back to our knees when we were done stripping. I was positioned to the right of Drew, kneeling there with my hands behind my back. My cock was still tucked securely in its locked cage between my legs, but I noticed that Drew's was fully erect.

"Petey," Matt said as he continued to stare at the television screen, "want you to kneel in front of the couch. Keep your hands behind your back and don't take your eyes off of me for one second."

"Yes Sir!" I responded and quickly crawled over to the place where I'd been directed.

"Get me an ashtray Drew," Matt said casually, as he inhaled a puff of smoke from the cigar. Drew jumped up from his position on the floor to head for the kitchen, but Matt was quick to stop him. "Did I say you could stand?" he asked rhetorically.

"No Sir!" said Drew as he dropped immediately back down to his knees and began to quickly crawl into the kitchen. Matt smirked as he awaited the sub's return, crossing his heels as he stretched himself out comfortably in the chair. When Drew returned moments later, Matt reached out to take the ashtray from him without even bothering to look down. "Now get me a beer."

Drew again immediately responded with respect, stating "Yes Sir!" and headed back into the kitchen on his knees. When he returned he handed the beer to Matt after first opening it and placing the bottle cap on the end table. "Go open the patio door ... let out the smoke," said Matt, and for a third time Drew complied with his orders unquestioningly.

When Drew returned, Matt did not acknowledge the sub's presence, but instead had become engrossed in a late-night talk show. Drew bowed his head and lowered himself humbly, pressing his face to the ground next to Matt's feet. He did not touch Matt, however, but merely awaited his instruction silently. Finally after three or four minutes Matt did speak. "I need a footstool," he said, and quickly Drew rose from his position to turn towards the stool that was a few feet behind him.

"No," said Matt calmly. "You be my footstool." Drew spun around immediately and crawled over towards Matt's feet. Matt pulled them back, allowing Drew to assume a crouched position in front of the recliner. Drew curled himself up, pushing his head down in front of himself towards his knees and resting his arms limply beside himself. Matt then brought his legs up, resting his feet comfortably on Drew's back as he continued to sip his beer and smoke his cigar.

I continued to obey Matt, while I knelt there in my statuesque position, trying not to even blink or twitch. I stared over at my owner, watching him sit there in absolute comfort. He was reclined and relaxed, his feet up on the back of the lowly subordinate. My cock throbbed within the chastity as I watched him bask in the luxury of his superiority. Drew was absolutely still, not moving so much as a muscle. In fact, I could not even see him breathing. He did not make any effort to reposition himself for the purpose of comfort or to adjust his posture in any way, but simply bowed there like a rock for the duration of the next twenty minutes.

I was astonished by all of this actually, for my own ankles were by this time going numb. Kneeling in one position without moving was remarkably painful and unpleasant. Drew's position, though, was even less comfortable, yet he did not flinch even once. Finally the show that Matt was watching concluded, and he chugged down the last of his beer. He already had snuffed out the cigar in the ashtray beside him, and he casually lowered his feet off of Drew's back.

"Look at me," he then said to Drew, and the sub quickly uncurled his body and assumed a kneeling position before my owner. He then stared up into Matt's eyes as he watched him attentively. "Do you know why I'm here?"

"Sir," Drew said to him in a hushed, respectful tone. "I believe you are here to be served, and I believe it is my duty to serve you as you desire. This is the instruction of my Master."

"... and?"

Drew looked up at Matt inquisitively, apparently unsure of the answer to Matt's question. "I'm sorry, Sir. I do not know," said Drew.

"And I want for my pup to watch. I want for him to see me served by another owner's boy."

"Yes Sir," said Drew.

Matt then stood up. Unable to control myself, I then let out a small gasp. Perhaps it was seeing my owner as he asserted himself, claiming his rightful position of superiority over his best friend's boy. Maybe it was the knowledge I held that Matt was truly the Alpha male, having been served previously by Drew's owner. Or it may simply have been that I was witnessing the coming together of the two people who meant the absolute most to me in my life–one my hero and savior and Master, the other my equal and my dearest friend. A feeling of incomparable excitement and anticipation washed over me at that moment, for I knew that something extremely significant was about to happen.

My very first encounter with Drew had been at a student union meeting on the campus of our school. At that time, I had not been aware that Drew was actually a faculty member of the college, and I was drawn to him almost instantly as he opened himself up to me. Being new in my relationship with Matt, I looked to my new, blonde friend for guidance. He was comfortable in taking the lead, offering me helpful advice and assurance as I continued to further submit myself to Matt's control. Drew not only brought into my life the wisdom of his years of experience, but also a calm voice of reason. He helped me sort through my emotions and understand things I previously had never considered.

Thrown into the mix was Drew's owner, Alex. In the very beginning I saw Alex so differently than I viewed him now. He seemed so commanding and confident, so much a leader. I prayed in my heart that my relationship with Matt would develop as had Drew's relationship with Alex. I considered Alex to be the ultimate, the role model for Matt to emulate. When Matt and Alex started to become friends I was pleased beyond expression, and I knew that it would only help strengthen my relationship with Drew.

It was not far into these new relationships that I started to realize that the dynamic was beginning to change. Within days, it seemed that a different hierarchy was beginning to develop that was significantly different than how I'd initially interpreted our status. Soon the roles of Alex and Matt started to shift, and Alex seemed to be deferring to Matt and looking to him for leadership and direction. It was very subtle actually. They were for all intents and purposes, equals, yet I saw it in the way Alex looked at Matt. I saw it in the way that decisions were made. Alex would not hesitate to assert himself as a dominant male, yet he always seemed to do so in a way that was less commanding than Matt.

When I walked into this very apartment one day to find Alex kneeling before Matt, humbly supplicating himself in a position of servitude, I knew that my natural instincts about who was most superior were very correct. It was Matt who was Alpha. It was my owner who was by far the most dominant.

Initially I'd been both thrilled and frightened by this revelation. On the one hand, it excited and pleased me to know that my owner was the highest in terms of status, yet on the other I was concerned what it would do to my relationship with Drew who was now my dearest friend. Would he ever be able to accept that his owner was beneath mine? Would he be hurt and disappointed, perhaps jealous?

Seeing Drew kneel there before Matt at that moment was the ultimate confirmation that my fears about Drew were baseless. When Alex had handed over his property to my owner for unsupervised use, it was definitive proof that Matt had the highest status. Drew accepted this reality and did so not merely as an act of obedience to his own Master, but also out of desire. I saw in Drew's eyes a yearning to serve. I saw how he craved Matt as he looked up from his humble position. There was no resentment there, only the purity of his submission and the power of his lust. It thrilled me to see it, which is why I then gasped uncontrollably.

"Take out my cock, boy," Matt commanded. "Use your hands."

Drew was quick to obey as he had been with every single order. He reached up quickly yet carefully and unbuckled Matt's belt. Then he unzipped the fly and pulled it apart reverently. Matt quickly grabbed his waistline and began to push his pants and boxers down. I believe he did so as an indication to Drew that he wanted them removed rather than to merely have his cock pulled out from the fly of his boxers. Drew took over, grabbing both sides of Matt's jeans and pulling them down over his thighs. He lowered them all the way to the ground, and as Matt lifted each of his feet from the floor, Drew pulled the pants off completely.

Matt then quickly removed his jersey and tossed it on the pile of clothes at his feet. Drew reached down and shoved the pile aside, clearing the floor for Matt. I stared at the perfection of Matt's body as he stood there, legs apart and towering over Drew. The beauty of his chiseled chest and cut abs was framed by the masculinity of his broad, authoritative shoulders. His stance was so commanding and confident, literally defining his status. I so envied Drew at that moment, wanting for nothing other than to crawl to Matt's feet and worship him then and there.

As Drew knelt and looked up at Matt's naked body for the first time, I saw that very same awestruck expression upon his face that must have been on mine when I first saw Matt that way. Drew's eyes fixated upon Matt's enormous, perfect-looking, cut cock. At this point it was semi-rigid, not near its full length, yet it was still an awesome sight. It was so thick and veiny, and his plump, round balls looked heavy and full of his superior cumload. Drew craned his neck back and stared up at Matt, taking in the perfect sight of his sculpted body.

"Kiss it," Matt then said to him, and Drew pressed his lips against the tip of Matt's cockhead, kissing it worshipfully. He then moved his lips over the bulbous head and up the topside of the shaft. He kissed it over and over as he inched his way towards Matt's pubes. He did not stop there, but continued kissing so gently and reverently, moving down to his nuts and then back up the underside of Matt's now stiffer hard-on. He kissed his way back up to the tip of his cockhead, returning to the position in which he'd started. "You like that boy? Huh?" asked Matt.

Drew nodded to him rapidly. "Yes Sir," he answered, in a breathy sort of whisper. "Yes Sir, oh god yes!"

"Use your tongue," Matt said. "Lick it."

Drew then proceeded to dart his tongue from between his slightly parted lips, starting with the urethra. As he licked Matt's slit he rolled his eyes to stare up at my owner. His lips parted a little wider, and he swirled his tongue around the bulbous head of Matt's cock. Then he began to bathe the shaft, running his tongue reverentially up and down the cock. He was making the entire fuckstick shiny and wet from his saliva. As he pressed his tongue against the underside of Matt's shank, he provided extra attention to the sensitive area just below the tip. I could see how much Drew was aroused by the privilege of tasting it. He was rock hard himself.

Matt was now hard also and finally reached down to grab Drew's head. He pushed the sub away from him, tilting his head backwards so that he looked up to him. "Say what you want boy," Matt said. "Beg for it."

"Oh Sir!" Drew whined. I'd never before heard his voice this way. He was literally whimpering. "Oh Sir. I'm begging you to feed me your cock! Please let me take it in my mouth. Oh please! Oh please!"

"Petey, get over here!" Matt commanded. It was the command I was waiting so desperately to hear, and I instantly jumped. I quickly crawled over and assumed a kneeling position beside my friend. Matt then shoved Drew backwards with a bit of force, causing him to topple over onto his behind and then said to me, "Suck my cock, pup!"

Immediately I slid my mouth around Matt's rock-hard prick and slid all the way down to the base. He moaned as he grabbed my head and thrust into me. I inhaled his scent as I devoured his shaft, greedily taking the entirety of him inside myself. I felt his pulsating and rigid cock against my tongue, and I cranked my jaw wide, ensuring a smooth entry into my tight throat. Matt held onto my head tightly and rocked his hips rapidly, several times jabbing my throat without mercy. Then finally he eased up and pulled me slightly back, allowing me to suck like a baby sucking a pacifier. Then without warning he slid out of me.

Matt then took a small step back and nodded towards the couch. He moved quickly, stepping between Drew and me as he swung around and dropped into a seated position on the sofa. He slid down to make himself comfortable and spread his legs wide. "Both of you, come here. Come and serve me!"

Eagerly Drew and I crawled to him, pressing our faces close together as we simultaneously began to lick his balls. I was on the left nut and Drew on the right, as Matt's rock-hard cock slapped against my face. The way our faces rubbed against one another was so beautiful to me. It felt for a moment I was kissing Drew as we worshipped together. I was so thrilled as I knelt there serving my owner and sharing this experience with my dearest friend. It seemed to me that he suddenly had become so much more to me than just a fellow sub and close confidant. It was as if he were now my brother, another of Matt's boys. This realization was so very touching to me, for it felt as if we were suddenly a part of something that was so much larger than a pairing of two relationships. We were linked together in a special way.

Alex was Matt's closest friend, and they truly were buds. I never for a second questioned Alex's authority over me or his position as a Dom, yet I knew his status was below Matt. Drew was my closest friend and was owned by Alex. I, of course, was Matt's pup. Now, though, the four of us were in a way melded together. Matt was the link that held us.

My eyes focused upon Drew's beautiful boyish face as I darted my tongue across my owner's ball sac. Drew did the same, gently caressing Matt's other testicle with the tip of his own tongue. I heard Matt moan softly as he relaxed himself, enjoying the sensation of the dueling tongues on his balls. This only encouraged us, and we focused our attention solely upon Matt's pleasure. Slowly Drew began to work his way up the shaft of Matt's cock, again lapping at it with his tongue. We both struggled to get ourselves as close to him as possible, intertwining our bodies at times with one another, gleefully sharing the object of our desire.

"Petey," I heard Matt say softly, and I immediately looked up to him. I wanted so much to listen to his commands and obey, yet was finding it difficult to pull myself away from him for even a second. "Tell him what to do," Matt said. "Tell Drew how to serve me."

My heart raced as I instantly became aware of Matt's intention with this command. He was allowing me the privilege of sharing my owner with my brother and friend. Whereas Matt certainly needed no approval from me to use Drew in any way he chose, Matt was affording me the opportunity to give my stamp of approval. He also was placing me above Drew in status. Although this may have seemed otherwise odd, with Drew being a mentor to me in so many ways, it was dramatically significant, for as Matt's pup I was above Drew. This was simply the way things were; it was the way it should be.

"Suck him!" I said confidently. "Suck his cock!"

Drew then reminded me of a marathon runner who was waiting to begin a race. My command to him was like the gunshot that went off signaling the runners to bolt. He eagerly slid his mouth around Matt's throbbing cock and impaled himself with it, sliding all the way down and devouring it with one smooth motion. Quickly I looked up to gauge the level of pleasure that Matt was expressing, and if I had not still been in chastity I think I'd have creamed myself right then. He was in heaven!

Matt relaxed himself completely, stretching his arms out across the back of the sofa and sliding his hips forward as he settled into a most comfortable position. Drew kept Matt's cock buried in his throat and used his tongue and mouth to stimulate it. He was sucking it hungrily and ferociously, and I could not help but smile up at Matt, realizing how pleased he must be at this moment.

"Slide on it!" I ordered Drew. "Bob up and down."

Drew began to pump himself up and down on Matt's nine-inch-plus pole, all the while keeping his lips wrapped tightly around it. He was pressing his tongue firmly against the underside of the shaft and went all the way to the base of Matt's cock with each downward stroke. I reached out and cupped my hands around Drew's head, holding it firmly with one hand over each ear and began to guide him. I wanted him to pump faster, trying to maximize my owner's pleasure. Drew, of course, made virtually no objection.

I looked up at my owner's face as I pumped my best friend's head on his rock-hard prick. Matt offered no gratuitous expression but appeared very nonchalant. Clearly he was enjoying the sensation, but he seemed to take for granted the fact that it was his right to be served. This observation was so very exciting to me. I became so aroused myself by seeing Matt's authoritative posture that I reached down reflexively to grope myself. This, of course, was a futile attempt, for my own soft cock was locked securely in chastity. I reached back up to grab a hold of Drew's head again as Matt leaned his head back against the sofa cushion and moaned softly. Then he brought his arms down quickly and placed his hands on top of mine. I pulled my hands away, slipping them out from under his, and allowed him full control. Then I dove for his nuts and began to lick them.

Having served Matt enough times by myself, I knew the signs well. He was about to dump his load. I continued to run my tongue across Matt's ball sac while he pumped Drew mercilessly up and down on his rock-solid prick. When he finally slammed Drew all the way down, forcing him to deep throat the entirety of the shaft, I knew he was blasting. I quickly pulled my face away from Matt's groin and looked up at my owner. He groaned loudly then. "Fuck yeah!" he said, and I knew he was shooting. After the first couple of blasts, Matt pulled Drew further up on his cock so that his load did not fire directly into Drew's throat. I realized he was wanting to pump some into Drew's mouth instead, for Matt then said to him, "Save some for Petey!" Then he pushed Drew away from himself, and I looked at my friend intently, staring directly in his eyes.

Drew looked as if he'd just won the lottery. I could see from the sparkle in his eye that he was just like me. He was born to be used, totally sub. I leaned into him then, bringing my hands up to grab Drew's smooth, delicate frame. I touched his chest and gently slid my fingers across it, moving my hands towards each of his shoulders. As I wrapped my hands around him, I felt Drew reaching out to touch me, leaning himself in, bringing his face towards my own. Our mouths opened as we pressed our lips together, and Drew slid his tongue into me. My own tongue met his, and I licked my owner's cum, lapping it up greedily. We knelt there together, our bodies entwined, and kissed ever so passionately in front of my owner. Kissing Drew was so very sweet and tender, a uniquely tantalizing experience. Every movement was so graceful and soothing. It was purely rapturous to share with him the precious reward of my owner's cum.

When we pulled ourselves apart from one another, he smiled at me sweetly and then turned to look at Matt. I did the same and knelt there beside my friend as we awaited my owner's further instruction. Matt held his hand out to me, and I placed my own smaller hand within his. He then pulled me towards himself, and I pushed myself forward, sliding myself up onto the couch beside him. Matt then kissed me as he wrapped his arms around me tightly, embracing me protectively. I snuggled myself against him, wanting to be as close to him as possible, wanting for him to be inside of me. I felt the contrast of Matt's embrace as compared to Drew's. Matt was so strong, so very much in control. His movements were urgent and demanding, and overpoweringly passionate. He was my world, my hero, my savior, my everything! I melted in his arms, surrendering every part of myself to him then.

Matt then rolled me over, positioning me so that I was lying on my back. My head was resting against the sofa pillow while I stared up into my owner's eyes. He looked down at me, meeting my gaze and conveying to me an expression of genuine desire. His body pressed against my own as he leaned into me, once again bringing his lips into contact with mine. My hands reached out for him, gently touching his face while he drove his tongue deep into my mouth. I shifted myself underneath him, moving my legs so that they encircled his body and wrapping them around his torso. My desire for him was so very urgent and compelling that I heard myself whimper involuntarily. I craved him so badly! I must have him in me! I absolutely must!

"Oh please Sir!" My voice was like a whisper, barely audible. The breathiness of its tone conveyed my overpowering desire to be consumed by him. "Please be inside me! Oh please!"

"Drew," Matt said offhandedly, while continuing to stare down at my face. "Get some lube."

Matt then slid his hands under my armpits and pulled me towards himself. He literally picked me up from my reclining position to bring my body over to him, placing me on his lap. His masculine arms encircled me as he buried his face in my neck, sending shivers throughout my body. My response was a sort of laughter mixed with a sigh. This encouraged him to continue. I felt his hands traverse my body as he ran his palms across my smooth chest. Gradually he worked his way down, gently caressing my abdomen, my thighs, circling back upwards to cup my buttocks.

Drew had returned, kneeling now between our legs. I looked down, watching him as he stared upwards while holding the tube of lubricating jelly expectantly in his grip. His cock was fully erect, jutting out in front of him as he voyeuristically observed the passion of owner and pup.

Matt's hands slid between my thighs, and he spread them apart, draping each of my knees over his own legs. He then opened his legs widely, stretching me to expose my hole to the sub friend who knelt before me. "Lube him, Drew," Matt ordered, and quickly Drew squeezed some of the gel onto his fingers.

I felt the hardness of my owner's cock pressing against my back. He had not gone even slightly flaccid after draining himself into Drew only moments before. In fact, he seemed to be throbbing against me. My own cock was unresponsive, being tightly locked away in its protective cage. I did not care, though; it was starting not to even matter any more. After so many days of chastity, my body was beginning to understand that my cock was not the only part of me that was sexually stimulated.

The moan that escaped my lips when Drew inserted his fingers into me seemed to begin at the core of me. It was a long, slow gasp of pleasure and anticipation. Matt's fingertips brushed my nips as Drew drove his slick fingers into my pussy. It had been ten days since I'd had my owner inside of me, and I was aching for him! Matt brushed his lips across my neck as he continued to run his fingers over my smooth chest. He was tweaking my nipples ever so gently, sending shivers throughout my body. I felt the firm yet gentle probing of Drew's fingers inside of me. The tentativeness of his touch was so erotic; it was almost loving the way he carefully inserted himself into me.

"Oh Sir! Oh god!" I whispered to Matt, as I felt the strength of his embrace. His hard body pressed against my back, and his powerful arms encircled me. I softly moaned uncontrollably within his arms.

"Turn around," Matt instructed me. His own voice was now hushed, lowered appropriately by the romantic shift in mood. "Turn around and look in my eyes, pup."

So gracefully then I repositioned myself, removing myself from this perched position of complete exposure and curling my legs up close to myself. I twisted my torso as I clung to my owner's neck, and then I pulled myself around to face him, remaining all the while seated on his lap. Then I positioned myself in a straddled kneel, my legs spread on each side of him. I stared into his eyes while I leaned back to rest my buttocks on his lap.

Urgently Matt reached up to cup my head in both of his hands. He tilted his head slightly as he forcefully pulled me into himself. I felt the powerful crush of his lips against my own, and I opened my mouth as we connected. His tongue entered me, and he twisted my head easily in his grip. It was so very passionate, as if he could not get enough of himself inside of me. His desire seemed insatiable, and the throbbing of his cock against my abdomen bore witness to his fervor.

I didn't need instruction at this point. I craved him as much as he desired me. I reached behind myself, groping for Matt's hard-on, but instantly realized that my sub friend behind me was already holding it. Drew guided Matt's throbbing prick towards my hole as I reached back up to wrap my arms around my owner's neck. I pressed my buttocks backwards slightly to align myself with the target. When I felt the bulbous head pressing against myself, quickly I thrust myself backwards. In a smooth and quick movement I instantly impaled myself while Matt kept his tongue buried in my mouth.

That beautiful moment of ecstasy washed over the entirety of my being as I rocked myself back onto him. We were so connected at this moment—owner and pup—our bodies joined together in a way that was so beautifully natural and appropriate. Matt's palms traveled down the sides of my face and neck, finally stopping at my shoulders. He gripped me tightly as he pushed me slightly away from him. My lips did not want to leave his; he actually had to pry me away from himself.

In that instant I suddenly became aware of my need to inhale, and I gasped for breath. He smiled as he looked up into my eyes. "Ride me, pup. Fuckin ride my cock!"

I then began to bounce on him, forcing my entire body up and down quickly. I reached up behind Matt's head and grabbed a hold of the sofa, steadying myself. Using my knees to raise myself upwards, I slid all the way up his shaft. Then I lowered myself quickly, mercilessly impaling myself again. Over and over I did this, increasing the speed of my actions with every single thrust. I worked it into a rhythmic dance, bouncing on my owner's lap as I buried him deeply inside of me.

His hands were all over my body, grabbing and pinching and tweaking. He caressed me and squeezed me and kissed me. I was acutely aware of every sensation, every part of myself experiencing an arousal unlike anything I'd ever known. Had I ever wanted him so badly? Had I ever felt such an intensity of emotion? Had my desire ever consumed me to this degree? If so, I was unaware of it at this moment. All that mattered was right now. The only significant thought in my mind was this connection I felt. He was inside me. I belonged to him. We were one entity.

As the passion intensified, my lunging became amplified to the point of frenzy. I was riding him now like a cowboy on a bucking bronco. I'm not sure he had ever thrust himself so hard into me as I was now allowing myself to be impaled. Never before had I been allowed to express my desire in this manner. Never before had I been allowed this control. I had to show him. I had to prove to him how desperately I craved him. I had to demonstrate the yearning within myself to be one with him!

Our gaze was locked upon one another as I felt him deep within me. His long shaft was a piston, firing in and out of my bowels. It was a mixture of pleasure and pain, passion and desire, yearning and need. It was heaven and hell. Oh god don't let it end! Oh god! Oh god!

Suddenly he placed his hands flat against the sofa cushions, one on each side of him. He pushed himself forward slightly and then reached around me to cup my buttocks. He leaned forward while embracing me with his masculine arms. In a smooth and effortless movement he used his legs to push himself up off the couch into a standing position. He was holding me in the air, his cock still inside of me. I wrapped my legs around him, grasping his waist tightly. My arms clung to his neck, trusting him to hold me.

Carefully he steadied himself, planting his feet firmly in a fixed position. Then he thrust! He was holding my body tightly, controlling my every movement, and he raised and lowered me onto his shaft with each thrust of his hips. It was amazing how quickly and easily he had shifted the balance of control. Only seconds before I was the one who was setting the pace. Now he was claiming this right as his own.

"Drew!" Matt gasped as he continued to rock himself into me. "Clear the table!"

I heard my friend behind me, scurrying quickly to his feet, racing out to the dining room to obey the orders given him. Then Matt began to move, taking steps towards his stated destination. With every single movement I felt him throb inside of me. As he took a step his hips would shift, and it would force him deeply into me. I locked my ankles together securely behind Matt's back, moaning as I clung to him trustingly.

Finally we approached the table, and Matt lowered me carelessly. His passion was so overpowering that it was way beyond the point of tenderness. I did not want him to be gentle though, not at this stage. I wanted his dominance, wanted to feel his power. I wanted to be small while he was larger than life. I wanted to be his tiny, defenseless puppy boy. I wanted him to take me, to take what belonged to him. I wanted him to fuck my tattooed ass like never before.

He did exactly that! He grabbed a hold of my hips then and pulled me right to the edge of the table. My buttocks were completely off the ledge, and my legs were spread eagled in the air beside his body. He then rammed himself into me. Over and over he thrust himself, forcing his cock as deeply into me as he possibly could. I cried out each time, whimpering helplessly. He owned me! He was my Master!

As I rolled my eyes to look behind me, I saw Drew standing there. He was on the opposite side of the table as Matt, his smaller hard-on only inches from my head. "Lick it!" Matt ordered me. "Lick Drew while I fuck you!" Drew stepped forward, positioning himself so that his ball sac was over my mouth. My view was obscured by his thighs as he straddled me. I knew he was leaning forward, reaching for Matt.

I darted my tongue out of my mouth, connecting with Drew's balls, gently touching him and tasting him for the first time. I heard my owner and friend above me, realizing they were also connecting. Matt was leaning in to kiss him. As he did so, his thrusting into me continued. I lapped at Drew's balls fervently. I wanted to please him. I wanted him to be a part of this beautiful, pleasurable moment. I knew the two had pulled away from one another when Drew repositioned himself. He brought his cockhead down to my lips. I still could only see the inside of his legs, but I felt his throbbing hard-on against my face.

"Suck him, Petey," Matt told me. They were the words I'd been waiting to hear. I craned my neck back and opened my jaw, allowing Drew to slide into me. He thrust himself forward, sliding deep into my throat with ease. I heard his moan of delight. It was a high-pitched squeal of sorts, and I devoured him hungrily. "Don't you dare fuckin cum in my pup!" commanded Matt. "Don't you even dare."

Then they proceeded to fuck me, Matt driving himself deep within me, burying his cock in my ass; and Drew raped my throat. I lay there naked and exposed, locked in chastity, my back against the hard, smooth surface of the wooden table. I was pup. I was property. I was owned. I was used!

As Matt rocked himself into me, pounding my ass in perfect rhythm with Drew's thrusts into my mouth, I knew he would soon be approaching orgasm. I wanted it so badly. I wanted to be filled by him, to have his precious seed inside me. I wanted my owner's cum so desperately. "Pull out!" Matt said to Drew, and instantly Drew backed away. It was only a split second later that I felt Matt erupt inside me. He buried himself balls deep and grabbed my hips ferociously. I felt his fingers digging into my flesh as he moaned animalistically. "Ungggh!!! Oh Fuuuuck!" He pumped himself into me, firing his load deep inside me. I whimpered, crying out to him, begging for it.

"Oh god! Oh Sir! Oh ... uh ... oh ... thank you Sir!"

Drew stood behind me, stroking his cock fanatically. I rolled my eyes to look up at him, realizing he was about to blast himself. Suddenly Matt spoke. "Stop!" he said. "Don't cum. Go get us a washcloth and towel. Now!" Matt's body lay against me as he leaned forward, kissing me tenderly all the while remaining inside me.

"I love you Sir," I said to him. "I love you so much!"

Matt then ordered Drew to clean me. "Get my pup cleaned up and ready for bed," he said. "I'm taking a shower. Petey, I want you sleeping when I return."

"Sir?" I said to him as I stared up into his eyes. "Are you leaving?"

"No, gonna wait for Alex to come home."

"May I please wait with you? ... Here in the living room, I mean."

"You can curl up on the loveseat," Matt said, "but I want you sleeping when I get out of the shower. And Drew, put on your shorts—no shirt."

"Yes Sir," Drew and I said together.

My friend then proceeded to wipe my bottom with the warm washcloth. My owner's cum was deep inside me, so it was merely the lube that he was cleaning. I lay back against the table, relaxing myself as I felt Drew touching me so tenderly. "Drew, you were awesome," I said.

"*He* was awesome!" Drew said. "Oh my god, I thought I was gonna cum."

I laughed. "I thought I was gonna myself ... and I'm in chastity!"

It felt so warm and comforting when Drew pulled me off the table and embraced me. He lovingly dressed me in my pajamas and walked with me over to the living room. Carefully he fluffed a pillow under my head and covered me with a blanket. "Sit with me Drew," I said. "Please." He then crouched down on the floor next to me, resting his head against the cushion. I reached out and grabbed his hand. "I love you Drew."

"I love you too, Petey."

Within seconds I was asleep.

It must have been the door opening that startled me awake. It was Alex returning home. At first I was confused, not remembering where I was. Then it occurred to me. I was on the loveseat. Matt had made love to me on the kitchen table and then let me curl up to sleep in the living room so that I could be near him. As I looked over across the room, barely able to focus, I saw Matt sitting comfortably in the recliner. Drew was kneeling at his feet. Drew was sucking Matt ... again.

Quickly I closed my eyes, being careful not to make either of them aware that I was awake. I opened them then only slightly, allowing myself to merely squint. Matt was relaxed and comfortable, and Drew was bobbing on his hard cock.

"Hey!" I heard another voice. It was Alex.

"Hey, dude," said Matt casually. "How was it?"

"Looks like I don't need to ask you the same question," answered Alex. "You're still goin at it, huh?"

"Yeah, I put the pup to bed, but my hard-on wouldn't go to sleep. Thought I'd use your boy one more time."

"Hmm, go for it. I'm gonna go to bed. Send him in when you're done with him."

"Sure," said Matt. "You all right?"

"Yeah, just tired. How was he? Do a good job?"

"Oh yeah, he did great. Can't ya tell?" Drew was continuing to suck Matt as if they were the only two in the room.

"Cool. Enjoy." Alex then exited the room, and I went back to sleep.

8

As much as I wanted to stay awake and watch my best friend Drew serve my Master, I couldn't help myself. Within seconds I dozed back off to sleep under my warm blanket. The next thing I knew it was morning, and as I awakened I found myself a bit disoriented. Then gradually I remembered the night before. I had fallen asleep on the love seat. I hadn't wanted to sleep in my bed while my owner was here. I wanted to be in the living room, close to him. It surprised me a little, because I expected that he would perhaps have carried me to bed when he was done with Drew.

I looked around the apartment as I slowly sat up on the mini-sofa. All was quiet. Everyone must still be in bed. Probably Matt had already gone home, and Drew must be in bed with Alex. That poor guy, I thought. He's probably worn out. I'm sure that after Matt was done using him, he had to then service his own Master. I was anxious to get every sordid detail from him, and I knew he'd tell all, for we were the best of friends.

Nobody on earth understood me the way Drew did. It's hard to describe the depth of love that I felt for him. Certainly Matt meant everything to me and was the most important person in my life, but even he did not possess the understanding that Drew and I shared. It was something special that we had developed, due partially to the fact that we both were subs, but even more than that we were connected emotionally. I remembered what had transpired a few hours before when I was allowed to tenderly and passionately kiss my dear friend. Yes, it was allowed for the sole purpose of pleasuring my Master—our Master, perhaps I should say—but it was also very significant to me. The softness of Drew's lips and gentleness of his caress were so drastically different from Matt's powerful manner of handling me. Even when Matt was being ever so gentle and tender with me, he was not as soft as Drew. Perhaps it was the vulnerability in Drew that I was feeling. Previously I had only ever experienced the power and force of my dominant Master's control. Now for the first time ever I knew how absolutely beautiful the suppleness of a tender boy actually was.

Maybe it seems odd that I refer to Drew in this way, especially being that he was quite a bit older than me. But honestly I knew that Drew was exactly that—a mere boy, just like me. He would always be a boy. He would always be soft and gentle. He'd always convey vulnerability both in his mannerisms and demeanor. By nature he was submissive, and by nature he craved the pleasure of serving a Superior Alpha Male like his owner Alex.

Now, however, things seemed a bit murky to me. There was no doubt in my mind that Alex still owned and controlled Drew, but with Matt having been served by him as well, I wondered if Drew would feel conflicted. What if he developed feelings for Matt similar to what I felt? It almost was a bit frightening to me as I thought about that possibility. On some level I feared that it was inevitable, for Matt was so absolutely powerful. How could a sub such as Drew not be drawn to Matt in this manner? How would he be able to refrain from obsessing about him and craving him the way that I did? And would this in any way interfere with Drew's future ability to serve his own Master, Alex?

The one thing that Drew did not realize, however, was that the situation was far more complicated than it actually seemed to be. Drew did not know that his Master had knelt and served my Master. I had watched one night from a place of hiding as Matt brought Alex to his knees and used him in the same way he would use any common slave boy. Alex had submitted, and he'd gotten no reciprocation whatsoever. For all intents and purposes, Alex was indeed a slave boy to Matt. And now here we were adding yet another twist to this already complex web of relationships, for Alex had submitted once again to Matt. This time it was in a much different manner. He had submitted his property to Matt. His prized possession. His boy. His Drew!

So at least in my mind it seemed that Matt had risen yet another notch in status. In the beginning he had been my Master. Now however, it seemed he was Master of All. He owned a piece of each of us. My heart skipped a beat as I contemplated this reality. I imagined what this must have meant to him. I imagined how he now must be relishing the fulfillment of his obvious plan. I was certain of it. He must have had this planned all along. He must have set out to own the group of us. To make each of us his property. To be the absolute authority within our group.

But then I also wondered if it would end here. Would this be enough power to satisfy such a power-hungry Alpha Male? After conquering the way he had, would Matt then set his sights even higher? Would he want to expand his circle of subordinates to a broader circumference? And if so, what would that mean? Who would he bring in next? Or would he simply go outside the circle to create new and different groups of subs to control?

My mind was racing too fast. I was getting so far ahead of myself and was allowing thoughts to enter my head which were certainly inappropriate. It was not a topic which should concern me, not now or not ever. It was Matt's business how and whom he would dominate. It was my job simply to love him and obey.

Finally I pushed myself up off the loveseat, realizing painfully the soreness of my bottom. He had really reamed me hard last night. Even my tattoo hadn't hurt like that. Slowly I eased myself back down, once again to a sitting position. "Whoah!" I sighed to myself. In spite of the discomfort, I smiled. If it hurts this badly to me now, it must have felt great to him. On my second attempt I began to move around a bit more limberly. Quietly and slowly I made my way to the bathroom.

After I was done, I headed down the hall to my bedroom, just to check and make sure Matt had not crashed in my bed. I pushed open the door and was not surprised to see an empty room and a perfectly-made bed. Again, it was a bit perplexing to me that he had chosen to leave that way, without holding me or sleeping with me, but it truly was not something that I had a right to question. So I padded my way into the kitchen and decided to start making some coffee and breakfast for the three of us.

I'd just gotten the coffee started when I glanced over at the dining room table, the very one that Matt had spread me across helplessly a few hours ago. The one upon which I lay exposed to him as he drilled me mercilessly. There in the middle of the table was a small square of notebook paper, folded over. A note. Curiously I walked over and picked it up, noticing that it had Alex's name written on it. It was undeniably in Matt's handwriting.

Knowing of course that I should simply leave the note on the table for Alex, my heart beat a little faster. I was so tempted to pick it up. I desperately wanted to see what it said. I was pretty sure that I already knew. It probably was merely a note of thanks. How odd that Matt would resort to a primitive means of communication, in this, the age of text messaging. Perhaps Matt knew that a text in the middle of the night would likely disturb Alex, who may have at the time been sleeping. In spite of my better judgment, though, I could not help myself, and I quickly yet furtively reached over and snatched it up.

As I unfolded the note and read the words before me, my mouth dropped open in shock, while at the exact same moment I heard my name being spoken behind me. "Petey, where the hell is Drew?" It was Alex.

Spinning around to face him, I could not speak but merely extended my arm, silently handing him the note. He looked puzzled as he snatched it from my hand. I looked up to see the impatience on his face. I knew he was angry, wondering where his boy Drew had gone. Wondering where he'd been taken. And why.

Now he knew.

I saw the look of impatience on his face instantly evolve into unadulterated anger. Rage, in fact. I thought for a second he was gonna punch me. He was gripping the note in one hand, but with the other he was making a tight fist.

"Wuh the fuck!" he exclaimed.

Instinctively I stepped away from him. He wasn't angry with me though. He apparently didn't give a shit that I'd read his note without his permission. His anger obviously was due to the content of the note itself, and understandably so, for the words it contained were quite shocking to say the least.

Alex, I took Drew to the cabin. Take care of Petey. Gonna be back in a couple days. Don't forget to do what I told you. And remember what I said—what's yours is mine. What's mine's my own.

Matt

Furiously, Alex turned and threw the note back down onto the table. "Get dressed!" he ordered me as he headed back to the bedroom. Quickly I scurried to my own room, not understanding exactly what was going to happen or why I needed to be dressed.

So many confusing thoughts raced through my head. It didn't make sense to me that Matt would sneak off with Drew in the middle of the night like that. Why didn't he take me with them? Why didn't he at least tell me about it beforehand? What was he trying to prove to Alex by just taking his boy from him and so smugly stating, "What's yours is mine. What's mine's my own!"? I felt a horrible knot in my chest and a lump in my throat, as if I were on the verge of tears.

I had been promising myself that I was going to be stronger. I was certain that no matter what my Master chose to do, I would trust him. But why this? Why my best friend? Matt knew how very much I loved Drew. Why would he use him in this way to hurt me? Or was it simply that he did not care whether I was hurt or not? He wanted to fulfill his own desires first, and if that meant that there would be casualties along the way, then so be it. But I was his pup! I was the one he loved most—or so I thought.

And this situation with Alex made no sense to me either. I thought I had had the dynamic of their relationship figured out. Both were Masters. Superior Alpha Males. But of course Matt established some time ago that he was in fact the most superior. Alex had accepted this fact, or so it seemed. Matt already had humiliated and humbled Alex by forcing him to kneel and serve like a common slave boy. Why was it now necessary to take from Alex the one single thing that he valued most—his Drew?

Matt had also reminded me the evening before that everything was cool between Alex and him. He'd stated that they were buds. He said Alex had just gotten a little "freaky", but they would work everything out. Then when the two had returned from the bar last night, Alex handed over his boy Drew to Matt for his use. Then Alex left and came back later. Of course Matt was still using Drew so Alex just went to bed, asking Matt to send Drew in when he was done with him. But then when Alex and I got up this morning Matt and Drew were gone, and we found this puzzling note. Matt told Alex in the note that he'd taken Drew away to the cabin for a couple days and reminded Alex to do what he'd instructed him. He also seemed almost to be goading Alex by his final remark about their personal property.

I was just pulling on my shirt when Alex's voice startled me. I turned to see him standing in my bedroom doorway. He was fully dressed, wearing jeans and a long sleeve tee, with a backwards-turned b-cap. He had a scowl on his face, and I noticed how his forehead wrinkled as he glared at me. "Hurry up!" he instructed me, and hurriedly I bent to snatch up my shoes. I was already very nervous about this whole situation, and his obviously sour mood was making things worse. He turned, and I quickly followed him back out into the living room.

As I sat on the sofa putting on my shoes, Alex began making a call on his cell phone. He walked away from me, but I could still hear him. Apparently he was leaving a message on Matt's voicemail. "Hey Matt," he said, clearly attempting to keep his voice calm and steady. "Dude, I got yer note. Man ..." He sighed before continuing. "Sorry man, but this is so not cool. I know what we agreed on. I got no problem with you usin Drew whenever you want, but come on! Don't ya think ya should've at least let me know you were takin him? Anyway, I'll watch Petey like you said. I'm about to take him over to the gym. Please call me. Let me know at least why you did this. Please!"

I looked over at Alex at this point and saw he was pacing back and forth. I sort of felt sorry for him in a way. He did not at all seem like a dominant Master at this point. It sounded almost like he was begging Matt. The way his voice rose as he pleaded for Matt to call him reminded me of the way I spoke when I talked to my Master. For a few seconds I felt a wave of excitement wash over me, imagining how Matt would feel when he heard that voicemail. It seemed so odd to me the way that Alex had started the message with the clear intention of expressing his anger at Matt. In fact, he actually did tell Matt that he was not cool with what happened. But then he calmed himself, forcing himself to remain respectful. This was not Alpha Male behavior. This was an act of submission.

If I noticed this, then I was positive that Matt would be fully aware of the significance. What I was witnessing with Alex right now was the exact same process that I had gone through so many times myself. When I had been given an order that I was not especially fond of following, the natural reaction was for me to want to rebel. I wanted so desperately to protest, to explain that it was not fair. I wanted to argue my way out of it. But I actually had to force myself to bite my tongue, swallow my pride, and simply accept the fact that a decision had been made which was not contingent upon my approval.

This had happened to me numerous times, perhaps hundreds. Eventually it got to the point that it became natural for me to obey and rare for me to want to voice my objections. I could not imagine how Alex must be feeling now, though. Matt had ushered me into my role as his sub, and it was all I had known. Alex, on the other hand, was not a sub. He was a dominant Master. It must be a thousand times harder for him to accept the fact that he was now in a position where he had to take orders.

I imagined that when Matt finally did listen to this voicemail he would be pleased. Certainly he would reprimand or possibly even punish Alex later for his initial tone of disrespect, but he would relish the way that Alex had ultimately bowed to his authority. There was a part of me that wanted to be indignant and offended by Matt's actions. I wanted to feel disappointed in him because obviously he was not acting like much of a friend to Alex. But then on the other hand, I was excited. It excited me in the same way that Ryan's humiliation had excited me. I loved seeing others brought into submission under my Master!

In spite of my excitement, however, I was feeling confused and worried. The thing that truly bothered me most was that Matt had chosen to take my best friend away.

Was he choosing Drew over me? Why wouldn't he have just included me? I was right there next to them in the living room. He could have easily awakened me or even just carried me out in his arms. Why did they sneak away like that and leave me behind?

When Alex and I got out to his Lexus, he did not hesitate to offer me an answer to this very question as to why Matt had not included me. "You do realize, Petey, that your Master is up at his cabin right now fucking the brains out of *my* boy, don't you?"

My mouth dropped open as I looked over at him. Immediately I began to shake my head. "No ... no Sir, Matt wouldn't do that. He promised me he would never fuck another sub ..."

"In front of you!" Alex clarified.

He was right! That was precisely what Matt had promised. He had said he would never make me watch him fuck another sub. He knew it'd be too hard on me. But even so, he would never fuck my very best friend. Never! "Sir, you are wrong. I'm sorry, but you're totally wrong! I know Matt. I trust him, and he knows what Drew means to me. He is not like that ..."

"Goddammit, Petey! You read what the fuckin note said. He said, 'what's yours is mine, what's mine's my own.' What the fuck you think he meant by that if not that he was gonna fuck Drew?"

"I don't know, Sir," my voice was starting to crack, "I don't know what Matt meant, but I do know Matt."

"I don't think you know him as well as you think you do!" I could feel the anger again rising within Alex as he sped out of the parking lot. "All you fuckin know is what he allows you to see. I fuckin cared about him too, Petey! I loved him, ya know." His voice was starting to crack.

My heart started to break for him right then. I understood exactly what Alex was saying. I'd seen him kneel to worship Matt the same way that I had done dozens of times. I knew he must have been totally infatuated by Matt. It must have been a horrific burden to bear, for it also was clear that he deeply loved Drew, but it was a far different kind of love. He was in a really unique position, trapped between being a dominant Master and a submissive slave.

At this point I was crying openly. "How do you know, Alex? How do you know he will fuck Drew?" My reversion to the use of Alex's first name had been unconscious, and he didn't even seem to notice.

"I just know that he had no reason to take Drew away like that. If he just wanted head, he'd have stayed home. He took Drew away so they could have privacy. He didn't want you or me seeing what they did."

"Why don't we go up there now?" I blurted out. "Alex, please! Let's just go up to the cabin and talk to Matt. Let's just work it out. It's probably just a big misunderstanding. Maybe he wants that. Maybe it's a test to see how strong you are. Maybe he is just trying to see if you ..."

"It's not a fuckin test, Petey!" Alex was getting angry again. "Just shut the fuck up, will ya?"

"I'm calling him!" I screamed as I reached into my pocket to pull out my cell. "I'm gonna just call and ask him."

Alex reached over and snatched the phone out of my hands, carelessly tossing it in the back seat. "You're not callin him. He's not answerin his damn phone anyway. I already tried calling. Plus you'd just get him pissed."

Well that was one thing that Alex probably was correct about. I knew I couldn't call Matt over this. He had given very specific orders to Alex instructing him to take care of me. If Matt wanted me to contact him, he'd have provided me with some form of communication to indicate such. Instead he left me in Alex's care.

"Alex please! Please try to call him again, or please let's just go up there to the cabin!"

"Shut up!" Alex screamed. "Just shut the fuck up! I'm not goin up there!"

"Dammit Alex! Fuck you!" I screamed, beside myself with hysteria.

Instantly I felt his fist connect with my face. The force of the blow was powerful, and my head spun around, my face slamming violently against the glass. "Don't ever fuckin talk to me like that, faggot!" he snarled. A gusher of blood erupted from my nose, and I reflexively pulled my hands up over my face. I panicked when I looked down to see them saturated by the bright red blood.

The pain from my broken nose ripped through my skull, and I cried out in agony. Alex pounded his palms furiously against the steering wheel and quickly pulled over. He grabbed my shoulder and spun me around to face him. At this point I was visibly shaking. This was not the first broken nose I'd ever had, but I was more afraid of what he was gonna do next. I tried pulling away from him, flailing my arms pathetically.

"Calm down!" he yelled. "Petey, oh God! Oh my God, I'm sorry! Let me see ... please calm the fuck down!"

9

After slugging me squarely in the face, blackening my eye and apparently breaking my nose, Alex was far more panic-stricken by the situation than was I. Initially I freaked out, mainly due to the blood, not to mention the searing pain that was shooting into my skull; but as I witnessed Alex have a near melt-down right before my eyes, I realized that I was gonna be the one who'd have to get the situation under control.

"Get me a towel or something! Please!" I yelled.

"Here! Here, take this!" Alex handed me a napkin that was apparently stuffed into the side pocket of his car door.

I snatched it from him but shook my head, "Not big enough!"

"Oh fuck, Petey! I'm so sorry! Oh god, I don't know why I did that. Oh fuck! Oh god, does it hurt?"

"Yes!" I screamed. "Yes it fuckin hurts like hell! Don't you have a towel or something in your trunk?"

Alex then opened the car door and jumped out. We were parked along the highway and I thought, *great, now he's gonna get hit by an oncoming car*. I turned and saw him run towards the trunk, then quickly turn around and open the car door, remembering that he hadn't pressed the release button. He reached under the dash frantically trying to locate the button as I pressed the tiny napkin under my nose. It already was completely soaked with blood.

A few seconds later Alex had found something. It was in fact a beach towel that'd been left in the trunk. He held it up to my face, trying to gingerly press it against a geyser that had erupted. I grabbed it away from him, sliding as close to the passenger door as I could. Apparently my body language spoke loud and clear, for instantly he backed off.

"Dammit!" he yelled. "Dammit to hell!"

I continued to hold the towel up to my face and looked out my window, tears now welling in my eyes. I now not only was aching inside myself from the pain of the words Alex had said to me moments before, but my face was also on fire. How could I have forgotten how horrific this pain was? It was exactly what had happened the very first day that Matt and I had met at the bus stop. But it was two thug gay bashers who had attacked me, not my owner's very best friend!

This whole situation had turned so quickly into a scene from my worst nightmare. I had discovered this morning when I woke up that Matt had taken my best friend away in the middle of the night to our special place. He left a note saying he'd be gone for two days and that Alex was to take care of me. Then Alex turns around and tells me Matt is probably up there at the cabin fucking Drew's brains out. I get upset and yell at him, and Alex hauls off and decks me!

At this point I did not know fact from fiction. In my heart I wanted to believe that Matt was not doing what Alex said, but in my head I knew that it must be true. As badly as my head was hurting at the moment, the pain did not begin to compare to my broken heart. It all made perfect sense, really. After I had fallen asleep on the loveseat, Matt must have continued using Drew for his pleasure. He probably wanted to fuck him, being as horny as he was at the time. He had promised me that he'd never do anything like that in front of me, so he took Drew away. It also was clear that he was sending Alex a clear message as to who was boss. He had sarcastically told Alex that he was entitled to any of Alex's property, but that Matt's property was his own.

As I sat there with the towel pressed firmly to my face and my head resting against the window, tears streamed down my cheeks. This whole situation was so awful. What was

Matt gonna do when he found out that Alex had punched me? Would he say that I deserved it for cursing at Alex? Would the situation make him angry at Alex and result in a possible fight between them? What I most feared was what all this would do to my relationship with Drew.

"Petey, oh my god, I'm so sorry! God! Why'd you have to disrespect me like that? I'd have never punched you ... Oh fuck!"

Had I not still been weeping uncontrollably I may have turned to him and apologized. In spite of my injury, I sincerely was sorry. I did not mean to curse him. I did not mean to show him disrespect. I had just freaked when he refused to let me call Matt. I knew that he'd freaked as well. He responded in a way that guys like him did. He responded with his fist, with his testosterone.

"I'm sorry, Sir!" I sobbed. "I'm so sorry ..."

"Oh Petey," Alex said. Now he too was crying. "God! I gotta take you to the hospital."

"No!" I screamed. "Please no!"

"But you're bleeding, and I think your nose is broke."

"It'll be okay ... Don't make me go to the hospital. Please. Matt will find out then. Please don't tell him!"

"Petey, you can't lie to Matt. Oh my god!" It was as if some major realization had dawned upon him. "He left me in charge of you! He told me to take care of you, and look what I've done!"

"We can say it was an accident!" I said. "That's not a lie. You didn't mean it, did you?"

"Petey, he'll know!" Alex shook his head.

"No, listen to me Alex ... um ... Sir. Please. We're both gonna be in trouble. If he finds out I told you to fuck off, he's gonna kill me. He's gonna kill you if he finds out you punched me. Remember when he told you that day not to ever discipline me ... that day you sucked him—"

Fuck! I had said it!

"What are you talking about?" Alex demanded. "What did Matt tell you?"

Damn, I could not believe I'd just said what I did. Alex did not know that I had seen him serving Matt that day. I had kept the secret for all this time, and now it just slipped out. "He didn't tell me, Sir. I saw."

Alex's face had turned beet red, whether from embarrassment or anger, I'm not sure. "Does Drew know?" he asked quietly.

"No Sir, of course not!" I replied. "I would never tell Drew, I swear."

"That's why you came in your pants, isn't it? You got your rocks off watching it. You loved seeing me humiliated like that!"

"No! It wasn't like that Al—um—Sir. It wasn't like that at all. I was turned on seeing my Master—seeing Matt—watching him being serviced. I had never seen another guy suck him before. I came in my pants but did not want to tell you why. I did not want you to be ... well ... humiliated."

"And so you let Matt paddle you for it? Why'd you do that?" Alex's voice had gotten so quiet as he stared straight ahead at the steering wheel. It was as if he could not bear to look me in the eye.

"I did it for Drew ... and for you. I did it because you are a Master. You are above me. I did not want you to think that I no longer respected you. Plus you were right. I shouldn't have sworn at you—not then and not now."

"Petey, you need medical attention. We at least need to go to urgent care or something."

"No, please. The bleeding's stopped. Even if it is broken, there's not much they can do. I get nosebleeds easy. It's probably not even broke. Let's just go to the gym like you planned. Why are we going there anyway?"

Alex sighed. I thought he was gonna start crying again. "There's something I have to do for Matt," he said.

"Can you tell me what it is, Sir? Please?" I asked meekly.

"Matt hired me about a month ago. It was before spring break. I designed a computer program for him. It's software for his dad's businesses—for the gyms. Well, he's opening that new gym this week, and I have to go there to get everything installed. He is gonna have me install the software in all the stores, but this one is the pilot. He is also negotiating to sell the software to other gyms all across the country."

"Oh my god Alex! That's awesome! Congratulations!"

"Thanks. Matt wants me to have everything done this weekend. We are gonna launch it on Monday, I guess when he gets back. The gym opens for business on Wednesday."

"So what are we waiting for?" I asked. "Let's go over there."

"What about Matt and Drew? What about them being at the cabin fucking? I don't even know if I wanna do this any more. And now that I know you saw me ... well, you know ... I just don't know."

"Alex ... I mean Sir ... you already told me you loved Matt. I understand, really I do. And Drew told me before that you used to be sub yourself. I understand why you'd be infatuated by a guy like Matt. We all are. I don't wanna think of Matt fucking Drew, but if that is what he chooses to do, I'm not gonna stop loving him. Are you?"

"I don't love him like you do, Petey. He's kind of like a hero to me, I guess. I love him like my bro, and I look up to him. But stealing my boy like that, taking him from me in the middle of the night. That shit's not right."

"Can we just wait and see ... please? Can we just try to give him the benefit of the doubt? Maybe he has some sort of plan. Maybe it's like I said—a test or a lesson. For you *and* me."

Alex sighed again. "He's gonna figure out I punched you and then he's gonna be ready to kick my ass. We'll never be friends again. There's no point in me even goin to the gym.

After this he'll probably never speak to me again. I mean, after he kills me."

"Alex, we're not tellin him! We'll just say it was an accident. He might not even know. I don't even think it's broke, and he won't be back for two days!"

"Okay ... I guess we can see. It *has* stopped bleeding. We'll go to the gym. Maybe we can find you some clean clothes while we're there. I'll buy you a new shirt at the mall, all right?"

"No, you don't have to do that. I deserved to get punched in the nose for what I said to you. Really, it was my fault."

"You know, Petey, I see why Matt's so crazy about you." He then reached over and pulled me into him, squeezing me carefully against his chest in a brotherly hug. I tried not to cringe from the pain as my face pressed against him but wrapped my arms around him with a display of genuine affection.

* * *

By the time we got to the mall my badly stained shirt had dried. I went into the bathroom and washed the caked on flakes of blood from my face. The injury really was not as bad as I'd initially thought. I was sure that my nose was not broken. I was, however, starting to show a black eye. This was just like when I'd met Matt. I'd had a black eye, which reminded him of the dog Petey from the Little Rascals. He had thought it was the wildest coincidence that it was my actual name.

Alex was waiting for me outside the bathroom door, and we walked together to the gym entrance. I remembered how only a few days before Matt had brought me here and fucked me while the gym was still being set up. Now it nearly broke my heart to think that he was off fucking my best friend, probably in a similar way.

Alex of course had a key to get into the store, and I stood patiently behind him as he turned the door knob and pushed the door open. No sooner did he take a step inside then I was startled by a rousing cheer of, "Surprise!" Instantly all the overhead lights came on, and Alex stood frozen in his tracks. Directly in front of us was a huge banner displaying the following message: CONGRATULATIONS ALEX! It was a surprise graduation party.

The very first two people we saw as we stepped through the doors were none other than Matt and Drew, standing there all smiles. Drew rushed up to Alex and wrapped his arms around his neck. "I knew you'd come! I knew our plan would work."

Matt just stood there beaming until he looked over to me. As he took in my shiner and my blood-soaked shirt, his smile instantly drained from his face. "My god, Petey! What happened to you?"

10

The room that I stepped into looked far different than it
had the week before when Matt had brought me here alone.
Just days before it had been nearly empty with drywall
covering the exterior. The floor coverings had not been
installed, and it even was lacking furniture or fixtures of any
kind. Now, however, it appeared to be ready to open for
business. A huge, marble countertop, which would surely be
the registration desk, stretched across the front wall. There
were exercise machines of every imaginable type strewn out
across the big open room. The store itself obviously
consisted of several rooms, though I could only at this point
see the entrance.

I didn't have much time to take a gander at my
surroundings, however, not with Matt standing directly in
front of me with a look of shocked horror on his face.

"What the fuck happened to you, Petey?" he repeated.

Quickly I glanced away from him and into the eyes of
Drew, knowing full well that both his fate and my own were
at stake, depending upon how I answered. "Oh nothing Sir,"
I said. "I, um ... I had a little accident."

"A little accident!" Matt exclaimed. "Petey, you're covered
in blood. Come here!" He grabbed my arm and pulled me
away from the crowd of people, ushering me into a back
room. I tried to glance back to see my best friend Drew. I
was hoping he'd follow. I saw Alex take a step in our
direction, but he was thwarted by the group of his friends
who now surrounded him. Drew was at his side.

Matt pulled me into a kitchenette area. It must have been
a break room or lounge for the employees who'd be working

here. The countertops were covered with food products, which had been used to prepare the spread for the party. Matt was holding tightly to my arm as he walked over to the refrigerator and opened the freezer. He grabbed some ice and quickly wrapped it in a towel that he pulled from one of the cabinets nearby. "Put this on your nose!" he ordered me. "What do you mean?" he demanded. "What kind of accident? It looks like you have a black eye too!"

I was shaking my head as I looked up at him, trying to figure out how to hold the ice pack in place and answer his questions simultaneously. I pulled the towel away from my face slightly and said to him, "Sir, it was no one's fault. You know how clumsy I am."

"You're not answering the question, Petey!" Matt's voice was rising. "Did someone hit you, and where was Alex? Why didn't he fuckin call me?"

"He called you this morning, Sir, but you didn't answer. We didn't think you had your phone on. We thought you and Drew were ..." I didn't finish my sentence.

"That was this morning, less than two hours ago. I got the message, and Alex didn't say anything about an accident. Here, sit down, for godsakes!"

"It just happened, Sir. I hit my head against the door of the car. At first I thought I broke my nose, but it doesn't hurt so bad now. There was just so much blood!"

"He should have called me. Dammit! Why didn't he take you to the hospital?"

"It's not his fault, Sir. I begged him not to. I didn't want to worry you. It was my own stupidity, as usual."

"Well never mind about that, pup. You're not stupid, but it seems like you think I am!"

I started shaking my head, "No, no Sir. Of course I don't think—"

"You expect me to believe you got a bloody nose and a black eye from falling into the car door? I can tell someone hit you. Who hit you, Petey, and why would you lie to me?"

Just then the door opened, and Alex walked in. "I hit him," he said flatly. Drew was standing behind him, his mouth agape.

"You hit Petey?" Matt repeated, the timbre of his voice rising slightly as he turned to face Alex eye-to-eye.

"Yes," Alex said meekly, looking quickly down at the ground, "and I'm so sorry."

"Sir, please!" I shouted. "Honest he didn't mean it! It was an accident, just like I said."

"Shut up, Petey!" Matt said sternly without even looking in my direction.

Within what seemed to be a split second, Matt had a hold of the front of Alex's shirt with both of his fists and hurled him against the wall, pinning him there helplessly as he stared him directly in the eye. Alex hung there, wide-eyed, making no attempt to struggle free of Matt's grip. "Man, I'm so sorry, I swear!" he whimpered. As Matt shoved his weight into Alex I heard his head thug against the wall, and he visibly winced from the pain.

"You fuckin *hit* Petey? You fuckin punched him in the face? What the fuck!"

Drew had rushed over to Matt's side, trying to force his way in between them, and I instantly dropped the ice pack on the ground and rushed to the other side. "Stop, Sir! Please! It's not what you think. He didn't mean it! He didn't mean to hurt me!"

"You've got five seconds to come up with one good fuckin reason for me to let you walk the fuck outta here alive, dude!" Matt snarled into Alex's face. "Five seconds!"

I was now crying, and by the looks of Drew, he wasn't far from it himself. "I deserved it, Sir!" I screamed. "I told him to fuck off."

My confession did not seem to be making any difference to Matt at all. In fact, it seemed to make him angrier. "Is that true?" he glared directly at Alex whose arms were stretched out flat against the wall as he remained pinned defenselessly. "Petey swore at you and so you fuckin decked him?"

In a situation like this one, I would think that Alex would realize that this was the time he should be coming up with something, anything, to defend himself. He should have offered some kind of explanation, some sort of rationale. He could have explained how freaked he had been when he found the note and how hysterical I was in the car. He could have explained how disrespectful I was being to him and how disobedient I was trying to be even to my own Master by insisting that he allow me to call him without permission. Instead of saying any of these things, though, Alex simply nodded.

When Matt released his grip on Alex with one of his fists, I was momentarily relieved but then equally stunned when he drove that same fist back brutally right into Alex's gut. Like a rag doll, Alex crumpled forward, moaning loudly.

"No!" Drew screamed. "Please stop!"

I saw the door to the kitchen open, and a couple college-aged guys rushed in, quickly grabbing Matt by the shoulders. He wasn't done throwing punches though. Before they could get him away he landed another punch directly into Alex's chin, and Alex's body was thrust backwards against the wall where he slumped over and slid down to the ground. The two guys who'd come into the room now had a hold of each of Matt's arms, dragging him backwards away from Alex. Drew dropped to his knees and grabbed Alex, crying hysterically.

I could not believe what was happening, and I knew it was all my fault. I had known how distraught Alex was about the situation, but I just made matters worse for him. I wouldn't listen to him, and then I had cursed him. He already was furious and confused and emotional. But I had to go and freak out on him and tell him to fuck off. Of course he reacted the way that he did. No true Dom is ever going to allow a sub to talk to him that way. I was lucky that a punch in the face was all I'd gotten out of the situation.

And now Matt had stepped in to protect me. I was his responsibility and his property. There was no alternative but for him to defend me against any and all physical threats. Regardless if Alex was right or wrong, of course Matt would automatically want to kick his ass for touching me. He had instructed Alex to take care of me, and instead he delivered me back to Matt covered in blood with a black eye. It was no wonder Matt freaked.

And now everything was ruined. This beautifully orchestrated party was completely destroyed. It was supposed to be an occasion that celebrated and honored Alex for his tremendous accomplishments. All of his friends and fellow students were present to recognize him for what he had achieved. It was a day of celebration, but now thanks to me it had become a day of tragedy.

Not only had this series of events driven a wedge between Alex and Matt which may prove irreparable, but I also knew it was surely to be the end of my relationship with Drew. How would Matt ever consider allowing me to continue associating with him so long as he was Alex's sub? And to make matters worse, I had just moved in with them. What was going to happen now? Where would I go? Back to Kathie's already?

It took four guys to actually get Matt out of the room, and all the while he was cursing at Alex, threatening him further. As they dragged him out he yelled for me, ordering me to follow, but one of the guys turned to me and told me to just stay where I was and put the ice back on my head. I did stay—not as an act of disobedience, but because I knew they were not going to allow me near him. I also needed to make sure Alex was okay.

Of course, Alex proved far tougher than me. He was back on his feet within a matter of minutes, and then finally he sat down in a chair. Drew remained by his side, repeatedly consoling him and asking if he was all right. Finally Alex smiled halfheartedly. Perhaps he was reflecting upon the irony of the situation. All this time he had been certain that Matt had betrayed him by stealing away in the middle of the night with his boy. He had been so confident that Matt had Drew up at his cabin fucking his brains out, but in reality the two had been preparing this grand surprise for him.

"I guess I don't need to worry about installing the computer software," he mumbled sarcastically as he rubbed his chin.

"Alex!" I sniffled. "I'm so sorry. It's all my fault."

What happened next then shattered my heart into a million pieces. It was not a comment or a sarcastic remark. It was neither a threat nor another demonstration of physical violence. It was something much simpler and much, much worse. It was a single look. An expression of disgust on Drew's face as he looked over at me and glared. I saw the utter disappoint in his eyes. Was it anger? Was it hatred?

I just stared back at him, feeling like a deer caught in headlights. There was nothing I could say. Sorry was not nearly enough.

"It's not your fault, Petey," Alex said calmly. "It's not Matt's fault either. I shouldn't have hit you. I deserved for Matt to kick my ass. Do you know what I'd do to someone who laid a finger on Drew?" As he said this he reached over and pulled Drew into his embrace. "I'd fuckin kill em."

"Why didn't you just tell him, Sir? Why didn't you explain what a little snot I was being?" My voice was shrill and whiney as I fought to hold back my tears. "You should have just blamed it on me!"

Alex laughed. "That'd 've just made him more pissed. It was my job to take care of you. If you were bein a brat, I should have disciplined you and let him punish you later, not haul off and slug you."

"Still," Drew finally spoke, "still everyone has their limits. Some people just don't know when to keep their mouth shut.

Some people don't know the fucking meaning of the word respect." He glared straight into my eyes as he leveled this indictment against me.

About this time the kitchen door again opened and in walked a girl I did not know. Apparently she was a friend of Alex. "Oh my god, are you all right?" she asked.

"Yeah, Greta, I'm fine. Really."

"What happened?" she asked. "You got into a fight with Matt? Why?"

"Not really a fight. I guess I just got what was comin to me."

She looked at him with the most puzzled look on her face. "Oh hon, are you sure you're okay? Where did he hit you?"

"He punched him in the face ... and the stomach!" Drew said.

"I'm fine," Alex repeated. "How's Matt? Is he still goin ape shit?"

Greta shook her head. "He's in the back room. They took him to some office, and he's not yelling any more. Does this mean there is no party?"

"No!" I said. "No, that's not what it means. There is still a party. Please don't go. Please let me go and talk to Matt now that he's calmed down. Please!"

"Haven't you done enough already?" snapped Drew. "Alex, can we just get out of here?"

"Please Drew!" I cried. "Please think about what you're saying. If you go, we might never see each other again. Please let me talk to him first. Let me see if – "

"Come on," said Greta, grabbing my wrist. "You guys just stay here, okay? You promise? I'll come back in a minute. I'll bring you a drink. What do you want?"

Before Drew could say anything, Alex answered. "We won't go anywhere. Yet. We don't need anything to drink."

"Okay, stay right there, and I'll be right back. Come on, I'll take you to Matt. What's your name? Petey?" I nodded and followed quickly behind her.

* * *

It was very awkward having to walk through the entire main room of the gym, past all the guests who were mingling with one another. Some of them I recognized, including Ryan and his new friend Eric. I simply looked towards the ground as Greta led me through the room and down a short hallway in the back. I knocked gently on the door but heard no response, and so I cautiously pushed it open and peered inside. The office was much more spacious than I'd expected, with a huge oak desk that seemed to take up a third of the room. Matt was sitting at that desk, resting his elbows on top and clasping his hands together in front of him. Was he praying?

As I carefully and silently stepped inside, it seemed as if he wasn't even aware of my presence, for he didn't at first acknowledge me. I let the door close behind me and stepped closer to him.

"Sir?" I said meekly. "Are you okay?"

Matt did not immediately reply, and I inched my way closer to him. Finally he sighed. "Think I fucked up this time," he said very quietly. At first I was not sure I'd heard him correctly and so I repeated myself.

"Are you okay, Sir?"

Matt then coughed and cleared his throat. He quickly looked away from me, seeming to be staring at a portrait on the wall to his right. He turned his chair so as not to be able to see me. It almost looked as if his eyes were moist, like he was about to cry.

"You didn't fuck up, Sir. Really, you didn't. Even Alex understands why you punched him."

He then shifted back around to make eye contact with me. "Not about that, pup. How could I not have reacted the way I did? How can I be your Master without being willing and able to protect you?"

"Then what, Sir? Why is it that you feel you've messed up somehow?"

"Come here," he said, holding his arms out to me, and as I quickly rushed to him I heard a sob involuntarily escape from my own throat. As I felt those strong arms wrap around me, I released all of my emotion into his chest and sank into the security of his embrace. "Let me see your face, pup. Let me see." It sounded as if he were speaking to a third grader. His voice was so soothing and so reassuring. He gently cupped my head in his big hands and slowly turned my head from side to side, carefully examining my injuries. "I'm going to touch your nose, little guy. Just relax cuz I won't hurt you." Gently he pressed his finger against one side, then the other. "Does that hurt?" he asked.

I shook my head. "No Sir, not much."

"I don't think it's broken this time," he said. "Still maybe it should be x-rayed."

"Sir why do you say you messed up?" I asked him, trying to divert the conversation away from my injury. "Why'd you say that?"

He had pushed his chair back about two feet from the desk and positioned me so that I was on his lap. He sighed once again and then looked me directly in the eye. "Pup, I forgot for a minute who you are and why I love you. I forgot how easy you get hurt."

"But you did not hurt me. It was Alex, and even so it was an accident!"

"I don't mean *this*," he said, gently touching my nose with his index finger. "I mean *this*." He moved his finger down to point at my chest. "Do you believe me when I say that I remember every promise I have ever made to you?" he asked.

"Yes Sir. Yes of course!" I assured him.

"What was the first thing I ever promised you, pup?"

"You will never hurt me. And you never have!" I insisted.

"When you thought that I took Drew up to the cabin, did that hurt you?"

I didn't want to answer him, but I also did not want to lie. I sat there for a moment looking him in the eye. Slowly I shook my head.

"Yes it did," he said, gently contradicting my gesture, "and I know why it hurt you. You thought that I was fucking your best friend."

"It is your right, Sir. I already know it, and so does Drew. You have a right to do that with whoever you want, even if I don't like it."

"Of course it's my right, pup, but that's not the issue. I'm not talking about my rights here. I'm talking about my responsibility. It was my job to protect you and to make sure you did not get hurt."

"You didn't even do what I thought you were doing, though, Sir. You didn't fuck Drew, or did you?" It was my voice now that had gotten quiet.

He shook his head. "No, the two of us went over to my house and fell asleep for a couple hours. Separate beds. Then we came over here early this morning and got ready for the surprise party."

"Why did you do it that way, Sir? Why didn't you just have Drew meet you here when he got up?" I wondered immediately if it were even my place to question him.

"That's a good question. I wish now I had done it that way, but at the time I wanted mainly to piss Alex off. I wanted him to be so fuckin pissed that he didn't think of anything except me taking Drew from him. I thought that way he'd never start to figure out what was really goin on."

"But that was really smart, Sir, and it worked! Alex had no idea, and neither did I."

"I thought about bringing you with us, but I knew it wouldn't have the same impact. And then I added the comment about his property being mine. I knew that'd just about send him over the edge." Matt smiled in spite of himself.

"Can't you see, Sir," I said, "that I'm the one who messed up? I was the one who freaked out and started yelling. I said 'fuck you!' to Alex. I deserved to get punched like that."

"Maybe," Matt agreed, "but not by him. He should have spanked your fuckin ass, is what he shoulda done."

Shamefully I looked down at my lap. "I'm sorry, Sir," I said. "Will you ever forgive me?"

"Does it look like I haven't forgiven you?" he asked, raising his eyebrows. I then wrapped both arms around his neck and hugged him so tightly. He gently squeezed me into his chest. "Did they leave?" he asked. "Alex and Drew?"

"No Sir, they promised to stay til after I talked to you. They're still in the kitchen."

"Want you to tell me the absolute truth pup, okay?" I nodded. "Do you need to go to the hospital? You know what a broken nose feels like. You think it's broke again."

"No Sir, honest I don't think so. I don't think it's broke."

"Still, you're gonna have a bit of a shiner there. You look like you did that first day we met."

"Like Petey. Like our puppy Petey!"

"Well, he's not so much a pup any more. He's getting big. Gotta take you to see him more."

I nodded quickly. "Yes! Yes Sir, you do."

"Okay, well you wanna have a party today or what? You wanna put all this shit behind us?"

"Oh yes! Oh Sir, please!"

"All right, go back to the break room and find Alex. Tell him I wanna talk to him alone. Then you tell Drew how sorry you are about all this mess. You understand?"

"Yes Sir! I understand!" I was already up off his lap and halfway to the door.

"And take Drew outside. I'm sure he's ready for a smoke." I smiled back at my Master as I turned to close the door behind me.

11

Drew and I were sitting together on the curb outside of the mall. He had his arm around me, pulling me tightly against his torso as he inhaled deeply on his cigarette. I didn't even mind the smoke. He took one final drag and flicked the butt casually into the drive, then wrapped both arms around me and squeezed me tight. He began kissing my forehead affectionately until I tilted my head back and gently pressed my lips against his.

"Eww ... you smell like smoke!!" I complained.

"I know. It's like kissing an ashtray," he laughed. "That's what Alex always says. Too bad though. That's your punishment."

"Drew I'm so sorry. Will you ever forgive me?"

"I'm only kidding, guy. Can't you tell? And there's nothing to forgive. Really. We all got a little out of control. Everyone said shit that we now regret."

"What if they don't make up, Drew? What if Matt and Alex start fighting again? They might never let us see one another again!" We had come outside while we were waiting for them to finish their conversation. The whole situation was very awkward, and I had to wonder what all of the party guests thought about the drama. I was surprised that they'd all stayed.

"Don't worry. Matt wouldn't have asked to talk to Alex if he wasn't ready to make up, and Alex wouldn't have gone to him if he wasn't. You know he feels real bad for hitting you. Your eye looks like hell too." He gently ran his finger across my swollen face.

"He didn't mean it," I offered. "I knew he was sorry as soon as he did it, and besides that, I think I really deserved to be hit anyway."

"I'm sorry for saying what I did to you Petey. You know I didn't mean that either."

"I know," I smiled at him, "but you actually were right. I should've kept my mouth shut and not got Alex so upset."

"Well I shoulda known better too. I should've warned Matt about Alex's temper when we played that trick on him. I should have just figured out some other way to come over and get this party set up without making Alex think I'd gone to the cabin with Matt."

"Did you like serving him ... I mean with me. And then after?" I asked.

Drew smiled. "I was ordered to serve him by my Master, remember?"

"That's not what I asked. I said, 'did you like it?'"

"I like obeying my Master. Period," he said.

"Well I liked it. I liked it a lot, and I could tell you did too."

"I wonder if Matt will ever let you serve Alex with me," Drew pondered. I didn't want to tell my best friend that I highly doubted it. Apparently he had not seen Matt's note, which stated his property was his and his alone. I didn't think Matt would ever agree to allow me to serve someone other than him.

"Maybe ..." I said.

"Hey, if you want you can help me with the party. We should get back in there and make sure there's enough food and shit. Gotta keep the ice full and cut the cake. And there's gonna be a lot of clean up."

"Yes, of course. You know I'll help!"

"Let's go get you some new clothes first though," he offered. "That shirt's all bloody."

"Okay, but I might have to wait for Matt. I don't have much money with me."

"Alex and I are buying your new clothes. You don't need money," he stated matter-of-factly.

"No!" I said. "You've already done enough for me."

"Shut up, or I'll do your other eye!" Drew said in the most threatening voice he could muster. I just laughed as we jumped up off the curb simultaneously. He then dragged me back into the mall and straight into the Eastbay store where he promptly picked me out a snug fitting polo shirt and a pair of shorts. He then used his credit card to pay the sixty-eight dollars and pulled me into a fitting room where he made me strip off my bloody clothes while he removed tags from the new items. He then smoothed out my shirt and pressed down the hairs on my head, which were sticking up every which way. He spun me around and examined my butt to make sure the shorts fit all right.

"Perfect!" he exclaimed. "Sit down and we'll get your shoes on ya."

I did as I was told, smiling at him contentedly. Drew then dropped to his knees and slipped my size 7 ½s on one at a time. I laughed at him. "I'm not a Master, ya know!"

"Sorry," he said, looking up into my eyes. "Force of habit I guess." I thought perhaps it was a matter of him expressing love in the manner in which he was most comfortable. I'd have done the same for him. "Petey, you are so cute, ya know. Even with your black eye, you just have the most adorable face. Sometimes I wonder if Matt even realizes ..."

I looked at him puzzled, wondering how he had originally intended to finish the sentence. Was he about to say that Matt did not realize how lucky he was? I found this astonishing, especially from the mouth of Drew. This was the same Drew who only a few weeks prior had counseled me as to how lucky I was to have a Master such as Matt. I guess if he genuinely cared about both of us it was natural for him to acknowledge that we each were lucky to have one another. Nonetheless, I knew in my heart that if Matt were to choose to end our relationship for any reason, he would be able to move on far more easily than would I. It was I who was so fortunate to have him. To have his protection and guidance. To be afforded the privilege of serving a man like him. It was quite literally surreal.

"... what a pain in the ass I actually am to him?" I stated, finishing Drew's sentence.

While still on his knees he then sighed and looked me directly in the eye. "Petey, don't sell yourself short. I thought I was gonna lose both you and Matt today from my life. And ya know what? I can live without Matt. I don't think I can say the same about you."

"Drew, we're a package deal," I said flatly, "and you're not gonna lose either of us. Ever."

It seemed at that moment that his eyes sort of sparkled as he stared straight at me. "Give me one more of your sweet kisses," he whispered. I did exactly that, and then we swiftly exited the store and headed back to the party.

* * *

It was not without an inkling of fear and some hesitation that we dared open the door of the gym and step back into Alex's party, but as we did we were greeted instantly by loud music and the sounds of pleasant conversations and laughter. It instantly felt like a real party, and as we stood there scanning the room I noticed Alex and Matt together over by the beverage table. Matt had his arm around Alex's shoulder and was talking animatedly with one of the guests.

"Look," I spoke into Drew's ear so he'd hear me over the music, and I pointed to our Masters. Drew then put his arm around me, mimicking Matt and Alex. He smiled broadly as he looked at me.

"I guess they made up!" he yelled. I nodded in response and then Drew grabbed my hand and pulled me after him as he headed across the room.

Suddenly I started noticing who all was at the party. Many of the students I knew from my college classes were there, but there were plenty of faces I didn't recognize. I smiled at Greta as we passed her, and she politely waved. There didn't seem to be any older guests, but there was a fairly even mix of male and female.

I finally was taking in the entire room, noticing the graphics on the walls and the impressive manner in which the room was decorated to honor Alex. There were two large easels set up containing bulletin-board-sized, framed collages, which depicted Alex at various stages of his life. There was a table next to the photo display containing yearbooks and several photo albums. A smaller table had a large wrapped box with a slot in the top. It looked like a big gift, but it was for the purpose of storing graduation cards from the guests. Next to the box were several other wrapped presents, which had obviously been deposited by guests.

Alex's high school diploma and several trophies and other awards were displayed on another table. As we approached the area where the food and beverages were located, I quickly noticed a huge sheet cake. It was very handsomely crafted, and I couldn't help but admire the cleverness of its design. It contained a replica of a computer screen, and on the screen was a photo of Alex with the inscription: CONGRATULATIONS ALEX, B.B.S.

There were streamers and balloons hanging from the ceiling, and the decoration colors were all gold and blue. Some of the balloons had graduation caps and diplomas on them, and others were simply plain. I knew all of this preparation must have been an enormous job, and there was little doubt in my mind that Drew and Matt had worked very hard to get everything set up perfectly.

The spread of food was also impressive, mostly hors d'oeuvres, sandwiches, and salads. I was sort of disappointed that Matt had not enlisted my help in the preparation, yet obviously he'd had this event catered.

As we approached Matt and Alex, they turned to see us, and Matt removed his arm from Alex to pull me into him. The guest he'd been chatting with had by then turned away. "Where'd you guys go?" he asked, speaking in a tone which would never have even hinted that there'd been any kind of a skirmish earlier.

"Drew bought me some new clothes," I smiled. "Do you like them?"

Matt quickly appraised them. "Yeah, pup looks cute," he smiled. Alex now had his arm around Drew, and as I looked over to them my heart swelled a bit. I was so happy to see that things were beginning to feel normal again.

"I can't believe you guys did all this!" I exclaimed. "What an awesome party. How come nobody even told me about it?"

"I didn't even know about it myself," said Drew, "not til Matt told me last night—early this morning, actually."

"I have never been so faked out," admitted Alex, "especially after our conversation last night. Matt had me thinking he was gonna hire me to install my computer program at his new gym."

"Well that part's true," Matt injected, "but not right now. We're here to have a party today."

I sidled up so closely to Matt as we stood there talking, pressing myself securely against his body, feeling suddenly as if the world were right again, as if everything that'd happened had been a ridiculous distraction. I just wanted more than anything to pull the other two into our embrace and be a happy family again. Instead I just smiled at Drew affectionately.

He looked as content as I felt, snuggled securely in the arms of his own Master, and I wondered if he had the same feeling as I. Did he also feel that all of this drama had been such an unnecessary distraction? Did he feel that the humanity associated with living had interfered with life? There were no three people on earth I cared about more than these guys, and it had all seemed to be on the verge of being snatched away from me. I had feared that Matt was stealing Drew from Alex, and that Alex would surely hate him bitterly for it. I did not understand how Matt could do such a thing, not to me nor to his best bud.

It made me feel so foolish as I reflected upon it. How could I have doubted Matt? How could I have ever thought he would so callously hurt the ones he loved so much? There was no question in my mind that he was the Alpha Male, and it was certainly his right to make decisions with which we did not fully understand or agree. Yet I also knew he was a man of principle. Everything he'd ever taught me had evidenced this reality about him.

We did not remain huddled together like this for long, for Matt quickly turned away to mingle with the guests. The questions that they asked about the initial disturbance were all handled very tactfully by Matt. He'd explained that there was a bit of confusion, a little misunderstanding, but everything was cool. People wondered if Alex had been upset by the surprise, and Matt simply replied, "Yeah, something like that."

I attributed my black eye to my clumsiness, and those who knew me well were not surprised. It seemed I always found a way to get myself injured. Alex had no visible injuries, unless you looked really closely at his chin, you may have noticed a bit of puffiness.

Eric and Ryan made their presence known by starting a conga line dance, leading a trail of followers back and forth through the maze of exercise machinery in the center of the big room. More guests arrived, including some of Alex's family. This was the first time I'd ever seen his parents, and he also had a younger sister.

The party had gotten off to a very rocky start, but it ultimately was a huge success. Alex was encouraged at one point to go open his gifts, and as everyone gathered around he made a big show of it, theatrically injecting an overabundance of gratitude for each gift he opened.

It was nearly five o'clock in the afternoon before the majority of guests dissipated, and by this time I had already begun the process of cleaning up the mess. Matt stopped me though, explaining he had hired someone to do it, and he informed me that we were gonna head over to a restaurant for a real meal in a bit. He invited Eric and Ryan to join us, so it was to be a party of six. Alex's parents had already left, politely declining Matt's invitation.

Drew and I gathered up all of Alex's presents as well as the photo displays and awards and stored everything in Matt's office. The two of us then went back out through the mall and outside to the parking lot, where Drew promptly fired up another cigarette.

"Wow," he said as he exhaled, "that first puff always tastes so good! Hey what a party, huh? Can you believe how it worked out?"

"No!" I exclaimed. "I thought this was gonna be the worst day of my life, but look at how it turned out."

"Well the days not over yet," said a voice behind us. I turned and saw Ryan standing behind me.

"Hey," I said, "what'd ya think of the party?"

Ryan shrugged his shoulders. "It was cool. You guys gonna tell me what all the fighting was about? How'd you really get that black eye? Looks to me like there's some trouble in Paradise."

Drew then interrupted. "There's no trouble, not unless someone decides to try making some."

"Hey man," said Ryan. "I don't have any interest in getting in your guys' shit. I'm happy now. After we met at Adam's party last month, I've started a very interesting relationship. I would've never thought Eric would be the kind of guy he is."

"What kinda guy is that?" asked Drew. I could tell by Drew's tone that he was almost as annoyed by Ryan as I had been the first time I'd met him.

"Well let's just say he makes me wonder what I ever saw in your *Master*." He said the last word in a tone dripping with sarcasm as he looked directly at me. I turned to Drew and rolled my eyes.

"Why do you say that, Ryan?" I shot back. "Did something leave a bad taste in your mouth the last time we saw you? Come on Drew, let's go wait at the car." We turned and walked away from Ryan, leaving him standing there alone.

12

My feelings towards Ryan became harder and harder to conceal, and although I knew that I had been very pointedly instructed by Matt to always be respectful and polite, he was one person that I found extremely difficult to even stomach. Our initial meeting had been several weeks prior when Matt took me to a gay club for the first time. Ryan had made no attempt to hide the fact that he was interested in Matt. To my chagrin, Matt had then taken me aside and severely scolded me for my own behavior, being that I was acting rudely and snottily towards Ryan. Matt had actually forced me to be polite to him and to apologize in spite of my own feelings of jealousy which were raging within me.

Our next encounter proved to be a very different situation. This occurred the very day that Matt and I had returned from our vacation. On the drive home we'd witnessed a horrific multiple-vehicular accident and had stopped to rescue several people who were trapped in their cars. A paramedic on the scene named Eric was impressed, and he invited us to spend the night at his house and attend a party, which was being thrown by his friend Adam. When we got to the party, Matt and I were both surprised to see Ryan in attendance.

Matt had promised me a surprise that night as a reward for the bravery I'd shown at the site of the accident, and he delivered me Ryan. At first I did not understand why he would bring this rival of mine into the privacy of our "bedroom" (so to speak), but I soon discovered that he was planning to order Ryan to service me orally. This was the very first and only time in my life that I had been sucked by another person. Previously I had only been afforded the pleasure of providing service, never receiving it.

It was obvious at the time that Ryan still desperately wanted Matt. He was so clearly attracted to him that it made me literally green with jealousy. It should have been virtually no surprise to me that other subs, or even women for that matter, would lust after Matt. After all he was the hottest guy that I knew, and I thanked my lucky stars about a million times per day that I had been given the privilege and honor of serving him as my Master. Yet for some reason Ryan just rubbed me the wrong way.

He always had some smart-assed remark to say, and he always made me feel as if he was trying to compete against me. In truth I would have just loved to be his friend. I did not consider myself to be the type of person who made a lot of enemies. Certainly there were haters like Devin who had beaten me up just because I was an easy target. Of course there would always be those religious nutcases who wanted to label all gay people as perverts and sinners. But for the most part, I had always felt that it was important to look for the good in other people, and by maintaining an attitude like this, it wasn't often that people despised me the way that Ryan seemed to.

Perhaps another reason why I disliked Ryan so much was because I felt threatened by him. He definitely was cute. I knew first hand that he was an expert cocksucker. He was intelligent and well spoken. There was no reason why a Dom like Matt would not look at him and desire to use him for pleasure. Frankly, I was surprised when I thought of it—that Matt had not chosen to use Ryan that night right in front of me. The only reason that he hadn't was because it was a promise he had made to me. He knew that it would hurt me too badly to watch him fucking some other guy.

It should have been a relief to me that Ryan had appeared to have finally moved on and hooked himself up with a partner. Eric seemed to be a good match for him. He was a good-looking guy who possessed a lot of self-confidence. He seemed far less authoritative or demonstrably dominant than Matt, but he wasn't someone that you'd ever be ashamed to call Master. But I had to wonder, if Ryan was indeed content in his new relationship, then why'd he decide to throw that little dig in about Matt. He must still be harboring some resentment about the fact that Matt had rejected him and chosen to be exclusive with me.

As we waited for Matt and Alex by the car, I told Drew about my feelings concerning Ryan. "That dude's a total flake," Drew assured me. "Don't waste a minute worrying about him. What you said to him was perfect." He laughed.

We were leaning against the car when Alex came bounding out of the building. "Hey Petey," he said. "I'm takin Drew with me over to Applebee's. Matt wants you back inside."

"Yes Sir," I said. "I guess we're gonna meet you over there?"

"Yup, I think he just wants to talk to you alone."

"Okay, thank you Sir," I said. "See you in a bit," I said to Drew as I squeezed his arm affectionately.

"Okay Petey-pup," he said. "We'll meet ya there."

As I headed back inside I passed Ryan, who was sitting on a ledge by the door. We both looked at each other briefly, but then I quickly looked down and headed straight inside. Neither of us said anything.

Eric was leaving the gym as I entered and told me that Matt was in the office. He also mentioned that he'd see me in a bit over at the restaurant.

It was dark when I walked into the gym. All the lights had been turned out except the security lights in the far corners. The front windows still had their coverings, not yet to be exposed until opening day Wednesday. It was quiet, and the cleaning crew had not yet arrived. It seemed that Matt and I were again alone here. This was the very same place where he'd bent me over a sawhorse the week before and plowed my ass mercilessly.

Slowly I closed the door behind me, but before I could take a step forward towards where I thought Matt was waiting, the lights came on again. This time they were not the bright overhead beams, but instead flickering and multicolored, and they came from a strobe located in the center of the ceiling. I froze in my tracks, waiting to see what was happening. Then slowly I heard music, very soft and romantic. I saw him, standing at the edge of the room right in front of the hallway that led into his office.

What I saw was merely a silhouette. It was definitely Matt, the man of my dreams, my knight in shining armor—but he was dressed much differently than I had seen him only moments before. Now he was wearing a suit—complete with sharply polished shoes, a crisply pressed shirt, and a tie. Of course the top button of his shirt was undone and the tie not pushed tightly against his neck. It made the look nearly perfect, just a hint of casual. Suddenly I felt self-conscious, as if I were a total slob standing there in my polo shirt and shorts.

As I slowly stepped closer to him, he spoke to me quietly. "Lock the door, pup." Quickly I turned and obeyed him. When I turned back around I discovered he had moved closer to me. He was now standing beside one of the weight benches. One of the security lights was on him almost like a spotlight. I nearly gasped at the sight of him for he was literally breathtaking. He didn't speak, but merely held out his hand.

It felt as if I moved in slow motion as I inched my way closer to him. "Why do you look so handsome, Sir?" I whispered.

He laughed and said, "Don't I always?"

"Oh yes, yes Sir. I'm sorry. I didn't mean it like that. Why're you dressed so sharp?"

"Got this suit for the grand opening. Wanted my pup to see it and tell me what he thinks."

I smiled back at him. "Can't you hear my heart beating Sir?" I whispered. "Doesn't my excitement tell you all you need to know?"

"Tells me my pup needs to be let out of his chastity," he said, reaching in his pocket and removing the small key.

"Oh Sir ..." I gasped, my heartbeat pounding in my ears.

"But first I need to know if you really do like my new duds. If I don't really excite you, no sense in un-caging ya. What'd be the point?" He looked down at me smugly. The way that he toyed with me was both maddening and thrilling. I smiled at him coyly.

"Tell me Sir, what do I need to do to prove it to you?" I think my voice had risen about an octave from the emotion I was feeling.

"Well, what about my shoes? These aren't cheap, ya know."

"Oh, they're awesome Sir. I bet they were at least a couple hundred bucks."

He laughed. "And then some. Try doubling it."

"And your suit Sir?"

"Custom made."

"And the silk tie, definitely not from K-Mart."

"Doesn't your Master deserve the best?" he asked. "Don't you think a guy like me should treat himself to the best of what life has to offer?"

Slowly I nodded. "You look so powerful Sir. To me you'll always be my jock hero, but right now you seem so much more than that. You seem so ... grown up."

He laughed right out loud. "I think maybe I'll just put this key away after all." He moved his hand back towards his pocket.

"No wait!" I exclaimed. "I just mean—well, I didn't mean you weren't grown-up looking before. You look like a powerful businessman now. Like someone who commands and deserves respect."

"I've always been all those things, boy," he said sternly.

"And now I'm reminded of them in the most powerful way." I maintained my eye contact with him, although everything inside of me said I should look away. "And I'm reminded of how unworthy I am to even be owned by you Sir." It was at this point that I did look down, staring directly at his brilliantly shined shoes.

"Do you want me to unlock it?" he asked flatly.

Again I nodded. "Yes Sir, please."

"Ask me the right way, and I may consider it." His tone continued to rebuke me. Without hesitation I then dropped to my knees.

"Please Sir!" I pleaded with him. "Please release me from my cage! Please give me the privilege of showing you my excitement." He stared down at me and casually pointed down to his shoes. Quickly I curled my body forward and pressed my lips against the shiny leather. He stood there statuesquely as I lapped at his imported shoes, bathing them ceaselessly with my tongue. I continued until he ordered me to stop nearly two minutes later.

"Stand up, boy," he ordered, "hands behind your back." Like a soldier I briskly complied and assumed the position. He then reached down and unbuttoned my shorts, roughly pulling them open and sliding down the fly. He let them fall to the floor. Then he cupped the bulge in my boxer-briefs, pressing his hand against the hard plastic encasement that surrounded my privates. He smiled evilly as he held me in his hand. "You know why I keep you locked in this cage, fagboy?" he asked.

I nodded as I looked up in his eyes once again. "Yes Sir," I whispered.

"You may think you know, little boy, but I doubt it. Tell me why I enjoy knowing you're all locked up." His tone was intended to taunt me, but having served him as long as I had, it merely excited me all the more.

"Sir, you enjoy keeping me in a cage because it protects me. You know I cannot do anything without your permission."

"And why would this matter? Why would I care?" His eyes were locked on my own.

I shivered a little as I felt the impact of his authority. "Because you love control."

And at this point he smiled very broadly. In fact he craned his neck back and laughed. A full-throated, straight-from-the-gut, hearty burst of laughter erupted from deep inside him. "Fuckin aye, I love control! I love every fuckin second of it! I love every single time that you squirm, knowing you're at my mercy! I love every single second that you wonder how much longer you have to endure your lock-down. I love being able to say 'yes' or 'no' based upon my whim and that alone, and you have absolutely no input in the matter whatsoever. What do you think of that, bitch boy?"

My eyes widened as I stared up at him, not knowing fully whether it was an honest answer he was seeking. Nonetheless it was honesty I provided him. "Sometimes I *don't* like it Sir. Sometimes I don't like it at all."

He continued to smile at me. "I know, little one. I fuckin know very well, and that's the beauty of it!" Without another word he then reached down and pulled my briefs outwards, sliding the key into place and unlocking the tiny padlock. He then casually tossed them both behind him. "Soon will come the day when we don't need these plastic cages. They're merely training devices. Eventually I will control you so entirely that it will take no more than a glance to bring you into submission."

"Please Sir, teach me to serve you better," I felt the tears welling in my eyes. "I wish for nothing more than to be under your absolute control as you describe."

"Take it off. Get rid of the chastity," he ordered, and I immediately complied. As I gingerly pulled it off of my flaccid penis, I felt the softness of the cotton briefs against my flesh. I was so sensitive that it tickled a little. He watched with amusement as I stifled the shiver that ran through my body. "Feel good?" he asked.

I nodded vigorously. "Oh yes Sir. Thank you Sir!"

He then pointed to my shorts, which were crumpled around my ankles. "Off!" he said, and I stepped out of them. As soon as I did so he pulled me close to him, wrapping his arms around me. I inhaled and took in the scent of his intoxicating cologne. I was wearing boarder sneaks, which I casually toed off my feet and kicked behind me.

"Dance with me, pup," he said, his voice suddenly so gentle. As I wrapped my arms tightly around him, I pressed my body against his deliberately. I wanted for him to feel my instantly growing arousal. I wanted him to know that he did indeed excite me. The music swelled around us as I stepped up and placed my socked feet on top of his expensive, crisply polished Italian shoes. He then swayed back and forth ever so slightly and wrapped me securely in his enormously protective embrace.

All of the day's drama then simply washed away. The music, the lights, the smell of his cologne, the feel of his hard body against my own, the security of his strength—these things all synergistically combined and swept away every trace of anxiety or worry. All was now again right in the world, as I clung passionately to my Master.

The feel of his lips upon mine as he leaned in to kiss me was like a drink of water to one who'd been wandering aimlessly in the desert. I devoured him, pressing my mouth firmly against his, forcing my tongue deeply into his eager mouth. Had there ever been a moment when I was more aroused, I certainly now could not remember when it was. As the romance of the moment was swept away by our passion, he too responded to me aggressively. He wrapped both hands around my cotton-clad buttocks and squeezed me, pulling me even tighter against his body. As I felt him pulling upwards, I lifted my legs and allowed him to pick me up off the ground. I wrapped my small legs around his powerful waist.

It took him only seconds to walk me over to the weight bench, his mouth never leaving my own. He leaned forward and pinned me on the bench beneath him, and I kept my legs wrapped tightly around him. I knew my hard-on was pressing against him. I knew that at this point my excitement was utterly undeniable. He pulled away from me, but not without protest from me. I so desperately needed his body next to my own that I nearly whimpered when he easily broke free from the clutch of my desperate embrace.

He reached down then and violently pulled the briefs from my body, tossing them behind us along with the trail of my other clothing. Then he stopped. He froze as he leaned over me and simply stared at my trembling body, which was lying there beneath him. He then reached down and ripped my polo shirt up over my head. I flopped back down on the bench, now lying there wearing nothing but my white crew socks. The look on his face as he stared at me, taking in every inch of my naked flesh, it was a look unlike anything I'd ever seen. It was so unfamiliar to me, and yet so amazingly hot! He was lusting for me!

My Master then leaned into me and began kissing me, starting at my neck. I writhed on the bench beneath him, feeling the weight of his body pressing against me. The feel of his light stubble tickled my neck and chin as he brushed his lips against my flesh—first gently and then more aggressively. He kissed me over and over, hundreds of times, back and forth across my neck, down my torso until he found my little brown nipples. The feel of his tongue as it darted across them was like an electric shock traveling through my body, and I arched my back involuntarily. A sound escaped my throat unlike any I'd ever uttered. It was laughter combined with moaning, and I thought for sure I would cum right then and there.

He did not stop. He continued to bathe my torso with his kisses, inching his way further down my body. He pushed my rock-hard cock gently aside and buried his tongue deep into my belly button, again making me go crazy. He kissed me and kissed me, as if he simply couldn't stop. And then he did something that I never in a million years would have imagined.

He took me in his mouth.

13

What happened after Matt—my Master, my hero, my protector, my everything—took me into his mouth for the very first time ever, was something that is beyond description. He obviously had no intention of sucking me the way I always sucked him. His intention was not to serve me or even to bring me to orgasm. It was a part of the passionate expression of his undeniable attraction to me. It seemed to me as if he was truly worshipping me the way that I had done to him a million and fifty times before.

I lay there disbelieving what I was experiencing, and though it lasted merely a few seconds it was heaven on the face of the earth to me. I was inside my Master! Was it right? Was it as it should be? Was it an indication that he was any less than I'd always imagined him to be?

Any doubts that I may have briefly had about his dominance were very quickly swept away when seconds later he plunged his cock deep inside my tight hole and began fucking me with abandon. He was fully dressed in his tailor-made Italian suit, raping my naked body mercilessly and savagely as I lay beneath him spread out on the weight bench. He held my legs by the ankles as he leaned over me and plugged me violently. He was moaning and grunting almost like a savage animal, yet looked so goddamned businesslike in his three-piece suit. Within a matter of minutes I was on the verge of erupting myself.

"Sir, I'm gonna cum! Oh god!! Sir!! Sir!!!"

"Shoot it pup!" he commanded. And then he fucked every drop of cum from my tiny body. His thrusting into my body seemed to drive it out of me as I screamed in orgasmic pleasure. It was volcanic in its intensity as it blasted all over my naked torso.

And then seconds later he too reached the point of no return and buried himself deep within me, grinding his hips forward to achieve maximum penetration. I felt the pump of his cock as he emptied himself completely into me.

We then cleaned ourselves up and headed for the shower. Within minutes we were at Applebee's in the company of our four friends. "What took you so long?" asked Drew casually.

"Oh, sorry. Matt wanted my opinion on a new suit he'd bought. He was showin it to me."

Drew raised his eyebrows. "And what was the verdict? Did you like it?"

"Should be just fine, I think. It's an awesome looking suit." I then leaned in to whisper in Drew's ear, "You wouldn't happen to know something that will get cum stains out of an expensive Italian suit, would you?"

Drew just smiled knowingly. We had a great dinner.

* * *

It ended up being such an incredibly long day, and I was frankly quite exhausted by the time we headed home. Eric and Ryan had stayed through dinner and were actually extremely courteous and social, but they left shortly after eating. Perhaps Ryan was on his best behavior being that three of our superiors were present. During the meal Matt invited the couple to join us the following weekend for some activity, which was yet to be decided. I wasn't thrilled by that news, but at least I knew it meant I'd again be with Matt.

It was odd that the events, which had transpired during the early part of the day, seemed to be completely forgotten. There was no further discussion of Alex hitting me or of Matt punching Alex. It just sort of seemed the whole drama had been forgotten. What we did discuss, though, was the success of the party and how much of a surprise it actually was to both Alex and me.

Finally when we got home, I made a beeline to my bedroom and changed into some comfy sleep pants and a tee. The four of us sat in the living room together, Matt and I together on the sofa while Drew sat at Alex's feet as he reclined in one of his comfortable chairs. Matt was the one who started the discussion.

"Drew and Petey, I'm giving you permission to speak freely," he began. "If we are going to get beyond the incidents that happened earlier today, we have to make sure we get everything out in the open right here and now. This is the time and place to say anything and everything that you feel or think. If you're pissed about anything, speak now or forever hold your peace." He looked at each of us one at a time, and Drew and I looked at one another.

I felt my heart begin to beat a little faster, fearing that what I had thought had been settled already may now suddenly reemerge and rear its ugly head. I had sensed earlier that Drew was not pleased with Matt, and I was afraid he may actually be brave enough to tell him so, especially now that he'd been granted permission to speak freely.

Quickly Drew glanced back at Alex, waiting to see if his Master was about to say anything, and when Alex did not speak, Drew turned back around and sighed. Then finally he spoke up. "Sir," he stated respectfully, looking directly at Matt. "I do have something I want to say."

"Go ahead. I said to speak freely."

Drew then looked down at the ground in front of him, appearing to fear direct eye contact with Matt. "I know it is not my place to question you or your judgment, but I am confused and ... well ... and honestly a little bit angry by what you did today. I mean by the way you handled the situation."

I couldn't believe Drew had the balls to say what he was now saying to my Master. I waited, expecting Matt to jump from his seat at any moment to put him in his place. Instead, though, Matt sat calmly beside me and responded. "Which situation specifically?" he asked.

"Sir, I'm talking about the surprise party. You must have known how upset and distraught that Alex was gonna be when he thought you'd taken me in the middle of the night to fuck me. I just think it was kinda mean."

I looked over at Alex, then back at Matt. I wondered if Alex would say anything at this point, but he just sat there listening. Again Matt did not seem upset in the least by Drew's criticism.

"Drew, I think you're right. It definitely was a mean thing to do. May not've been the smartest thing I've ever done either. Never said I was perfect, and if I had the chance to do it over again I probably would do some stuff differently."

My heart suddenly was breaking, hearing my Master offer up such a confession. I couldn't remain silent any longer. "Drew," I said, "Matt just threw your Master the most awesome graduation party in the history of the world, and you think he was mean? I don't think that's right for you to even say such a thing!"

Matt put his hand on my shoulder, obviously sensing that I was about to rise to my feet. "Calm down, pup," he said quietly. "Drew has a right to say what he thinks. I gave permission for everyone to speak freely."

"I'm sorry, Petey," said Drew sincerely. "I'm not criticizing Matt. I just gotta say how I feel." He then looked back at Matt. "Sir, I think if you hadn't decided to do it that way, none of this fighting would've happened. Alex wouldn't have gotten so upset and hit Petey."

Finally Alex spoke. "Drew, I shouldn't 've ever hit Petey, no matter what. No matter what Petey said to me or how pissed I was, it was not my place to lay a hand on him, at least not like that. I'm responsible for my own actions." I then noticed how Drew reached between Alex's leg and placed his hand affectionately against his calf, rubbing it tenderly. He was such a devoted sub to his Master, I thought.

Matt then again responded, "Alex and I had a long conversation about all of this shit already. We are cool with one another. We know why we both did what we did. The issues I have with Alex concerning how he handled Petey we will deal with Master-to-Master. You two don't gotta worry bout it. Understand?"

We both nodded and said simultaneously, "yes Sir."

"Drew, you're right. If I hadn't made Alex think that I had you up at the cabin fuckin your brains out, he probably wouldn't 've freaked the way he did. We could have figured out a way to get you over to the gym to help with the party setup without making him think I was betraying his friendship."

"Sir," I then said, "wouldn't you have been upset if another Master took me away somewhere to fuck me and just left you a note?"

Matt smiled at me and thought for a minute. "I'd track him down and rip him apart limb-by-limb," he stated matter-of-factly. "But I'm not just some Master. I think the situation is a little more complex than that. Alex and I already had an agreement that Drew would serve me last night. I just was pushin the envelope a little further."

"If you really thought that Alex had a right to be so upset like that, Sir," Drew stated, "then why did you haul off and punch him the way you did?"

For the first time since our conversation started Matt's voice took on a much sterner tone. "Didn't punch Alex cuz he was upset. Punched him cuz he decked my pup!"

"Drew," Alex said, "I would've done exactly the same thing if *any*one ever hit you. I swear I would kick their fuckin ass, and that is exactly what Matt did. It was completely a reflex. Petey is his sub, and it's Matt's job to protect him. It's his instinct to do so."

"And it's *my* instinct to get pissed when I see someone punch my Master! Twice!" Drew was now on the verge of tears.

"Drew, I'm so sorry!" I said, now starting to cry myself. "It was my fault, not Matt's. I was the one who swore at Alex. I was the one who got him upset, not Matt!" Matt put his arm around me and pulled me next to him.

"It's not your fault, Petey," he said calmly. "And Drew it's not your fault for being pissed and for wanting to defend your Master. Subs are supposed to be loyal. Always." I looked up at Matt through my tears and realized that I could not have ever been more proud of him than I was at that very moment. "Petey and I haven't yet had our conversation about his backtalk to Alex. What he said to Alex is not acceptable, and he will be punished, but that's not the purpose of this conversation now. What I want to make sure of is that from this point forward we make an agreement that we deal with our issues maturely, that we talk things out instead of throwing punches."

All of us nodded in agreement. "And no disrespect. No swearing at your Masters. No arguing when a Master tells you no." He looked directly at me as he said this, and I hung my head shamefully.

"Yes Sir," I said meekly.

"This means that when Alex is responsible for looking after you, you'd better show him the same level of respect that you show me. Understand?"

"Yes Sir," I repeated.

"Same applies to you, Drew," Alex said. "Understand?"

"Yes Sir," Drew responded.

"Okay," Matt said seriously. "Gonna ask each one of you, startin with Alex, do you have anything else you need or want to say about this topic? If nobody has anything else, we are cool and don't ever need to discuss it again. But if there are any other unstated feelings or gripes, say em now. Got it?" We all nodded. "Alex?"

"Just that I'm glad we worked this out, and again that I'm sorry for hittin Petey," Alex said with sincerity.

"Okay, Drew?" Matt said.

"Sir, I am sorry for being mad at you today. I was pissed about the whole situation and I think I blamed you unfairly. Plus I was afraid of losing Petey. He's my very best friend." Tears were now streaming down Drew's cheeks.

Matt smiled at Drew affectionately before moving on. "Petey?"

I still had my gaze upon Drew and wanted more than anything to just get up and go to him right then. I wanted to hug him so tightly. "Sir, I am so proud to have you for my Master. I'm ashamed I was such a bad pup, talking back to Alex the way I did, and I think I deserved this black eye. Please forgive me."

"Everything's forgiven, pup," Matt said. "Okay, my turn. When I agreed to let Petey move in here I knew it was the best thing for both him and me. Of all the sub guys I have met so far, none have even compared to Drew. He is the perfect example of how a sub should be, and Petey you're lucky to have him as your friend. Alex is also a cool peep, my best bud. I sort of think of the four of us as bein a family in a way. I think it's important to work shit out. Life's not perfect, but when people care about each other, they gotta make the effort.

"I feel like I might not have made all the right decisions with this whole situation. I'm a fuckin awesome Master, we all know that, but I'm not perfect. I'm still human. If I could go back and do shit different, I would not have put Alex and Petey in that situation where they were upset enough to get all freaked the way they did.

"Still Petey was wrong to backtalk Alex, and Alex was wrong to hit Petey. I think all of us agree on that. I'll talk to Petey alone about his punishment later.

"Okay, I guess that's all I got to say. Case closed."

Drew then snuggled up against his Master's legs, and I slipped back into Matt's arms as Alex turned on the television. The four of us sat there together and watched *Queer As Folk* and then the first part of an HBO movie, but I was so tired that I fell asleep against Matt's body. At some point he must have carried me to bed. I woke up in the morning and rubbed the sleep out of my eyes, trying to remember all that had happened the day before. I slipped out of bed lazily and padded my way to the kitchen. I guess I'd make some coffee and start breakfast for Alex and Drew. As I glanced in the living room I noticed Matt sleeping on the sofa.

Apparently he had decided not to try squeezing himself alongside me in my little twin bed. I stopped and took the sight of him in. His size-twelve, socked feet were draped over the armrest of the sofa, and he was lying there fully clothed. I tiptoed over to him and pulled his blanket up around him. It had all but slid completely off of him. Carefully I spread it out and gingerly tucked it around his masculine body. I wanted so badly to kiss his beautiful face right then, but I feared waking him. As I quietly stepped back away from the couch and turned to go to the kitchen, he spoke.

"No morning kisses?" he said.

"Oh Sir, I didn't mean to wake you. I'm so sorry."

"Come ere," he said, holding his arms out to me. "Nah, didn't wake me. I'm gonna buy you a bigger bed. This sucks sleepin on this couch," he laughed as he kissed me tenderly.

"Why didn't you sleep in my bed, Sir?" I asked. "I could've slept on the floor beside you."

"Pup needed his rest after a long day," he yawned. "Sides, you got another big day ahead of you today."

"I do Sir?" I asked, waiting to hear what he meant.

"Yeah," he had pulled himself up into a sitting position. "The first part of your punishment is today."

I quickly looked away from him and stared at the ground, feeling a wave of shame wash over me. "Yes Sir," I said quietly.

"Don't ya wanna know what it is?" he asked. I nodded slowly but did not speak. He then pointed to the floor. "Kneel down pup," he said, and I instantly slipped into the servile position before my Master. "What time is it now, pup?" he asked.

"It's about 7:30, Sir," I said.

"Okay, so you're gonna get yourself cleaned up and be ready to go by nine. Understand?"

"Yes, Sir," I said. "May I ask where I'm going, Sir?"

"Don't know," said Matt casually. "It's not for me to decide. You're not gonna be spending the day with me."

I glanced back up into his face. "With Alex, Sir?" I asked meekly.

He shook his head. "Nope. Ryan's gonna be here to pick you up. You'll be spending the whole day with him. He's gonna have charge of you and you're gonna respect him just like you would a Master. Then he's gonna bring you back to me and report how you did. Understand?"

My mouth nearly hit the floor when he said these dreadful words. I simply knelt there, feeling my face redden as I tried to force myself to somehow respond.

"Pup, do you understand?" Matt repeated more sternly.

"Yes, Sir," I whispered. "Yes, Sir, I understand."

"Good. Now get over here and blow me before you start getting ready."

14

I was standing in front of the bathroom mirror brushing my teeth when Drew walked in. He said good morning and went about his business of relieving himself, yawning as he did so. When he finished up and turned to face me, he suddenly had a startled look on his face. "Petey, what's wrong? Why are you crying?"

I motioned for my best friend to close the bathroom door, and he quickly did so. "Ahm bee-en punissed to-aye," I cried, with the toothbrush still in my mouth.

"I don't understand you, hon," Drew said, placing his arm around my shoulder. I removed the toothbrush and spit into the sink, wiping my mouth with the back of my hand.

"I'm being punished today," I said. "Matt is making me spend the day with Ryan."

"Aw, well don't cry, Petey," Drew said compassionately. "It might not be so bad." The horrified look on his face betrayed him though, in spite of his attempt to offer me reassurance.

"And he said ..." my voice was now cracking, "that I have to treat him as if he were my Master."

Drew's mouth dropped open. "No way! You have *got* to be kidding me!"

I shook my head, confirming the incredulous reality. "Why would he make me serve Ryan, the one single person on the face of the earth who hates my guts?"

Drew sighed. "I don't know, Petey. I'm so sorry. That punishment would suck."

"It *does* suck!" I exclaimed. "How can I possibly take orders from that—"

235

"Asshole," Drew finished.

"Exactly!"

"Sit down," Drew instructed me, pushing me over toward the toilet as he lowered the lid with his free hand. "Petey, you probably think that I'm such a good sub that I've never had to be punished." He smiled at me and paused. "But really when I was younger, I was a shit. I used to have a Master who punished me all the time, and it was awful."

"How'd he punish you?" I asked.

"Used to get spanked a lot. I had to do extra chores. Chastity. Got privileges taken away. There were a lot of different ways, but he finally realized that the best way for him to punish me was to force me to do things I hated most."

"Like Matt's doin to me," I said.

"Right. He knows that you and Ryan don't like each other. He knows that Ryan's the one person above all others that you'd never wanna spend time with, so he is forcing you to do it. The punishment was for showing disrespect to Alex, so he's making you show respect to someone you really can't stand. It sort of makes sense."

"But it'll be so hard," I whined.

"Yeah, hon, it's gonna be hard, but that's kinda the idea, right?" I nodded.

Just then I was immediately startled by a loud knock on the bathroom door. "Petey, get out here!" It was Matt.

"Shit!" I whispered to Drew. "I'm coming, Sir," I hollered back towards the door as I quickly planted an affectionate kiss on Drew's cheek and then shot up and bolted towards the door. As I swung the door open I was a bit startled not to see Matt on the other side of the threshold but instead Ryan. He had a smirk on his face, looking smug as ever, and he crossed his arms over his chest cockily as he looked down at me.

"Hey, Petey pup," he said, "you as excited as me bout spendin some quality time together today? Huh?" He waited a couple seconds as if he expected me to answer. "I hope so

...” His voice went up an octave or two and his smirk morphed into a broad grin.

I glanced over at Drew and saw him glaring hatefully right at Ryan as if to say, “Petey might have to respect you, but I sure as hell don’t.”

“Um, yes Sir,” I said quietly, looking down at Ryan’s feet. I couldn’t bring myself to look him directly in the eye, especially with him acting so cocky the way he was.

“Good, cuz I’m real excited about it. Couldn’t believe it last night when Matt called me. He said it was a special assignment, and then when he explained exactly what it was, well ... let’s just say I got *real* excited!” He reached down and groped himself then in an obscene way, which nearly made me wanna puke.

Drew could remain silent no more. “I thought you said yesterday that you didn’t even like Matt. Why’re you acting now like the two of you are best buds?”

“Never said I didn’t like him,” Ryan responded. “I said I was glad I met Eric. He’s the perfect Master for me. Doesn’t mean, though, that Matt is any less hot than he’s always been.”

“Yeah, well just remember that today when you’re responsible for his most prized possession—Petey! You better treat him good and take care of him!” Drew was pointing his finger at Ryan defiantly.

Ryan laughed. “Don’t go pointin at me, Drew. I don’t take my orders from you. And as for Petey, I’m gonna treat him *exactly* the way Matt told me to. Maybe you should just mind your own fuckin business for a change.” He then roughly grabbed hold of my bicep and pulled me through the door, shoving me down the hall in front of him. I stumbled then quickly steadied myself so as not to trip. As I turned to glance back at Drew I saw him standing in the doorway with his fists clenched tightly, obviously ready to throw a punch. Thankfully, he remained in control and I headed straight for the living room, praying my Master was still there to witness all of this.

Matt was indeed in the living room, sitting comfortably in the recliner. I wanted more than anything to run to him and have him wrap his protective arms around me, but I knew it wasn't going to happen. He had told me yesterday how much he loved the complete control that he held over me, and today his actions evidenced this claim. It was precisely as Drew had just stated to me in the bathroom. Matt was forcing me to do the one thing I hated most. He was forcing me to obey the one person on earth that I resented most.

The reason that I disliked Ryan was not really because he recognized how awesome my Master was. I truly hoped that everyone saw this about Matt. I loved him with all my heart, and for him to be respected and admired was my goal, not something that I was in any way jealous of. But in my heart I did not so much believe that Ryan's feelings about Matt were genuine. Had I felt they were, then I would have been far more likely to be tolerant and understanding of Ryan's antics. I knew more than anything that I was the luckiest sub in the world to have a Master like Matt. Of course it would be natural for other subs like Ryan to envy me for this.

It was the fact that Ryan seemed so disingenuous to me. He seemed pretentious and phony. He was this way not only about Matt but with everyone else as well. Almost every time I was around him he was sugary sweet to me in the presence of Matt, and then he'd say cutting things to me behind Matt's back. He also had made that remark about Matt yesterday, implying that my Master was inferior to his own. I wished that I'd have told Matt about it yesterday, and then perhaps he wouldn't have sentenced me to my upcoming Hell Day.

Matt pointed to the ground as I approached his chair, and I immediately assumed my humble position at his feet. As I slid to my knees I felt my eyes welling with tears, but I willed myself to be strong. I wanted to take my punishment like a man, to somehow make my Master proud of me. Were I to begin crying, he would realize just how weak and immature I really was. So I knelt there silently, my hands clasped behind my back and my head bowed in submission.

What Matt did next was horrifying to me, and it not only humbled and shamed me, but it also nearly broke my heart right in two. He reached beside himself in the chair and pulled out my collar. Then he held it out to Ryan. "Put it on him," he said curtly.

I heard Drew's gasp behind me as Ryan eagerly snatched the collar from Matt's hand. "Thank you, Sir," Ryan said enthusiastically as he stepped over to position himself directly beside me. I lifted my head up to expose my neck to him but continued to focus my gaze downward at the ground. I would not look up at him at all. I didn't want to even see his face. Then I felt the leather around my neck as his long, feminine fingers snapped the buttons together, securing the collar snugly. It was the sound of those buttons as they snapped together that humiliated me most.

"Petey," Matt spoke to me sternly, "do you understand your instructions?"

I nodded and then quietly answered, "Yes Sir, I understand."

"And they are what?" Matt asked, forcing me to verbalize them back to him.

"I will obey Ryan today as if he were a Master, Sir."

"That's right. Ryan will have charge of you for the next eight hours. When he is done, he'll return you to me safely. You will be unharmed. You will have no new bruises or scrapes or broken bones." It was as if Matt were stating these things as much for Ryan's benefit as my own. "And he will report to me whether or not you were obedient. If you have failed him in any way, you will have also failed me. Do you understand?"

"Yes Sir," I whimpered, now right on the verge of bursting into tears.

Matt then turned his attention to Ryan. "Okay, guy," he said, "take good care of my pup, and remember the things we talked about. Don't worry about whether or not Petey is enjoyin himself. Suppose ta be punishment. But don't hurt him either. If you do, you'll have me to answer to."

"Oh no Sir, don't worry," Ryan stated confidently. "I'm not gonna hurt him, and I bet he'll end up enjoyin it more than he'll ever admit." I could only imagine what that comment was supposed to mean.

"Get up and get your shoes on, Petey," Matt instructed. "Time to go."

Quickly I scurried over to the front door where my shoes were and slipped them on, too ashamed to look up at anyone though it felt as if all eyes were on me. Suddenly Ryan was beside me pressing the palm of his hand against the small of my back, ushering me out the door. I glanced back quickly to see Drew standing behind us staring wide-eyed. I wondered what he thought of all this after our family meeting the night before. I hoped it wouldn't in any way cause him to again resent or mistrust Matt.

As sad and nervous as I was about spending time with Ryan, I truly did understand why my Master had chosen to punish me. Alex after all was his very best friend, and I had certainly breached the bond of trust that the two of them shared by cursing Alex. If Matt did not have confidence in the fact that he could know with certainty I would obey him when he instructed me to respect his friends, then how would he ever regard me as a loyal pup?

Since I had failed to obey and respect Alex in the manner I was ordered, it was only logical that Matt would reassign this lesson to me. This time he was trying to teach me that it did not matter whether I liked the person or not that he chose. All that was important was the fact that he had chosen them, and that I was to simply obey. It was not my place to question them or their judgment. Matt also knew that by placing Ryan in a position of temporary superiority over me, he was indeed doling out a fairly humiliating punishment to me. He knew how much Ryan irritated me. He knew that my feeling of jealousy towards Ryan was an issue with which I struggled. And he also knew that Ryan very well may have been waiting for the day to come when he'd be able to exact a little revenge upon me for the time he'd been ordered to give me head.

It was that last factor that made me most nervous of all. As the two of us walked out of the apartment complex towards Ryan's car, I kept thinking of the cocky way he had stood in the bathroom doorway, groping himself obscenely. My heart beat a little bit faster as I thought about what that gesture had meant. If Ryan did indeed plan to serve up a little bit of revenge, his would be the very first cock I had ever sucked other than my Master's or Drew's.

If Matt did allow this to happen, then what would it mean for me in the future? It surprised me that Matt would even condone the notion that his pup was sexually serving anyone other than him, let alone a sub the likes of Ryan.

Of course I did not know at this point exactly what Matt, or Ryan for that matter, had in mind for me that day. Perhaps Ryan was merely going to use me as a domestic servant. Maybe he would give me orders to clean his dorm room or wash his car. Maybe he was going to take me in public and make me display my collar as a means of humiliating me. Maybe he was going to spank me or tickle-torture me or place me in bondage. The fact that Matt had pointedly stated that Ryan was to make sure I was not injured or bruised led me to believe that there may be some sort of pain involved. Otherwise why would Matt have to caution Ryan about limitations?

As I crawled into the passenger seat of Ryan's car I felt like a prisoner who was being hauled off to jail. It was all that I could do to keep myself from becoming emotional, for I felt like simply bursting into tears. I wanted more than anything to just bolt from the car and run back into the apartment. I wanted to throw myself at my Master's feet and beg him to reconsider my punishment. Wasn't it enough that I had this big black eye? Wasn't it enough that I had almost lost my very best friend? Wasn't it enough that I had truly learned my lesson already? If I reasoned with Matt, perhaps he would see things differently. Perhaps he would show mercy on me.

As I thought of these things a tear trickled down my cheek. I did not bolt out of the car, though. I just sat there staring blankly out the window as Ryan started the engine and backed out of the parking place. I glanced up towards Drew's apartment and saw him standing there on the balcony. He was watching us pull out and puffing nervously on a cigarette. He stared down at me, and we locked into one another's gaze. I wondered what he would say about all this tonight after it was over. I wondered if it would in any way change the way he felt about me.

Ryan drove a small, sporty car, but it wasn't expensive. It had a spoiler on the back to give the impression that it was cool, but like Ryan, his car wasn't all that. Although he didn't immediately speak to me as we pulled out of the lot, he continued to maintain a cocky, shit-eatin grin on his face, obviously enjoying every second of my humiliation.

His first comment to me was when he pulled into the gas station. He handed me a fifty and said, "Fill it up. Clean the windows too."

I looked at him directly in the eye, wanting more than anything to tell him to bite me, but I simply replied "Yes Sir." As I was cleaning his windshield, I noticed he was talking on his cell phone, completely ignoring me. I decided to simply take my time. I carefully used the sponge to soap up every square centimeter of the window and then slowly scraped off the water with the squeegee. When I was done with the front windshield I moved to the side windows, cleaning each of them as meticulously as I'd done the first. When I was all done and had thrown away the blue towels

I'd used and hung back up the squeegee, Ryan rolled down his window.

"Do the windshield again. You left streaks on it, and hurry up!" Before I could respond, he'd rolled up his window.

I could see how this day was gonna go already. I sighed to myself and returned to my duties while Ryan sat comfortably in his car. When I got completely done I went inside and paid the cashier. She looked at me rather strangely, obviously noting the dog collar around my neck, but didn't say anything. I returned to the car and gave Ryan his change. He was still on the phone and did not even acknowledge my presence.

"Listen, I gotta go. See you in class tomorrow, okay? ... All right, talk to ya later, bye." He then started the car and pulled over to the side of the building. There was a large canister vacuum next to the wall. "Did you get any quarters when you were in there?" he asked me.

"No, Sir. Sorry, I didn't know I was supposed to."

"Go back and get some then. Jesus Christ!" I looked down at my lap, feeling my face redden. I was waiting for him to hand me some currency but instead he simply said, "Hurry up!" I jumped out of the car again, digging into my pocket as I did so. Luckily I had a five-dollar bill. I wondered briefly if I could get away with removing my collar before I went in there again, but since he'd instructed me to hurry I figured I shouldn't take any chances.

Just as I rounded the corner of the building and headed for the entrance door I looked up to see a familiar face. It was my coworker Jason. It was too late for me to turn away. "Oh my God, Petey!" he exclaimed. "What'd ya do to your face?"

Obviously he was referring to the black eye. "Oh hi Jason," I said, trying to sound light hearted. "Can you believe it? I hit my eye against the car door yesterday." I laughed.

"Wow! I thought someone punched you or something. Doesn't it hurt?" He held the door of the store open for me, waiting for me to walk through.

"Oh, it did, but not now. What're ya doin? Do you have to work today?"

"Tonight. Dude, that's kinda int'resting," he pointed to my collar, and I felt myself blushing again.

"Oh ... um ... yeah. It's just something I wear sometimes." He raised his eyebrows as I said this and smiled.

"Whatever floats yer boat, man," he said. I quickly stepped up to the counter to get my change.

"Good seein ya, Jason." Just as I said this and turned away from him, the entrance door opened and Ryan stepped in.

"I thought I told ya to hurry up, Petey!" he said. The cashier and Jason both stared at him disbelievingly. "Come on! I don't have all damned day."

At this point he was just starting to sound silly. It seemed to me that he was trying a bit too hard to act dominant. This realization did not in any way lessen my humiliation, though. I could only imagine what Jason must have been thinking. And with him making note of my black eye, I wondered if he was starting to put two and two together and drawing conclusions that were not exactly correct. He probably was starting to assume that Ryan was my boyfriend—that he beat me and made me wear a dog collar. I smiled a little to myself as I thought about it.

"Sorry SIR!" I said loudly, "I'm coming." Then I glanced quickly behind me to see that Jason was still looking. He was hatefully glaring right at Ryan. I'm not sure why I enjoyed myself so much in that brief moment, but it just felt really good to see that yet one more person disliked this bastard who was my Master-for-the-day.

After I got my quarters, Ryan instructed me to go vacuum out the car. He stayed inside and got himself a beverage and some snacks. I knelt down on the ground beside the car and thoroughly vacuumed the floors and seats. It made me feel so humble to kneel that way, knowing that my assignment was part of my punishment. Oddly it did not make me angry at all. In fact, it almost felt right in a way. Kneeling to serve my Master was something I had always enjoyed doing, and now if wrapped my mind around it the right way, I knew that this was exactly what I was doing now. I was serving Matt, not Ryan. I was obeying my Master and complying with his instructions.

I heard Ryan step up behind me just as the vacuum was turning off. He placed his hand on my shoulder. "You like it, don't you Petey?" he asked. "You like being on your knees serving."

"Don't you?" I asked. "I mean, don't you SIR?"

He laughed. "Yeah, I do like it. You're right. In fact, I guess you could say I need it."

"No offense, Sir," I said, "but it's kind of obvious you're not used to giving orders."

"Really?" he sounded genuinely surprised. "Why would you say that?"

"Ryan, you're trying too hard. You keep yelling at me, ordering me to hurry up when you know I'm already hurrying."

"And it pisses you off, I bet," he smirked, "cuz you know you gotta take it. You gotta take everything I dole out to you."

"No Sir, I mean it did sort of annoy me at first, but right now it just seems a little bit silly. Think about it. Do you really think that Matt or Alex or Eric would act like that?" As I turned to look up at my pretend Master, I saw that it now was his face that was reddening.

"Just shut the fuck up, bitch, and do your work. And from now on, don't talk to me unless I give a direct order or ask a question. Got it?"

I looked back down at the floor, "Yes Sir."

When I finally finished vacuuming the car, Ryan took me over to his apartment. I had thought he lived in a dorm room but was surprised to discover that he and two other guys from school shared their own apartment. Neither of them was home at the time, so I had no idea what they were like. I wondered if his roommates were gay, and if they were, I wondered if they were subs like him.

Once Ryan introduced me to their bathroom, though, I was fairly certain that he did not have gay roommates, and if he did, they were by far the biggest slobs I had ever seen. Granted, the assumption that gay men are neater and cleaner than straight guys is a stereotype, but I truly did not see how any self-respecting fag would ever be able to tolerate a bathroom such as this one. For one thing, it reeked of piss. It seemed to me that whoever had been using it did not take the time to even bother aiming before they began emptying their bladder. In addition to the smelly condition of the commode area, the sink looked as if it hadn't been scrubbed in months, and so did the shower. There was debris and junk piled up everywhere, and the mirrors were spackled with toothpaste spittle and various other unidentifiable smudges. The trash was overflowing. It appeared the guys had just continued to throw garbage into it even when there was no room left, creating a mountain on top of the canister and a stack of trash all over the floor.

I stood in the doorway staring at the mess as Ryan waited behind me. He began to laugh. "This oughta keep ya busy for a while, dogboy," he said. "That's what ya are, aren't ya? Matt's little *dog*boy."

Now at this point I was genuinely pissed, and it had nothing whatsoever to do with the bathroom. I wanted more than anything at that moment to just knee the bastard right in the nuts, but I instead turned to look up at him, gritting my teeth. "Sir," I said slowly, "please don't call me that. I am Matt's *pup*, not his dogboy."

Ryan shrugged. "Well today you're *my* dogboy, so get used to it." He was glaring at me hatefully, and for a second I thought he just might smack me. "And don't be tellin me what I can and can't call you! If you don't fuckin start showin me a little more respect I'm gonna call Matt right now!"

"Sir," I said nervously, "please don't call him. I'm sorry. You're right—you can call me whatever you choose."

"Good. Glad we got that straight. Now before you start cleanin up this mess I want you to go fix me some lunch. When you're done with that, you can start on this pigsty of a bathroom and then the kitchen. Don't take all day either, cuz I have more work for ya when you're done."

I looked to the ground as he doled out my orders and said quietly, "Yes Sir."

The condition of the kitchen was slightly better than the bathroom, but not by much. I found some boneless chicken breasts and a few vegetables in the fridge, and so I decided to whip Ryan up a stir-fry. At least it was something easy. I could only imagine what he'd do if he didn't happen to like it. It actually kind of surprised me to see that the guys had decent food in the house. They seemed to live like typical straight bachelors, and I expected to find old pizza boxes and leftover fast food containers. Instead it seemed their kitchen was stocked with some pretty healthy staples. Perhaps it was Ryan who did the grocery shopping.

I also noticed when I was walking through the hallway that Ryan's room was extremely neat and tidy. It seemed to be the one place in the apartment that was actually inhabitable. I was a little confused as to why he wouldn't have made a greater effort to keep the bathroom clean. My questions were soon answered, however, when Ryan got up out of his easy chair and strode down the hallway to his room. A few moments later I heard a toilet flushing and water running. He had his own bathroom in his room. What a creep! He was making me clean up this pigsty bathroom, which wasn't even his.

It was only a matter of about twenty minutes for me to prepare Ryan's lunch. When it was ready, I dished up a large serving and carried it into him in the living room. "Sir, would you like to eat your lunch in here or at the dining room table?"

"Set it down there, dogboy," he said, pointing to the coffee table in front of him. "Then go get me a tray. They're in the corner of the dining room. And I want a Diet Coke. Hurry up!"

Oh cripes, he was starting again with that crap. I did not say anything this time, though. I simply complied quickly with all of his orders. He had the television on and his feet propped up comfortably on an ottoman when I left him and began the daunting task of tackling that bathroom.

It took me well over an hour to get the bathroom clean. I found a bunch of supplies under the sink and some sponges, scrubbers, and paper towels in the utility room. As I cleaned, I employed the same strategy I had used when vacuuming Ryan's car. I just kept telling myself that I was doing all of this for Matt, not Ryan. I also allowed myself to imagine that the guys who had trashed this place were hot-looking, straight, college jocks; although I had no idea what they actually looked like.

At one point during the whole cleaning ordeal, Ryan called me back out to the living room. He was in need of another Diet Coke and he wanted his plate cleared. Being his domestic servant did not particularly even faze me at this point, however. I was starting to get used to it, and I knew that it would only be a matter of a few more hours until the whole nightmare was completely over.

After I finished with the bathroom, I stood back and assessed my work. It was amazing really. That bathroom was shining from top to bottom, and it even smelled clean. I smiled to myself, feeling rather satisfied by my accomplishment. I then made my way quickly back to the kitchen and began doing dishes. The kitchen was really my comfort zone, and it didn't take me long to make myself at home there. I got it spiffed up in no time and was almost to the point of being ready to inform Ryan that I was done and ready for his inspection. Before I actually did this, however, I looked up to see Ryan standing there.

He had a look in his eyes that suddenly concerned me. It reminded me of the way he was when I'd opened the bathroom door earlier that morning, and he was standing there groping himself. In fact, he was now making the exact same gesture. I just stared at him silently and heard myself gulp. "Sir ... um ..." I was stammering. "Sir, I think I have all my duties completed. I'm ready for your next ... um ... order, Sir."

"Ya know Petey, that night at Eric's party, when we went to the motel room together—you remember that night don't ya?" I nodded but didn't say anything. "I knew at the time that the day would come when our roles would be reversed. I knew that one of these days you would be serving me. Guess what? Today's the day." The smugness of his facial expression was almost evil. "Do you remember how Matt told you to use me? He told you to grab a hold of my head and pump it, to force me to deepthroat ya. Well I don't think you quite understood what he meant by that, cuz you weren't all that aggressive. Maybe you just need a little hands-on demonstration."

I started backing away from him as he said this, feeling my heartbeat quicken. I was in an apartment kitchen though, and what I actually was doing was backing myself into a corner. With each step I took away from Ryan, he moved in closer to me. Soon I was against the kitchen wall, and he was directly in front of me. He placed the palms of his hands flat against the wall above my head so that he was leaning over me. "Let's not do this in here," he whispered. "It's just too crowded in this little kitchen." Then he quickly reached down and grabbed a hold of my dog collar, jerking my neck violently towards him. He stepped aside and hurled me with all his might across the kitchen floor. As he released the grip he had on my collar I flailed forward and stumbled awkwardly, tripping over my own feet. Before I knew it I was on the floor.

Ryan stepped over to me, the entire time remaining in his perfectly-postured, upright stance. He pointed towards the living room. "Get over there, bitch. Over to my chair, now!"

Everything that Ryan had done to me so far during the course of this god-awful day had thus far seemed to border upon the absurd. His attempts to dominate me had felt more like play-acting or role-play than genuine domination. At this particular moment, however, he really was beginning to frighten me. It was as if the hatred and rage that he'd always felt towards me was finally bubbling to the surface. How could Matt not have anticipated that this may happen? How could he have trusted Ryan enough to leave him completely alone with me?

It was right about this moment when I was struck with the realization that Ryan was slipping into a state of uncontrolled rage. He actually seemed to completely snap. I saw it in his eyes. He suddenly became a mad man, and it was only a split second later that I felt the force of his Doc Marten boot connecting with my ribcage. I never realized that when a rib snapped like that, you'd be able to actually hear the breaking of the bone.

The pain was unlike anything I had ever felt, far worse even than when my nose was broken. In addition to the stabbing inferno that slashed into my chest, I also was terrified to realize that I now had virtually no ability to inhale. I couldn't breathe! Ryan was totally oblivious to my plight, however, and he hauled off and kicked me again, this time in the gut. "Move it, bitch!" he screamed.

My eyes flooded with tears as I tried unsuccessfully to gasp. I couldn't even make a sound, however, because it was not possible at that moment to take in air. Helplessly I wrapped my arms around my torso and rolled onto my back, pulling my knees up towards my chest reflexively.

When the force of Ryan's body landed on my already-injured chest, it felt right then and there as if I were having a massive heart attack and dying. He was on top of me and pinning me in a position, which many refer to as the schoolboy pin. He straddled my chest with his legs on either side of my head and cruelly trapped my arms beneath his knees.

I finally was able to suck in my first gulp of air, but when I did so I honestly wished I hadn't, because it felt like a spear slashing into my chest. "Please!" I cried, trying desperately to beg for mercy, but I couldn't even manage to do that.

Ryan was reaching down to unbuckle his khakis, and it was obvious that he had not been exaggerating when he said he'd give me a hands-on demonstration of how to be aggressive. He was already rock hard and both his pants and underwear were soaked with precum. Within seconds he had his dick out and in his hand, pointing it menacingly at my tear-streaked face. He slid up further on my chest—which actually was a blessing because it took some of the pressure off my ribcage—but then he very smoothly thrust himself forward so that my mouth was aligned directly with his rigid prick. He pushed it forcefully against my lips.

"Open up, bitch, or I'll finish beatin the fuck outta ya! Suck it dogboy!!" Although I still was barely able to breathe I was terrified of not obeying him, and I did indeed open my mouth to invite him in. In fact, if all I had to do to get him to stop beating me was to suck his dick, I would gladly oblige.

I didn't honestly have a problem with accommodating the size of his dick, being that it really didn't even compare to Matt's. The real problem, however, was that I was in such horrific pain, and it still was almost impossible for me to breathe. He drove himself deep into my throat, nonetheless, and quickly assumed a position over me as if he were doing push-ups. At least this released my arms from their imprisonment and allowed me to again clutch my enflamed chest.

It was undoubtedly the pain of my injury that prevented me from servicing him the way that a good little sub would be expected to do. I was gagging and choking and apparently scraping Ryan with my teeth. He continued his assault, nonetheless, warning me to watch the teeth, until finally he decided that he'd had just about enough of my obvious refusal to cooperate with him.

He then pulled out of my mouth and resumed a position once more sitting atop my chest. This time my arms were pinned beneath him along the sides of my body. Then he started slapping me, using each of his hands, one-at-a-time. "What the fuck's wrong with you dogboy? Didn't your Master ever teach you the right way to suck a dick? You're a fuckin joke! You're a pathetic little excuse for a sub! You make me sick, you dogboy bitch!"

It was then that Ryan finally made the decision to cross the ultimate line. As I lay there beneath him, pinned helplessly with tears and snot running down my reddened face, he informed me point-blank what he was about to do. "If you can't take it down your throat bitch, you're getting it up the ass!"

15

I was gasping for breath and sobbing as I lay flat on my back pinned beneath Ryan. When he moved off me and grabbed my shoulders to roughly flip me around on my stomach, the jarring effect of this sudden movement sent yet another stabbing pain directly into my chest. This time I actually had enough breath to scream in pain.

"Shut up! Shut the fuck up dogboy!" he said. "I haven't even hurt you – yet!" He obviously had no idea that he'd injured my rib when he kicked me.

"Please Ryan," I begged, "I hurt my side. Please stop!"

"Shut up!" he screamed, "Quit your baby-assed whining. If you're half the sub Matt thinks you are, you'll take it like a man. You should be beggin me to fuck your boy pussy." He then grabbed the belt loops of my pants and began jerking them downward, trying to rip them off of me.

"No! Please stop!" I cried, but he didn't seem to care about anything but getting what he wanted, and that was his cock up my ass.

Finally Ryan reached around me and unbuttoned my pants, allowing him to at last get them pulled down to my knees. He also quickly finished taking off his own pants and then positioned himself over me. He used his palm to shove me down flat against the floor. Apparently since his cock was already slick with my spit and phlegm, he didn't even feel the need to get any lube, or a condom for that matter.

In only a matter of seconds he completely impaled me. As I felt him slide into me another wave of pain swept through my body. The force of his cock ramming violently up my un-lubed hole was excruciating. I had never before experienced a dry fuck and certainly had never been entered in such a brutal manner, completely against my will. It felt almost as if I was being ripped apart, but I was trapped and unable to offer even the slightest resistance. I bucked beneath him, screaming and pounding my fists wildly against the carpet. "Aaaagghh! Oh puh-leez, Ryan ... pleeeze," I was now sobbing.

I could smell Ryan's sweat as he rutted into me, and as he groaned in pleasure it reminded me of a wild animal. His weight pressing against me was not only horrifically painful but also degrading in the worst imaginable way. Previously I had felt as if his attempts to dominate me were silly and inane, but now there was no question that he was crushing me beneath him. He had undoubtedly proven his superiority, at least in the physical sense. This awareness apparently had dawned on him as well, for he laughed excitedly. "You still think I'm just acting, bitch?" he snarled.

All of a sudden Ryan started to pull out of me. I felt the weight of his body begin to lift off my back. I tried to lift myself up somewhat, and as I did so I noticed the entrance door had opened. Someone had entered the apartment. I had no idea who it was, and frankly I didn't care. "Help me! Please help me!" I screamed. Ryan was already on his feet, scrambling to grab his pants.

"What the fuck's goin on?" it was Eric's voice.

"My side," I cried, rolling into a fetal position. "I hurt my side." I closed my eyes and clutched myself futilely, trying to alleviate the pain any way possible. Every single intake of breath was like stabbing a knife into my chest, though.

Then I realized that Eric was not the only one who had entered the room. When I felt his touch I knew instantly that my Master was here. "Matt?" I cried, opening my eyes to see his beautiful face.

"Oh my god," he said. "Petey, are you okay?"

"Hurt my side," I repeated. "My ribs. Can't breathe."

"Fuck!" he screamed. "Dammit to fuck! Oh god Petey, I can't fuckin believe this. This was *not* supposed to happen!"

"What the fuck are you doing here anyway?" Eric said to Ryan. "You were supposed to be over at your dorm room, and you were supposed to get Petey to help you with your term paper. Why're you here in *my* apartment?"

"I'm sorry Sir," Ryan whimpered. "I'm sorry. We were cleaning ... we wanted to surprise you."

"You were *not* fuckin cleaning!" Matt yelled back at him. "You'd better deal with your boy, Eric, before I rip his fuckin head off." He then scooped me up in his arms ever so gently. Although he was making every effort to be careful, it still hurt terribly, and I moaned in spite of myself. "How did he hurt his rib like this? What the fuck did you do to him?"

Eric stepped over and helped Matt by pulling my pants up while Matt held me as still as possible. "I'm ohh-kay," I cried. "Put ... me ... down."

"I'm not putting you down Petey, and you're not okay. Eric, deal with your boy. I'll be back!" He then quickly rushed out the door with me.

Once again we were on our way to the emergency room. I wondered to myself if I was ever going to stop getting hurt. Matt had been the one who rescued me so many months prior after a brutal attack by some fag-bashing bullies. He also had taken me to the emergency room the day we returned from vacation and I got glass in my leg when we rescued a car-crash victim alongside the highway. Then just yesterday he was going to once again take me to the hospital after Alex had hit me.

There was no doubt this time, though, that I had to get some help. I had never felt such horrific pain, and with every breath I attempted to take, that stabbing sensation repeated itself. I did not know which was worse—being unable to breathe or enduring the pain. I tried holding my breath as long as possible.

Matt had laid me in the backseat and was driving as fast as he possibly could. I wanted to tell him to just slow down and be careful, but it was so difficult for me to even talk. I heard him on the phone. He was calling Alex and Drew, telling them to meet us at the ER. Finally I forced myself to speak, regardless of the pain. "Not ... Kathie!" I croaked.

"No, pup," he said reassuringly, "don't worry. We'll call her later. Just relax and don't try to talk, okay?" I could hear the strain in his voice, and I wondered if he was about to start crying himself. "I just can't believe this happened, pup. Ryan knew exactly what he was supposed to do. He was gonna make you clean out his car and then take you over to his dorm room where you were gonna help him with his term paper. Then he was supposed to meet us back at Eric's apartment later tonight. We were gonna ... well I think you can imagine what we were gonna do."

They were gonna use Ryan and me as their subs, I was sure. It was going to be similar to the way that Alex and Matt had used Drew and me. It would have been hot, two subs serving their Masters simultaneously. It all made such perfect sense. Matt was making me spend the day with Ryan, knowing that although I really didn't much care for him I would at least respect him. He probably had hoped that we would in some way bond with one another, especially since we were to be working on a project together.

Matt may even have planned to actually force me to suck Ryan and return the favor so-to-speak for that night at the motel room. But he hadn't given Ryan permission to initiate this on his own. He certainly hadn't authorized him to rape me.

Other than the horrific physical pain that I was feeling at the moment, the only concern that I really had was for Matt. These past few days had been a series of missteps for him, or at least I feared that is how he would see it. It had begun with an argument he'd had with Alex. The two of them had made nice with one another and Alex had agreed to allow

Matt the use of his boy Drew. The result was a beautiful and intimate session of lovemaking, which involved my Master, my dearest friend, and me. Then it all turned south when Matt decided to sneak away in the middle of the night with only Drew in an attempt to throw Alex off his guard so he wouldn't suspect the surprise graduation bash that Matt had planned later that day. Alex had become furious at Matt for stealing away with his boy in the dead of night, thinking Matt was boffing Drew at his family cabin getaway. In a state of rage he'd hauled off and decked me because I had gotten out of control, becoming hysterical and emotional. This resulted in a fist fight between Matt and Alex and nearly ruined the party. It also nearly destroyed my friendship with Drew.

Of course it all seemed to have worked out so well in the end. Matt made passionate love to me in a way unlike ever before. He and I stayed behind after the party, and he fucked me on a weight bench in the middle of his newly remodeled gym. Afterwards we gathered at our apartment and held a family meeting to rehash all that had happened. Matt informed me that I was not off the hook for cursing at Alex and showing such a lack of respect. The next morning I discovered exactly what Matt had meant. I was to be punished and would have to spend the day in the company of my chief rival, Ryan. Not only was I to remain respectful of him, but I was to respond to him as if he were my Master. Matt had even handed over my collar to Ryan and had allowed him to personally place it around my neck. He collared me as his own—if only for the day.

And what a day it had been. I served Ryan as best as I could in spite of his ridicule and absurd over-the-top attempts to humiliate me. I cleaned his car, scrubbed his bathroom (at least I'd thought it was his), cooked him lunch, and scoured his kitchen. This was not enough though. He then demanded that I service him sexually. He was hell bent on exacting revenge upon me for a night a few weeks prior in which he had been forced to kneel in service to me. Had it been that simple, all would have been fine. Had it been a scene in which my Master had either chosen to participate or given his seal of approval, I would have humbled myself gladly. I would have done it for Matt. Of course I would.

But this was not how it all played out. Instead Ryan had chosen to take it upon himself to overpower me physically. He had become irate and hostile. He was enraged and consumed with jealousy and hatred towards me. He knocked me to the floor and began kicking me, breaking my rib mercilessly. Then he'd throat-fucked me and finally began to rape me.

Had it not been for the intervention of Matt and Ryan's Master, Eric, I do not even know where it would have ended. But now here I was lying in the backseat of Matt's vehicle as he rushed me to the ER. I felt like my chest was collapsing. I could barely take in breath, and even when I did it felt as if a spear were slicing through my lungs. It was as if I was suffocating.

What could Matt have been thinking at this moment? He had blamed himself for my injury the day before when Alex hit me. This of course was why he'd sentenced me to my punishment with Ryan. He was trying to teach me to control my emotions. He wanted me to learn how to be respectful even when it was extremely difficult. And now this plan backfired on him. It had failed miserably, even worse than the surprise party ruse.

I knew that Matt regarded himself as being in control at all times. He was an extremely self-confident individual. He took quick and decisive action when it was necessary. He made wise decisions. He was young, but he was smart. He was not all that experienced, but he demonstrated impeccable judgment that went well beyond his years. All of these realities must now be in question, at least in his own mind.

How could he have placed me in danger like this—twice in as many days? How was he going to answer to my sister who had already warned him to take care of me? How was he going to justify to himself that his good intentions were all that really mattered? He was the type of person who measured success or failure by the end result. Motivation was not enough. Good intentions did not in any way compensate for bad decisions.

I recalled how Matt had held me on his lap the day before in his office. He had told me that he'd failed me. He felt as if he had not done his job of protecting me. How must he now feel? What was this tragedy going to mean to us as a couple? What would it mean to him as a Master?

Honestly I should have been more careful in the situation. I knew something was not right with Ryan. I could tell by the way he acted at the gas station that he was beginning to go over the deep end. He was being ridiculous with his over-the-top commands and insults. Instead of remaining respectful the way Matt had instructed me, though, I had back-talked Ryan. I had made it clear to him that he was no Master. I'd told him that it seemed as if he were acting, merely role-playing. This was perhaps the moment at which he snapped.

Yes, that was it. That was exactly what had happened. We started the day together exactly as planned by Matt. Ryan had taken me to the gas station and made me fill his tank, clean his windows, and vacuum his carpets. It was humbling to do this, especially for another sub. But when Ryan became aware of the fact that this act of humility was not something that degraded me but rather was something that came natural to me—he was pissed. I didn't mind kneeling there and vacuuming out the car. I simply reminded myself that I was doing it out of obedience to my Master. Ryan wanted me to suffer though. If this was not enough to humiliate me, he'd find something more severe that actually would.

If I had kept my mouth shut and allowed Ryan to believe that he truly did have the power to denigrate me, then all would have been fine. Instead I did what I always do. I ran my mouth and messed everything up. Now it was my Master who was going to shoulder the blame. I knew he would once again feel that he had used poor judgment. He would on some level blame himself for my injury.

"Sir," I said, trying to breathe as normally as possible so that I could somehow fool him into believing I was not in such excruciating pain. "I'm sorry about this. It's my fault. Not yours."

Matt glanced back at me over the seat, "Don't talk, pup," he scolded me. "Just lie still, and of course it's not your fault. I don't know how I ever allowed myself to believe that Ryan could be trusted."

"It was like yesterday, Sir," I said. "I didn't respect him enough. I pissed him off."

Matt just sighed and shook his head. "We're almost there. Stop stressin about it. Right now we gotta make sure you're okay, then we can deal with all that other shit later." When Matt pulled into the parking lot of the emergency room, I expected him to find us a parking space as one would do in most situations, but instead he pulled the vehicle right to the front door. Then he came around and scooped me into his arms again and carried me inside. I winced as he picked me up because the movement once again sent a stabbing pain right through my chest, and as I tried to take in a breath it felt as if I were a fish out of water. It now was nearly impossible for me to breathe, and that suffocation sensation was intensified exponentially. It was frightening me to the point of near panic.

The emergency room staff actually allowed Matt entry right into one of the examining rooms where he carried me and gently placed me on a gurney. Immediately a male nurse came over, and Matt informed him of the nature of my injury. The nurse proceeded to then cut my shirt off of me.

Matt sucked in his breath as he stared down at my side. "Oh little guy," the nurse said. "You more than fractured that rib; you broke it right in two. Don't move, just lie here as still as possible."

Suddenly there was a flurry of activity around me, and in the confusion, Matt was gone. They placed an oxygen mask over my mouth, and suddenly I began to panic in earnest. Why were they acting like this was such a big deal? Why were they rushing around me as if this were a life-threatening emergency? Maybe I really was suffocating to death. Why were they sticking needles into me? And where was Matt? Where the hell was Matt? I tried to sit up and then to cry out for him. I attempted to clutch the face mask but someone grabbed my arms and pulled them down.

At last I was able to breathe a little better, but I didn't care. I wanted Matt. Where was he? Where the fuck did he go? And then finally he was there again, by my side and holding my hand. "Calm down," he said soothingly. "I'm not going anywhere. I promise I won't leave you, but you just have to lie still. Please." I tried to tell him I loved him, but I couldn't speak, not with the mask.

I couldn't understand what was happening and why there was such a flurry of activity around me. It made no sense that everyone was acting as if I was having a massive heart attack when I was there for a minor injury, just a cracked rib. The confusion was more than I could take. It felt as if I was in the middle of a nightmare, and the entire room around me was spinning. Everything was spinning out of control, and all I wanted was to be with Matt and no one else. I didn't want these people around me, touching and prodding me. I didn't want the noises and the needles and the chaos.

I wanted my Master! I wanted him and only him! Make it all go away, please. Oh god, why is this happening?

And then suddenly I awakened.

I recognized immediately where I was but didn't understand how it was possible. I was home again, in my room. Apparently I was alone. It was not my room at Drew's apartment, though, nor was it my room at Kathie's place. I was in the home where I grew up, where my parents had last been with me.

I looked around and everything was exactly as I had remembered it. The wall hangings were identical, including the Harry Potter posters and my honor roll plaques from school. There was a picture on my dresser of the four of us— Mom, Dad, Kathie, and me—taken at Disney World when I was nine.

I could hear a voice, and it sounded almost like an angel. It was coming from downstairs. Of course I recognized it. It was the voice I heard every morning when I awakened. My mom always sang in the kitchen as she was preparing breakfast. Sometimes she just hummed. Sometimes she whistled. What you never heard from her when she was cooking was silence. She'd always been such a morning person, cheerful and wide-awake the instant she rolled out of bed.

I could smell the sausages cooking. I figured it must be pancakes and sausage she was making. Everything seemed so perfect to me all of a sudden. For some reason it didn't even occur to me that none of this could be real. I didn't even remember all that had happened. I completely forgot about the funerals and the way Kathie and I had been forced to move from the house. I forgot about the sense of abandonment I had felt, about the overwhelming grief. I forgot that long ago I had resigned myself to the reality that Mom and Dad were gone forever and never coming back.

All that mattered was that I was here now in my old home, and that mom was downstairs cooking breakfast. Quickly I threw back my covers and bounded out of bed. I looked down at myself, not surprised to see I was clad in my most comfortable pajama bottoms and a tee shirt. I grabbed my glasses off of the bedside stand, the exact place I always had stored them when I slept, and I headed briskly out the bedroom door, down the hallway, and then descended the stairs to make my way down to the kitchen.

When I saw her again for the first time, I simply stopped in my tracks. I stood there in the doorway unable to speak. I didn't want to even move because I was afraid that any attempt I made to confirm the reality of the situation would backfire. I was afraid that Mom would go away. It was so odd, for I knew on some level that none of this made any sense, but I also couldn't allow myself to even begin imagining that this may be only a dream.

"Mom," I whispered so quietly that I could barely hear my own voice.

She turned to me and smiled sweetly. "Good morning, honey. Sleep well?"

I simply nodded.

"Breakfast is almost ready. Wanna holler for your sister?" She then turned and refocused on her culinary tasks, acting as if all was fine.

"Mom," I said again, this time a little louder. "What's going on?"

"What's going on?" she repeated back to me, somewhat confused. "Why nothing dear. Nothing but breakfast. Now hurry up. Go get your sister; it's almost ready. And tell your father to get a move on. He's gonna be late for work again."

Before I could do or say anything, my father and Kathie stepped up behind me. Kathie slid along side of me, nudging me out of the way as she made her way towards the table. She had her face buried in a romance novel and was reading it intently as if she were the only person in the room.

"Petey," my dad said casually, "don't forget to put out the garbage when you leave for school. It's Friday." He then walked past me and over to my mother. The two kissed each other sweetly the way that married couples do. It was just a quick peck, a gentle little token of affection to greet one another early in the morning.

I was so confused at this point. My emotions were playing tricks on me. I wanted so much to be happy. Could it be possible that I had gone back in time? Could it actually be true that my parents were still alive, and that I was—what? Twelve? Thirteen years old again? What had brought me here, and why didn't anyone but me know the truth about all that had happened?

Suddenly it did not matter. Why should I care? For all these years I had begged God to allow me to go back and spend just one more day with Mom and Dad. I had prayed for just an hour, a minute even. And here it was. It was happening. I ran over to them, wrapping my arms around them both at the same time, squeezing as hard as I could.

"I love you! I love you both so much!" My dad reached around me and pulled me into himself. He seemed a little bewildered by my sudden display of emotion but did not discourage me.

"We love you too Petey," he said, smiling down at me. My mom bent over and kissed me sweetly on the forehead, gently smoothing out my messed-up, morning hair.

And then I heard Kathie behind me. "Petey!" she was saying. "Petey, are you okay?" I didn't care about her though. I reached up and wrapped my arms around my mom, pulling her against me. I could smell her sweet femininity as it surrounded me. "Petey," Kathie said again. "I love you Petey. Oh god, please be okay."

Then it all was gone, and as I opened my eyes, I saw Kathie staring down at me kindly. "Petey I love you," she repeated.

"I love you too, sis," I said. I was in a hospital room, and it all came back to me. They were doing stuff to me in the emergency room. That was the last I had remembered, and then the next thing I knew, I was back at home with mom and dad. "I thought I was with Mom and Dad," I whispered, my voice trembling as I said the words.

"Honey, they are always with us," Kathie said. "You *were* with them. Of course you were. They've been watching over you."

"What happened to me?" I asked. "And where is Matt?" I began trying to look around the room. "I wanna see Matt!"

"Honey, he's not here, and you just need to rest right now. You were hurt pretty bad last night. Your lung collapsed, and they had to put a tube in your chest to inflate it again. You had some ruptured veins they had to repair. You were unconscious while they did the surgery, and you probably were dreaming about Mom and Dad."

"It wasn't a dream!" I screamed. "It was real, and I was with them. They told me they love me. Where's Matt? I need to see Matt *now!*"

"Sweetie, listen to me. You need to calm down and rest. Matt can't be here right now, but I'm here with you. There's gonna be a man coming to see you in a little bit. He needs to make sure you're all right and ask you some questions."

I looked at her suspiciously. "What do you mean?" I asked. "What man and what kind of questions?"

"He works with the police, Petey. We need to find out exactly who did this to you. You were beat up pretty badly. You have a black eye and a fractured nose, and several of your ribs were cracked, one of them snapped right in two. Did someone attack you?"

"Kathie, didn't Matt tell you? Didn't he tell you what happened? Where did he go? Where's my cell phone?"

"Honey, listen to me! Matt is not coming back. He is not coming anywhere near you, not until I find out the truth about what happened. Did he do this to you, Petey? If he did, why would you protect him this way?"

"This *way*?" I asked. "What do you mean, 'protect him this way'? Matt did not hurt me. He never touched me. He's the one who brought me to the hospital."

"Please, Petey." Kathie now had tears in her eyes. "I talked to your friend Jason from work. He called me yesterday afternoon. He saw the way that Matt was treating you, and he was very concerned about your safety."

I shook my head. "Jason's never even met Matt. That wasn't Matt who was with me. It was someone else."

Kathie reached down to hold my hand, but I jerked it away from her. "Let's not talk about this now, honey. Please just try to rest and not let yourself get so upset. You really do need to get rest right now."

"I know what I need. I need him. I need my M—" I was gonna say "Master" but I stopped myself. "I need Matt!"

It was right at this point that Carter walked into the room, and he was escorted by a young blonde guy who was dressed rather casually. He had on a white polo shirt and khakis, and his hair was crested in the front. His model-like features made him look almost like a movie star, and he was tall and broad-shouldered. He smiled at me warmly.

Carter spoke. "Hi," he said quietly, sharing a knowing look with Kathie. "How you feelin little guy?" he asked me.

"I'd feel better if I knew where Matt was," I said, "and my chest hurts really bad."

"I bet it does," Carter sympathized. "Petey, this is Detective Murray. He's here to ask you some questions and to help us find out what exactly happened to you."

I looked up at the detective as he extended his hand to me to shake. "Nice to meet you, Peter. You can call me Rick."

"Thank you, sir," I said quietly. "Nice to meet you too. Sir, Matt did not do this to me. I swear he didn't."

The detective nodded as I spoke. "Okay. No need to get upset at all. Nobody is making any accusations here. We only want to find out the truth and to do everything we can to keep you safe. Who is this Matt, by the way?"

"Matthew Porter," Kathie blurted out. "His father owns that chain of gyms in Tampa. He's a big, tall muscular jock guy, twice the size of Petey."

"And Petey," the detective redirected his attention to me, "what's the nature of your relationship with this Matt?"

"He's my friend," I said cautiously. "He's a very close friend."

"You mean like a boyfriend?" he asked. I'm not sure why, but just the way that he said this to me put me at ease a bit. He had such an understanding tone to his voice.

I nodded.

"Do you mind if I talk to Peter alone for a bit?" he asked the others. I could tell how irritated Kathie was by this request but she nodded.

"Oh sure, certainly. We'll just go get a cup of coffee. We'll be in the cafeteria. If you'd like, call my cell when you're done."

"Sure," the detective smiled at her. "Won't be long."

After they had left, Rick pulled up a chair beside the bed and sat down.

"Sir, you can call me Petey if you like."

"Okay Petey," he again smiled at me. "I *would* like that. I want you to know I'm not here to get anyone in trouble. It's not my job to make judgments about you or your boyfriend or anything like that. My job is to find out if there has been a crime committed against you. If there has, we want to make sure it never happens again, cuz nothing is more important than your safety. Would you agree with that?"

"Sure," I said. "But sir, there was no crime committed. I mean, at least not by Matt. He has never hurt me in any way. He l—um, he looks after me."

"Do you think he loves you? Is that what you were gonna say."

I smiled in spite of myself. "Yes sir, he does love me. He loves me very much, and I love him to. I love him more than anything."

"You know I have someone that I love like that too. His name is Tim. We've been together for almost five years now."

"Really?" I asked. "What's he like?"

"Well, in some ways I guess he's like you. He is a littler guy. He's real smart. He writes plays."

"Wow. I've always wanted to be a writer. I've never thought of writing a play though."

"What kinda stuff do you write, Petey?"

"Oh just essays and stuff like that. One time I won an award for one of my essays, back when I was in school. Someday I wanna write a story. Maybe like a book. I'd like to write about Matt and me maybe."

"Well if you ever do, I definitely wanna read it. What can you tell me about Matt? Tell me what he's like."

"He's really smart, sir. He has his own gym now. It's gonna open in two days over in Sarasota. His dad's made him manager of it. He's really good looking too. I don't know where my wallet is, but there's a picture of him in it. I bet he could be a model or a movie star. I'm lucky to even know him, let alone be his boyfriend!"

Rick laughed as I said this. "He really sounds pretty awesome. So you think he treats you pretty good then? He's not ever mean to you, is he?"

"Oh no sir, never. He sometimes is strict, but he's never mean."

"Strict? Whata ya mean by 'strict'?"

"Well, I'm not sure how to explain this exactly. He knows its um, well, it's his job sorta to protect me. It's my job to do what he says. He watches over me in a way."

"Kinda like a big brother or something?" He raised his eyebrows slightly, but his question seemed very sincere.

"Yeah, I guess it is kinda like that. And like a big brother, he is sometimes a little bit bossy too. But he is not mean. Never."

"Would you say Matt has a temper?" Immediately I thought of the way he'd punched Alex just a couple days earlier.

"I have seen him get mad, but I don't really think he's hot tempered, sir. He gets mad if someone tries to hurt somebody he cares about."

"Someone like you, ya mean?"

"Yeah, exactly. He's protective of me, I guess."

"Has he ever hit you, Petey? And please be honest with me about this. I can only help you if you tell me the truth."

"I swear, sir, Matt has never hit me. I mean he's hit me, but not to be mean. Oh god! No, that's not what I mean. I mean he's spanked me before ... in a situation." Fuck! I was saying all the wrong things.

The detective had a wry grin on his face. "It's okay Petey. Don't be embarrassed. When you say he has spanked you, are you talking about discipline or sex?"

"Both really, sir. But in a way I guess it is the same sort of thing."

"So discipline is sometimes part of your sex play?"

"Yes sir," I said as I felt my face starting to redden.

"Do you ever do anything in your sex play that hurts you? I mean do you let him beat you and punch you or whip you? Anything like that?"

"No sir! Never has he done anything at all like that. Only spanking, and that's it."

"How'd you get that black eye? Did that happen during one of your sessions with Matt?"

"No sir, it really didn't. Matt wasn't even there when I got it. I was with Alex. He's a friend of ours."

"Did this Alex hit you?"

"Yes sir, but it was an accident. He didn't even mean to hurt me. And when Matt found out about it he was so mad that he punched Alex twice, once in the chin and once in the stomach."

"Hmm, why'd Matt do something like that if it was just an accident?"

Dammit! What was I supposed to say now? If I said that he didn't know it was accident, then Matt would appear hot-tempered. If I said it wasn't really an accident it would make Alex look bad. "Well, I guess it wasn't *exactly* an accident, but Alex felt really bad about hitting me, and in a way I sort of deserved it."

For the first time during our conversation, Detective Murray scowled a little. "I don't quite follow, Petey. I'm sorry, but what would make you think that you deserved to be hit so hard that you have a broken nose and a black eye."

"I don't think my nose is broke, sir. I mean it doesn't even hurt. I was really upset and was screaming at Alex. I said something really bad. I said the "f" word to him."

"Oh," Rick nodded and leaned back in his chair a bit, "so since you cursed at Alex you feel you deserved a black eye?"

I was starting to get a little bit frustrated, more at myself than the detective. I just didn't seem to know the right things to say. "I didn't really mean it like that. I'm sorry about it. I'm sorry I'm not explaining this right." I heard my voice starting to break, and I was afraid that before long I'd be crying.

"Hey, you're not sayin anything wrong. Don't worry, I'm just tryin to understand is all. I just try to gather all the facts, ya know. You've heard that before, haven't ya? 'Just the facts, ma'am'." He laughed a little, and I smiled at his attempt to lighten the mood.

"Sir, I guess I don't think I actually *deserved* to be hit, but I understood why Alex did it. It was a mistake, and he regrets it a lot. All of us had a meeting afterwards and he told me how sorry he was. Even Matt wasn't mad at him any more."

"All of you? You mean the three of you?"

"Alex has a boyfriend too. His name is Drew, and we are best friends. Drew and me, I mean. Right now I live with Alex and Drew. I moved in with them about a week ago."

"You like it there so far? I mean other than when you got hurt?"

"I love it there, sir. I love being with Drew every day, and I know Alex is a really good person."

"Did Alex break your rib too?" I shook my head slowly but didn't say anything. "Well do you think you'd feel comfortable telling me how it happened? It was a pretty serious injury. The doctor told your sister he'd never seen a break like that. The bone was broken right in two and bulging out of your side."

I winced as I thought of it. "I guess it was kind of my fault too. I mean it wasn't really my fault. It wasn't anyone's fault."

"Did someone hit you with something? A baseball bat or a club maybe? Did someone maybe kick you?"

My eyes were now again brimming with tears. I nodded my head slowly. "Someone kicked me," I said.

"Matt? Did Matt get angry and kick you, Petey?"

"No! I told you he didn't do it, and neither did Alex. Please you gotta believe me!" Quickly I covered my face with my hands and turned my head away from him.

"Hey, it's okay, if you say they didn't do it, I believe you. Petey, look at me. Please. Please tell me who did this to you. If it wasn't Matt and it wasn't Alex, who was it?"

"Did you know about how Matt and I met?" I asked. "Did Kathie tell you?" He shook his head and continued to intently stare at me. "These guys attacked me at the bus stop, and Matt was there. He saved me from them and took me to the hospital. Matt would never hurt me. He'd never beat up someone like me, someone so much smaller than him."

"Who was it Petey? Who kicked you?"

"If I tell you it was an accident, then why does it matter, sir?" I hated the whiney sound of my own voice.

"You haven't told me that, Petey. You never said it was an accident. You said it was your fault. Let me tell ya something, and I want you to listen real carefully to me. You do not deserve to be beaten, not by Matt or by any of his friends. Your sister loves you very much and wants you to be safe. I want you to be safe, but you have to help me here. Please won't you let me help you?"

"It was someone else, but it wasn't Matt's fault."

The detective again looked confused. "If it was someone else, Petey, why would you think that I'd assume it was Matt's fault?"

"Everyone seems to think everything is Matt's fault!" I shot back defensively. "He was only trying to do what was best for me. He was trying to teach me something."

"He was teaching you something and this is why he had someone beat you?"

"No, it's not like that sir! I swear! Matt did not tell Ryan to beat me—" Fuck! I'd said his name.

"Okay," the detective said, leaning into me, "tell me who Ryan is. What is his last name?"

I shook my head, tears now streaming down my cheeks. "Please, please don't ..."

"Petey, listen to me. Please don't protect this guy. This guy hurt you really bad, and he doesn't deserve your protection."

"Sir, it's not like what you think. I swear it's not. I know my sister thinks that Matt is abusing me and beating me up, and now you think that it's this other guy Ryan. But really it is all just really bad luck. A bunch of bad stuff's happened to me lately. That's all! Honest!"

Detective Murray then sighed audibly. "All right Petey, let's try something different. Why don't you just start from the beginning and tell me exactly how you got these broken ribs. Can you do that for me?"

I nodded. "Yes sir, I can tell you." I scooted myself up slightly in the bed, trying to sit more upright, but my efforts at repositioning proved futile. A stabbing pain shot through my chest and I winced.

"Let me help you," Detective Murray said, and he raised himself out of the chair, grabbing my pillow and fluffing it behind my back. While he did this, he wrapped his other arm around my shoulder, holding me upright. Being so close to me, his scent was nearly overpowering. He was wearing some kind of very provocative cologne, or was it merely the smell of very masculine body wash from his shower? "Is that better?" he asked, and I nodded.

"Thank you … Rick." He smiled at my use of his first name. "Okay, I'll tell you exactly what happened, but I'm not sure you will understand it completely." He looked at me puzzled.

"Try me," he said, smiling.

"Well, first of all, I haven't lied to you sir. Everything I've told you so far is the honest-to-god truth. But there is something you don't know about Matt and me, and the reason I haven't told you is because I'm sort of afraid you won't understand. It's something Kathie doesn't even know."

"Well, I'm glad that you feel you can trust me, Petey. And like I already said, I'm not here to judge you. I'm only here to help."

"Thanks. I'm not quite sure how I should explain this. It's not an easy thing to say to someone who doesn't know me – who doesn't know Matt."

"Just say it," he urged me.

"Matt is my boyfriend, just like I said. But he's more than that."

"What do you mean, Petey? You mean you think of him as your spouse? Your husband?"

I shook my head. "Well, not exactly, sir. Matt is more like my Master. Well, actually he *is* my Master."

"Okay," he said, "so if he's the Master, then that would make you the slave?"

"No sir, he doesn't think of it like that, and neither do I. I'm not a slave boy. I could never be a slave. There is a big difference between being a slave and being what I am."

The detective was staring at me so intently now, and from his expression he actually seemed genuinely interested, though I sensed he was puzzled. "And what is it then that you are, Petey?" he asked.

"Matt calls me his pup. I'm his sub, sir. I am submissive to him."

"So if you are a pup, does that mean that he treats you like a dog?"

I laughed at this question. "Sorry sir, but that question seems so funny to me. It reminds me of something. There was one time when Matt had me kneel on the floor and beg like a puppy, and he fed me. But we were just playing. He doesn't treat me like a dog usually."

"Then where does the 'pup' come from?"

"Well it was a nickname he gave me when we first met. I had a black eye after the attack, just like I do now. He said I reminded him of Petey, the dog on Little Rascals. Then when he became my Master, he said I was loyal to him like a pup is to its Master."

"I see," Rick said, "and since he is your Master, you have to obey him? He gets to tell you what to do?"

"Yes sir, but I like obeying him. He takes care of me. He protects me and makes decisions for me. He gives me advice."

"Okay, well I think I understand, sort of anyway. But you haven't told me what this has to do with your broken ribs."

"Well Alex is one of Matt's close friends. Alex is a Master also, and his sub is my best friend Drew." I looked over at Rick to gauge his reaction and he seemed rather nonplussed. "Matt was planning a big surprise party for Alex on Saturday, and I knew nothing about it. It was because Alex was graduating from college, and Matt had hired him to design a computer program, which Matt was buying from him to use in his new gym. The whole thing was this big surprise for Alex. So what Matt did was trick Alex."

"Oh really? How'd he do that?"

"He took Drew in the middle of the night and left Alex a note. Alex thought that Matt and Drew were off doing … um, well, doing stuff together, ya know."

"Having sex?"

"Yes, sir, that's what Alex thought, and it made him really pissed. He was very, very upset. The truth, though, was that Matt and Drew were over at the gym setting up for this big party.

"Well, when Alex got all upset that got me upset too. We kind of had an argument. I ended up swearing at Alex. I told him to 'F' off. When I did this, he punched me and gave me the black eye.

"Right after he did it, though, he was so sorry. He was really freaking out, cuz he knew Matt was gonna kill him. When Alex and I got to the gym, we thought that Alex was just there to install the computer program. We didn't expect to see Matt and everyone else. We walked in and my shirt was all soaked in blood from my nose. Matt saw it and knew right away that I'd been hurt. He got into a fight with Alex, and he punched Alex in the stomach and the chin."

"Wow, right there in front of everyone?"

"No sir, it was in the back room. In a kitchen or something. Still everyone knew about it. It was a big dramatic scene."

"I bet."

"Well, Matt was so upset. He blamed himself for the whole thing, and for me getting hurt. He made up with Alex and then after the party all of us went out to dinner together. The four of us had a meeting at home afterwards, and we all apologized to each other for everything, and I thought everything was fine again.

"But it wasn't?"

"Well, Matt felt that I should be disciplined for swearing at Alex like that. For showing disrespect, since Alex is a Master."

Rick raised his eyebrows. "Well, don't you think your black eye was punishment enough?"

"It is not for me to decide, really. Matt is my Master, and it's his choice."

"And what did he choose? How did he punish you?" The detective was now scowling, as if he were very angry.

"Sir, please don't be mad. Don't be mad at Matt. He only disciplines me to teach me stuff. It is to help make me better."

"Okay, but how did he do it?"

"Well there is this kid Ryan. He's in some of my classes at school. He is a sub just like me, but the two of us don't like each other very much. Matt knows this. He knows I don't care for Ryan. As a punishment he ordered me to spend the day with Ryan. I had to show him respect as if he was my Master. I had to take orders from him."

"Hmm, bet that really sucked."

"Yes sir, it did kinda. But it wasn't too bad. I just kept pretending that it was Matt giving the orders and I was fine."

"Did you do something wrong? Something that pissed Ryan off?"

"I think Ryan felt like I was not showing him the respect that he wanted. He was pissed that I wasn't getting upset when he tried being mean to me."

"So he beat you up?"

"I think he just went kind of crazy. He was like a mad man or something. He threw me on the ground and started to kick me. Then he tried to force me to have sex with him."

"Oh my god," he gasped. "And this was Matt's punishment for you?"

"No! No, not at all! Matt thought I was helping Ryan with a term paper. He never gave Ryan permission to do that stuff to me."

"When you say Ryan tried forcing you to have sex with him, what do you mean? Oral sex or the other?"

"Both," I said, looking down at the bed sheet.

"And did he succeed?"

The memory suddenly came back to me in vivid detail, and I recalled how Ryan had pinned me so mercilessly, evilly ignoring my excruciating pain. I recalled the way I had felt like a fish out of water, unable to breath and in a state of complete panic. He had been oblivious to all of this as he'd rammed his cock into my mouth.

"A little," I confessed, "but I didn't really do too good of a job pleasing him."

"Good!" the detective said, "but that's not the point."

"What happened afterwards? Who brought you to the hospital?"

"Matt brought me. He came in just as Ryan was ... um ... just as he was starting to have anal sex with me."

"So why didn't Matt call the police? When Ryan did this to you, it was a rape. That's a crime."

"I think Matt was worried about my injuries, sir. He might not have been thinking about whether or not there had been a crime. Plus, I wouldn't have wanted him to call the police. I doubt they'd even have believed me. It would have been my word against Ryan's."

"Well, I believe you, Petey."

"Thank you, sir," I said, now beginning to tremble. I'm not sure why, but I became so overcome with emotion that I just started crying very hard. The cries turned to sobs, and I covered my face with my hands, trying to turn my body away from the detective as I did so.

His arms were then around me, and he was sitting on the side of the bed. He was pulling me into his embrace. I clung to him then, feeling my weakened body wracked with uncontrollable sobs. As I tried to control my emotions, it seemed that it all got worse. I just cried and cried.

"Please!" I begged. "Please don't let anything happen to Matt!"

"Shhh," he said reassuringly. "Don't you worry about Matt. This isn't even the time for you to worry about anything or anyone other than Petey. And don't worry about Ryan either. I swear to you he's gonna get what's coming to him."

"Can I talk to Matt? Can you please call him for me? I don't know why he's not here. I'm afraid Kathie is keeping him away from me."

"Petey, I don't think you should see Matt just now. I think you need to be away from him for a little bit."

"No! How can you say that?"

"Petey, listen to me! You have been hurt really bad, and Matt is at least partially to blame for that."

"No he's not! He loves me; he'd never hurt me! I want to talk to Matt! I need to talk to Matt!! Please!"

"Petey," the detective sighed, "I couldn't let you talk to Matt even if I wanted to."

"Why?" I pulled away from him and looked him in the eye.

"Petey, Matt's in jail."

16

The unimaginable reality that my Matt was behind bars was beyond my comprehension. Surely this must be a mistake. After all, the detective had not even known who Matt was when he began questioning me. It was my sister Kathie who had told him Matt's last name. She even went on to state that he was that guy who's father owned all those gyms in Tampa.

Why had they done this? It obviously was an attempt to deceive me. They were trying to trick me into giving them information that they could use against Matt. How sweet Detective Murray had been when he coaxed me to open up and confide to him the nature of my relationship with Matt. Now here I was crying in his arms, begging for my Master only to be told point-blank that I cannot see him. He's in jail!

"What do you mean he's in jail?"

"Petey," the detective said to me soothingly, "Matt was arrested last night. The officer had no choice."

"What are you talking about? This is a mistake! Matt hasn't done anything wrong, certainly not anything *illegal*!"

"It was actually the hospital who contacted the police. They were rather solidly convinced that you had been the victim of domestic abuse. When we tried questioning Matt about this, he became rather irate. Hostile, in fact."

"So has he been charged with domestic violence or with something else?"

"He was taken into custody on suspicion of domestic assault and is also being charged with resisting arrest and inciting a public disturbance."

I could feel the anger rising from inside of me. At this particular moment I was feeling anything but submissive. "How can you arrest him for assaulting me without even asking me about it first?"

"We no longer need the permission of the victim to make such an arrest," he informed me. "For years we found ourselves in situations where we had to let abusers off scot-free because their victims were too frightened to testify against them. The law now protects victims whether they want that protection or not."

"Well I don't *need* any protection from Matt. Matt has never hurt me. Never!" How many times did I have to keep repeating this fact before someone would believe me? "What's gonna happen to him? He has to open his new business this week. Can't I just go tell the judge or someone that it's all a mistake? You can't keep someone locked up like that when they didn't do anything wrong!"

"Petey, stop worrying about Matt," he was actually starting to sound irritated at this point. "Matt's family has money, and he's gonna be just fine. They probably have bailed him out already. I'm sure they'd have done it last night if not for the fact that it was a Sunday evening and no bail had yet been set."

"So he might even be out already? I need to see him! I need to talk to him right away. I've got to find my cell phone!"

"Kathie has your cell phone and all the rest of your belongings, including the dog collar you were wearing." Was he now trying to embarrass me? "Matt is not going to be able to talk to you though. He will be served with a restraining order. We have petitioned the court for an order of personal protection on your behalf. Matt Porter will not be allowed to make contact with you in person or by phone until that order has been rescinded."

"No!" I screamed. "You can't do this!"

"I'm sorry Petey, but it's for your own good."

"Sir, didn't you hear anything I told you? Matt is the one who saved me. He is the one who has always saved me. He protects me!"

"Well he obviously puts you in situations where he can then turn around and make himself out to be your hero, but there is just too much evidence to ignore. Your black eye, your broken nose and ribs, the eye witness who saw and heard Matt verbally abusing you."

"That was not even Matt! That was Ryan who Jason saw! He's the one you should be arresting, if anyone."

"Don't worry, Ryan will have his day. Look Petey, I know you're not happy with me. I understand, really I do. But all I can hope for is that at some point you'll see that everything I've done is for your well-being. If it's true that Matt hasn't hurt you and that he only protects you, then it'll all be cleared up soon enough. In the mean time, you need to just rest and get yourself better. Let Matt worry about defending Matt. He's a big boy, and he can take care of himself."

"Can I at least see Drew?" I pleaded. "Has he been here? Does he even know about all this?"

"Yes, Drew has been here. He's downstairs in the waiting room, and he wants to see you. I needed to talk to you first, though. Would you like me to send him up?"

"Yes! Oh god, yes." If only they'd have let me talk to Drew first then maybe I wouldn't have said so many of the wrong things to the detective. Wasn't that the plan though, to get me to trust him enough to tell him things I wouldn't otherwise share?

"Okay, I'm gonna go find your sister, and I'll send Drew up. I hope you will try not to be angry with me and especially not with your sister. She really does love you, Petey. I'm gonna leave my card here on the stand. I want you to call me anytime if you need anything. Okay?" I wondered if I could call him and tell him I needed Matt. I didn't say that though, but simply nodded. "Okay," he repeated and placed his hand on my shoulder. "Get better, and I'll be back soon." He then turned and left the room.

I could only imagine what must have happened the night before when Matt was arrested. Perhaps they had tried to force him to leave my side and he refused. Maybe they had accused him of hurting me and he became angry. I also knew, however, that Matt did very much blame himself for all that had happened. I hoped he had not said anything to implicate himself in any way. I hoped he hadn't stated he was responsible for my injuries.

It would be just like Matt to shoulder the blame for everything. In his mind, he was responsible for the bad things that happened to me because he was my guardian. He took credit for the good and reaped the rewards thereof, but by the same token he also bore the burden of responsibility for the bad. Isn't that what a Master did? For good or bad, he was always accountable.

Although I was so groggy from the pain medication, I tried to watch television while I waited for Drew. I wanted so much to just doze off to sleep, but I was just too anxious. I was terrified of the thought that Matt was in jail. I wondered what it must be like. It was just not right, thinking of my Master in jail, taking orders from other people. Tears were streaming down my cheeks as Drew stepped into my room. He did not immediately rush to my side, though. He just stood there staring at me.

"Drew," I whispered. "Matt." All I could say was his name, and of course Drew knew what I was feeling.

"I know, honey. I'm so sorry." Very cautiously he inched his way closer towards my bed. "Oh baby, does it hurt real bad?" I think he was talking about my ribs, but he could have meant my broken heart.

"No, they have me on pain medication. It makes me tired though."

"Want me to come back later so you can sleep?" he offered.

"No!" I cried. "I want you here now!" He immediately rushed to me and we embraced, clutching one another as if we hadn't seen each other in years.

"Oh Petey, I was so scared. When they said you had to have surgery I was terrified!"

"I'm okay, Drew. Don't worry," I could smell the sweetness of his shampoo as his golden hair brushed against my cheek. I wanted him to crawl right in bed with me and curl up beside me as we did at home. "Please sit here with me, on the bed. Don't leave, okay?"

"No, never. I'll stay as long as you want. I promise."

"Where is Alex?" I asked.

"When they um, well ... when they took Matt, Alex went down there to the jail. He couldn't really do anything though, so he came back here to be with me. We waited here all night and then once we found out you were going to be okay, he took me home and we ate and showered. I came back here this morning, and Alex went down to the jail again. Matt's dad was gonna be trying to get him out, and Alex wanted to be there for him."

"Good! I wish I could be there too. I can't believe they took him to jail!"

"Oh it was so horrible, Petey. It was just like a nightmare happening right before my eyes. They put him in handcuffs."

"No!" I was crying so hard now. "They put him in handcuffs? They dragged him out like he was a criminal." How could they have done this to him?

Drew smiled in spite of the situation. "Well I guess that *is* how they arrest people usually. It's just hard to see when it's someone like Matt. Please don't cry, Petey. It's gonna be okay."

"I won't even be able to talk to him when he does get out. They won't let me."

"Who won't?" Drew asked.

"The police! The detective said he's putting a restraining order on him."

"Didn't you tell him what happened? Didn't you tell him that Ryan's the one who did this to you?"

"Yes, Drew! I told him like a million times, and he won't believe me. He thinks Matt is to blame somehow."

"Do you think it's cuz your sister? She probably told him stuff about Matt. I don't think she trusts him."

"I know she doesn't," I said. "She thinks it's her job to protect me from Matt."

"Why don't you talk to her? Maybe you need to tell her the whole truth about you and Matt."

I shook my head. "It'll just make it worse. Can't you imagine how she'd be if I told her Matt was my Master? She'll say he brainwashed me or something. Don't you remember how she tried to break us up before when she introduced me to Cameron?"

"Well there is nothing that says I can't talk to Matt. When he gets out I'm gonna talk to him and ask him if he can get you a lawyer. There's got to be a way to get that stupid restraining order cancelled."

"What did Matt say when they arrested him? Did he tell them he'd hurt me or something? Why did they just assume he was the one who had beat me?" My voice was quivering again. It was so difficult to even think about how they hauled him off in handcuffs.

"They didn't even ask him anything other than his name. They just came up and said, 'Are you Matthew Porter?', and when he said yes they told him he was under arrest. He got pissed off and told them he hadn't hurt you. He kept sayin it over and over, but they didn't listen. He started getting more and more angry at them, and they pushed him against the wall and forced him into the handcuffs."

"Detective Murray told me he was charged with resisting arrest," I cried.

"Oh that is such bullshit, Petey! Matt never resisted them at all. He just argued with them ... or I mean he tried to argue with them, but they wouldn't even listen. He did not fight them or anything though. He didn't even raise his voice that much."

None of this was making much sense. Why would the police detective have told me that Matt was charged with resisting arrest when he had not so much as raised his voice? "Matt has a lawyer, doesn't he?" I asked.

"Yeah, don't worry hon. Matt's dad will get him a really good attorney. He's not gonna be in trouble over this. In fact, I bet the police will eventually be more concerned about facing a lawsuit for false arrest, especially after they find out what you told the detective about everything."

"But the detective said he has a lot of evidence. He thinks Jason was an eye witness to Matt abusing me."

"Who's Jason?" Drew asked.

"He works with me down at the bookstore. He saw me with Ryan yesterday, and I guess he thought Ryan was Matt."

"So Ryan was abusing you in public and Jason saw it?"

"He was just yelling at me. Ryan never hit me in public. Jason was gonna be working last night, and he must've called Kathie from the store. My phone number is still listed as her apartment. Maybe he was just trying to call me, actually, and she happened to answer. He told her that he'd seen me with my boyfriend and that he was abusing me."

"Wow," said Drew. "I guess Jason must've been really worried about you."

"I guess so, but by telling Kathie that, she just naturally assumed it was Matt that was yelling at me in front of Jason. The detective also said that the hospital called the police. They were the ones who thought I had been beaten, and they must've told them they suspected Matt for some reason."

"Yeah, well probably cuz he just was beside himself when you were in surgery. He kept sayin shit like he was responsible for this. If they overheard him, I bet they thought he meant he had personally kicked the shit out of you."

"Oh my god, Drew! He *didn't say that?* Did he?"

"He said, 'Please let him be all right. It's all my fault; I'm responsible for all this.'"

"Oh Drew! I knew that he'd blame himself. I just knew it! And so now he is in jail because of me."

"No! Not because of you, Petey. Because of that asshole motherfucker Ryan!"

"If I hadn't gotten Ryan so mad at me, he never would've done this to me, and Matt never would have been blamed for it. How can you not see it's my fault?"

Drew sighed. "Dammit Petey, you're as bad as Matt. It is *not* your fault, and it's not his fault. It's Ryan's fault. He's the one who disobeyed Matt and who attacked you. Don't you remember what Matt specifically told him? He said he'd better not hurt you in any way—no broken bones or bruises. Well look at yourself! You have plenty of both."

"I wish I could just tell them I don't wanna press charges. I don't even care if he gets away with it."

"Well I care!" I looked up and saw Kathie standing at the foot of my bed. "And Matt is *not* gonna get away with it this time."

Drew and I looked at one another in stunned silence for a moment, and then I responded. "I wasn't talking about Matt, Kathie. I was talking about Ryan. He's the one who broke my rib."

"Listen Petey, I know you love Matt, and I know it has been so hard on you since Dad died, but you don't have to be with someone who abuses you like this. I know Matt did it. I heard him confess to it." She glared at Drew as she said this, as if to drive the message home to him that she'd go to any lengths to protect her brother. "And if you are not strong enough to stand up for yourself, Petey, I will do it for you!"

"Do you two need to discuss this privately?" Drew offered, but immediately I shook my head.

"Don't go anywhere, please! Please stay with me. Kathie, I'm not protecting Matt. He honestly didn't do this to me.

When you thought he was confessing, he was just saying that he was responsible for my safety. He feels like he has failed."

"He has!" she snapped back at me.

"Well that may or may not be true, but it is not the same thing as beating me."

"Honey, whether you realize this or not, I'm on your side. Some day I pray you will look back at this and ask yourself why you ever thought you were deserving of this kind of abusive treatment. But for right now, since you can't seem to love yourself enough to break free from this bully, I'm gonna do everything in my power to keep you safe." She stepped over to the other side of the bed, opposite where Drew was sitting.

"Kathie," Drew said calmly, "I know we don't know each other very well, but I do know Matt. I see Matt and Petey together every day, and I know Matt would never hurt him. Matt loves him so much." Just hearing this testimony brought fresh tears to my eyes.

Kathie sighed. "Okay, well let's not talk about this any more right now. It's upsetting Petey. If Matt is innocent like you both say, the police will find that out."

"If you really love me like you claim to do, Kathie, you'd believe me! I'm not lying to you, I swear!"

"Honey, I *do* love you. I love you with all my heart, and I never thought you were lying to me. It's just sometimes when we are in love with someone so deeply we don't see the bad things that they do. I don't think you even realize how many ways he has abused you."

Before I could respond to this last volley of insults to Matt, Drew again interjected. "It is obvious how much you love your brother, but please understand that I love Petey too. I might not be his blood relative, but I feel like he is a little brother to me. I would do anything to protect him, but I don't think that keeping him from Matt is helping him at all. Matt hasn't ever hurt Petey, and I know in my heart that he never would."

"How do you know this? Look at him! Look at his black eye, his bandaged ribs! Don't you know what this does to me to see him like this?" She let out a little sob as she asked the last question. "It kills me!"

And it was at this point that I realized where all of this overprotective behavior was coming from. It made such perfect sense. When we lost Mom and Dad, Kathie and I grew so close to one another. We both had realized that we were all that the other had, and now Kathie feared that she was at risk of losing me. I couldn't imagine what it must have been like for her when I was in surgery. What if something did happen to me? What if I died and left her completely alone? It was no wonder she was so scared.

"Kathie, I love you too, and if I thought that Carter was hurting you, I'd try to do everything possible to get you away from him. I don't think I'd even have the strength to go on living if I had to do it without you. But you have to trust me about Matt. He really has never hurt me. In fact, the very first promise he ever made to me was that he never would hurt me, *ever*!"

"Sweetie, even if he never laid a finger on you, he still has hurt you. He's taken away your independence. He's stripped you of your self-confidence. He's actually made you feel as if you are someone inferior, and Petey, *that's* abuse."

I knew that Kathie wouldn't understand my need to serve Matt. I knew she had no concept of what a Dom and a sub were. She didn't realize that the nature of the relationship was such that it benefited each of us. Matt and I both got what we needed from one another. Yes, it was true that I did feel inferior to him, but it was because of the fact that this superior person had selected me and chosen me as his own that I felt wonderful about myself. It didn't strip me of my self-confidence. Contrarily, it bolstered my ego. It made me feel special. As for having no independence, I didn't want any. I guess you could argue that this was a weakness, but how was it any different than any other couple? Do married heterosexuals have the same level of independence as they did before, when they were still single?

From my point of view, it was I who reaped the most benefits of this relationship. I did give up my right to make certain decisions for myself, but along with this sacrifice I also gave up all of the worry and headache of wondering whether or not I was doing the right thing. Matt was the one who bore the burden of responsibility for all major decision-making. All I had to do was obey him. And truly this was not really a sacrifice to me at all. If Matt were to suddenly be removed from my life, I would feel so lost. All of that responsibility would suddenly fall completely upon my shoulders.

This was exactly what was happening. Matt was being removed from my life, and it felt as if there wasn't a damned thing I could even do about it. "Kathie, Matt doesn't make me feel inferior; he makes me feel *special*," I said to her quietly. "Every single moment I'm with him I feel like I should be pinching myself to make sure it's not a dream. How can someone as wonderful as him love me the way that he does? How could I have ever been so lucky to have him in my life?"

"No honey," she said, as she gently placed her palm against my cheek, "he's the lucky one. He's lucky to have you, and he doesn't deserve your devotion."

"They're both lucky," Drew said, "and they both deserve each other."

Just as Drew said this, an orderly entered the room carrying a tray. It was apparently my lunch. Kathie pointed to the L-shaped, portable bed stand behind Drew. "Can you get that?" Drew pushed it over so that it went across my lap, and the orderly set down the tray in front of me.

"There ya go, honey," she said. "Smells pretty good."

"Oh thank you," I said, smiling up at her. "I guess I *am* kinda hungry." When she left, I lifted the lid off my plate and stared down at the offering before me. "On second thought ..." I said.

"Petey, if you want I can go get you something else," Drew offered. "I'll buy you anything you want. You name it."

"No, I just want you to stay right here, Drew. Please just stay, and you can help me eat this ... whatever it is."

He then leaned in and kissed me sweetly on the lips, right there in front of Kathie. "I love you, Petey. I won't leave you. Never."

* * *

Kathie didn't stay long at the hospital that afternoon. She looked as if she were about to drop over from exhaustion, having been up the entire night before. I encouraged her to go home and get some sleep, for I was myself quite tired. I was so stiff from the incision they had made, and the tenderness made it difficult for me to even move much. I assured her that all I wanted was to get some rest. When Drew volunteered to stay with me so that I wouldn't be alone, Kathie finally agreed and went home for some much needed shut-eye.

Even though I was so sleepy and a bit groggy from the pain medication, I immediately urged Drew to call Alex to see what the status was on Matt's incarceration. I sat beside him listening eagerly, trying to discern any clue as to if he'd been released and if he was all right. Drew looked over at me and smiled, mouthing the words, "He's out!" Oh thank God! I knew now it would be merely a matter of time until Matt got everything all straightened out. I hated that there was this ridiculous restraining order, but I also knew that Matt had resources, which I was sure he would capitalize on. I suspected he was working now on a resolution to our problem so that we could soon be better.

When Drew signed off from the call, he leaned into me and grabbed hold of my hand. "Well, he's out," he heaved an audible sigh of relief. "His dad bailed him out this afternoon finally, and Alex did get to talk to him."

"Oh my god, Drew. What did he say?"

"Well the first thing he did was ask about you, of course." I smiled, and felt for a second as if I were gonna again begin crying. "Then he said he wanted Alex to make sure that you just chilled out and got all the rest you needed. He says to just not worry about anything other than getting better."

"Of course he'd say that, Drew," my voice cracked, for at this point I was indeed crying.

"Don't cry, sweetie," Drew said. "Everything is fine."

"I know," I whimpered, "but it makes me so sad that even after being thrown in jail because of me, all he cares about is whether or not I'm all right."

"He loves you, silly. He loves you so much."

"I love him too. I wish I could talk to him ... be with him."

"Soon. Just be patient. Do what he says and just concentrate on getting rest and healing. He also said that when they release you he wants you to go stay at your sister's for awhile again."

"What?" I couldn't believe what he'd just said. "Why?"

"Because of the restraining order."

"I don't understand, Drew. That should be all the more reason he'd want me away from my sister. If there are no witnesses around to call the cops, he'd be able to see me a lot easier if I were at your apartment."

"Matt's gonna be staying at our apartment himself."

"Why?" I was almost afraid to hear the answer.

"His dad was sort of pissed about the whole thing. They got into an argument I guess, and now Matt needs a place to stay."

"You mean Matt's dad kicked him out of the house?"

"I'm sorry Petey. I'm not sure I should even tell you all this."

"Tell me!" I insisted.

"Just calm down, all right? You know Matt wouldn't want you getting upset."

"Matt got thrown in jail and then kicked out of his own house, and you don't expect me to be upset?" Could there possibly be any more bad news? It didn't take long to get the answer to that dreadful question.

"Of course you're upset. I'm so sorry, Petey. I'm just trying to break this to you gently, and I know Matt wouldn't want me telling you anything that is gonna keep you from getting the rest you need to get better."

"What else is there then?" I demanded.

"His dad knows about the two of you now, obviously. He knows about Matt, about his sexual preference, and he doesn't much like it."

"I don't think most parents like it too much when they find out their kids are gay. This was definitely not the best way for him to find out, either," I conceded.

"Yeah, exactly. His dad kind of overreacted a little, I think. He's threatening to disown Matt. He hasn't even hired him a lawyer yet, and he fired him from the gym."

"Oh my god!" I screamed. "No!"

"Petey, calm down! It's gonna be okay; his dad just needs some time to cool off. Matt doesn't think his dad will seriously disown him, and he says his dad doesn't even have anyone else to run that gym. He thinks after his dad gets over being mad, that he'll come to his senses."

"But what about Matt in the mean time? What about this legal stuff? What about the restraining order?"

"Give him a little bit of time, Petey. I think this is why he wants you to go back to your sister's. He doesn't wanna get himself thrown back in jail by getting caught with you. He needs to get this shit worked out with his dad and his mom too. She hasn't even talked to him yet."

"Maybe she will help him convince his dad not to disown him."

"Right, and I'm sure no matter how angry his dad is, he won't let Matt go back to jail. You have to just do what he says, though, and trust him. Matt said to go stay at your sister's and not to worry. Can you at least try to do that?"

"Of course I can *obey* him. How could I *not*? But I'm not sure I'm capable of stopping myself from worrying."

"Just try, Petey. Do it for Matt, okay?"

I was crying again now, unable to believe that all this horrid stuff could have happened within the course of the last forty-eight hours. "Do you think Matt will talk to me if I call him from your phone?"

Drew shook his head. "No Petey, he specifically said not to call. He promises you that he'll call you soon though. He needs to get everything worked out first."

As I lay there in the bed, barely able to even move, my body was wracked with uncontrollable silent sobs. I simply began to tremble and buried my face in my hands. I couldn't bear the thought of being away from Matt for days at a time, possibly weeks. How long would it take for him to solve these problems? What if his father did disown him? Would he choose to give up his relationship with me in order to placate his dad? I certainly couldn't expect him to give up his inheritance and the relationship he had with his parents for me. He had suffered enough for me already.

Drew climbed onto the bed beside me, kicking his shoes off onto the ground. He wrapped his arms around me ever-so-gently, avoiding any pressure on my incision or tender ribcage. I snuggled next to him as he held me and repeatedly kissed my cheek. His gentle hand stroked my face lovingly, wiping away my tears. "It's gonna be okay, Petey. I promise. Don't cry baby. Don't cry."

17

It was dark when I woke up, and I was alone in the hospital room. At least I thought I was. The dim light made it difficult for me to see, but as I looked up I saw there was a hospital employee standing next to my bed, perhaps a male nurse. He had his back to me and appeared to be checking the medication bottles on my IV stand. It seemed he had a face mask around his mouth, which surprised me a bit because I hadn't realized that I suffered from anything contagious. Perhaps it was he that was battling a cold or something.

"Excuse me," I croaked. "Sir, could I please get some water?"

The way he was standing there, almost completely immobile, was very odd. It started to concern me, and I thought perhaps he didn't hear me. He was tall, about the same height as Matt. By the looks of his broad shoulders and firm body, I would guess that he probably was about Matt's weight as well. It was sort of hard to tell, though, because he was wearing that loose-fitting, blue nurse's uniform. Scrubs are what I think they're called.

Just as I was about to repeat myself, the nurse reached over to the bedside table, still not turning to look at me. He picked up a Styrofoam cup and poured some water into it from a small plastic pitcher that had been sitting there. He handed it to me, and as he did so, he finally turned to look at me. It was so dark in the room, and all I could see was his eyes. Those eyes! Those beautiful eyes!

I knew unmistakably who it was! It was my Master. It was Matt!

"Sir!" I gasped, and as I did so he quickly pulled down his face mask, holding his index finger up to his lips.

"Shh" he said, immediately silencing me, and then he smiled.

"Oh Sir, I knew you'd come! I knew you'd find a way to be with me!" I whispered.

"My name is Doctor Porter," he said calmly in a very hushed tone. His voice sounded so sexy to me. When someone with a voice as deep as Matt's speaks in quiet tones, it is beyond sexy ... it's seductive. I noticed for the first time he was wearing a stethoscope around his neck. "I'm here to give you an examination." He smiled at me wryly.

I beamed.

"I haven't been feeling too well lately, Sir," I admitted. "I think an exam is a good idea."

"Oh really?" he asked. "What seems to be the problem?"

"It's my lips, Sir. They feel like they are dry or chapped or something. Not soft like they usually are."

"Hmm," he pondered. "Well I think I know what the problem might be, but it's gonna require a close inspection."

"Of course," I said, concurring that a close inspection would indeed be necessary. "Would you like me to pucker them for you, Sir? Like this ..." I then ever-so-slightly pursed my lips as he leaned in closer to me.

"Odd. I don't notice any chapping," he stated quizzically. "Are you sure there's something wrong with them?" His face was merely inches from my own.

"Oh, Sir, I'm absolutely certain of it. I know it's hard to see, but you'd certainly know what I meant if you were to touch them."

He was staring me directly in the eye, and without breaking his gaze, he reached up with his index finger and gently brushed it across my very soft, un-chapped lips. I desperately wanted to wrap those same lips around that finger and suck it into my mouth, but I simply lay there staring into his eyes. Slowly he ran his finger back and forth across my lips, tracing them from side to side, first the top and then the bottom.

"Very soft," he concluded. "Still I don't see there being a problem." He was speaking so quietly to me, still whispering, and as he did so he had inched himself even closer to me.

"Sir, maybe if you touched them with your ... um ... with your own lips, perhaps then you could feel what I'm talking about."

"You want me to examine your lips with my own?" he asked. He couldn't help himself; he broke into a smile.

"Yes Sir!" I pleaded. "Please do it. I don't think I can go on much longer like this."

"Well it is a somewhat unconventional method of examining a patient," he rationalized, "but if you feel it may help me understand your problem ..." He then leaned the rest of the way in and pressed his lips so carefully against my own. I was afraid to move or respond in any way at first. I just wanted to savor the softness of his touch. I just wanted to breathe his sweet breath and smell his masculine scent. I moaned just a little bit, barely more than a whimper, as he pressed his mouth fully against my own.

Instantly all of the anxiety and heartbreak of the past three days simply disappeared. I reached up and wrapped my arms around my doctor, clutching him desperately as our mouths remained locked together. His own strong embrace encircled me, and I slid my small hands up to the sides of his face, kissing him passionately and violently as I did so. I groped at him savagely, frustrated that I could not get myself as close to him as I wanted to be ... as I *needed* to be! I clutched his head, pulling against the surgical cap he was wearing, slipping it quickly off his head and discarding it. I began running my fingers through his cropped hair. I could smell him, taste him, feel him ... and my god did he feel wonderful.

I moaned as he slid his tongue deep into my mouth, and I of course responded in kind. I felt the forcefulness of his passion pressing against me, the weight of his body pinning me to the mattress beneath him. He turned his head from side to side as he continued kissing me, mauling me, and evilly drilling his tongue deep into my hungry mouth.

He gripped my shoulders with each of his hands—holding me there in place like a prisoner—and then slid his mouth downward and buried it in the crevice of my neck. I giggled momentarily as he found my erogenous zone, licking and sucking as I struggled beneath him. As he toyed with me in this manner so mercilessly, I continued to writhe beneath him, unable to keep myself from wriggling my legs and kicking my feet.

"Sir, if you'd just allow me to ..." I was gasping, barely able to speak. "If you'd just allow me to kiss you all over, then you'd see. You'd see how my lips feel."

He pulled himself away from my neck and cupped my head gently in both of his hands. "Well I think I've got a fairly clear diagnosis at this point already, and I also have a recommended treatment."

"Doctor, please tell me," I pleaded. "What must I do? Should I drink lots of fluids?"

Matt could remain serious no longer and burst into laughter. Then he regained his composure. I smiled up at him, a little too proud of myself for my lame joke. "Indeed, that may help, but I was merely going to suggest more kissing."

"Shouldn't we commence with the treatment plan immediately, Sir?" I asked.

The return of his lips to my own was his answer. This time he delivered multiple loving kisses, more than I could count. Over and over he kissed me, pulling away slightly between each one. It was maddening and divinely romantic at the same time. I couldn't get enough of him. I wanted him so desperately, so madly.

Finally his kisses stopped and he spoke again. "You seem a bit excited. Maybe I need to check your vitals."

"Oh dear," I feigned concern. "I hope my blood pressure isn't elevated."

He was now kneeling at the side of the bed, and he looked down at my body, pulling the bed sheet completely off of me. "It seems that your blood pressure is not the only thing that's elevated at this point." He then stood up. "Sit up so I can listen to your breathing," he instructed.

"Yes Sir!" I said and immediately complied. He placed the stethoscope in his ears and leaned in to hold it against my chest.

"Unfasten that gown," he ordered.

I reached up behind my neck and quickly untied the strings. "Yes Sir," I repeated. I allowed the gown to slide down my arms, exposing my bare chest to him.

Oddly it never occurred to me to wonder where my bandages had gone, not to mention the excruciating pain from my now non-existent incision. The doctor gently placed the cold metal of the stethoscope against my smooth bare chest and instructed me to breathe deeply. Slowly I inhaled. He moved it to various locations on my chest, listening very carefully. Finally he pulled away and ordered me to lean forward.

The doctor then placed the stethoscope against my back, once again listening to my breathing. As he did so, he reached around and brushed his fingers against my chest. Ever so slowly he encircled my hard little nipples. I wanted to squirm but knew I must remain perfectly still.

"You seem to be easily excitable, and this may be cause for concern," he surmised. "Hold out your hand and let me take your pulse." He pressed his fingers against my wrist and listened, acting as if he was actually counting my heartbeats.

"Yes, I do believe there is an issue with your heart rate."

"Is there something wrong with my heart?" I asked sincerely.

"I'm not quite sure just yet, but I fear it may be broken," he stated compassionately.

"Oh Sir, I think it was. I think it was broken right in two."

"Oh really? Why do you make such an assumption?" He was staring down at me with the most compassionate look on his face. His eyes penetrated me, and I felt as if he was staring directly into my soul.

"I guess I wasn't getting the care I needed, Sir. I felt alone and abandoned, but that's all changed now. I now have you to care for me, and you're a very competent doctor."

"Indeed you do," he agreed, "but still that does not answer my question. How was your heart broken?"

"Someone was taken from me, Sir. Someone I loved with all my heart. But it was my own fault because I had failed him, and that's why they took him from me."

The doctor looked confused. "Who took him?" he asked.

"The police, Sir. They came and took him to jail."

"And this is your fault?" he questioned.

"Yes Sir. I'd been hurt, and somehow they blamed him, but it actually was not his fault at all. It was my own disobedience that led to my injuries." Suddenly I was again aware of the dull ache in my side, the soreness where my ribs had been fractured.

"Well as your doctor I must advise you, and it is your responsibility to listen very carefully and do as I say. Are you capable of doing this?" His expression and his voice were very stern and authoritative.

"Yes Sir, of course I will try."

"You must stop blaming yourself because this is not good for your little heart. It seems that your heart is very soft, and it can be broken quite easily."

"I've been told, Sir, that I have a big heart."

"Indeed you do. I stand corrected. Nonetheless, you must ask yourself, were you ever really disobedient to the one they took from you?"

"Not on purpose Sir, but I *did* fail him."

"How so?" he asked.

"It was the way I spoke to Ryan, Sir!" I felt the teardrops stinging my cheeks. "I got him so angry, but I was supposed to be serving him. Instead all I ended up doing was making him mad."

"This Ryan sounds very troubled. Why would he get so angry at you when it was obvious that you were trying only to please him?"

"He hates me Sir. He hates me so much because he's jealous."

"I think you're right," Matt said, "and it was his jealousy which caused all of this, not your disobedience. Am I not correct?"

I nodded. "You're always correct Sir."

He smiled at me lovingly. "If only that were true." He then reached down and pulled the hospital gown completely off of me. I was wearing only a pair of boxer briefs underneath. I watched as he scanned the entire length of my body. "You're so smooth," he observed.

"Why are you looking at my feet, Sir?" I asked. "Is there something wrong with them?"

"You have cute little feet," he said. "No, there's nothing wrong with them." I wiggled my toes a tiny bit as he stared at them. "When I see them I'm reminded of how small and vulnerable you are. I'm reminded of the fact that you need protection."

"My feet remind you of *that*?" I asked, laughing a little to myself.

"To me, everything about you seems like your feet. So delicate. So fragile."

"I wish I were stronger, Sir," I said.

"Oh it's not a lack of strength on your part. It says more about me as your doctor. I get very attached to my patients. I feel the need to protect them."

"That's what makes you such a good doctor, Sir."

"Will you promise me that you'll stop blaming yourself? Otherwise your heart will never heal."

"Yes Sir," I said, now instantly again on the verge of tears. "I promise."

"Good, then perhaps you're ready to commence with the remainder of this examination."

"Oh ..." I said. "There's more?"

"We've barely even started," he said.

"Well what part of me do you need to examine next, Doctor?" He opened a drawer beside my bed and removed a pair of latex gloves. He held one up with his right hand and slid his left hand into it, snapping the latex against his wrist once it was in place.

"You may need a prostate exam," he said.

"A prostate exam?" I asked. "Even at my young age?"

"Good prostate health can never begin too early," he said, sounding almost like a spokesperson on a television commercial. He snapped on the other glove. "Now, I'm gonna slide this pillow under your behind. Lift up." I obliged him as he picked up a pillow from an adjacent chair and slid it under me. "Take off your underwear and assume a position with your legs spread, knees up."

Quickly I slid off my shorts and then spread my legs. My knees were bent with the soles of my bare feet pressed flat against the mattress. "Like this, Sir?" I asked.

"Yes, very good. Now don't be embarrassed by your *obvious* erection. I assure you it's very normal."

"When you're the doctor, Sir, I'm sure it is," I smiled. A serious look from him quickly wiped that smile from my face though.

"So by your comments I will have to assume this is your first-ever prostate exam. Correct?"

I nodded. "Yes Sir."

He was now holding a tube of some sort of gel. He squeezed a bit onto his left index and middle fingers. "I need you to answer a few basic questions for me. First of all, do you feel that you urinate frequently?"

"Um ... well ... no Sir, I don't suppose any more than normal."

"Good," he said as he slid his left hand down between my legs, rubbing his lubed fingers against my exposed ass-crack. "And is there any discomfort while urinating?"

"No Sir ... ungghh," he slid one of his fingers into my tight hole. "None that I've really noticed."

"That's good," he said, as he wiggled his finger into my hole. It was difficult for me to remain still in this position, especially as he eased his way deeper into me. "Any difficulty in achieving orgasm?" he asked in a dry, monotone voice.

"Actually Sir ... oh god, that feels ..."

"Just focus, boy, and answer the question." He was now all the way in with one finger.

"Um ... sorry Sir, um ... well, no actually I find the opposite to be true. Often it's difficult for me to hold back from cumming, even when I know I'm not supposed to yet."

"Ahh ..." he said. "Perhaps you have not been properly trained."

"Oh, no Sir. I had a very good trainer."

He then used his right hand to squeeze a small glob of the gel onto my very-erect cock. With his left hand he continued to drive his middle finger in and out of my tight, boy pussy; with his right he began to stroke my boner. "Are you experiencing that urge right now, young man? Are you finding it hard to resist ejaculation?"

I sighed and gripped the bed sheet beneath me with both of my hands. "Ahh ... well I think I might have some difficulty very soon. I mean, if you have to continue for very long with ... ahh ... unnngh ... with this examination."

He then pulled out of me for merely a split second before re-entering, this time with both fingers. "That's a very tight little hole you've got there," he said. "If I didn't know better, I'd almost think it'd never even been used."

"Only one person's ever used it," I said, but then immediately I remembered Ryan. The doctor must have seen the distressed look on my face. He commented.

"I'd say it is still in perfect condition. Don't you worry, and I must admit, it seems to be very neatly shaved and clean."

"Thank you, Sir," I said, smiling at him briefly. I so wanted to thrust my hips upwards as he increased the speed of his stroking. The grip of his hand around my cock had initially been somewhat loose, but as he continued, it seemed to tighten.

"Just relax," he encouraged me. "I need to feel around up here with both my fingers. Gotta make sure your prostate gland is healthy."

"Oh Sir, it feels very healthy to me!"

He laughed in spite of himself. "Is this examination bothering you?" he asked. "We can stop now if you wish."

"No Sir!" I pleaded. "No, please don't stop yet."

"Better continue a while longer to be on the safe side, then?" he offered.

"Yes ... ugghh ... yes Sir, just to be ... ahhhh ... safe!"

He had now quickened the pace of both his inward thrusts into my hole and of his stroking of my throbbing cock. "It almost seems to me as if you're kind of enjoying this."

"Oh Sir! It feels so good!"

"Oh so you *do* like it, huh? Well it's too bad that I have to stop then." He immediately pulled out of me and stopped stroking. He still had his hand wrapped around my dick though.

I stared up at him, gazing intently into his eyes. "Sir, I almost ... well you know ..."

"You almost ejaculated, and without my permission."

"I'm sorry Sir," I said quietly.

"Well I just can't get a real good feel for what is going on up in that hole of yours. I may need to use another instrument to examine you."

"Another instrument?" I asked. With his left hand he then pulled the cord on his waistband. My eyes widened as I realized the instrument to which he was referring. "Oh, I think that might be a good idea Sir!"

He released his grip on my now-throbbing cock and took a step backwards. "You'll need to slide to the edge of the bed," he said, "facing me." I quickly obliged him, pulling the pillow out from beneath me and tossing it aside. He rapidly shucked off the pants he was wearing, revealing that he wasn't even wearing underwear.

My gaze suddenly was riveted on his own throbbing prick. It was the single physical characteristic of him that turned me on the most. The beauty of it was breathtaking, and it seemed to me then that it'd been oh so long since I'd touched it, tasted it, felt it inside of me! I reached out to him, but he gently pushed my hands aside.

"Is this an examination of me or of you?" he asked.

"Of me, Sir. I'm sorry."

"Very well. Let's not forget who the patient is here, and who's the doctor."

"No Sir. Of course."

He then reached beside me and again picked up the tube of lubrication. He squeezed a generous amount onto his cock, and then some more onto his fingers. I was now positioned with my buttocks resting right on the edge of the bed, my legs draped over the side. "Lift up your legs, boy," he said, and I obeyed. I spread them wide apart for him, feeling suddenly like a baby who was about to endure a diaper change.

Slowly he smeared the warm gel against the inner sides of my butt cheeks. He slid his fingers back and forth, making me feel real slick and slimy. I felt his fingertips again brush against my pucker. I wanted him inside me so badly! "Oh

Sir!" I gasped, even before he'd made any indication of his plans to enter me.

"You're just an eager little thing, aren't you?" he teased. "You know, perhaps you've had enough for the day. Maybe we should just call it good. I have a pretty good feel for your overall prostate health at this point."

"Oh Sir!" I cried. "Please, you can't stop now!"

He raised his eyebrows as he stared down at me. "Are you telling me how to do my job?" he asked.

"No, Sir ... um ... I'm sorry, Sir! Please though ... I'm begging you!"

An arrogant grin now graced his face. "You call *that* begging?" he asked sarcastically.

"Oh PUH-LEEZ!" I cried. "Please continue the exam!" I was pulling my knees back as far as they would go, spreading myself wide for him. I knew of no more obvious an invitation than this to encourage him.

Then in what seemed to be a split second, he was on top of me. Without another word he aimed his cock at my exposed hole and drove it into me. In one smooth thrust he'd completely impaled me, burying himself balls-deep. "Oh god!" I screamed. "Oh fuck!"

He grabbed my ankles and lifted them in the air, spreading my legs wide apart. It was almost as if he were using them to steady himself. Then he began to thrust. He crinkled his face a bit as he rammed himself into me, but then asked rather seriously, "How's that prostate feel now?"

"Oh Sir! It feels so good!"

"And now ...?" he drove himself all the way in again, grinding himself into me.

"Oh fuck! Oh god yes! It feels awesome Sir!"

Then he began fucking me. He pumped himself in and out of me rapidly, almost like a wild animal. I looked around him and saw a mirror on the closet doorway. I could see the tightening of his ass cheeks as he pounded his way over-and-over into my tight hole. I saw his broad shoulders and his neatly trimmed conservative haircut. I saw his narrow waist and strong legs as they flexed with each thrust. Oh god, he was so fucking hot!

I reached up to him, trying desperately to touch his chest. I wanted to feel the firmness of his body against me, but he seemed to be intent upon one thing alone ... fucking my tight hole. He tilted his head back and closed his eyes as he continued his wild thrusting. Over and over and with increasing speed he plugged my hole with his rock-hard prick.

I moaned uncontrollably as he impaled me. My own cock was throbbing, and it bobbed up and down, slapping against my belly as his thrusting continued to jar my whole body. "Oh Sir!" I shouted, "it's gonna make me cum. I'm so close!" I was whimpering, reduced to barest form of my existence. I was completely exposed to him, and I wanted nothing more than to have all of him within me.

"Shoot it pup!" he commanded. "Shoot your fuckin load!" He then released my legs and leaned into me, grabbing my head with both his hands. He planted a passionate kiss on my open mouth, driving his tongue deep within.

I cried uncontrollably, "Ohhhhh!" I felt myself reach the point of no return as his cock rooted inside of me. He began to moan as well. I felt his body tense against my own and we both began to tremble. "Fuck! I screamed, and he continued to kiss me. We came at exactly the same moment.

"Oh god! Oh god!" I cried. "Thank you Sir! Thank you doctor!" My eyes remained tightly shut as my body shook with pleasure.

Suddenly it was over. I opened my eyes and my doctor stood before me. It wasn't Matt though. It was someone I'd never seen, and my chest was again bandaged. I again felt the soreness in my ribcage. There was daylight in the room.

"Good morning," he said. "I'm Doctor Straight, your attending physician. You were having quite a dream I see."

Bewildered, I stared up at him. "I'm sorry, sir," I said.

"Are you all right?" he asked.

"Yes, oh yes, I'm fine. Was I screaming?"

"You were moaning quite a bit. Are you in pain?"

"No sir, definitely not."

"Ready to go home today?" he offered.

"Yes sir! I'd like that very much."

"Good. I think we've kept you prisoner long enough."

If only I could get Kathie to recognize that reality, everything just might go back to normal. I needed to see Matt. I needed to make my very vivid dream a reality.

"What's that mark on your neck?" the doctor asked. "If I didn't know better I'd think it was a ... um ... what do u call them? A hickey?"

"I don't know, sir," I said. "Perhaps something that happened to me during an examination."

"Not likely," he said, and then he proceeded to make notations on his chart.

18

I was so ecstatic to be getting released from the hospital. I had a nurse call my sister for me, but I had no way of calling Drew. Kathie had specifically requested that no phone be hooked up in my room, fearing I would attempt contacting Matt, and of course she'd taken my cell phone from me. This was extremely frustrating to me because I was overjoyed about getting out yet had no one to share it with.

I was only just beginning to be able to get up and walk around the room a bit. My side was so sore that it truly hurt me even to move my torso ever so slightly. Lying still in bed, it was easy to convince myself that I was doing well, but as soon as I tried getting around like a normal person I realized how much of an invalid I actually was.

It was around ten o'clock that Tuesday morning when Kathie strolled into my room. She was smiling broadly. "Petey!" she greeted me, spreading her arms wide, "you ready to go home?"

"Oh my god, yes!" I said. I already had my clothes on and was sitting in a chair beside my bed.

"Well, sorry, but we can't leave yet," she frowned.

"Why not?" I asked. "The doctor said I was free to go, and the nurse has me all checked out. She's gonna come and have me sign some papers and give me some prescriptions. Then I can go."

"Yeah, but we have to wait for someone first," she informed me.

"Who?" I asked.

"There's a lady from the prosecutor's office named Michele. I spoke with her this morning, and she wanted me to bring you down to her office. I told her you were still in the hospital, and she agreed to meet us here."

"I don't wanna talk to any more cops!" I snapped back at her.

"Hi!" a young African American woman said as she stepped through the door. "I'm Michele Montgomery from the prosecutor's office, and I promise, I'm not a cop."

I felt my face redden with embarrassment. "I'm sorry Ms. Montgomery," I said. "I shouldn't have said that."

"It's cool," she smiled down at me. "I know you must be getting tired of all these questions."

"It's not that, ma'am; it's just that I wish people would believe me when I answer their questions." I stared up at Kathie as I said it.

"May I have a seat?" Michele asked.

"Of course!" offered Kathie, and she pushed a chair over to the prosecutor. "I'm Kathie, Petey's sister. We spoke on the phone earlier." They shook hands and exchanged pleasantries.

"Peter ... Peter Drinkell, right?" she asked me as she looked down at a clipboard that she was holding in her lap.

"You can call me Petey," I said.

She smiled. "Okay, Petey. Well I've read all of the information I received from Detective Murray including your statement. I reviewed the eyewitness testimony of Jason Scruggs. I believe he's one of your co-workers, correct?"

"Yes, but he did not actually witness anything!"

Again she smiled. "I noticed that," she replied politely and nodded. "I reviewed the information I received from the hospital about your injuries, and I have testimony here from your sister Kathie." She pointed to my sister briefly. "She reports to have overheard Matthew Porter confessing to being responsible for your injuries."

"It's not true!" I retorted. "He meant he's responsible for my well-being. He said that cuz he was so worried about me. I was in surgery at the time."

"Honey, it's okay. Don't get upset. I'm just giving you all the information I have. I'm not making any accusations."

"Well that's what the detective said too," I responded, looking away from her out the window. I was afraid I was gonna start crying again. It seemed I did so every time I got upset or emotional about anything.

"Well you may be pleased by the news I have for you then, Petey," she said, and quickly I turned to look at her. "We're not charging Matthew with any crimes."

"You're not?" I was so ecstatic I wanted to leap from my chair. "So he is free? He isn't in trouble any more?"

She shook her head. "Nope. He was released from jail yesterday and all charges were dropped this morning. I cannot see that we have the evidence to charge him with domestic abuse when you insist it was someone else who did this to you."

Kathie sighed audibly in exasperation. "I can't believe this!" she said.

"Kathie, he *didn't* do it!" I replied. "Do you want him to go to jail for something he didn't do and let the real attacker get away with it?"

"That's a good point, Petey," the prosecutor said, "and that's why I'm really here. I need to talk to you about what did happen. I'd like to go after this Ryan Connors. He's the one who did this to you, right?"

I nodded. "But I don't want you to go after him. I'm sorry, but I just want to put this behind me. I already had to go to court over those guys who beat me up last year. I don't wanna go through it again."

"If he's done this to you once, Petey, he surely will do it again, if not to you then to some other victim."

"But it's just his word against mine. I know what he'll say. He'll say I wanted it."

"You wanted to be kicked in the ribs and then raped?"

"He'll say it wasn't rape, and he'll say the broken ribs were an accident."

"Petey, we have the eyewitness testimony of Matt. He walked in when the attack was occurring, didn't he?"

This time I sighed. "He walked in and saw Ryan on top of me, and he saw I'd been hurt. He didn't see Ryan forcing me to ..." I couldn't bring myself to say any more.

"Did Matt hear you ask Ryan to stop?"

I shook my head. "I don't think so."

"Well I hate to push this one to the back burner. We do have a case against Connors, but we need yours and Matt's testimony. I'm gonna give you my card, and I want you to call me. When you're ready you need to come down to the office and fill out a report, the sooner the better."

"And what if Matt says he didn't hear or see anything?"

"I've talked to Matt. His testimony will be sufficient. I need yours though."

"I want to talk to him first, to Matt."

"Why do you need to talk to Matt? For god's sakes, Petey!" Kathie shouted.

"I just do!"

"It's okay, Petey," Michele said. "You can talk to him first. There is no longer a restraining order; it was removed this morning."

"It was?" I asked. "I wonder why he didn't come here, or try to call me. Kathie, do you have my phone."

"I'll give it to you when we're done," she said curtly, and I glared at her.

The prosecutor again smiled. "Well! I guess I don't really have anything else. If Ryan Connors should attempt to make contact with you, please either call my number or 911. I hope you'll decide to pursue this, Petey. You don't have to allow people like him to victimize you."

"Thank you," I said, and reached out to shake her hand.

She stood up. "Good luck, and I'll expect to hear from you real soon."

"Thanks."

As soon as she was out the door I held my hand out to Kathie. "I need my phone, sis. Please."

"Can't you at least wait til we get home?"

"No, what if he's on his way up here now? I need to let him know I've been released. Plus I need to talk to him about that other thing."

Reluctantly she dug in her purse and retrieved my phone, handing it to me. "I'm gonna go find a nurse while you call him."

"Okay, thanks." I was grateful for the privacy actually. I quickly pressed Matt's speed dial and waited as the phone rang. After about four rings he finally picked up.

"Yeah?" he said.

"Sir, it's Petey! It's your pup! I heard the great news, and I'm ..."

He interrupted me. "Petey, I don't want you callin me any more."

"What? Sir, what do you mean?"

"You heard me," he said. "Don't call me any more. I'm over it. I'm sick of all this drama."

"Sir, I'm sorry, but I don't know what you mean. They're releasing me from the hospital today."

"Good, cuz I just got released from jail. I got my ass thrown in jail cuz of all this shit, because of your bullshit. I almost lost my job and my dad nearly disowned me."

"I'm so sorry Sir!" I cried, the tears instantly pouring out of my eyes. "I didn't mean ..."

"You never mean it! You just can't help yourself, I know. You are just like all those other little fag bitches. Everything is all a big drama. You're not happy until you've fucked up everyone else's life. Well like I said, I'm over it."

"Matt, why are you saying this to me?" I cried. "I don't understand."

"Petey, ever since I met you, you've been nothing but a sponge. You take and take and take, demanding every second of my attention. All I get in return is headache. I get my ass thrown in jail. I get in trouble with my family. Even your sister blames me for all your problems."

"I'm sorry, Sir. She's wrong. I've told her she's wrong, I swear."

"And stop calling me Sir. I'm not your Sir any more. You're free. Enjoy it."

"No! Please don't say that ... please, Matt!"

"Go find someone else's life to fuck up!"

The phone went dead.

19

I didn't bother to call Drew for I knew he was working. He'd already missed the previous day of work in order to be at the hospital with me. After trying multiple times to call Matt back, I realized it was futile. He had his phone off, and the messages I left him were utterly pathetic. I was sobbing, begging him to forgive me, to give me another chance.

I barely remember the ride home. Kathie was offering me empty assurances, prattling on about how she knew how much it must hurt me but that it was for the best. I tuned her out, staring blankly out the window. It really didn't matter what she said to me. I didn't care what anyone said to me, actually. My world had come to an end, and there was nothing anyone could say that would change that.

When we got back to Kathie's apartment, I went to my empty room and closed the door. All my personal belongings had been moved out and were over at Drew's. I didn't even have a computer. It wouldn't have mattered, though, for I was so utterly exhausted. My side hurt terribly, and even taking a deep breath was excruciating. I couldn't remember a time in my life when my energy was so low.

I lay on top of the bed, not even possessing enough strength or motivation to pull a blanket over myself. I simply lay there staring up at the ceiling. My chest hurt, and I did not know really whether it was from the grief I was feeling or from my surgery. It was real, nonetheless, but I did not care. I didn't care at all that it hurt. The pain allowed me to feel something other than emptiness.

It seemed like a movie playing in my head as I recalled the way Matt and I had initially met. I remembered the way

315

he had rushed to my rescue, fending off my attackers and ushering me to the emergency room. I saw it all in my mind's eye, the day I had run into him on the sidewalk as he'd walked his dog, Petey. I'd knelt there petting the dog, and it felt so right to me to be at Matt's feet. It was a foreshadowing of how my entire world would soon change.

It had changed most dramatically that day I went to his house and knelt before him in submission for the first time. My confession of who I was and what I craved had brought tears to my eyes. He began the process right then of leading me to acceptance of myself. He had promised never to hurt me. It was a promise he had reiterated numerous times over the many months we were together.

I remembered the very first time he made love to me. In my mind he was a larger-than-life figure who dominated me in every way, yet that evening he'd been so tender and so gentle. He hadn't dismissed my fear but had instead helped me face it. In so doing he introduced me to a beautiful experience.

The day he took me shopping, I was so proud. I smiled as I recalled it, though the tears continued to trickle down my cheeks. He could have called me his mini-me, for I was a carbon copy of him in miniature. I ended up with the same clothes, the same haircut, even the same shoes. Eventually he'd even given me his letter jacket.

In those early days I was so terrified that he would choose a woman over me. I was insanely jealous of the fact that he'd continued to see Tracy even after he made me his pup. She eventually disappeared from his life though. As Matt and I became closer, he no longer seemed to even care about her, nor about any girl.

The day he'd collared me was the proudest day of my life. I recalled our lovemaking in the shower that evening; after which we had gone to the gay bar together for the first time. It was here that we'd stumbled upon Ryan for the first time.

How was I to have known back then that it would be he who'd eventually be our undoing?

During the course of our relationship, I had met and fallen in love with my dearest friend Drew. He had taken me under his wing and taught me what a sub was. He had soothed my broken heart, offered me reassurances, and calmed my fears. He'd shared in my joys and my sorrows. Now I didn't even know if he'd still be allowed to remain in my life. Matt and Alex were the best of friends. How would Drew be able to maintain contact with me while continuing to be obedient to his Master? Surely this would cause too many conflicts.

I wished I could simply sleep. Perhaps it would bring to me more dreams of Matt, like I'd had the night before in the hospital. Sleep would not come, though. It felt to me as if the world had stopped spinning. There was no more reason to go on with life. Matt was my life, and now he was gone.

How could it have happened? It must be a misunderstanding. Perhaps it was a lesson Matt was trying to teach me. Maybe he was testing me in some way. Twice during as many days, Matt had gone out of his way to protect me and had made passionate love to me as well. He had told me he loved me. He had reminded me of his promise never to hurt me. Then out of the blue, all of a sudden, he dumped me. It didn't even fit with his character. These actions were quite the opposite of anything I'd have ever expected of him.

But then again, hadn't this always been my deepest and darkest fear? I had always known in the back of my mind that there was a possibility that Matt would one day tire of me. He would eventually become annoyed by my emotionalism and my neediness. He would finally weigh the benefits and liabilities of our relationship and conclude that it just wasn't worth it any more. Wasn't that what he'd said to me on the phone? He just was tired of the drama.

Of course it was no real surprise to me that he'd be upset about being falsely accused of beating me and subsequently being thrown in jail. Then his father had threatened to fire him from his job and disown him. Why would I have ever expected him to be able to make such a sacrifice for me? Given the choice of a comfortable life with a guaranteed job and a wealthy family to back him up or a life with never-ending headaches and drama that he would have with me, he would logically *have* to choose the former.

I had heard the exhaustion in his voice when he said those horrible words to me. He sincerely was just worn out, beaten down, used up. He'd given so much to me and had gotten so very little in return. *You're nothing but a sponge!* It was true. Oh god, it was so very true!

From the moment I'd met him I had soaked up his attention, his protection, his guidance, and his love. I had taken money, gifts, clothing, even a cruise. I had required of him constant reassurances. I was so emotional and weak, and I continuously had tapped into his strength merely to sustain myself. I fed off of him. Yes, I was a sponge in every sense of the word. A parasite!

Why wouldn't the sleep come? Why wouldn't the darkness just overtake me? Why wouldn't all the pain just go away? Maybe if I did fall asleep I'd awaken later in my hospital bed and realize it all had been a dream. Just like the doctor-patient fantasy I had dreamt of, perhaps this horrendous breakup was also illusionary.

Darkness did indeed eventually come. Kathie had not bothered me, assuming me to be asleep. I just lay there, immobile. It had to have been for hours. I stared straight ahead, memorizing the lines in the wallpaper pattern in front of me. Even that didn't seem real to me. All of this was so unbelievable that I could hardly wrap my mind around it.

I should have expected that Drew would arrive. He'd done exactly the same thing when I was depressed once before. He'd come to me and taken me away with him, stuffing me with chocolate and junk food. We'd snuggled together in bed and talked about our two hot Masters. This remedy wouldn't work this time though. There was no cure for losing Matt.

He did arrive, however, rapping lightly on my bedroom door. When he stepped inside I think it surprised him to see me lying there with my eyes wide open. There were no tears. How odd was this? I cried over literally everything, yet now when the worst thing in the world that could possibly happen to me did occur, I merely lay there like an emotionless statue.

"Petey?" he whispered. "Are you awake?"

I nodded, not knowing whether or not he could see me in the dim light. He made no attempt to brighten the room, though. Instead he merely closed the door quietly behind him and slid over to the side of my bed. "Can I lay with you, Petey?" he asked. Again I nodded. Then he slid his warm body behind me, spooning himself around me and held me.

At last the tears came. They merely flowed silently from my eyes and down my cheeks. There was no sobbing, just a torrent of unstoppable acrid tears. Drew just held me and allowed me to cry. He never told me everything was going to be all right. He never suggested to me that I was better off without him. He never told me I should not feel bad because I was sure to find someone better. He never said any of those cliché remarks that friends tell you when you get dumped. He just held me.

It had to have been at least an hour we lay there spooned together like that, when finally I rolled over to face him. "I love you, Drew," I whispered.

He smiled so meekly. "I know," he said, "and I love you too, my sweet pup." He gently brushed my cheek with the tips of his fingers. He called me Matt's special name, but it was okay. Drew was the only person on earth who could do so without devastating me.

"Honey, I have to talk to you," he said. "There are some important things I have to tell you."

"About him?" I asked.

He nodded. "Yes, about Matt."

"I don't blame him, Drew. I really don't. I understand …"

Now he shook his head. "No, sweetie, you don't." I just stared at him. What was he saying? I hadn't the energy for games. I didn't even have the motivation to request that he explain himself. He did, nonetheless. "Petey, I was with Matt today when he broke up with you."

Drew was with Matt? How was this possible? Why would he then have waited so many hours to contact me? Unless Matt had ordered him not to speak to me.

"Are you here without permission, Drew?" I asked.

"I didn't ask permission, Petey. Had I been ordered to abandon you, I would've had to disobey." There were tears now streaming down his cheeks.

"Where were you? I mean where were you and Matt when he …"

"We were at my apartment, honey. And I stayed there for the next four hours afterwards, waiting for Alex to get home."

"Why?" I asked. "You didn't want Matt to be left alone in your apartment?"

"Matt was crying, Petey. I'd never seen him cry before, and he was so sad."

I then *did* sob. It was like a spear slicing through my soul. "Oh Drew!" I cried. "No! Then why? Why has he done this to me if it hurts him so badly?"

"Petey, he loves you so much. He loves you with all his heart."

"Drew!" I screamed. "You have to tell me! Why?"

"Petey, I need to show you something, but you have to swear to me that it will always and forever be our secret."

"Yes, of course, Drew! Why would you have to even ask?"

"Because it is going to be nearly impossible for you to keep it a secret, but you have to. You have to swear. You have to swear for Matt's sake, and for mine."

"For yours?"

"Yes, if Matt finds out I've shown this to you, we will all lose. We will lose everything forever."

"Show me Drew. I swear I won't tell him ..."

"Or anyone."

"Or anyone," I repeated.

He sat up on the side of the bed and turned on the lamp. It took a moment for our eyes to adjust to the light, and I reached up and brushed the dampness from his cheeks. He was so beautiful, even when he cried. After a few moments of silence, he finally reached into his pocket and removed an envelope. "Petey, I stole this from Matt."

"What is it?" I asked.

"It's a letter. It's from Matt to your sister."

"Oh my god!" I gasped.

"Wait til you read it, but remember what you promised me."

"Give it to me, Drew ... please." He looked a little scared as he handed it over. "Will you go lock the door?" I asked. As he did so, I opened the envelope and pulled out the notebook paper. I began to read....

Kathie,

I'm not sure when I'm gonna be able to talk to you again. I'm writing this from jail, and I don't know exactly when I'll be let out. When we spoke last night you made some things very clear to me about the love you have for your brother. I respect that. Honest, I totally do. It kind of pisses me off, though, that you don't give me that same level of respect in return.

I know that I'm the newcomer here. I know you and Petey have been everything to each other ever since your Mom and Dad passed. It makes sense to me that you'd be protective the way you are. Wouldn't be much of a sister if you weren't. Petey's been lucky to have you.

I also appreciate the fact that for all this time you've kept the secret of the abortion from him. We both know that it would be something that he'd have a really hard time understanding, and believe it or not, the last thing on earth I wanna do is hurt the little guy.

For most of my life I have pretty much gotten everything I ever wanted. I'm sure you think I'm spoiled and arrogant and very selfish. You're probably right about all those things. What you don't know about me, though, is that when I started to fall in love with your bro there were a lot of things about me that changed. For the first time ever I had someone else to think about besides myself. I got so swept up by this need to protect and help him that it sort of became an obsession.

The problem with Petey and me is not Petey. He is just Petey. He's innocent, emotional, trusting, loyal, generous, kind-hearted, and of course cuter than fuck. During the course of our relationship we followed a set of rules. These were rules, which I made up and Petey followed. He trusted me completely, and he believed with all his heart that by obeying me he would become a better person. That's the irony of it, really. He never needed to be any better than he was. He was pretty damn near perfect to begin with.

Of course there were times when he got under my skin. Sometimes he needed so much affection and reassurance that it was exasperating. I didn't exactly know how I could teach him to love himself the way that I loved him. If only he could've seen who he was through my eyes then he'd have been the happiest little guy in the world.

It was my desire to make him stronger that led to most of my blunders. I wanted him to see how much better of a person he was than that son-of-a-bitch Ryan. Instead I ended up sending my little lamb into the lion's den. I wanted to teach him that he was strong enough to face uncomfortable situations but that as long as he trusted me, things would work out. Instead I placed him in a volatile situation where my best friend busted up his nose. Every time I tried to help him get stronger, I put him in danger.

Kathie, you don't need to threaten me into doing what I know is right for Petey. Telling him about Tracy's abortion would not have changed anything between me and my pup. If anything, it would've only turned him against you. But your threat has influenced me in the sense that it's placed me on a timetable. I do not want Petey to go through all of the hurt and questioning of himself and his worth that this revelation will do to him only to then also have to face the reality that I have dumped him.

The reason I'm ending my relationship with Petey is not because I fear losing my family or my job or my reputation. It's not because you have tried to blackmail me with the threat of telling Petey how awful I am. And I'm not arguing that I'm not awful. When I pressured Tracy into that abortion, it was probably the most horrible thing I've ever done. But I'm not one to be backed into a corner. I don't do things I haven't chosen to do. Period.

The reason I'm ending my relationship with Petey is because I love him too much to continue hurting him and placing him in danger. I know that based on everything that has happened so far, Petey is only gonna keep getting hurt if we stay together. He will not only have to cope with this abortion revelation but he's also gonna be under fire from my parents, especially my dad. I also won't have the financial means to help him the way I've done in the past. And worst of all, I'll know in my heart that every time he looks at me in the eye he will know that he's seeing the man that sent him to be raped!

My heart ripped straight in two as I read these words, and I cried out, "Oh Matt! Oh my Master!" I held the letter up next to my chest and curled myself into a crouched position on the bed, sobbing uncontrollably. Within seconds Kathie was pounding on my bedroom door but I shook my head violently, "Don't let her in!" I cried.

Drew wrapped his arms around me and held me, pulling me into his chest. "It's okay, Kathie," he said. "He wants us to be alone right now. I promise it's okay. We'll be out in a minute."

"It's not okay!" she screamed through the door. "Open this fuckin door now before I bust it open!"

"Stop it!" I screamed. "Just leave me alone! Leave me the fuck alone right now!" Suddenly everything got quiet, and after a few seconds it appeared as if she'd gone away from the door. "Oh Drew," I whispered. "He does still love me!"

Drew nodded. "Of course he does, honey. He loves you with all his heart. Can you finish the letter?" I wiped my eyes with the tips of my fingers while Drew scanned the room for some tissue. "Here," he said, handing me a box of Kleenex.

"I can finish it," I said. "I *have* to finish it." I began to read again.

I beg you to be there for him now like you never have before. I know that merely by asking this of you it is somewhat an insult. Of course you will be there. You'll be there for him like you have been all these years before Petey even knew I existed. He's gonna need counseling to get past what has happened to him. He's gonna need so much assurance that he was the victim and that he did nothing wrong. He's gonna need you to remind him constantly that he's better off without me. You're gonna have to convince him he's too good for me.

I'll do my part, Kathie, to make it easier. I'll try to be the coldest and cruelest bastard that I've ever been. If I can force myself to do it, then maybe he will learn to hate me enough to be able to move on. I know it will hurt him, but I'd rather hurt him one time now than a thousand more times in the future.

If I do not get out of jail by tomorrow, I will mail this to you. If I'm released I will have already called you by the time you ever see this.

Take care of him.

M.

"Drew, how did you steal this from him?" I demanded. "Did he tell you about it?" I held the letter out to him, waving it in his face dramatically.

"He fell asleep on the couch, and I went into your room. That's where he's gonna be stayin. All his stuff is just like strewn everywhere in that room. He got to go to his parent's house and take out the bare essentials of what he needed. I don't think he was in the mood really to do any unpacking."

"And the letter was just sitting there?"

"I was trying to help him, Petey. When I saw the mess I started gathering up the clothes and shit he'd thrown on the floor. I was gonna wash them."

"And this envelope was in the pocket?"

He nodded. "Yes! And once I saw it was to Kathie, I had to read it. I'm sorry, but I just had to!"

"Thank God you did, Drew!"

"This was like an hour ago. Matt didn't even sleep for long, and after he got back up it almost seemed like he was gonna cry again. It was terrible cuz I knew the truth about everything then but had to act like I didn't know shit. When Alex got home I told him I had to go to the store."

"What do I do?" I cried. "I have to talk to him!"

"Yes, but you can't tell him you know about the letter. He will be so angry that he'll order Alex to forbid me from seeing you. Then you'll end up losing me too."

I shook my head. "I'm not ever gonna lose you Drew. And I'm not fuckin losin Matt either!"

* * *

That revelation about Matt from my best friend Drew was a turning point for me. Of course it was true that I was the one single person other than Matt's parents, perhaps, who knew him best. In many ways I probably knew Matt even better than his parents or the rest of his family. Prior to this day, I had felt I'd known all sides of him, which was why his sudden act of cruelty when he dumped me was so surprising, not to mention devastating. It had seemed out of character for him, and I began to wonder if I ever really knew him at all.

Yet in a way it had made sense to me that he would reach a breaking point. His comment to me about the endless, intolerable drama that my association with him brought into his life was a realistic statement. It had always been a fear of mine. I had always known that I was far more emotional than a guy my age should be, and this would be a factor that would be taxing on any relationship. Being that ours was a same-sex relationship and a Dom/sub one at that, it made it even more challenging. So for him to conclude as he was sitting in jail alone, facing ostracization from his family as well as a possible loss of employment and maybe even a jail sentence ... that he just couldn't take it any more; this was feasible to me.

Had I not seen the letter, I probably would have ultimately bought the explanation. Even though I felt in my heart that he did love me, and even though I knew he was the strongest and smartest person I'd ever met, I would have eventually accepted that a dramatic and emotional pup like me was just too high maintenance for a free spirit like Matt. In a nutshell, I had always known how lucky I was to have him, and it wouldn't have surprised me that he finally realized the same exact thing. I almost believed that he was over it, and that he was ready to finally kick me to the curb.

The one single thing that changed everything about how I viewed Matt and me was one seemingly minor reality. Matt had cried.

Matt cried!

Seeing my mom die was horrific to me. Losing my dad to a sudden and unexpected heart attack was devastating. Being beaten senselessly by Devin and his cohort Kyle was agonizing. Fearing that Matt had chosen the likes of Tracy over me was excruciating. Being punched in the face by Alex, being punished into the service of that bastard Ryan who then raped me—that had been unimaginably painful and humiliating. But nothing I had ever endured, no experience I had ever encountered, and no emotion I had ever felt was even half as heartbreaking to me as Matt's tears!

He was my Master! He was my bastion of strength. He was my stabilizer. It was he I turned to when I myself was emotional. He was the one who rescued me from danger, soothed my fears, calmed my troubled heart. He was my rock, and he didn't cry. He didn't fuckin cry! But he did.

When I say that it changed everything about how I felt about Matt and me, I'm not saying that it in any way made me think less of him. My God, I'm certainly not suggesting that it made him any weaker, any less capable, or in any way inferior. Not for one second did I fear that he'd ever been in any way phony.

The change that I'm referring to was a realization of what exactly a genuine Master is. A Master is not someone who merely revels in the benefits he reaps from the power and control he wields over his sub. A Master is not just an automaton who emotionlessly doles out orders and watches with amusement as his minions perform his bidding. A Master is not a person who only relishes the benefits that his superior status entitles him.

Certainly all of these characteristics could and often do exist within a Master. He may be demanding and at times selfish. He may genuinely enjoy and even be aroused by the power he holds over a sub. He may be able to expertly control his emotions, issuing his commands and enforcing his discipline with stone-faced determination.

But a true Master, a Master such as Matt, was so invested in his sub that he was actually in a way a slave himself. He was a slave to his love for me. He was a slave to his responsibility. He was a slave to the passion and the commitment. He was a slave to his overwhelming desire to protect his property at all costs. He was a slave to his slave. I knew without question that he loved me so much he'd literally lay down his life for me. He owned me, and his ownership owned him.

That was why he'd cried.

Matt cried because it broke his heart to give me up. He was laying down his life for me. He was sacrificing everything he'd invested himself in. He was giving up his control, his power, his own happiness, and he was doing it out of love for me. He had made a decision that he'd do anything and everything necessary to ensure my success and my growth and my safety, even if it meant he no longer would be a part of any of it.

And now it was my turn to master my Master. It was my turn to allow him to grow as he had so many times done for me. It was my turn to dry his tears. It was my duty and my obligation and my privilege to set his world aright as he had so many times done for me. Could I do it though? Could I really convince him that he was the Master I knew him to be?

20

I didn't rush out of Kathie's apartment to return immediately to Matt. I made no attempt to call him on his cell phone or to contact him on Drew's landline number. I didn't keep the letter but tucked it snugly back into Drew's pocket and instructed him to return it precisely to where he'd found it. I made no mention to Kathie of anything Drew had said to me.

That week I did not return to work. My boss Mr. Bartlett had assured me that my job was safe and that I could take as much time off as I needed. I was doing well in my classes, and Kathie had contacted my instructors to inform them of the reason for my absence. I merely had to complete my assignments from home and show up for my upcoming finals.

What I was supposed to be doing that week was getting a lot of rest. I was supposed to merely heal.

I was sad to have learned that Matt had kept Tracy's pregnancy and abortion from me, but what Matt had said to Kathie in the letter was very true. I had known all along that Matt was having sex with Tracy. I also knew he was no friend of condoms. A pregnancy had always been a dangerous and distinct possibility. I personally did not feel that an abortion was either the most ethical or the wisest solution to an unwanted pregnancy, but it would never have been my decision in the first place. I hated the fact that Matt had hidden this information from me, yet I also understood why he'd done so. He knew that I was so emotional and sensitive that I'd question his desire to remain with me. He may have even feared that I'd blame myself for the abortion.

I wasn't going to focus on the abortion at this point, nor was I going to worry about anything that had happened in the past. I wasn't going to allow the horrible thing that Ryan did to me to cripple my spirit. I wasn't going to face another minute of my life in fear of bullies like him or Devin.

Thursday morning I picked up the phone and made a call. "Hello?" I said, "Detective Murray? I need to talk to you."

* * *

Kathie had agreed to take me over to Drew's apartment on Saturday to pick up my belongings. I'd told her that Drew had it all arranged so that we could get in and out as quickly as possible without fear of running into Matt or Alex. Drew was going to be the only one home at the time.

Eric was shocked when I called him Thursday afternoon, yet he was very glad to hear from me. He stressed how terribly sorry he was about what Ryan had done to me, and of course he assured me that it had all been a misunderstanding and a terrible accident. Apparently Ryan had convinced him that I'd broken my rib in multiple places when I accidentally fell against a coffee table. Eric was concerned as to why Matt was not returning any of his calls, and I told him in a rather matter-of-fact manner that Matt and I were no longer together. He expressed how sad he was to hear this but added that after having witnessed Matt's temper he was not entirely surprised by the news. I stated that he really didn't know the half of it and asked if he and Ryan would be willing to testify as to what they'd witnessed concerning Matt's erratic behavior and temper tantrums. He readily agreed.

When I called Jason that same Thursday afternoon, he told me that he had to work on Saturday. When I stressed to him how desperately I needed his help, though, he agreed to check with Tim or Carrie to see if one of them could cover his shift. I gave him Drew's address and asked him to meet me there. I thanked him for calling my sister the day of the attack and said that if not for him, my ex-boyfriend probably would have never been arrested.

Saturday morning I made my final call, and it was to Drew. "Hey," I said casually into the phone.

"Petey, why haven't you answered my calls? I've been emailing and texting and leaving voice ..."

"Sorry, Drew. You know I love you, but I've been so tired. It's like all I can even do is sleep. I think it's these pain pills."

"I was gonna come over there and check on you if I didn't hear from you. It's been so awful here. You just wouldn't believe how depressing it is. It's like Matt doesn't really even talk or anything. He just doesn't seem like ... well like Matt."

"What are you guys doing today?" I asked.

"Well I'm doing laundry. Alex and Matt are gonna go shoot hoops later I think."

"But they're both home now?" I asked.

"Yeah, do you want me to see if Matt will talk to you?"

"No, it's okay. I just wondered. Maybe I'll see if Kathie can bring me over later, after they've left."

"You want me to come get you?" he volunteered.

"No, it's okay. She said she's gotta go out anyway, and I wanna pick up some of my stuff while I'm there."

"Petey, why don't you at least try to talk to Matt? How can you not try to work it out with him after you saw the letter?" He was whispering into the phone.

"He lied to me, or he might as well have. He kept the truth about Tracy from me, and it just makes me wonder what else he's lying about."

"Oh my God, Petey! How can you say that? You know how much he loves you! He cried!"

It was all I could do at this point to keep from crying myself right then and there, Drew's words driving a stake right through my heart. "I don't wanna talk about it Drew. Can we just drop it?"

He sighed into the phone. "Sure. Okay, well if you change your mind about needing the ride, just call me."

"I love you, Drew."

"I love you too, Petey-pup."

This was gonna be the very first time I had seen Matt since the night I went into the hospital. It was difficult enough for me to maintain my composure and function in a seemingly normal way without my Master, but the anticipation of a reunion with him had been the sustaining factor for me. I was able to focus upon the tasks that I knew I had to do, and to thus suppress my emotions, but I knew inside my heart that once I saw him face-to-face all of this bravado would immediately dissipate. I feared I would crumble there right in front of him and be reduced to the dependent, sniveling crybaby that I knew myself to truly be.

Somehow, though, I knew that I had to stay in control. If I didn't do what needed to be done, then I would lose everything. Worse than that, though, Matt would lose. He would lose not only me, his pup, but also a degree of his self-respect and his self-confidence. The very characteristics that made him who he was were at stake.

So why couldn't I just call him? Why couldn't I simply tell him I knew the truth about everything? To do that would be the ultimate form of humiliation. He could never know that I had seen this vulnerable side of him. He could never know all that I now truly understood about him.

"Kathie, can we just go now and get this over with?"

"You sure, honey? If you're not comfortable, Carter and I can just go over there later."

"I need my computer, sis," I said. "If I don't get that term paper typed up, I'm screwed."

"I told you, just use my computer." She stood in front of me with her arms crossed in front of her chest.

"No, all my research is on mine. Plus I just want this over with. I want to put it behind me and move on with my life. I'm tired of being a punching bag."

"Amen to that!" she said, stepping towards me and extending her arms to embrace me. "Oh Petey, I'm so glad to hear you say that!"

I cringed as she pulled me into herself. I hoped I'd be able to actually forgive myself later for even implying such a thing about Matt, but I knew the reason why I had to do it.

"Okay, then, let's go. I don't want you doin any lifting though, not with your incision and broken ribs. Let Drew and me do it, okay."

"I'm fine," I said, "but don't worry. I've gotten good at taking orders. I'll just do as I'm told."

"You know it's not like that," she scolded me. "I'm just concerned about you getting re-injured."

I smiled up at her. "I know. I'm just kiddin."

There didn't seem to be any activity at the apartment complex when we pulled in. It just felt so strange to me, especially since I knew that if everything did not work out this could be the very last time I'd ever come here. A wave of emotion swept over me as I noticed Matt's car in the lot. Kathie saw it too. "I thought Matt wasn't gonna be here," she said.

"He went somewhere with Alex. They probably took his car."

"You want me to go to the door first, just to be sure? Then I can come back and get you if the coast is clear."

I shook my head. "No, so what even if he is here. I'm not a complete baby ya know. I can handle seeing him."

She gave me a disdainful look. "I don't like this Petey."

"He's not here!" I insisted. "I just talked to Drew on the phone, and Matt is with Alex over at the gym."

"Okay," she sighed. "I'm sorry."

"Let's go," I said, opening my door and stepping out of the car.

I used my key to enter the building, and we made our way down the hallway, but I didn't even have to knock as we approached the apartment entry door. It opened and Drew stepped out, pulling the door shut behind him.

"Petey, someone is here for you!" he whispered.

"Who?" demanded Kathie.

"Some police detective. He's got a lady from the prosecutor's office with him."

"That's Detective Murray," said Kathie. "What're they doing here?"

"I dunno," said Drew, "but when I told them Petey wouldn't be here until this afternoon he still wouldn't leave. He said he wanted to talk to Matt then."

"Is Matt in there?" she asked. Drew nodded.

"He's talking to the police right now."

"Dammit!" said Kathie. "Petey, go wait in the car."

"I can't!" I insisted. "The detective said he wants to talk to me."

"I'll send him out to the car then. I don't want you facing Matt just yet. You're not ready."

"Stop it!" I said. "Stop bossing me around! I'm going in there whether you like it or not ..." I pushed my way past Drew and pulled the door open.

As I stepped into the apartment entryway and turned towards the living room, I saw him sitting there. As I had anticipated, my heart was suddenly in my throat. I felt my eyes welling with tears, and I forced myself to quickly look away. I trained my gaze away from my Master and instead towards the detective.

"Hey Petey," he said, standing up and stepping towards me. He extended his hand to shake my own.

"What are *you* doing here?" Matt exclaimed. His voice almost sounded a bit shaky, but I'd have never noticed had I not known him so well.

"I'm here to get my belongings, if that's all right with you ... *sir*." The tone of my reply was dripping with sarcasm.

"The real question is, 'What the fuck are *you* doing here?'" Kathie stated.

"I live here now," he said. She glared at him contemptuously.

The detective spoke. "We need to get a statement from both Matt and Petey. If we are gonna take any action on the charges against Ryan, we need to get this thing rolling right away." He looked over at the prosecuting attorney Michele as he said this. She was also now on her feet.

"I understand you're ready to give us a full statement," she said to me.

"I'll tell you what I know happened. That's all I can do."

"Well that'll be enough, I'm sure," she smiled at me and placed her hand on my shoulder. "Why don't you come over here and have a seat?" She motioned towards a chair positioned adjacent to Matt.

I could feel my knees wobbling as I stepped in front of him. On the inside it felt as if my whole body was shaking, but I forced myself to be calm.

The detective then turned to Kathie and Drew. "Could we possibly have a few minutes alone with them?" Kathie again looked pissed, but she reluctantly exited the room with Drew. They waited outside on the patio. I glanced out the window briefly and almost laughed as I saw Drew immediately light up a cigarette. One more thing to piss her off.

"Okay Petey, I know this is not gonna be easy to talk about," Michele said to me as she sat down in the big recliner. She was on the edge of her seat rather than sliding all the way back the way that Matt did when he sat there. "Do you want a drink of water or something before we start?" I shook my head and thanked her. "Okay, why don't you tell me everything that happened that day, the day you were injured?"

I wanted desperately to turn to Matt before I spoke, but I kept my gaze focused on the prosecutor. "Well, it wasn't the best day of my life," I laughed nervously and then looked down at the floor in front of me. "I was being punished that day."

"What do you mean, 'being punished'?" she asked.

"I had been bad, and I was being disciplined by my *Master*!" I stated emphatically. I heard Matt shift a little in his seat on the couch across from me, but I didn't look at him.

"Who's your Master?" Detective Murray asked.

"I don't have one now, but it was *him*!" I pointed to Matt and looked up at him for the first time, staring him directly in the eye. His expression was one of bewilderment and possibly even terror. He must have thought I was insane to be saying what I was.

"I'm not Petey's *Master*," he choked out. "Petey's got a very vivid imagination."

I reached in my pocket and pulled out my collar, handing it to the prosecutor. "Matt owned me, and this is the collar he made me wear to show that I was his property. He made me wear it like I was his dog."

I could almost feel the embarrassment and anger emanating from Matt's body as I imagined how irate he must now be by my sudden willingness to betray and expose him this way. "He called me a pup and gave me orders constantly, which I knew I had to obey."

"Petey, do you want to discuss this matter privately?" the prosecutor asked. "We can question Matt separately when we're done.

"No, I want him to hear everything I have to say," I retorted snidely. "*Every*thing!"

"Petey, what the fuck are you doing?" Matt demanded. "Are you crazy?"

"Why are you ashamed of it, Matt?" As I looked him in the eye this time I did begin to weep. I couldn't help it; the tears just came, flooding my vision. "You owned me. I was your prized possession. You should be proud!"

He shook his head and looked away from me. I could tell he wanted desperately to just get up and leave, but I also knew that he wouldn't go anywhere for fear of missing some other incriminating remark I might possibly say about him.

The detective had gotten up from his chair and was now crouched beside my own. He placed his hand on my shoulder. "Petey, are you all right?" I nodded and wiped my eyes with the back of my hand.

"Yeah, I'm fine. Can I have a tissue?" The prosecutor grabbed a box of Kleenex from the stand beside her and handed it to me.

"Are you okay to continue?" I smiled meekly and nodded.

"Okay," the detective said, "tell us about this punishment. I know you told me this earlier in the hospital, but we need to get your statement on tape." I looked down at the coffee table and noticed the recorder. "I'm sorry," he said, "is it okay with you both that we record his." I nodded and Matt just sat there glaring at me.

"Like I said, Matt was my Master. He owned me and called me his pup. I had to do everything he said, no matter what. If I disobeyed him or messed up in any way, he punished me, and sometimes those punishments were ... um ... horrible."

"Petey, when did I ever punish you horribly?" Matt responded. He had scooted to the edge of his seat, leaning forward. "This is bullshit!"

"Like a week ago. Like last Sunday when you had that Ryan *rape* me!" The emotion that flowed out of me into my hurtful words must have very convincingly appeared to be a result of the agony I felt re-living the nightmare of what had happened to me, but in truth it was from the pain in my heart caused by hurting the one I loved most. I saw the life literally drain from his face as the unthinkable guilt and regret swept over him. If only I could leap into his arms at this very moment ...

Before Matt could respond to my unforgivable accusation, the detective stood up and placed himself between the two of us. He turned to Matt and said, "You'll have your chance to give your side of the story. Just sit there and listen. Let Petey say his piece; then you can respond. Got it?"

Matt leaned back against the sofa. I saw him clench his fists in exasperation. "Yeah, fine, but for the love of God, Petey, *why?*"

I turned away from Matt at this point and faced only Michele. "Honey, are you all right?" she asked. I nodded and waited for her to continue. "Okay, so Matt was punishing you that day? He had sent you over to spend time with Ryan Connors, and you believe it was something the two of them had planned? You think that Matt told Ryan to rape you?"

"Well, it's kinda hard to explain to someone who doesn't really ... um ... who doesn't understand our ... our relationship, Matt and mine's. It's like I said, he's my Master. He was. And I gotta do what he says. If he tells me to do something for somebody else, then I have to do it."

"And what did he tell you to do for Ryan?" Detective Murray asked.

"He told me I had to obey him and respect him as if he was my Master."

"Did you interpret this to mean that you had to have sex with Ryan if that was what he wanted?"

I looked down at the floor in front of me, and in a voice barely more than a whisper, I responded with one word, "Yes."

The detective and prosecutor looked at one another without saying anything for a moment. Then Michele again spoke. "Petey, tell us what happened once you were alone with Ryan."

"He took me to a gas station, that one just around the corner. He was being real mean to me, bossing me around and trying to humiliate me. He kept callin me names like loser and the "b" word."

"Bitch?" she asked. I nodded.

"Yeah. And then he made me vacuum his car. At first it was really annoying to me. I was starting to get pissed by the way he was acting, but I just kept reminding myself that I wasn't doing it for him. I was doing it for Matt. I pretended it was Matt who was bossing me around and not Ryan, and then I was able to keep obeying him."

"Was Ryan talking to you the same way that Matt usually did?" she asked. "Did he call you those kinds of names?"

"Sometimes," I said.

"Dammit Petey!" Matt yelled. His outburst startled me and I jumped a little in my seat. "I have *never* talked to you that way. Never!"

Rick immediately turned to Matt again. "This is your last warning! If you can't keep your mouth shut, you're gonna have to go wait outside." I looked over to the patio window and saw Drew standing there staring in as if he were trying to discern what was happening. I couldn't look him in the eye.

"Can I at least respond to that last thing Petey said, please?" Matt said. I'd never heard him speak like this. He almost sounded submissive.

"No! Not yet. Like I said, you'll get your turn. Go on Petey," the detective said.

"Well, after the gas station we went over to Ryan's apartment. I thought it was his apartment anyway, but it actually was his boyfriend's. His name is Eric, but Eric wasn't there at the time. It was just Ryan and me."

"And what happened once you got there?" the prosecutor asked.

"Well Ryan made me fix him some lunch. I made him a stir-fry. I learned to cook after my mom died, so I'm pretty good at it."

"I bet you are," Michele smiled warmly at me. "So the two of you had lunch together?"

"No, Ryan had lunch, and I served it to him. He ate in the living room and ordered me to go clean the bathroom. It was a pigsty. Then I came out and cleaned the kitchen afterward. He kept yelling at me and making me wait on him. I had to bring him sodas and stuff."

"So he was treating you like you were his slave?" she asked.

"Exactly. I thought it was gonna be fine though, cuz once I got used to his name-calling it didn't bother me so much any more. I'd told him when we were back at the gas station that he didn't need to go so overboard with it. I told him that it just seemed phony when he acted all stupid like that."

I couldn't help myself; I had to glance over at Matt. He had a slight grin on his face as I made that last remark.

"How did Ryan respond when you told him that?" Michele asked.

"He was pissed and threatened to call Matt. I apologized and then he didn't say any more about it, at least not then. But then after I finished cleaning the kitchen he came out from the living room to inspect my work. It seemed like he was in a really grouchy mood again, and I guess he was."

"Why do you say that?" she asked.

"Cuz he backed me up against the wall and told me what he was gonna do to me."

"What did he say, Petey?"

"He said he was gonna teach me how to be aggressive. And then ..." Suddenly I felt the emotion sweep over me as I remembered the event so vividly. "And then he grabbed a hold of me and threw me across the room. I slipped and fell, and I landed on the floor in front of him. He started kicking me."

"Oh my god, Petey," Matt said. He didn't even care about his so-called last warning. "Please don't make him go on!"

"Are you okay to go on?" Michele asked. I couldn't even turn to look at Matt now. I knew if I did that I would completely lose it.

"Yeah, I'm okay." I sighed loudly before I continued, not so much for dramatic effect but merely to regain my composure. "When he kicked me the first time, I'd never felt anything like that before. He was wearing these heavy boots, and he slammed them right into my ribcage. It hurt worse than anything I'd ever felt. It was sort of like someone had shoved a spear or something into my side, and I could even hear the bone breaking as he did it."

"Do you think he heard that too?" she asked.

"I don't know. I'm not sure how he could have *not* heard it. He was just so mad at that point. He was like a crazy person. He didn't stop after the first kick. He kept right on doing it. He kicked me in the stomach too. Then he dropped down on top of me and pinned me to the ground."

"Were you able to talk? Did you tell him to stop?" she asked.

"That is a stupid question!" Matt screamed. "That's the stupidest fuckin question I've ever heard! Of course he couldn't talk! He was getting the shit kicked out of him. Look at him! Look at how small he is!"

"That's it!" said the detective. "Go wait outside! Go! Now." He was pointing to the patio door.

"I'm not goin anywhere. You go right ahead and arrest me again, but I'm not leavin. Why are you making him go through this again anyway? We already gave you our statements."

Just then we heard the apartment entry door open, and in walked Alex, but he was not alone. Two people were with him, Eric and Ryan. For a split second you could have heard a pin drop in that apartment. The three newcomers stopped in their tracks and stared at us. We all looked at them, not saying a word. Then instantly Matt leapt from the couch, lunging towards Ryan.

"You motherfucker!" he screamed. "I'll fuckin kill you! You motherfuckin bastard!" He moved so fast, and it was such a shock to all of us that nobody reacted quickly enough.

He was about to land the first punch when Alex and Rick quickly pulled Matt away and restrained him.

Eric had his arms around Ryan and was holding him in the corner by the front door. Alex and Rick had Matt pinned against the opposite wall. "Calm down!" Rick screamed. "Get a hold of yourself, man!"

I just sat where I was, not moving a muscle. Kathie and Drew had re-entered the room, and Kathie was immediately beside me. Just when it seemed that the drama had peaked, we heard the sound of the doorbell. Nobody moved to respond to it though, for we were all focused on Matt. He was still shouting and was struggling against his captors, trying to free himself. I truly believe he would have literally ripped Ryan limb-from-limb as he'd earlier threatened if not for Alex and Rick.

Drew rushed over to the door to see who was there. He glanced beside himself disdainfully at the cowering Ryan who was inches away from him in the corner. He whispered a remark to him, but I couldn't hear what it was, and then he peeked through the eyehole in the door.

He turned and looked at me, obviously bewildered by who he'd seen. I nodded to him, as if to say it was okay to let him in. Of course, it was Jason.

"Is Petey here?" he asked.

"Well, he doesn't live here any more, but he does happen to be here right now. Not sure this is the best time though."

"Come in, Jason!" I shouted. "This is the perfect time for you to be here." Finally I stood up from my chair and walked across the room to greet my coworker. "Jason Scruggs, I think you might have already talked to Detective Murray?"

He looked at me puzzled. "Yeah, I talked to him last weekend on the phone."

"Well this is him." I said, pointing to Rick. "And this is the prosecutor, Michele Montgomery. And this is Matt Porter, my boyfriend."

"*That's* your boyfriend?" he asked, smiling broadly as he assessed Matt.

"Yeah, well he was, until he got arrested last week. I guess they thought you'd seen him abusing me."

"Not him. It was some other guy. Some skinny, gay guy. That's why I thought he was your boyfriend."

"Thanks," I said sarcastically. "I think you might recognize him. He's standing behind you." I pointed to Ryan.

"Yeah!" he nodded to Ryan. "You're the one."

"This is the guy you saw with Petey last Sunday?" Rick asked Jason. Alex still had his hand on Matt's shoulder, but Rick had released him.

"Definitely. He was like being a total jerk too. He was bossing Petey around and calling him names. I thought he was gonna start hittin him next."

"He did," Rick said. "He did exactly that."

"Wait," Eric interjected. "This is all a misunderstanding. Nobody hit anyone."

"Are you outta your fuckin mind?" Matt screamed. "You were with me. You saw what your boyfriend there did to Petey. He almost killed him!"

Then Michele spoke up. "Petey, is this the Ryan Connors who beat and raped you last Sunday?"

Without any hesitation and with complete confidence I looked Ryan straight in the eye. "Yes, he is the one who raped me!"

"Read him his rights," she said to Rick, who immediately stepped over to handcuff Ryan.

Of course Eric was beside himself, protesting angrily. It didn't matter, though, because the decision had been made, and Rick was not about to be dissuaded. Ryan was instantly reduced to a fit of crying, looking desperately at Eric hoping to find some way out. Once he was handcuffed, the detective called for a squad car and sat Ryan down on the sofa where Matt had been. He asked everyone else except Matt and me to leave.

Even Alex and Drew left their own apartment, but when I saw the look of joy on Drew's face, I knew he didn't mind too much. "I'll call you in a little bit, when it's over," I said.

It took a good half hour for the police car to show up. Eric had protested, demanding that he be allowed to wait with Ryan, but they told him he could see his friend later after he had been booked and released on bail. I walked out into the kitchen to wait until after they took Ryan away. After a few moments, I meandered down the hallway to my room.

As I stepped inside, I immediately smelled the scent of my Master. He'd been staying in the room, and it was his cologne that I was smelling. I looked around me and saw his personal belongings strewn around the room. It seemed unlike him to be so messy. I busied myself and began to tidy the room when suddenly he was standing there behind me.

"What are you doing?" he asked.

"Sir, my room ... er, I mean your room ... it's such a mess. I was just tryin to clean it up a bit."

"Don't gotta pick up after me any more, Petey," he said. "And you don't have to worry about me ordering you around or calling you names either."

"Do you think I meant that?" I asked. "Do you really think it ever bothered me to take direction from you? And do you think there was ever any name you called me that I did not consider an endearment?"

"Sounded like you meant it. Sounded like you were out to run my ass right under the bus."

"Well you know me. I'm nothing but a sponge. I'm so selfish that all I ever do is take and give nothing in return. Of course I'd just run you under the bus, since I only care about myself."

"Petey, why? Why'd you say that shit?"

"Why did you dump me?" I screamed. "How could you abandon me like that?"

"After this little stunt you just pulled in front of the police, I'm not sorry I did," he said. But then as he stood there watching me, seeing the tears stream down my cheeks, his angry expression began to soften. "I'm sorry I hurt you, Petey. I'm really, really sorry."

"You know you should've never made me that promise. You should've never said you'd never hurt me."

"You're right. I shouldn't have. How can anyone make that promise? It's not even possible to keep a promise like that. We all hurt the ones we love at one point or another. But do you at least realize that I never hurt you on purpose?"

"Sir, I did believe that. I believed that with all my heart, until Wednesday."

He looked away from me and then began to pace, taking a couple steps towards the door, but then turned back to again face me. "You planned this whole drama, didn't you? You invited all these people here ..."

"I wanted to make sure they knew who did this to me. I wanted to make sure you knew it was Ryan's fault and not yours ..."

"Then why'd you say I had him rape you?"

"To get you mad!" I shouted. "When they saw how angry and how protective of me you were, how could they ever think you'd hurt me? When they saw that look on your face when I described how he'd hurt me, there was no question about it. You'd never in a million years hurt me. I had to do it, Sir. I had to piss you off enough to make you defend yourself ... and me!"

"But that's just it, Petey. I *did* hurt you. Over and over again you got hurt when I was supposed to be protecting you."

"You're not God!" I said. "I mean you practically are ... to me, but it's like you said. You don't have control of everything. Sometimes you can't help it. Sometimes you do hurt the ones you love. That's life."

"But I was your Master!"

"Matt, you will always be my Master. I can't stop loving you, no matter what you say or do at this point. A hundred years from now I'm gonna be loving you."

"Don't say that Petey. I've done a lot of shit you don't even know about."

"So have I!" I said. "One time when I was eight I stole a candy bar from the gas station."

Matt laughed right out loud. "Petey, you're so innocent." It seemed almost as if he wanted to pull me into his arms and hold me. "I did a lot worse than steal a fuckin candy bar."

"I don't care what you've done, Sir. We all make mistakes. I just think it's not really fair to you. This whole situation isn't fair cuz you think you've gotta be like this perfect person. You make all the decisions and shoulder all of the blame for every little thing that goes wrong."

"But I take the credit for what goes right too," he countered.

"As you should. You should get credit for everything! I have no problem with that."

He was again smiling. "Petey, I'm broke. My dad disowned me."

"I thought you dumped me so he wouldn't disown you," I said.

"Well it's not your fault. My dad's an asshole. I didn't want you blaming yourself for that too. But the point is I can't take care of you any more. I don't have any money. Well, I have a couple cars and a little bit of savings."

"So you'll be like the rest of the college kids in the world. Whoopty-do! Do you think I am in love with your money?"

"Of course not, but ... oh Petey." He placed the palms of his hands against his forehead and turned away from me, bending at the waist. "Dammit Petey!" he said.

I stepped over to him and placed my hand on his back. "Matt, I love you," I whispered. "I love you with all my heart. Please don't shut me out of your life. I beg you."

Instantly he swept around and scooped me into his arms, violently clutching me against his chest. I felt his entire torso convulse as he sobbed. "I love you too!" he cried.

Matt and I sat on the sofa together, his arm wrapped around me, as I recounted the remaining events of my assault to the detective and prosecutor. It wasn't so difficult to explain what had happened with Matt by my side. I wondered how he could have ever doubted just how much the security of his strength meant to me.

While it was always true that Matt was a larger-than-life figure in my life, I honestly had never expected perfection from him. Yes, he was my Master, but this did not mean he wasn't entitled to his humanity. He made mistakes just like everyone else. To be honest, if everything had worked out in the situation with Ryan, and he hadn't attacked me the way he had, then it would have all been very hot. Ryan and I would have gained a little better understanding of one another and possibly even become friends, and we would have been granted the privilege of servicing our Masters side-by-side in a hot four-way session.

Matt's reasoning had never been flawed. If he was guilty of anything at all it merely was the fact that he ascribed too much responsibility to himself. He couldn't control or predict the actions of a psycho like Ryan. How was Matt to know that Ryan would turn so crazy? Matt was teaching his pup to be in control and to respect people even when it was difficult to do so. That all made sense.

We didn't have all the answers to our problems yet. I had no clue about what Matt was now going to do with his future. I suspected that he would begin looking for a job and continue with his college classes. We still had the abortion issue to discuss and deal with, but I knew I'd have to wait for

Matt to tell me about it when the timing was right. There was also the challenge of coping with my sister and her over-protectiveness and control issues. The biggest obstacle for Matt, though, was certainly going to be dealing with his own family. They had just found out he was gay, and they were led to believe he was abusing his boyfriend.

In spite of all these concerns, there really was only one thing that mattered to me at that moment as I sat there wrapped within Matt's embrace. All I cared about was that the world was right again. We were together where we belonged. I really didn't care one iota about whether we would be rich or poor. I didn't care if Matt owned a chain of fitness centers or worked as a cashier at McDonald's. I also didn't care if Kathie or Matt's parents or anyone else for that matter approved or disapproved of our relationship. He loved me, and I loved him. That was what mattered. That was what life was about.

So after we had wrapped everything up and Rick and Michele had left us, Matt and I continued to sit there together. He didn't say anything to me but merely held me. And then without warning he pulled me onto his lap and grabbed my head with both his hands. Looking me straight in the eye, he whispered to me, "What would my life have been like without you, pup?"

His kiss was magical. It melted away every anxiety, every worry, every imaginable question in my mind. The taste of his breath, the feel of his lips and tongue, and the powerful force of his passion were enough to completely overwhelm me. I squirmed on my Master's lap as I felt the frustration of not being able to get close enough to him and yet enjoyed the excitement of trying. As he held my head in place with his powerful hands, I used my own small hands to explore his chiseled chest. The contrast of his masculinity to my vulnerability was the most powerful of all aphrodisiacs. I wanted nothing more than for him to simply ravage me.

Within seconds I was beneath him, lying flat on my back on the sofa. He was on top of me, kissing my neck, unbuttoning my shirt, grinding himself into me, and all at the same time. I moaned and cried out, begging him not to stop. "Oh please, Sir, make love to me!" It was such a pointless request, though, for I really at this juncture had little choice in the matter.

Once he got my shirt unbuttoned and looked down at my body, he immediately stopped himself and pulled off of me. "Oh my god, pup ... I forgot. I forgot about your bandages, about your surgery." This was the first he'd seen me since the operation.

"It doesn't hurt. I promise it doesn't," I whispered. "Please don't stop."

He then wrapped his arms around me ever-so-gently and picked me up, quickly spinning himself around and trading positions with me so that I was on top. "I don't wanna crush you," he said. "Let's do it this way."

"With me on top?" I smiled as I looked down at him.

"Yeah," he said, smiling back at me. "You on top."

I giggled. "You're in trouble now!" I taunted him. "Cause you know what they say about paybacks."

"Oh no!" he feigned panic. "Have mercy on me, please." Then I began kissing him, almost as passionately as he'd done moments before to me.

One-by-one our articles of clothing disappeared until we were completely exposed to one another. I positioned myself on top of him, sitting in an upright, kneeling position, straddling him. "Sir, I need you inside me," I said as I stared down at his face. "Oh please ..."

He reached behind the arm of the couch towards the lamp stand. "There's lotion in that drawer," he said. I leaned over him and opened the drawer, frantically groping for the bottle. Generously I squirted a glob into my palm and then reached behind myself to find his throbbing cock. When I wrapped my fist around it I delighted at the look of pleasure on his face. "Are you sure, pup?" he asked. "Are you sure it's not too soon after ..."

I looked down at my own throbbing erection, which was practically staring him in the face. He looked there as well. "Does it look like I'm not sure?" I asked.

Then I hoisted myself backwards just a bit to align my hole with his cock. I ran my finger up the crack of my butt, smearing some of the lotion against my pucker. Then quickly I grabbed his cock again and shoved myself backwards, smoothly impaling myself.

"Ahh fuck!" he moaned.

I also cried out as I felt the fullness of him plunge deep inside of me. I forced myself all the way down, wanting him to feel his cock completely surrounded by my tightness. He thrust his hips upwards as I slid down, and it was all I could do to keep from shooting a load right there on the first thrust.

Quickly regaining my composure, I began to ride him. I used my legs to pump myself, sliding my body up and down on his shaft. I placed my palms against Matt's smooth hard chest as I bobbed on him frantically. He was grinding himself upwards, matching my movements rhythmically. We both were like wild animals, moaning and screaming, humping one another as if we were in heat.

Within a period of less than five minutes I knew he was about to unload. I was trying to hold off my own orgasm in order to time it perfectly with his. I was so close! I had to cum! I had to do it! I couldn't hold back! "Oh God! Oh fuck!!" I cried. The force of his cock mercilessly stabbing my insides seemed to literally fuck the cum right out of me. The eruption was volcanic, firing everywhere, across Matt's gorgeous chest, onto his chin and face, even in his hair.

He crinkled his face into an expression of agony and then he moaned loudly. I felt his cock swell inside me as he released his load. He was literally shaking beneath me as he drained himself. "Oh yeah! Oh fuck yeah!" he cried.

We were gasping and panting and laughing as I leaned in to kiss him. Then suddenly the door opened and in walked Alex and Drew.

"Well," Drew said, raising his eyebrows slightly. "I guess you two got everything all worked out."

TO BE CONCLUDED ... IN BOOK THREE